Susanna Gregory was a police officer in Leeds before taking up an academic career. She has served as an environmental consultant during seventeen field seasons in the polar regions, and has taught comparative anatomy and biological anthropology.

She is the creator of the Matthew Bartholomew series of mysteries set in medieval Cambridge as well as the Thomas Chaloner books, and now lives in Wales with her husband, who is also a writer.

Also by Susanna Gregory

The Thomas Chaloner Series

A Conspiracy of Violence
Blood on the Strand
The Butcher of Smithfield
The Westminster Poisoner
A Murder on London Bridge
The Body in the Thames
The Piccadilly Plot
Death in St James's Park
Murder on High Holborn

The Matthew Bartholomew Series

A Plague on Both Your Houses
An Unholy Alliance
A Bone of Contention
A Deadly Brew
A Wicked Deed
A Masterly Murder
An Order for Death
A Summer of Discontent
A Killer in Winter
The Hand of Justice
The Mark of a Murderer
The Tarnished Chalice
To Kill or Cure
The Devil's Disciples
A Vein of Deceit
The Killer of Pilgrims
Mystery in the Minster
Murder by the Book
The Lost Abbot
Death of a Scholar

THE CHEAPSIDE CORPSE

Susanna Gregory

SPHERE

First published in Great Britain in 2015 by Sphere

Copyright © Susanna Gregory 2015

1 3 5 7 9 10 8 6 4 2

A CIP catalogue record for this book is available from the British
Library.

ISBN 978-0-7515-5280-5

Typeset in Baskerville MT by Palimpsest Book Production Ltd, Falkirk,
Stirlingshire
Printed and bound in Great Britain by Clays Ltd, St Ives plc

Papers used by Sphere are from well-managed forests
and other responsible sources.

MIX
Paper from
responsible sources
FSC® C104740

Sphere
An imprint of
Little, Brown Book Group
100 Victoria Embankment
London EC4Y 0DY

An Hachette UK Company
www.hachette.co.uk

www.littlebrown.co.uk

In loving memory of Sarah Rippetoe (née Pritchard)
whose devotion to her family, joyous spirit and generosity was
an inspiraration to us all.

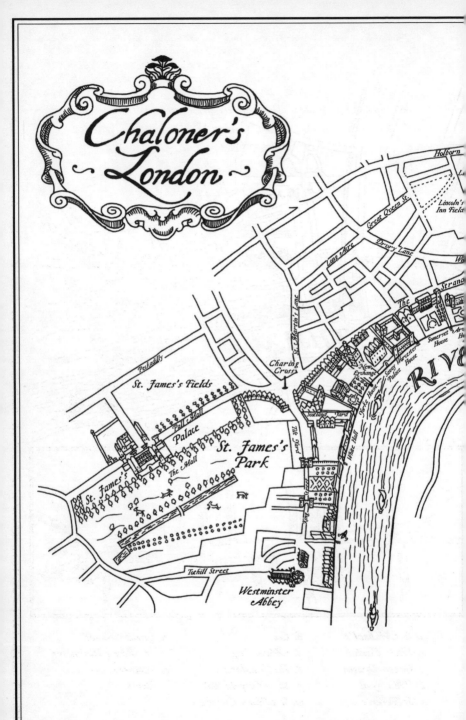

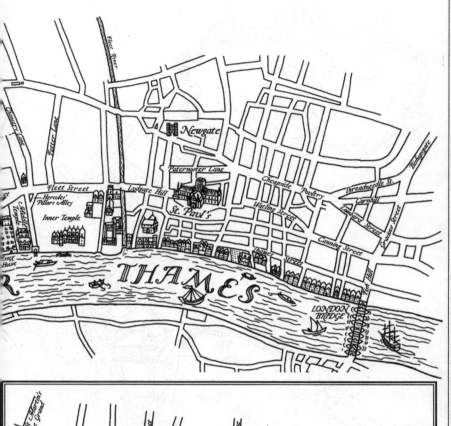

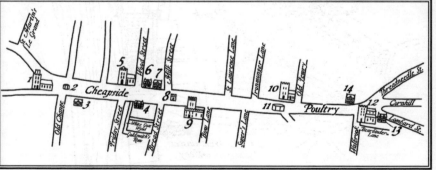

1. St Michael's
2. Little Conduit
3. Green Dragon
4. White Goat
5. St Peter's
6. Coo
7. Music Shop
8. The Standard
9. St Mary-le-Bow
10. St Mary Colechurch
11. Great Conduit
12. St Mary Woolchurch
13. Feathers
14. Baron

Prologue

It had been a terrible night for Nicholas Colburn. He had been a wealthy man, proud owner of a country estate, founder of a reputable wine business, and fêted as a shining beacon of virtue by his fellow vintners. Now he had nothing, and he doubted that even his most loyal friends would hold him in very high esteem once they learned what he had done.

As he left the illicit gambling den the sun was rising, presaging the start of another crisp, blue winter day. Then he saw the man who had introduced him to his vice, and who had been whispering for weeks that his luck would change. The fellow was smirking. Colburn stared at him. Was that vengeance in his eyes – that he had wanted this to happen? Colburn shook himself irritably. No, he would not blame his ruin on someone else. He had always had a weakness for cards, and the higher the stakes, the more exciting and irresistible he found them. It had been his own choice to continue playing in the face of all reason.

As his fortune had dwindled, he had applied to the goldsmiths for loans – goldsmiths were also bankers, men who stored money for some clients and lent it to others. They had been astonished that such a rich man should need to borrow, but he had invented a tale about expanding his business, and had offered to pay twice the usual rate of interest. Naturally greedy, they had scrambled to accept his terms. However, being gentlemen of discretion, not one had discussed the arrangement with his colleagues. And that was unfortunate, because if they had, they might have prevented what was about to happen.

It was too late now, of course. The previous night had seen Colburn lose the last of the enormous sums he had begged. Unbeknownst to each other, virtually every goldsmith in the city had accommodated him, and many had overreached themselves to do so, flattered that they should receive the patronage of such a prestigious customer. Many of the smaller concerns would not survive when he defaulted. Indeed, even the larger ones would suffer a serious blow.

Bowed down with remorse, Colburn began to trudge home, for once grateful that he had no family – he had never married, so at least the disgrace that was about to come crashing down would not have to be endured by a wife and children. It would be his alone to bear.

He turned into Cheapside. As usual, the road was bright, lively and chaotic. And noisy – the sound of iron-shod wheels on cobbles, and the honks, bleats and brays of animals being driven to market was deafening. It reeked, too; the hot stench of dung mingling with the contents of the drains that ran down either side of the road – slender ribbons of water that were wholly incapable of coping with the volume of rubbish tipped into them.

As he passed the church of St Mary le Bow, a royal herald climbed the steps, resplendent in his fine uniform. Two trumpeters blared a fanfare to attract attention, and Colburn went to listen, although he did not know why – what heralds proclaimed could not matter to him now.

In a penetrating bawl, the man announced that war had been declared on the United Provinces of the Netherlands. Colburn wondered why the King had waited so long to say so – the news was weeks old, and had already been thoroughly discussed in the coffee houses. He experienced a familiar, sharply agonising stab of guilt as the little procession marched away to its next destination. Wars were expensive, so how would His Majesty pay for one? The answer was that he would expect help from the goldsmith–bankers. Except that many of them would not be in a position to oblige, thanks to Colburn and his gambling.

He hid behind a cart when he saw several bankers in the crowd that had gathered to hear the herald. Taylor, Wheler and Backwell headed the most powerful enter-prises, while Angier and Hinton were smaller, but still influential. They stood talking in low voices, no doubt discussing how best to fund the looming conflict. Misery engulfed Colburn. What if the Dutch invaded because the King could not afford to defend his realm?

Sick with shame, Colburn stumbled away. How could he live with the knowledge that his fondness for cards had put his country in danger? He could never repay what he owed, and no one would ever spare him a smile or a friendly word again. He would be a pariah, shunned by all until the day he died. Gradually, he began to see what he must do. He waited until a particularly heavy cart was lumbering past, and flung himself beneath it.

There were cries of horror as the wheels crunched across him, and people hurried to stand around his mangled body, shaking their heads in mute incomprehension. Some were the bankers.

'It is Nicholas Colburn,' said Backwell, unsteadily. 'One of my biggest clients.'

'And mine,' added Angier. 'In fact, he owed me a fortune, so I hope his estate can pay, or I shall be ruined.'

Blood drained from faces as others said the same and the awful truth dawned. The sum total of the loans Colburn had taken out were far greater than the value of his assets, and he had offered the same collateral to all. No one would receive more than a fraction of what had been lent.

'The war,' gulped Backwell. 'How shall we finance the war?'

Goldsmiths' Row, February 1665

Dick Wheler was the richest goldsmith in London. He was also the most ruthless, and thought nothing of lying, cheating, scheming and even ordering the occasional death to expand his empire. He had lost a substantial sum to the selfishly irresponsible Colburn, but it had not taken him long to recoup his losses. He had simply tightened the thumbscrews on his clients, and was pleased to say that now, just a few weeks later, his coffers were bulging once more. Few of his colleagues could claim the same – most were still reeling from the disaster.

He eyed the man who stood in front of him, a squat, ugly brewer named John Farrow, who quailed in trepidation and wrung the hat he held so hard that it seemed he might rip it in two.

4

'You have paid me nothing for four months now,' Wheler said sternly. 'Therefore, I have no choice but to take possession of your brewery.'

'No!' cried Farrow in dismay. 'How shall I dig myself out of this trouble without it? Please! Give me a few more days. My wife has been unwell and—'

'Yes, yes,' interrupted Wheler. He had heard the excuses a thousand times: business was bad because of the cold weather; the Dutch war meant customers were less willing to spend money; there had been an unprecedented hike in the cost of coal; a loved one was ill and medicines were expensive. 'You have told me before.'

Farrow opened his mouth to press his case, but Wheler snapped his fingers and two henchmen materialised out of the shadows. The brewer struggled and howled as he was manhandled through the door, but his pleas fell on deaf ears – Wheler was actually rather pleased by what had happened: the brewery occupied a strategic position on Cheapside, and could be turned into a profitable tavern.

The next defaulter was ushered in, and the process began all over again.

'Ah, yes,' he said. 'Widow Porteous. You borrowed money to start a laundry, but you have repaid none of it so far.'

'Because no one told me that coal prices would rise so high,' she stammered. 'But I have to buy fuel to heat up my water, and there—'

'You left a ring as surety,' recalled Wheler. He walked to a cabinet and took it out. It was a pretty thing, silver studded with garnets. Perhaps his wife would like it. He brightened. It would distract her for a while, and she might relent in her campaign to be given a role in the running of the business. Joan had a good financial head on her shoulders, it was true, but Wheler did not want to work with her, and wished she would stop pestering him about it.

'My late husband's,' whispered Widow Porteous, a tear rolling down her cheek.

'It is forfeit,' declared Wheler briskly. 'You have a month to make the next repayment; if you fail, you will lose a lot more than this little bauble.'

'But it is the only thing I have left of him! Please give me another week to—'

'I *have* given you another week,' snapped Wheler. 'Several times. But you do not honour your promises. I, too, have bills to pay – the rugs in here are little more than rags, while my wife is in desperate need of new winter shoes.'

Widow Porteous stole a glance at the office's opulent decor, which included a portrait of Joan in finery fit for a queen. When her gaze settled on the banker again, there was a good deal of reproach in it. Irked, Wheler barked an order and his henchmen ushered her out. When she had gone, he made a note of the transaction in the ledger that lay open in front of him.

As he wrote, he was wracked by a deep, phlegmy cough that hurt. His physician had diagnosed lung-rot, which would kill him in a few weeks, although that fate held considerably less terror for him than the prospect of catching the plague. There had been three cases near St Giles, and while most Londoners had grown complacent about the possibility of a major outbreak, Wheler had seen what the disease did to its victims. The thought of his pustule-ravaged corpse tossed in a pit with hundreds of others was almost enough to make him turn to religion.

He supposed he should spend the little time he had left with Joan, but that was a dull prospect when compared to the heady delights of high finance. It was no secret that he loved money more than people, and he would far rather pass his last days confiscating the assets of defaulters than sitting at home waiting to die.

He was still coughing when there was a knock on the door. It opened to admit James Baron, his top henchman, a great bull of a fellow with a rakish smile. Baron was resourceful, greedy and cold-blooded – exactly the kind of person Wheler needed to manage the less pleasant side of his operation. It was Baron who would take possession of the brewery, and who would visit those who had missed appointments that day. He was very good at what he did, and Wheler could not have managed without him.

'Widow Porteous was your last client today,' Baron reported. He frowned when he saw his employer's pallor. 'Do you want me to fetch Dr Coo?'

Wheler shook his head. 'It will pass, and there is nothing more he can do anyway.'

'As you wish. Is there anything else, or can I go home?'

'I want you to visit the linen-drapers first. They promised me fifty pounds tonight, but they only brought forty. Perhaps one might have an accident, as a warning to the others.'

Unusually, Baron hesitated. 'My brother-in-law is a linen-draper, and business *has* been bad of late. They lost a lot of money when their ship was attacked by Dutch privateers and—'

'Not you as well,' groaned Wheler. 'They made an agreement and they broke it. Now do as I say, or I shall dismiss you and appoint someone else.'

Baron inclined his head, but not before Wheler had seen the flash of rage in his eyes. Many would call him a fool for challenging a brute like Baron, but Wheler knew it would be more reckless to let him gain the upper hand. Like all dangerous animals, it was necessary to let them know who was in charge. The two men nodded a cool goodnight, and Baron left.

Wheler pored over his ledgers for another hour, then stood to walk to the meeting he was due to attend – a gathering of the Goldsmiths' Company, where fine food and drink would be served in sumptuous surroundings. He was looking forward to it, as he would be able to gloat over those colleagues who still floundered in the wake of the Colburn Crisis.

He heard the soft tap of footsteps behind him as he strode down White Goat Wynd and turned in annoyance, assuming it was a debtor come to beg for a reprieve, so when the knife plunged into his chest, his first reaction was indignation. Who dared raise a hand against him? An embittered client? Baron? A fellow banker, jealous of his success? The long list was still running through his mind when he died.

Chapter 1

London, late April 1665

It was easy for travellers to know when they were nearing London because of the stench – three hundred thousand souls living in unhealthily close proximity could be detected from a considerable distance. The city could be seen from afar, too, first as a yellow-brown smear on the horizon from countless belching sea-coal fires, furnaces and ovens, and then as a bristle of towers, spires and turrets, with the lofty bulk of St Paul's Cathedral looming majestically over them.

Despite the city's drawbacks, filth and reek being but two, Thomas Chaloner was pleased to see it again. Since taking employment as intelligencer to the Earl of Clarendon three years before, he had spent more time away than at home, and his latest jaunt of six weeks had told him more than ever that he wanted to settle down. He had married the previous June, but had spent scant few nights with his wife since, and as their relationship was turbulent to say the least, he needed time to work on it if he did not want it to end in disaster.

9

He returned his hired horse to the stable in Westminster, and began to walk the short distance to his house on Tothill Street. It was warm for the time of year, which was a relief after a long and unusually bitter winter, and everywhere were signs that spring had arrived. There was a blaze of flowers in the grassy sward around the old abbey, while blossom covered the trees in St James's Park. Birds' plumage brightened as the breeding season got underway, and London seemed a happier, more hopeful place than when he had left it in March.

Striding along made him hot, so he unfastened his coat, a thick, practical garment of an indeterminate shade of beige. Like Chaloner, there was nothing about it to attract attention. He was of average height, weight and build, his hair was brown, his eyes were grey, and his face was pleasant but unremarkable. He had worked hard to make himself unmemorable, to blend into the background of any situation or gathering of people, and that was one reason why he had survived so long in the turbulent, shifting world of espionage.

As he walked, he reflected on the assignments he had just completed. There had been two of them. The first, for his friend John Thurloe, had been to visit members of the Cromwell family – no small favour, given that the Lord Protector's kin had become *personae non gratae* after the fall of the Commonwealth. He had helped Cromwell's son to catch a thief in the Fens, then had travelled to Northamptonshire to ensure that Cromwell's widow was being properly looked after. He had completed both errands, including travel, within a week.

The second task had been for the Earl, and had taken rather longer: there had been rumours of an uprising in Hull, and Chaloner had been charged to put it down.

It had been a ridiculous order. The local sheriff was more than capable of tackling a handful of deluded fanatics who were more danger to themselves than the stability of the nation. Moreover, the sheriff resented someone from London looking over his shoulder, and had avenged himself by sending Chaloner on foray after foray into the sodden countryside, forcing him to endure weeks of muddy tracks, sleeping under hedges and poor food. Chaloner suspected the 'rebellion' had been crushed at least a fortnight before the official announcement was made, and the delay had been purely to make him suffer a little longer.

Thus he was delighted and grateful to be home. Tothill Street had a heartening familiarity about it, and he quickened his pace. His house was the big one in the middle, far larger than he and Hannah needed, but she was lady-in-waiting to the Queen and appearances were important to her. The extravagance worried Chaloner, though, who felt they should put aside at least some of their earnings for a rainy day. She disagreed, and some very fierce arguments had ensued.

A hackney carriage was parked outside, which meant she had guests. Chaloner's heart sank. He disliked the hedonistic, vacuous courtiers Hannah chose as friends, and he had hoped she would be alone. He bypassed the front door and headed for the back one, aiming to slip up the stairs and change his travel-stained clothes before she saw him – more than one quarrel had erupted because he had joined a soirée in a less than pristine condition. With luck, by the time he was presentable, the visitors might have gone.

He strolled into the kitchen and was met by the warm, welcoming scent of new bread. All the servants were

11

there. The housekeeper sat at the table with her account book, the cook-maid fussed over the loaf she had just removed from the oven, the scullion swept the floor, and the footman and the page perched on a window sill, polishing boots.

It was a comfortable scene, yet Chaloner immediately sensed an atmosphere. The staff were a surly horde, and he had often wondered how Hannah had managed to select so many malcontents. The housekeeper was inflexible and domineering; the cook-maid, scullion and footman were lazy and dishonest; and the page, old enough to be Chaloner's grandfather and thus elderly for such a post, was incurably disrespectful. But even by their standards, the kitchen was not a happy place that particular day: all were uneasy, and the girls had been crying.

'Oh,' said the housekeeper disagreeably, when she saw Chaloner. 'You are back.'

It was no way to greet the master of the house, but she was secure in the knowledge that her long association with Hannah's family meant she would never be dismissed, no matter how discourteously she behaved. She was a lean, cadaverous woman whose loose black clothes and beady black eyes always reminded Chaloner of a crow. He did not check her for impertinence that day, however, because she was so wan that he wondered if she was ill.

'Who is with Hannah?' he asked, startled and suspicious when the others came to offer a variety of curtsies, bows and tentative smiles. They usually followed the housekeeper's example of sullen contempt, and he was unused to deference from them.

'They did not leave their names,' replied the footman.

'But they have been here before. The mistress owes them money, see.'

Chaloner felt the stirrings of unease. Hannah had accrued some serious debts the previous winter, and it had not been easy to settle them all. Appalled by how close they had come to fiscal disaster, she had promised to be more careful while he was away. Chaloner had believed her assurances, and was alarmed to learn that he might have been overly trusting.

'Money for what?' he asked.

'Everyone at Court is in arrears with payments for things these days,' said the housekeeper evasively. 'So she is not alone.'

'No, indeed,' put in the scullion. 'Will Chiffinch and Bab May owe tens of thousands.'

Supposing clean clothes would have to wait, Chaloner aimed for the drawing room. Hannah was proud of this chamber. It boasted a French clock, a Dutch chaise longue, and the walls had been covered with paper, an extravagance that had been decried by Cromwell's Puritans, but that was a very popular fashion among the reinstated Royalists.

He arrived to find Hannah sitting on a chair looking frightened, while two louts loomed over her. The knife he always carried in his sleeve slipped into his hand, and he started towards them, but he had not anticipated a third man lurking behind the door. He jerked away in time to avoid the blow directed at his head, but it left him off balance, which gave the other two time to launch an attack. He deflected one punch with a hastily raised arm, but another caught him on the chin and down he went. Hannah's cry of relief at his appearance turned to a shriek of alarm.

13

Blinking to clear his vision, he saw a cudgel begin to descend. He twisted to one side, ramming his blade into the fellow's calf and kicking the feet from under another, just as Hannah sprang into action and dealt the last man a wild clout that made him stagger. The cosh-wielder released a howl of pain and hobbled towards the door, while his cronies, loath to tackle anyone who fought back, were quick to follow. Chaloner scrambled upright, but he was still giddy, and by the time he had recovered enough to give chase, the three men were long gone.

'Oh, Tom!' wailed Hannah. 'Thank God you are home. You have been gone so long and—'

'Who were they?' demanded Chaloner.

'No one to worry about,' she replied unconvincingly, and flung herself into his arms so vigorously that she almost sent both of them flying. She snuffled into his shoulder, while he held her rather stiffly, supposing he should say something to comfort her, but not sure what. Eventually, she pushed away from him and went to stand in the window.

'I had my portrait done by Peter Lely while you were away,' she said in a muffled, distracted voice that made him suppose she was hurt by his failure to dispense the necessary solace. She pointed to the wall above the fireplace. 'Do you like it?'

Chaloner stared at the picture. It captured perfectly her laughing eyes, snub nose and inconvenient hair. The quality of the work was no surprise, though, because Lely was Principal Painter in Ordinary to the King, and thus the most sought-after artist in the country. His popularity meant he could charge whatever he liked for a commission, and it was common knowledge that his prices were far beyond the reach of all but the richest of patrons.

14

'Oh, God!' gulped Chaloner. 'So that is why we are in debt again!'

It was not the homecoming he had hoped for. Chaloner sat in his extravagant parlour, sullenly sipping expensive wine, while Hannah perched at his side and chatted about all that had happened since he had left – she was rarely cool with him for long. There had been another comet that presaged a major disaster – even astronomers from the Royal Society thought so, and they were no fools. Then there had been an ugly purple mist with leprous spots, followed not long after by a coffin-shaped cloud.

'Some folk say these things foretell an outbreak of the plague,' Hannah explained. 'Because there have been a dozen cases in the slums near St Giles-in-the-Fields since February. But I think they are wrong. It has not spread to other areas, so the danger is probably over.'

Chaloner had lost his first wife and child to plague in Holland, and although it had been more than a decade ago, the memory was still painful.

'Those men,' he began, keen to think of something else, even if it was a matter that was likely to annoy him, 'what did they—'

'Your Earl has been the focus of a lot of scurrilous talk,' Hannah interrupted, equally keen to postpone the spat that both knew was likely to follow once the subject of debt was broached. 'As you know, people were starting to call his new mansion Dunkirk House, because he sold that port back to the French at a ridiculously low price, but now *everyone* is doing it. They are angrier than ever with him, as Dutch pirates are using it as a base from which to harry British shipping.'

'It was not his idea to sell it,' Chaloner pointed out.

'Perhaps not, but he oversaw the arrangements, and people think he let the French bribe him, because we *should* have got more for it. The *douceur* he took to let them have it cheap probably did pay for his fine new house.'

Chaloner was more interested in their own affairs. 'What did those louts want with—'

She cut across him a second time. 'Our housekeeper has been ill. Surgeon Wiseman has been treating her, but she has needed several visits to Epsom for the waters, which are costly . . .'

Chaloner regarded her in alarm. 'How much do we owe?'

'A few thousand pounds,' mumbled Hannah, rather indistinctly.

'*What?*' It was far worse than he had anticipated. 'How much Epsom water did she drink? Or is it the Lely portrait that has ruined us?'

'We are not *ruined*, Thomas,' said Hannah irritably. 'We are temporarily embarrassed. And it is not the housekeeper or Lely who put us there – she paid for most of her treatment herself, while Lely agreed to defer payment until next year.'

Chaloner regarded her accusingly. 'You promised not to spend more than we earned. In fact, you swore an oath.'

'And I have kept it,' declared Hannah indignantly. 'I have not spent a shilling more than we agreed – other than the Lely, which I knew you would not mind. He was free for a few weeks, and it was too good an opportunity to miss. The painting is an investment, you see.'

'So why are we in debt? Again.'

16

'Because I inadvertently defaulted on the loan I had to take out when I bought my post with the Queen. I had no idea the conditions had changed until the demands came for the arrears.'

Chaloner blinked. 'You *bought* the post? I assumed you won it on merit.'

'Oh, really, Thomas! That is not how things work at White Hall. You may have unique talents that earls clamour to purchase, but the rest of us are rather more ordinary.'

Chaloner almost laughed at the notion that noblemen were falling over themselves to hire his services. He had fought for Parliament during the civil wars, and had worked for Cromwell's intelligence services thereafter. Employment was scarce for such men in Restoration England, and he was fortunate that the Earl had been willing to overlook his past loyalties and take him on.

'I hardly think—' he began.

'Anyway, it cost three thousand pounds, which obviously I did not have, so I had to borrow from Edward Backwell. But the King asked the bankers to donate a million pounds for the Dutch war, and as they do not have such a huge sum to hand, they have to raise it by any means they can. Most do it by selling their debts – Backwell sold his to Rich Taylor.'

'I have heard of Rich Taylor. He was one of few goldsmith–bankers who remained a Royalist during Commonwealth.'

Chaloner knew this because such loyalties had been deemed suspect when Parliament was in power, so Taylor was one of those whom John Thurloe – then Cromwell's Spymaster General – had been obliged to monitor.

'Well, he is a terrible rogue,' said Hannah. 'And I am now in debt to him.'

Chaloner was puzzled. 'You must have had this arrangement with Backwell when we married. You have been a lady-in-waiting for more than three years now but I have never heard of it before. Why not?'

'Because the money was always taken directly from my salary, so I never had cause to think about it. Many courtiers are in the same position, and handling "standing orders" is a service that White Hall's accompters offer. They gather all the payments together, and deliver them to our creditors on the first day of every month.'

'So what has changed? Did the clerks forget?'

'No – the problem came when Taylor revised the agreement I made with Backwell, which I only discovered when I received a letter informing me that I was in arrears. I went to the Solicitor General, expecting to be told that Taylor had acted illegally, but it seems he *was* within his rights to change the terms.'

'How did he change them?'

'Instead of the five per cent interest that Backwell charged, Taylor wants fifteen. I refused, of course, but all that means is that my debt has mounted, and I am now in rather a muddle.'

'But that is extortion – usury. Which *is* illegal, no matter what the Solicitor General says.'

Hannah sighed. 'Unfortunately, there is a clause in the contract that lets any new lender do as he pleases. I queried it when I signed with Backwell, but he told me not to worry, as he would never sell the arrangement.'

'But he did sell it,' said Chaloner heavily.

She nodded. 'He apologised profusely, but I could see he was in a bind – he cannot refuse a "request" for funds from His Majesty. Unfortunately, Taylor has demanded so much that I have been unable to pay the butcher, the grocer, the baker, the milkman . . .'

'So who sent those three louts? Taylor, or one of the others?'

'Taylor. But all will be well now that you are home. You have not drawn your salary for two months, which might appease him for a while.'

From that remark, Chaloner surmised that his outstanding wages would not cover all that was needed. Unless Taylor could be persuaded to agree to more reasonable terms, of course, which he might, once informed that sending henchmen to the homes of ladies while their husbands were away was not the best way to enhance his reputation as an honourable man of business. Chaloner looked at the painting, and wondered if anyone would buy it.

'No,' said Hannah, reading his mind. 'Prices for works of art are low at the moment, because of the war – no one wants to buy any, just in case the Dutch invade us and steal it all. We need to wait until the crisis is over. Besides, we shall never win recognition at Court unless we flaunt a little wealth. As I said, the Lely is an investment.'

'It will be a redundant investment if we are arrested for debt,' Chaloner pointed out. 'I doubt the Queen will keep you if you are obliged to live in the Fleet Prison.'

'She might, because I should be in very good company,' Hannah flashed back. 'Any number of courtiers are in the same position. But this is not my fault, Tom! How was I to know that Backwell would sell my debt to someone like Taylor? And there is Colburn, of course.'

Chaloner regarded her in alarm. 'Who is Colburn? Another creditor?'

19

Hannah eyed him stonily. 'He was a gambler, who took massive loans from virtually every banker in the city, which he cannot repay because he killed himself. A number of the smaller concerns are ruined – which has put even greater pressure on those who weathered Colburn's sly dealings, as there are fewer of them to fund the war.'

'So is that why Taylor is charging so much interest? To raise money for the King?'

'Oh, no,' said Hannah bitterly. 'His Majesty has not demanded a contribution from *him*, because he remained loyal to the monarchy during the Commonwealth. His coffers are safe, unlike all the others, who declared for Parliament. But we will survive this nastiness, Tom. The housekeeper is going to stay with her mother in Shoreditch, which will be one fewer mouth to feed.'

Chaloner doubted the departure of one person was going to make much difference to their predicament. 'I did not know that loans could be bought, sold and renegotiated.'

'Nor did anyone else at Court, and Taylor's antics are doing nothing to make bankers popular. But this is tedious talk for your homecoming! I am delighted to have you back, and to prove it, I shall bake you a cake.'

Chaloner's heart sank. Hannah was the least talented cook he had ever encountered. A cake would mean a sticky mess for the staff to clean up afterwards, and some inedible offering that he would be obliged to praise.

'I have a letter to deliver to the Earl,' he said, standing quickly lest he was invited to watch her at work – invariably a fraught experience. 'I should go to White Hall.'

'He prefers to lurk in Dunkirk House these days,

because everyone at the palace hates him so. You will have to go there if you want to see him.'

Chaloner left Tothill Street with a mind that teemed with worry. He was so preoccupied that he forgot to change his grimy clothes before visiting the man who lived in the newest and most extravagant stately home in the capital.

He walked to Clarendon House wondering what had possessed him to marry a woman with whom he had so little in common, and who was about to land him in debtors' gaol into the bargain. And there was little that unsettled him more than the prospect of a spell behind bars – he had once been caught spying in France, and the following incarceration had been so harrowing that it still haunted his dreams. Even the thought of being in prison brought him out in a cold sweat, and he determined to visit Taylor as soon as possible, to see what could be done to avoid it.

He cut through St James's Park, a pleasant expanse of formal garden and woodland, and emerged on the semi-rural lane called Piccadilly. Clarendon House had stood in glorious isolation when he had left London six weeks before, but now it seemed the Earl was to have neighbours. Two more mansions were rising out of the mud, although neither was as grand as Clarendon's with its fluted columns, ornate balustrades and lofty windows. The Earl's home screamed of wealth and privilege, and he was not surprised that Londoners resented it.

He was standing at the gate, regarding the place with dislike, when something slammed into the back of him, almost knocking him from his feet. He spun around to

21

find himself staring down a roll of cloth. It was being toted by two men who grunted and sweated under its weight, and who did not seem to care that they posed a considerable menace to others. A quick glance down the lane told him that he was not the only one who had been butted – a number of people rubbed shoulders and heads.

'You should have moved,' said one of the men, unrepentant. 'We called out to tell you to mind.'

Chaloner was sure they had not, but the load looked heavy, and he would not have wanted to lug it around on such a warm day, so he let the matter pass unremarked.

'Curtains,' explained the other, more contrite. 'All the best houses have them.'

'Do they?' Glumly, Chaloner wondered how long it would be before Hannah wanted some.

'There is much to commend them over shutters,' added the first. 'They exclude draughts, look pretty in a window, and do not need painting.'

'Before the year is out, all fashionable houses will have them,' predicted the second. 'You mark my words.'

Chaloner began to walk up the gravelled drive, and they fell into step behind him, chatting as they went. They informed him that their names were Gabb and Knowles, and that they worked for a person named James Baron.

'He buys and sells,' elaborated Gabb with a meaningful wink. 'And he is a powerful force along Cheapside. Ask for him if you need anything – anything at all – and he will get it for you.'

'I see,' said Chaloner, wondering if the Earl, who prided himself on his morality, knew that his fashionable

22

new drapery hailed from such a dubious-sounding source.

'Here,' said Gabb, shoving a card into Chaloner's hand. It was an advertisement for the services Baron offered to potential clients. Such notices had been rare in Cromwell's time, but there had been a proliferation of them since the Restoration, as every businessman hastened to legitimise himself with the printed word. This one read:

Jaymes Baron, purveyor of Fyne Cloffs and other Superiore Items to Howses of Qualitye and Fashon, including curtaynes, linin, goode furnichure, piktures, cloks and ornamentals.

Aske for Jas. Baron, at the Sign of the Feathers on Chepeside.

Anythinge bawt or solde. No Questyons Askd.

Printed by Thos Milbourn of St Martin le Grand

Personally, Chaloner thought that Thos Milbourn should have advised his customer to reword the last part, as it screamed of criminality. A little editing for spelling would not have gone amiss either. He started to hand it back, but Gabb indicated that he should keep it.

'You might want something yourself one day,' he said. 'And if you do, tell Mr Baron that you was sent by Gabb and Knowles, because then you will get a

23

better price, and we will get what is known as a *commission*.'

'Of course, we are unimpressed that Mr Baron treats with Dunkirk House,' said Knowles, nodding towards Clarendon's stately pile with considerable disapproval. 'Cromwell worked hard to get that port off the French, and Clarendon was wrong to sell it back to them.'

'He let them bribe him,' stated Gabb with such authority that anyone listening might have been forgiven for thinking that he had been there when it happened. 'He sold it out of self-interest.'

'Is that so,' said Chaloner flatly, thinking they had no right to denigrate the Earl when they worked for a man who offered to buy and sell property of debatable provenance.

Gabb nodded. 'Of course! How else could he afford this fine house? Or do you think he earned it all from being Lord Chancellor?'

Chaloner agreed that the Earl's current post was unlikely to generate sufficient income to fund an expensive project like Clarendon House. However, his employer's finances were not for discussion with delivery men, so he led them to the back of the building, where such goods were received.

Because the Earl wanted his new home to be at the forefront of fashion, he had hired a man to ensure that it never lagged behind. John Neve was a thin, harried perfectionist whose finicky attention to detail was likely to drive him to an early grave. He was an upholder, which meant he was not only qualified to fit furniture with material, but was also an expert in interior design. He was waiting at the door, and gave a relieved smile when he saw the curtains.

'Good,' he said, waving them inside. 'That is the seventh pair. Two more to come.'

'No, these are the last,' said Gabb, dropping them on the floor and mopping his sweating face with a grimy sleeve.

'Nonsense,' said Neve impatiently. 'There are nine windows in the Great Parlour, and I ordered a set of curtains for each. I am unlikely to have miscounted.'

Gabb shrugged. 'Take it up with Mr Baron. Lord! It is hot for such labour. Would you happen to have a cup of cool ale for two tired and thirsty men?'

'No, I would not!' cried Neve indignantly. 'And certainly not until you have brought everything that we paid for. Well? What are you waiting for?'

Chaloner was amazed by how much Clarendon House had changed since he had left. Then, it had been lavish, but now it was unashamedly ostentatious. Every wall was hung with priceless paintings, sculptures abounded, and ceilings and doors had been slathered in gilt. It was more opulent than White Hall by a considerable margin, and he wondered what the King thought about being upstaged by his Lord Chancellor. The two no longer enjoyed the easy relationship they had once shared, mostly because His Majesty disliked being treated like an errant schoolboy, and the Earl deplored the merry monarch's licentious lifestyle. Moreover, the King did not have as much money as he thought he should, and Clarendon's brazen affluence was bound to rankle.

'I am glad to see you back, Chaloner,' said Neve, once the curtains had been toted upstairs and he and Chaloner were watching them being unrolled ready for hanging. He looked tired and out of sorts. 'You have been missed.'

'I have?' asked Chaloner doubtfully. 'By whom?'

'By the Earl. His suppliers have been causing problems, as you just saw, and he says almost every day that he wishes you were here to sort them out.'

'Oh,' said Chaloner despondently. He had been a very good intelligencer during the Commonwealth, and his analyses of enemy shipping and troop movements had earned him praise from princes and generals. But the Earl wanted him for handling awkward traders!

'It is important,' Neve assured him earnestly. 'He will not be happy until his Great Parlour is perfect, and he will be furious when he learns he is still two pairs of curtains short.'

'Perhaps you should buy them from someone else,' suggested Chaloner, thinking of the blatantly felonious notice in his pocket, and sure the Earl would not approve if he knew what manner of 'linen-draper' his upholder had engaged.

'Why should we, when we have paid for these?' said Neve crossly. Then he noticed Chaloner's less-than-sartorial appearance, and his eyebrows shot up. 'Lord! If you intend to see him today, you had better come to my office while I sponge off your coat. And when was the last time you shaved?'

Chaloner ran a hand over his jaw, and was startled by the amount of stubble there. No wonder the likes of Gabb and Knowles had regaled him with details of their master's dodgy dealings! He must look thoroughly disreputable.

He followed Neve down two flights of stairs – so as not to spoil the fine symmetry of the house's façade, all the rooms allocated to the staff were below ground level – and through a maze of dim corridors to the upholder's

26

chamber. It was near the buttery, and smelled of bad milk. It was barely large enough for the desk and two chairs that were crammed into it, and every available surface, including the floor, was covered in plans and receipts.

Within moments, they were joined by Thomas Kipps, the Seal Bearer, a bluff, friendly man who, unlike most of the Earl's household, did not care that Chaloner had sided with Parliament during the wars. He always wore the Clarendon livery of blue and yellow, and was never anything less than immaculately attired. His duties were minimal, and involved standing around at ceremonies with as much pomp and dignity as he could muster.

He took one look at Chaloner and called for soap and hot water. While Chaloner shaved and removed the more obvious dirt from his face and hands, Neve set about the mud-spattered coat with a damp cloth. Kipps perched on the table and regaled them with Court gossip.

There was a lot of it, because White Hall was a lively place with many flamboyant characters, and someone was always sleeping with someone else's wife. Then there was the usual gamut of rumours – an imminent Dutch invasion, omens predicting disaster, and one that claimed bankers were embezzling their depositors' money.

'And are they?' asked Chaloner.

Kipps shrugged. 'Probably. They are a dishonest rabble, interested in nothing but making themselves richer. Personally, I consider them a curse, and wish them all to the devil.'

From that, Chaloner surmised that Kipps was in the same boat as Hannah apropos finances.

'I doubt Satan will want financiers in the dark realm,' said Neve acidly, pointing at Chaloner's boots, to remind him to scrape off the mud.

Kipps laughed and turned to another subject. 'Clarendon will be pleased to see you, Tom, but I doubt he will show it. He is irascible at the moment.'

The Earl was always irascible as far as Chaloner was concerned, and although the spy had proved himself loyal on countless occasions by saving his life, reputation, money and family, it was never enough. The Earl needed Chaloner to help him stay one step ahead of his many enemies, but deplored the necessity, and treated him with a disdain that bordered on contempt – he had awarded him the title of Gentleman Usher purely so it would look more respectable in the household accounts. The dislike was fully reciprocated, and Chaloner would leave the Earl's employ without hesitation if another opportunity arose. Unfortunately, it was unlikely that one would.

'He will be pleased,' agreed Neve. He glanced at Kipps. 'I was just telling Chaloner that he might be asked to speak to Baron – those curtains were ordered weeks ago.'

He stood back to assess his handiwork with the cloth. Unfortunately, even sponged clean, Chaloner's travelling coat was not something that should appear in the august company of lord chancellors of England.

'Baron is a scoundrel,' averred Kipps. 'You should never have done business with him.'

Neve was annoyed by the censure. 'He was the cheapest, and the Earl told me to cut costs.'

'He is only the cheapest if he actually supplies what he promised,' Kipps pointed out caustically. 'Have you heard of him, Chaloner? He was the chief henchman of a very corrupt banker called Wheler, but when Wheler was stabbed two months ago, Baron took over the criminal side of his operation. He is now known as the King of Cheapside.'

Chaloner raised his eyebrows. 'I am sure the Earl's

28

enemies will be delighted to learn that he buys goods from felons.'

'Baron is not a felon,' snapped Neve irritably. 'He has never been convicted of a crime.'

'Not yet, perhaps,' harrumphed Kipps. He turned back to Chaloner. 'And if the Earl does order you to treat with the fellow, I recommend you take your sword.'

Chaloner was grateful for the warning. The Earl had a nasty habit of sending him into dangerous situations armed with only half a story, so he appreciated Kipps's concern.

'This is a peculiar headpiece,' said Neve, picking up Chaloner's hat and beginning to slap the dust from it. 'It looks as though it is made of cloth, yet the crown is as hard as steel.'

'It is steel,' replied Chaloner. It was a gift from a Spanish lady he had once loved, and had saved his life on more than one occasion, protecting him from sly blows, and even an attack from a persistently violent gull. 'I always wear it when I travel.'

'Very wise,' said Kipps. 'Incidentally, Secretary Edgeman has just arrived with this month's payroll. Claim yours now – he ran out of money last time, and some of us were obliged to wait two weeks before we were given what we were owed. There is a shortage of coins at the moment, because of the rumour about the bankers mismanaging their clients' funds.'

'It is probably untrue, but people are withdrawing their cash at a tremendous rate.' Neve snickered spitefully. 'The faint-hearted fools think it is safer under their beds.'

'Then I imagine burglars will be pleased,' said Chaloner. 'Large sums of money under beds is always a boon for them. It is the first place they look.'

29

Kipps regarded him in alarm. 'Really? I had better move mine somewhere else, then.'

For all his faults, the Earl of Clarendon worked hard, and was always either at his offices in White Hall, or the grandly named My Lord's Lobby in Clarendon House, surrounded by papers that represented affairs of state. My Lord's Lobby was a frigid, marble monstrosity with windows that looked out across what would eventually become a park, but that was currently an expanse of weed-infested mud.

The Earl had always been plump, even when he had shared the King's exile on the continent and regular meals had not been guaranteed, but high office and a sedentary lifestyle had combined to make him fatter still. He was balding under his luxurious blond wig, and the profusion of lace at his throat accentuated rather than concealed his flabby jowls. He favoured a T-beard – a thin moustache on the upper lip with a tiny sprout of hair on the chin below – and even at leisure, he liked to wear the elegant robes that marked him as Lord Chancellor. It was a vanity that his many enemies loved to mock.

'There you are at last,' he said coolly, when Chaloner knocked on the door and walked in. 'I was beginning to think you had abandoned me these last few weeks. What took you so long?'

'The Hull rebels were not dangerous, sir,' Chaloner explained, supposing the letters he had written outlining the situation had not been read, 'but it still took a while to root them all out. Here is the sheriff's report.'

The Earl tossed it, unopened, on to the table, where Chaloner suspected it would suffer the same fate as his missives. 'Did you visit your uncle's kin when you were in the north?'

Chaloner hailed from a very large family. His father had had twelve siblings, and his mother nine. Most had married, some more than once, so he had enough relations to populate a small village. However, none lived near Hull.

'My uncle, sir?' he asked cautiously, not sure why the question was being put.

'The regicide,' snapped the Earl. 'Your namesake.'

This was a sore subject. Thomas Chaloner the elder had been one of the fifty-nine men who had signed the old king's death warrant, which impressed diehard Parliamentarians, but that had earned his family the eternal hatred of Royalists. The younger Chaloner had been a teenager at the time, powerless to influence events one way or the other. However, he had never thought that executing a monarch was a very good idea, and deplored his kinsman's role in the affair. His uncle had died in Holland several years before, but his radical politics still continued to haunt the surviving members of his family.

'I have not seen my cousins in years,' replied Chaloner warily. 'And—'

'They live in Yorkshire,' interrupted the Earl, and added pointedly, 'Near the alum mines.'

The Guisborough alum mines were the reason why the Chaloner clan had sided with Parliament in the first place. His grandfather had discovered rich deposits of alum – a mineral used for medicine and dyeing – on his land, and had turned them into a profitable business. This had attracted the envious attention of the old king, who had promptly decided to take them for himself. It was brazen theft, and the family had never forgiven the outrage, although Chaloner thought it was time the matter was forgotten – there was no point brooding over something that had happened so long ago and that was unlikely ever to be rectified.

'Yes, they do,' he conceded guardedly. 'But the mines are nowhere near Hull.'

The Earl regarded him balefully, and Chaloner felt a stab of alarm. While he disliked working for the man, he could not afford to be dismissed, especially now that Hannah had debts to pay off. 'They did not support the insurgents?'

'Of course not! My family do not involve themselves in politics these days. We are all tired of rebellion, and none of us want more of it.'

'Buckingham claims otherwise,' said the Earl with a grimace. 'But he does not like you, and I should have known better than to believe him.'

Chaloner's last London-based investigation had caused the Duke some embarrassment, so he was not surprised that the nobleman had avenged himself with a few spiteful stories. 'The sheriff has included a complete list of rebels with his letter,' he said, nodding towards the table. 'You will see that none of my family are on it.'

'Good. I could not have kept you on if your kin were plotting to overthrow the government. Which would have been a nuisance, as there is something I need you to do for me.'

'Talk to Baron about your last two pairs of curtains,' predicted Chaloner heavily.

Neve had reported the shortfall before the spy had been granted an audience, and it had been impossible not to hear the angry tirade that had blasted through the closed door.

The Earl nodded. 'I want them delivered tomorrow *at the latest.*'

Chaloner had a sudden vision of his flamboyant, accomplished uncle, and was glad he would never learn what his nephew was reduced to doing for a living. He would certainly be unimpressed, and perhaps even ashamed. It was not an easy thought to bear.

'Are you sure it is a good idea to do business with Baron, sir?' he asked, aiming to duck the assignment. 'He is almost certainly a criminal.'

The Earl gaped at him, and Chaloner could tell his shock was genuine. 'A criminal? No! Neve told me that he is a linen-draper.'

Chaloner pulled the card from his pocket, feeling it was ample evidence of the kind of operation that Baron ran. The Earl read it, then handed it back.

'I suppose he does sound a little unethical,' he conceded. 'I should have known that three thousand pounds was rather too cheap for such fine quality material.'

'Three thousand pounds?' Chaloner was stunned. It was an enormous sum and not cheap at all – at least four hundred times what the average labourer earned in a year. 'For *curtains?*'

'They are brocade,' said the Earl, as if that explained everything. 'I suppose you had better visit the man, and make it clear that the purchase was made by my upholder, *not* by me. I shall deny any involvement with him, should anyone ask.'

'Very well,' said Chaloner, wondering how to do it in such a way that the villainous-sounding Baron did not immediately scent an opportunity for blackmail.

'But before you offend him, make sure our order has been delivered in full. Those curtains go beautifully with my new carpets – red with a hint of gold.'

Chaloner regarded him askance. 'It might be wiser to end the association at once, sir, before it causes you problems.'

'But no other linen-draper has that particular shade, and my wife has set her heart on it. I *must* have them.'

'As you wish.' Chaloner was careful to keep his voice neutral, but was unimpressed that his employer should persist with the arrangement when it was clear that it should be terminated immediately. Moreover, Lady Clarendon was a sensible woman, who would place her husband's political safety above the colour scheme in her Great Parlour, so it was almost certainly the Earl who was determined to have the things. And it was reckless.

'I do wish, Chaloner,' said the Earl sharply, as if reading his thoughts. 'I cannot undo the fact that my household has done business with Baron, and my enemies will attack me for it anyway, so I might as well have what I have paid for.'

'But it will be easier to defend yourself if you can claim that you renounced the association the moment you learned that Baron might not be entirely respectable.'

'I have learned nothing of the kind, Chaloner,' snapped the Earl crossly. 'Or will you stand in a court of law and bear witness against me?'

Chaloner might, as he disliked the notion of lying under oath, but fortunately the Earl did not expect an answer, and only stared across the desolate, muddy expanse of his garden, stroking his chin thoughtfully.

34

'I think you had better investigate Baron for murder,' he said eventually.

Chaloner blinked his surprise. 'Murder, sir?'

'He was in the employ of a banker named Dick Wheler, who was stabbed to death. If I arrest Baron for the crime, no one can accuse me of anything untoward in my relationship with him.'

Chaloner suspected the Earl's enemies would see straight through such a transparent ruse. Moreover, once in custody, Baron was likely to tell all and sundry about his dealings with the Earl, if not in an effort to wriggle out of the charges levelled against him, then for spite. The whole notion was absurdly flawed, but the Earl continued speaking before Chaloner could say so.

'The Spymaster General investigated Wheler's killing, but failed to catch the culprit.'

He referred to Joseph Williamson, who had the unenviable task of running the country's intelligence network – unenviable, because not only did Williamson now have a war to concern him but also because the monarchy was still weak and half the country would rather have a republic. Plots were rife, as Chaloner's recent foray to Hull attested.

'Did he have any particular suspects?' asked Chaloner, seeing from his employer's growing enthusiasm for the plan that he was not going to be dissuaded. There was no choice but to do as he was instructed – and hope the affair did not end in disaster.

'Oh, yes, dozens! That was the problem. Wheler was hated by his clients for his rapacity, and by his fellow bankers because he was richer than them. And Baron benefited greatly from his death, so he was on the list as well.'

'Lord!' muttered Chaloner. He recalled what Kipps had said: that Wheler had been killed two months ago. How was he supposed to catch the culprit after so much time had passed, especially given that the crime had already been explored by the authorities?

'And there is one last thing,' said the Earl. 'On Friday, three days ago now, a Frenchman named Georges DuPont became ill in a house at the junction of Drury Lane and Long Acre.'

Chaloner knew the building, because he rented rooms on Long Acre – a safe place to hide was useful in his line of work. It was also somewhere he could play his bass viol, or viola da gamba, as Hannah did not like him doing it at home.

'Despite his sickness,' the Earl went on, 'DuPont was able to stagger to a tenement in Bearbinder Lane, which is an alley off Cheapside. He died there a few hours later.'

'Died of what, sir?'

'That is what I want to know, and it is important, because he was a spy. He was introduced to me by a mutual acquaintance – a person who then reported DuPont's suspicious demise.'

'What mutual acquaintance?' asked Chaloner warily. His employer rarely dabbled in espionage, but when he did, naivety and ineptitude invariably led to trouble. It was possible that DuPont's death was the Earl's fault, simply by virtue of his inexperience in such matters.

'I cannot tell you,' replied the Earl haughtily.

Chaloner suppressed a sigh: looking into the matter was going to be a challenging business if he was unable to question key witnesses. 'What kind of spy was DuPont?'

The Earl frowned. 'There are different types?'

36

'I mean was he one of ours? Or was he an enemy agent, working for the French?'

'He was French, as I said, but he was going to supply intelligence for us. On the Dutch.'

'You mean he was one of Spymaster Williamson's people?'

'He was mine,' replied the Earl loftily, then grimaced. 'Or he would have been, had he lived. That is why I want you to find out what happened to him. His death is a serious blow, as we are in desperate need of the kind of information that he offered to provide.'

'Quite,' pounced Chaloner. 'Which is why it is imperative that I speak to the person who brought him to you.'

'Impossible! I promised him anonymity. Have you heard about poor George Morley, by the way? The Bishop of Winchester? He is one of my closest friends, as you know.'

'He is not dead?' asked Chaloner, alarm overriding the irritation he felt for the abrupt change of subject. He liked the gentle-spoken churchman, and he did not take to many of the Earl's cronies, as they were all much of an ilk – pompous, dull and censorious.

'Worse – he is in debt. Yet he is in august company. The Lord Mayor is also in trouble, and so is Prince Rupert. Apparently, their bankers have recalled monies that are owed.'

'Recalled them?' queried Chaloner, thinking of Hannah's plight. 'Or sold them to other financiers, so that the loans can be renegotiated at disadvantageous rates to the borrower?'

'I see you are familiar with the tactics of these leeches. They should be ashamed of themselves. Damned vultures!'

'Do you know anything about a vulture named Rich Taylor?' asked Chaloner, supposing he might as well learn as much as he could about the man who now owned Hannah's debt.

'He is current Master of the Company of Goldsmiths, and a widower with three grown sons named Evan, Randal and Silas. He was great friends with Wheler – the man whose murder I want you to explore – and he has copied Wheler's more unscrupulous but successful methods. However, I hope you do not learn that *he* is the killer, because he will not like it.'

'Few murderers do.'

'Well, Taylor will be angrier than most, because he has so much to lose. He married his son Randal to Wheler's widow, and has thus united the two houses in a vast financial empire. Raw power is why he can do what he likes with his clients, and no one dares stop him. If you have to question Taylor about Wheler, I recommend you tread with care.'

Chaloner invariably felt low after interviews with his employer, and that day was no different. Why did the Earl refuse to reveal who had put him in contact with DuPont? Moreover, he was not looking forward to tackling Baron, suspecting the man would object to being ordered to provide two more pairs of curtains and then dissociate himself from his prestigious customer. And how was he to solve a two-month-old murder that the Spymaster General, with all his myriad resources, had been unable to crack?

But it was a pretty afternoon, with soft white clouds dotting a bright blue sky, and the sun was shining. It was good to be home, and he felt his spirits lift as he savoured the familiar sounds of the city – iron-shod wheels and hoofs on cobbles, the cries of street vendors, the clang of church bells. He slowed to a saunter, enjoying the hectic bustle after the damp stillness of the country, and stopped to buy a venison pastry from a pie-seller. It was surprisingly good, and a definite improvement on army rations in Yorkshire.

He went to Long Acre first, feeling that exploring the death of a spy was the most urgent of the tasks he had been set. The street had once been fashionable, but had grown seedy since the Restoration, its houses redolent of better times. Many were architectural gems, but their timbers were rotting, their shutters needed paint and their roofs leaked. The whole area smelled of bad drains, fried onions and manure.

Chaloner's garret was in the middle of the row, but there was no reason to visit it that day, so he continued on to the building where DuPont had been taken ill. He knocked on the door, but an elderly man from the alehouse next door informed him that everyone had gone cockfighting. Chaloner wrinkled his nose in distaste. He liked birds, and considered that particular 'sport' an affront to decency.

'Did you know a resident here named Georges DuPont?' he asked.

'Not really. You know he died recently? Dr Coo came to tend him when he was ill. That man is a saint. Have you met him? He lives at the Sign of the Bull on Cheapside, near the Standard. He might be able to answer your questions.'

It was a fair walk, but Chaloner did not mind re-acquainting himself with the city. As he went, he over-heard snatches of conversation from passers-by. There

39

was a lot of silly talk about the Dutch, the kind of nonsense that always circulated during a war – the enemy roasted babies on spits, slit the noses of children and assaulted pregnant women. Then there were tales about the King's debauches and the fecklessness of his courtiers. Chaloner rolled his eyes. Nothing had changed since he had been away.

When he arrived at Cheapside he stopped for a moment to survey it. It had the Royal Exchange and the market known as the Poultry at one end, while the great gothic mass of nearby St Paul's Cathedral presided over the other. It was wide, spacious and full of the smells of the trades that were practised in the adjacent lanes – the bakers in Bread Street, the dairymen in Milk Street, and the darker, ranker stench of hot metal from Ironmongers' Lane.

The Standard, a tall structure containing a cistern, stood in the middle of the road, about halfway down. A spiral staircase led to the balustrade on its roof, and there was a fountain at street level – an uninspiring series of spouts that emptied into troughs to provide water for locals. Cheapside was punctuated by churches – mighty St Michael le Querne, followed by St Peter Westcheap with its lofty steeple, stocky All Hallows, St Mary le Bow and its noisy bells, pretty St Mary Colechurch and at the far end, bustling St Mildred Poultry and St Mary Woolchurch.

Chaloner began to look for the Sign of the Bull, but had not gone far before he became aware of a rumpus. The south side of Cheapside, particularly west of the Standard, was the domain of the goldsmith–bankers, and fine carriages with matching horses were not an unusual sight. One had pulled up outside the White Goat

Inn, where it promptly attracted unwanted attention – stones were lobbed by apprentices, and its driver was struggling to keep the animals from bolting.

'Serves them right,' muttered a butcher to a companion as he watched. 'I hate bankers.'

'So do I,' agreed the friend. 'They have far too much money, which is an affront to the poor; and they lend it out at shamefully high rates of interest, which is an affront to us. They—'

He stopped speaking when the carriage door was flung open and a man climbed out to stand glowering with his hands on his hips. He was fashionably dressed with deep-set, dark eyes in a haughtily handsome face, and although he was not very large, there was something about him that commanded attention. The apprentices promptly dropped their stones and slunk away, while the two butchers, evidently afraid that he might have heard their remarks, were not long in following. Chaloner marvelled that a simple scowl should have such a dramatic effect.

As the man was a banker, a trade he was going to have to investigate if he was to learn what happened to Wheler, Chaloner ducked into a doorway to observe unseen. He watched the fellow turn to help a woman alight from the coach. She was considerably younger, and jewels glittered in her hair, and on her earlobes, neck, fingers and wrists. Her skirts were so richly embroidered that he suspected they cost more than he earned in a year, and her shoes were tiny and ridiculously impractical. Yet not even all her finery could make her pretty, and her small, sharp-eyed face immediately put him in mind of a ferret. Moreover, there was an arrogance in her demeanour that was distinctly unattractive.

Once she was out, the third and final occupant of the coach clambered down: a man remarkable only in that he wore no wig – his long yellow hair, which was as fine as a baby's, lay greasily across the top of his head. He was portly, and like virtually everyone else in the city, he had a narrow moustache of the kind currently in vogue at Court.

Unfortunately, Chaloner was not the only one who aimed to stay out of sight, and he started in surprise when a man and a woman joined him in his hiding place. The man had one of the surliest faces Chaloner had ever seen, while the woman was giggling like a schoolgirl, even though she and her companion were in their fifties.

'Forgive us,' she chortled, while Chaloner struggled to extricate his foot from under the man's boot. 'We do not want to be spotted by Mr Backwell either.'

'Backwell?' queried Chaloner, thinking to have stern words with the financier who had sold Hannah's debt and put her in such an uncomfortable position. 'Which one is he?'

'You do not know?' asked the man. 'Then you must be the only fellow in London who does not recognise one of the richest people in the city! He is the one who stepped out last.'

'He is organising an outing for tomorrow evening,' confided the woman. 'He will want us to join him, but we would rather stay at home. We have music planned, you see.'

'Music,' sighed Chaloner wistfully, questions temporarily forgotten. It was his greatest love, his refuge when he was confused or unhappy, and little gave him more pleasure than playing his viol. There had been scant opportunity for such pastimes in Hull, and he had missed them badly.

42

'We aim to sing airs by Dowland and Jenkins,' she elaborated. 'As long as Mr Backwell does not spot us, of course, in which case we shall be obliged to stand around and make awkward conversation with others who wish they were somewhere else. He feels sorry for us, unfortunately, and thinks he is being kind by including us in his invitations.'

'But we wish he would leave us alone,' said the man sourly. 'Taylor does not bother with us any more, so why must Backwell persist?'

'Do you mean Rich Taylor?' asked Chaloner keenly. 'The Master of the Goldsmiths?'

The man pointed at the handsome, charismatic fellow who had driven off the apprentices with a glare. 'There he is – a man whose name suits his status, as he is indeed *Rich* Taylor, and has grown even more so since February.'

'Because of the lady with him,' explained the woman. 'His daughter-in-law Joan, whose first husband was stabbed. She inherited a vast fortune, and formed an alliance with Mr Taylor by marrying his son. Their pooled resources created the biggest bank in London.'

'Then her first husband must have been Dick Wheler,' surmised Chaloner.

The woman nodded to the lane that ran along the side of the tavern. 'He was killed over there, walking down White Goat Wynd. He was alone, as he assumed that no one would dare raise a hand against him, so he never bothered with guards.'

'It is a lesson the other bankers have taken to heart,' said the man with a smirk. 'None take that sort of chance now. And they are wise to protect themselves, as there is no more hated profession than banking these days.'

Chaloner stared at the alley. It linked Cheapside with Goldsmiths' Row, and there was nothing to distinguish it from any other passageway in the area. It was too narrow for anything bigger than a handcart, and comprised walls with a few well-secured gates. It would be very dark at night, so was the perfect place for an ambush.

'We should introduce ourselves,' said the woman. 'I am Lettice Shaw, and this is my husband Robin. He was a goldsmith once, too.'

'Thank God we are out of *that* dirty business,' said Shaw, casting a disapproving eye at the elegantly clad group on the other side of the road.

'Now we run a music shop instead.' Lettice waved towards a nearby building that, while strategically placed to snag passing trade, was an unprepossessing place. 'We have the honour of supplying instruments and books to Court, which is much more fun than high finance.'

'And a good deal less fraught,' agreed Shaw, his glum expression lifting slightly. 'Would you like to see it, Mr . . .'

'Chaloner – Tom Chaloner.'

The couple exchanged a glance. 'Not Hannah Chaloner's husband?' asked Lettice.

Chaloner nodded cautiously. 'Do you know her from Court?'

Lettice inclined her head. 'She bought a flageolet from us last year.'

'A silver one,' added Shaw, a little pointedly. 'With a jewelled case.'

Chaloner did not like the flageolet at the best of times, but it had taken on a particularly shrill quality in Hannah's hands. Fortunately, she had soon tired of it,

44

after which the thing had been tossed in a chest and forgotten. Then he looked from Shaw to Lettice, and groaned.

'I suppose she neglected to pay for it.'

Hannah was not dishonest or especially forgetful, but she took her cue from her aristocratic colleagues, who were notoriously bad at settling their accounts. Chaloner was always amazed that tradesmen were willing to deal with them at all, and could only suppose that they were compensated for the inevitable lack of payment by the kudos accruing from being able to count so-called 'people of quality' among their clientele.

'A matter of forty pounds,' shrugged Lettice, looking away uncomfortably. 'A mere trifle.'

It was a long way from being a mere trifle, and Chaloner did not have it to give them – and he doubted he would be able to raise such a sum very soon if he was obliged to satisfy Taylor first. He supposed he would have to dig the instrument out and see if they would accept it in return for a smaller repayment. Unfortunately, he recalled Hannah flinging it across the room in frustration at one point, while the jewels on the box had fallen prey to dishonest servants. A dented flageolet and a despoiled case were unlikely to be received with great enthusiasm, but Chaloner was desperate enough to try anything.

'Hannah told us that you own alum mines in Yorkshire,' said Shaw. 'They are the only source of the stuff outside Rome, and thus a very lucrative concern.'

'They are,' said Chaloner, thinking the first King Charles would not have stolen them if they weren't. 'But I hope she did not offer them as collateral, because they have not belonged to my family for decades. And I have never been anywhere near them.'

'Oh,' said Shaw, frowning. 'Are you sure? Only she told us that they earned you a fortune.'

'Did she?' Chaloner was unimpressed that she should have fabricated such a tale. 'Well, I am afraid it is untrue. They belong to the Crown.'

'No matter,' said Shaw with a benign smile, giving Chaloner the distinct impression that they did not believe him. 'I am sure she will bring us our money soon.'

'My mother used alum to reduce her freckles,' confided Lettice. 'It is a very useful mineral. But do come and see our shop, Mr Chaloner. You will not be disappointed.'

Chaloner wanted to resume his monitoring of the bankers, but felt it would be churlish to refuse the invitation under the circumstances. And it took no more than a glance to realise that the shop's shabby exterior concealed a veritable Aladdin's Cave of riches. Not only did it have seven or eight very fine viols, a large display of lutes and three virginals, but it sold sheet music by all his favourite composers, including some he had never seen before. He scarcely knew where to look first, and his investigations flew from his mind.

'You will have to excuse the smell,' said Shaw, although Chaloner had been so enraptured that he had barely noticed the aroma of sewage that pervaded the place.

'Our neighbour's cesspit has overflowed into our cellar,' explained Lettice.

Chaloner would not have cared if they had been standing knee-deep in ordure, because he had found a fantasia by Dowland, and was playing it in his mind.

Scenting a possible sale, Shaw took a lute and strummed the first few phrases, indicating with a nod that Chaloner was to pick an instrument and join in. Chaloner selected a bass viol, and joy surged through him as he bowed the first notes he had played in weeks. Lettice leaned over his shoulder and began to sing, although he would have enjoyed her performance more if she had not filled the rests with sniggers. Even so, time passed quickly, and Chaloner was shocked when he heard the Bow Bells chiming for the four o'clock service.

'Please stay,' begged Lettice, as he stood to leave. 'We have much more to show you. For example, have you heard of Dietrich Buxtehude? He is young, but will be famous one day.'

Chaloner was sorely tempted, but duty called. 'I have to visit Dr Coo.'

'He lives five doors along,' supplied Shaw, his harsh features softening. 'When I had a fever last winter, he tended me like a son. He is a true saint.'

It was the second time Chaloner had heard the physician so described.

There was a large sign depicting a bull swinging above the entrance to Coo's home, but Chaloner would have recognised it as belonging to a *medicus* anyway. The door was carved with an image of Aesculapius, the Roman god of healing, complete with serpent-entwined staff, and the place oozed the sharp, clean scent of herbs. The door was open, so he stepped inside.

'I will not be a moment,' called a voice from within. 'Please take a seat.'

A low murmur of voices suggested that Coo was with a patient, so Chaloner perched on a bench and thought about the music he had just played. Notes and melodies drifted through his mind, and he was so lost in them that the client leaving Coo's surgery stumbled over his outstretched legs. Chaloner shot upright to catch him.

The fellow promptly closed his eyes, gulped in a breath and held it for so long that Chaloner wondered if he should summon help. Then he sneezed, right into Chaloner's face.

'Sorry,' he muttered with a wet sniff. Another sneeze followed, along with an unpleasant snorting sound, after which he shuffled out. Chaloner wiped his own face dry with his sleeve.

'I apologise for the wait,' said a tall, thin man with a large bald head. 'Will you come in?'

Chaloner rarely took an instant liking to people, as a life in espionage had taught him that this was unwise, but he experienced an immediate partiality for Abner Coo. The surgery was a warm, comfortable place, and exuded the sense that here was somewhere a person could feel safe – as opposed to the lairs of most *medici*, which tended to reek of urine and blood, and made no bones about the fact that terrible things happened in them.

'How may I help you?' asked Coo, waving Chaloner to a chair before taking the one next to it. This was also in marked contrast to other physicians, who preferred their victims squatting submissively before them on low stools, or better yet, prostrate.

'Your last patient sneezed on me,' said Chaloner, voicing what was uppermost in his mind.

'The rogue! I told him to wear a scarf. I suppose you are worried about the plague? Many folk are, but I tell them the tale of poor Dick Wheler, who was more frightened of it than the lung-rot that was killing him. But in the end neither claimed his life – he fell victim to an assassin's blade, and all his apprehension was for nothing. Such is life.'

'I do not suppose you know the assassin's name, do you?' asked Chaloner hopefully.

Coo shook his head. 'Spymaster Williamson tried to find out, but with no success.'

'The Earl of Clarendon has asked me to investigate Georges DuPont's death,' said Chaloner, unreasonably disappointed that a solution for Wheler's murder was not to be had so easily. 'And I am told that you tended him before he died. Is it true?'

Coo sighed and rubbed his eyes. 'I wondered how long it would be before an envoy from the government arrived. I am afraid that DuPont died of the plague.'

Chaloner stared at him. 'Are you sure?'

'Yes. I have never seen a clearer case: swellings in the armpits and groin, high fever, mottled skin, and death within hours.'

Chaloner edged away. 'And you tended him? I thought that anyone in contact with a victim was to be sealed up for forty days.'

'That does not apply to me, because I am immune,' explained the physician. He saw Chaloner's scepticism. 'I was in Venice during the last outbreak, and I stayed in the hospital the entire time. I never became ill, despite physicking hundreds of sufferers.'

Chaloner wondered if he was immune, too, because he had tended his dying family, then looked after servants and neighbours. Nine people had breathed their last in his arms, but he had not suffered so much as a sniffle. 'Is that possible?'

Coo shrugged. 'How else can you explain my continued good health in that place of death? But I have a theory about the plague: it is not propagated by a miasma, which is the current thinking on the matter, but spread by worms so small that they cannot be seen with the naked eye.'

That notion sent a chill down Chaloner's spine. How could people fight something they could not see? At least a miasma was visible, especially at night when it rose through the ground as a mist, stealing into houses, shops and churches. Coo's theory was so unsettling that he did not want to dwell on it, and returned to its victim instead.

'I am told that DuPont became ill in Long Acre, but died in Bearbinder Lane. It is a distance of a mile and a half. Do you know if he walked or had some kind of transport?'

'He walked – and might have infected dozens as he went. But God was watching over us that day, because the disease remains confined to St Giles.'

'Why did he make such a journey, knowing the risk he posed to others? Or did he not understand what was wrong with him?'

'He was perfectly lucid when I broke the news. I left to fetch him some medicine, but he had gone by the time I returned. I was summoned to Bearbinder Lane a few hours later, but the disease was in its final stages and there was nothing more I could do. He died soon after my arrival.'

'Did you seal up the houses he was in?'

'There was no point. They were tenements, and people came and went from both the whole time I was there – it would have been like trying to block the flow of the Thames. I did not attempt what would have been both futile and impossible.'

Chaloner was seriously unsettled. Coo should have notified the authorities at once, and keeping the news until 'an envoy from the government' came to question him had been unforgivably reckless. He said so.

'Why?' asked Coo with quiet reason. 'Could *you* shut every house and shop that DuPont walked by? Identify every person he might have passed? No, of course not. And as I told you, the disease is confined to the purlieus of St Giles—'

'But it will not stay confined if infected people wander around the city,' Chaloner pointed out. 'You have seen what it can do – you do not need me to remind you of the dangers.'

'No,' acknowledged Coo. 'But Cheapside heaves with unrest at the moment, because of the greed of the gold-smith–bankers who live here, and slapping quarantines on it will do nothing to soothe the situation. I do not want riots and mayhem if they can be avoided.'

Chaloner itched to remark that riots and mayhem were preferable to an epidemic that would kill everyone, but why bother when the deed was done? 'What else do you know about DuPont?'

Coo shrugged. 'Very little. I am told he was French, but I could not place his accent. He was not wealthy, or he would not have been in those particular tenements, although he did mention the possibility of earning a lot of money in the future.'

From the Earl, surmised Chaloner. 'Did you know that he was a spy?'

Coo blinked. 'Was he? There was—'

He was interrupted by a knock on the door. He excused himself and went to answer, but the moment he pulled it open, there was a sharp report and a thud. Chaloner was on his feet with a knife in his hand almost without conscious thought. Two masked men stood on the door-step, and Coo lay in front of them, eyes open but sight-less. One held a still smoking handgun – an elaborate

51

piece with an intricately engraved barrel and an ivory butt. The killer wagged it at Chaloner tauntingly, almost as if daring him to notice what a fine weapon it was.

Chaloner lunged at him with the knife. The gunman hissed his alarm and shied away, but his companion was made of sterner stuff. He also had a firearm, although it was an ancient thing, quite unlike the elegant affair held by the first. There was a flash, a ringing crack and then nothing.

Chapter 2

Chaloner had no idea how long he lay sprawled on Coo's floor, although he sensed it was no more than a few moments. He became aware of a buzz of excited conversation, and opened his eyes to see a number of silhouettes looming over him. All jerked back in alarm when he moved, clearly having thought him dead. There was a persistent ringing in his ears, and the bright flash of the discharge still marred his vision, no matter how many times he blinked.

He sat up and removed his hat to discover the metal marred by a dent. Fortunately, the old gun had not been very powerful – or perhaps its owner had been niggardly with the powder – so although the impact had stunned him, it had done him no serious harm. Gradually, his senses returned to normal, and he saw that Shaw and Lettice were among the horrified onlookers.

'We thought you were dead,' Shaw murmured, helping Chaloner to his feet. 'Which would have been a pity. Not only would it be a waste of a decent violist, but it would be unseemly to ask a new-made widow for forty pounds.'

Lettice giggled, although Chaloner suspected it was more to conceal her embarrassment than because she had found the remark amusing.

'We heard two sharp cracks from our shop,' she explained. 'I thought it was gunfire . . .'

'But I told her that was impossible,' finished Shaw. 'Not in broad daylight on Cheapside. This is London, not the United Provinces. What happened?'

Before Chaloner could reply, others hastened to relate what they had seen. Backwell was first. He was standing with Taylor and Joan, and Chaloner supposed they would have had a clear view of events, given that they had been in the tavern directly opposite.

'After the shots, I saw two men running away,' Backwell said. 'One was waving a gun, which was rash – most killers would have hidden it. They disappeared up Milk Street.'

'Roundheads,' added Joan. Up close, her face was pinched and sour, and her tiny pointed teeth and small pink nose were definitely redolent of a ferret. 'Troublemakers, like all their breed.'

'You were one once,' Backwell reminded her. 'As was I.'

'But *I* was not,' put in Taylor haughtily. Chaloner had sensed the power of the man from a distance, but close up it was almost overwhelming, and he noticed people were careful not to stand too close. 'I was *always* a Royalist.'

'I was led astray by my first husband,' averred Joan. 'But he is dead, and now there is no more loyal servant of the Crown than I.'

'She has changed her tune,' murmured Shaw in Chaloner's ear. 'And I know why: she is afraid the King will use her former loyalties as an excuse to demand a

54

donation for the war, as he has all the other financiers who once loved Cromwell.'

'Which is probably why she married Mr Taylor's son with such unseemly haste,' put in Lettice. 'Wheler left her fabulously wealthy, and she does not want to lose it to a money-hungry monarch. As Mr Taylor was a Royalist, the King leaves him and his riches alone.'

'Who would want to harm Dr Coo?' asked a man whose clothes identified him as a brewer, although not one who earned a very good living. 'He was a gentle man.'

'He was indeed, Farrow,' sighed Backwell. 'He will be missed among the poor – he treated them for free.'

'I advised him against that,' said Taylor. His eyes were hard, like brown buttons, and there was no kindness in the handsome face. He looked, Chaloner thought, exactly like the kind of man who would turn others' misfortunes into profit for himself. 'It was asking to be abused by lazy beggars who cannot be bothered to work.'

'No beggar killed Coo,' stated a laundress angrily. 'A banker did, jealous of his popularity.'

'Who cares about popularity?' shrugged Taylor. 'Especially from paupers. I would rather have the money they owe than their love.'

'We know,' said Farrow sullenly. 'That greedy rogue Wheler stole my brewery, and now I am forced to borrow from you to—'

'This is not the place to discuss such matters,' interrupted Backwell sharply. 'Not with Coo lying dead in front of us. Now, first things first. Is there any money in his pockets?'

'Money?' blurted Chaloner, startled by the question, especially after the curt reprimand that had been snapped at Farrow.

'Coins,' elaborated the banker, and his eyes took on an acquisitive gleam. 'Pounds, shillings and pence. Cash. Currency. Legal tender. Lucre. Specie.'

Chaloner was not the only one who grimaced his distaste when Backwell knelt next to Coo and began to rifle through the physician's clothes. Three shillings and sixpence were found, which Backwell held up reverently, like a clergyman with the Host.

'I shall keep them safe until his next of kin comes to claim them,' he said, placing them in the purse he wore around his neck; it was already bulging. 'Now we can discuss his murder. Who were those two men?'

'I could not tell – they were wearing masks.' Taylor addressed Backwell arrogantly, as if no one else was there. 'But I wager anything you like that they were minions of Baron. We all know that he is not beneath murder if it suits him. *He* sent these men to dispatch Coo.'

'But Coo physics his trainband,' said Backwell doubtfully. 'I doubt he—'

'Trainband!' spat Taylor contemptuously. 'His men are not a company of militia organised to rally in the event of trouble, but a gang – a rabble of thieves, robbers, cut-throats and felons.'

A wave of resentment rippled through the onlookers, making Chaloner suspect that some might be trainband members themselves. He glanced at them. There were one or two merchants among the throng, but most were either obviously impecunious or were like Farrow – people who struggled to make an honest living, and who were compelled to borrow to make ends meet.

'Regardless, Coo tended them when they were hurt or ill,' Backwell was telling Taylor. 'So Baron has no reason to harm him.'

'Then I suppose the murder will remain a mystery,' said Joan with callous indifference. 'Now, let us all be about our own business. Shaw will not mind seeing to Coo. He is no longer a goldsmith, so he can have nothing better to do.'

She turned on her heel and flounced back to the tavern. Taylor followed, although not before he had taken the opportunity to run his eyes over the spectators, giving the impression that he was looking for debtors; Farrow was suddenly nowhere to be seen. Chaloner watched Taylor go, wondering whether to run after him to discuss the murdered Wheler – not to mention Hannah's debt – but decided it was hardly the best time.

'I cannot abide that Joan,' muttered the laundress. 'She was a greedy vixen when she was wed to Wheler, and marrying into the Taylor clan has made her worse than ever.'

There was a murmur of agreement, followed by a lot of vicious remarks about goldsmith–bankers in general. Chaloner turned back to the Shaws, but they had been cornered by Backwell, much to their obvious consternation.

'My outing,' Backwell was saying, blithely oblivious to the unfriendly mood of the onlookers. Personally, Chaloner thought he was reckless to stay there alone. 'I have planned a meal of anchovies, followed by shopping. What time will you and Lettice arrive?'

'Seven,' replied Lettice, although her husband had opened his mouth to decline. Chaloner did not blame him: the excursion sounded dreadful.

'Good,' beamed Backwell. 'It will be a celebration, as the King has just appointed me to oversee the finances for the Dutch war. I am delighted! There is nothing nicer than counting money and my new duties will involve a lot of it. I shall not only buy arms, ammunition and naval supplies, but see to the sailors' pay. All those little packets of coins! What could be more fun?'

'Music,' said Lettice firmly. 'Or listening to birdsong.'

'And cockroach racing,' added Shaw. Chaloner had no idea if he was serious.

But Backwell was warming to his theme and did not hear. 'Coins deserve to be handled by someone who *loves* them, which is why I became a banker, of course. Nothing gives me more pleasure than money – the feel of it in my hands, its delicious scent, the way it glitters.'

He continued in this vein for several minutes, then turned and strode away without giving the Shaws a chance to respond, humming happily to himself.

'Lord!' muttered Chaloner, watching him go. 'Is he in his right wits?'

'He loves money more than life,' said Shaw, then glared at his wife. 'I was looking forward to singing tomorrow. Why did you let him bully you into accepting his invitation?'

Lettice sighed. 'We cannot offend a powerful man – especially one who is friends with Joan. We do rent our shop from her, after all.'

When the bankers had gone, Shaw took control of the situation, albeit reluctantly. A messenger was sent to notify the authorities, Coo was carried inside his house, the laundress was paid to scour his blood from the step, and the remaining gawpers were dismissed with a few pithy words.

'Could Taylor be right?' asked Chaloner, feeling *he*

58

had a right to linger, given that he had almost shared the physician's fate. 'Coo was shot on Baron's orders?'

Shaw shook his head slowly. 'Baron might be a ruthless criminal with a powerful trainband at his disposal, but he would never kill a popular fellow like Coo – the culprit will earn the undying enmity of all Cheapside, and he is too canny to incur that sort of dislike. Unless Coo refused to pay the Protection Tax, of course. Then Baron might strike.'

'The Protection Tax is what we on Cheapside pay to ensure we are not burgled, burned down or vandalised,' explained Lettice in response to Chaloner's questioning look. 'It is extortion, of course, given that Mr Baron's men will be doing the burgling, burning and vandalising.' She turned to her husband. 'But Dr Coo was exempt, Robin – his reward for tending the trainband.'

Shaw shrugged. 'Well, even if Baron was rash enough to kill Coo, no one will ever prove it. He kept Wheler's nasty operation – *his* nasty operation now – running smoothly for years, and he knows how to hide his tracks. He will never be charged with a crime.'

He would, if the Earl had his way, thought Chaloner. 'You say Wheler's operation is now Baron's, but how did Baron win control? Or does he work for Joan?'

'When Wheler died, she inherited everything,' explained Shaw. 'But Baron seized the *illegal* side of the venture – the brothels, gambling dens and Protection Tax – before she could stop him. She was livid, but what could she do? She can hardly take him to court, given that the concerns she wanted to reclaim are criminal.'

'It was probably his antics that encouraged her to marry Randal,' added Lettice. 'No one will steal from her now she is under Mr Taylor's wing.'

'So who killed Wheler?' asked Chaloner, ever hopeful for an easy solution. 'Baron?'

'Perhaps,' replied Lettice. 'Unfortunately, there are lots of rumours but no evidence to support any of them. No one actually *saw* him stabbed.'

'When the body was found the next morning,' Shaw continued, 'it had been stripped completely naked. That suggests to me that it was the work of opportunistic thieves.'

'Not an unhappy client?' pressed Chaloner. 'Or a colleague? Or even a wife who wanted to inherit his business?'

'All are possible,' shrugged Shaw. 'But as Lettice said, there is no proof.'

'The affair has caused much discord on Cheapside, though,' sighed Lettice. 'Everyone is using it to accuse everyone else – paupers blaming bankers, bankers suspecting their clients . . . I suppose that is what happens when a man so universally hated is dispatched.'

'Wheler led the way in setting very high interest rates,' explained Shaw. 'Along with ruthless methods of collecting – an example that is now being followed by Taylor. I deplore such tactics, personally. It would never have happened in my day. Then, bankers were gentlemen.'

Chaloner could only suppose that had been a very long time ago. 'Do you think Wheler was killed by the same people who shot Coo?' He glanced to where the laundress was still scrubbing stains from the step. 'Or are there two murderers on Cheapside?'

Lettice chuckled. 'I suspect there are rather more than two! Mr Baron does not recruit angels for his trainband.'

'The two deaths are not connected,' said Shaw irritably,

60

while Chaloner wondered why such a morose fellow had wed a woman who could not stop laughing. 'How could they be? A much-loved physician and an unpopular banker? One shot, the other stabbed? One killed in an alley, the other on his doorstep? One now, the other two months ago?'

He had a point. 'Plague,' said Chaloner, thinking that as Coo was now unavailable for questioning, he would have to quiz others instead. 'Have you heard that an infected man named Georges DuPont became ill in Long Acre, but came to Cheapside to die?'

'Of course,' replied Shaw. 'But there have been no other cases, thank God. It was a selfish thing to have done, and I cannot imagine what he was thinking.'

Chaloner asked more questions, but although Shaw and Lettice were willing to talk, they knew little of value. Then the parish constable arrived, and it immediately became apparent that the fellow was more interested in returning to the beer he had abandoned than gathering information – he would not be investigating the physician's death.

'I am not surprised,' said Shaw, when he and Chaloner were standing out on the road together; Lettice was helping the laundress lay Coo out. 'He probably thinks Baron is the culprit, and dares not rile him.'

'Why are you no longer a banker?' asked Chaloner, somewhat out of the blue.

Shaw's expression was far from pleasant. 'Tulips.'

'I beg your pardon?'

'They fetched extraordinarily high prices a few years ago, and I, like many others, traded in them. But it was a bubble – a speculative plan that collapsed. At its height, a single bulb was worth twelve acres of land. I might have weathered the storm had we bankers stuck together, but it was every man for himself. Yet losing all was a blessing in disguise.'

'It was?' asked Chaloner doubtfully.

Shaw smiled, the first genuine one Chaloner had seen him give. 'Selling music to the Court is a far more rewarding existence than banking could ever be. It is not just the war and this terrible scramble to raise money for the King, but there was the Colburn Crisis.'

'My wife mentioned him. He gambled, and lost thousands of borrowed pounds.'

Shaw winced. '*I* would have lent him money, had I been a goldsmith. He was a respectable vintner, who offered houses and land as collateral. Unfortunately, he had already lost these at cards, so bankers who expected a field or a cottage when he defaulted found themselves with nothing. Several have been ruined.'

'Were Backwell and Taylor badly affected?'

'Yes, but they are wealthy enough to weather the crisis. However, Percival Angier committed suicide, while John Johnson went mad. My heart goes out to their families.'

Chaloner spent the rest of the evening talking to Cheapside residents about Wheler, Baron, Coo and DuPont, but learned nothing he did not already know. Wheler had been greedy, vicious and unpopular, and most people seemed glad he was no longer alive. By contrast, no one had a bad word to say about Coo, who was loved for his kindness and generosity.

When the daylight had faded, and he was sure of not being seen, Chaloner walked to the New Coffee House on Gracious Street, which he knew to be a favourite haunt of Spymaster Williamson. It was not that he was keen to seek out such disagreeable company, but he needed to know more about DuPont if he was to discover what had possessed the dying Frenchman to wander across half the city. A conversation with Williamson might save him some time.

The New Coffee House was a small but elegant establishment that attracted clerics and the wealthier kind of merchant – the sort of men who, unlike Chaloner, did not mind being seen hobnobbing with a person whose remit was to spy on the general populace. Its decor was discreetly affluent, and although it still reeked of pipe smoke and burned beans, there was also an underlying aroma of furniture polish and the lavender that had been set in bowls on the window sills.

Chaloner walked in, appreciating its cosy warmth after the chill of a spring evening, and saw he was in luck: Joseph Williamson, Under Secretary of State and the current Spymaster General, was lounging by the fire. Williamson was a tall, aloof man who had been an Oxford academic before deciding to dabble in politics. He was smooth, ruthless and devious, and while he and Chaloner had been forced to work together in the past, it was an uneasy alliance, and neither trusted the other.

Williamson's eyebrows shot up in surprise when Chaloner sat next to him. 'You!' he exclaimed. 'I thought you were chasing insurgents in Hull. Or, if Buckingham is to be believed, fomenting rebellion with your kin in Guisborough.'

'Then Buckingham is mistaken. My family are peaceful folk.'

'Perhaps so, but they are bitter over losing their alum mines, according to the Duke,' Williamson went on.

'Especially now that it is in such great demand for plague remedies. But do not worry about him – he needs to travel north himself soon, to pay off his debts by selling some land, and will soon forget that he is irked with you.'

Chaloner regarded him sombrely. 'Do *you* think the plague will come?'

Williamson grimaced. 'It is already here – a dozen cases in St Giles. Unfortunately, there have been rumours about an outbreak for so long now that the terror has worn off, and the foolish think we have escaped. But I sense it is just biding its time.'

Chaloner shuddered and changed the direction of the discussion. 'What do you know about Georges DuPont, the French spy who was diagnosed with the disease in Long Acre, but who went to die in Bearbinder Lane?'

Williamson regarded him in alarm. 'What French spy?'

'He offered to supply intelligence on the Dutch, apparently.' Chaloner was careful to conceal the Earl's involvement – Williamson would not appreciate meddling in his domain.

'Well, he was not one of mine, although all manner of worms are emerging from the woodwork these days, hoping to earn a quick profit by selling information. Few know much of value. However, I am rather more concerned about people wandering around with the plague. Did the fellow set out to spread the contagion deliberately?'

'I do not know, although a physician named Coo assured me that no new cases have arisen from the episode. Or he *was* assuring me, before he was shot and killed.'

Williamson eyed him balefully. 'You do lead an exciting life, Chaloner. You cannot have been home many days, yet you are already embroiled with spies, plague and murder.'

'Hours, not days,' said Chaloner ruefully.

'Coo was a popular man on Cheapside, and people will want vengeance. May I assume that you plan to look into his death, given that he seems to be connected to your DuPont?'

'I suppose so.' Chaloner half wished he was back under a hedge in Yorkshire. It had been uncomfortable, but at least his mission had been straightforward.

'Good. The Dutch war has left me very short of operatives, and I do not have a man to spare. Find out who killed Coo and what this DuPont was doing, then report to me.'

'My Earl will not—'

'Your Earl will be delighted with an opportunity to serve his country, and will not demur when I inform him that you are working in both our interests.'

Chaloner stood to leave. The visit had been a waste of time: DuPont was not known to Williamson, and he had learned nothing to further his enquiries. Worse, he now had the Spymaster expecting answers from him. He sincerely hoped the Earl would not object to Williamson being briefed, too, as he had no desire to be caught in the middle of two such powerful men.

It was late by the time Chaloner left the coffee house, and although he knew he should tackle Baron, it had been a long day and he was not in the mood. He started to walk home, but then thought of something he would far rather do – visit John Thurloe in Lincoln's Inn. Feeling his flagging spirits revive at the prospect of seeing an old friend, he set off at a jaunty clip, and was just passing the Poultry Market when a coach drew up beside him.

It was the aspiration of every ambitious Londoner to own a private carriage – an expensive commodity that required not only purchasing the vehicle itself, but also horses, stabling and staff to care for them. This one was new and shiny, and its horses had been chosen for their matching colours. There was a coat of arms on its side, but not one Chaloner recognised, although he was relieved to note that it did not belong to Buckingham. He peered at it in the light from a nearby tavern, then recoiled in astonishment when he saw what the bear rampant was doing to the hart.

'It is a joke, Tom,' said Temperance North, pulling aside the carriage's curtain to laugh at his shock. 'Do you not think it amusing?'

Chaloner supposed it did have a certain style, although he suspected there would be some who would take offence at such ribaldry. Cromwell's Puritans might no longer be in power, but that did not mean they had gone away.

He had met Temperance three years earlier, when she had been a shy teenager. Her parents had died not long after, and she had startled everyone by using her inheritance to establish an exclusive brothel – although she preferred the term gentlemen's club – which had made her very wealthy. Dining on expensive delicacies with her patrons had taken its toll on her figure, and she was now a very large young woman, something her costly clothes failed to conceal. She was losing her teeth, too, presumably from all the sweetmeats that were readily available.

'Do you like my coach?' she asked, waving a plump hand at it with undisguised pride.

'Very nice,' replied Chaloner, dutifully admiring the smart black paint with the gold trim. The driver wore a scarlet uniform, as did the footmen who stood on the back. One jumped off to open the door, revealing one of the most luxuriously appointed interiors Chaloner had ever seen, all plush satin and lacy curtains. Its opulence told him that the club was continuing to make Temperance richer and richer.

'Now that you are home, I need you to talk to Richard,' she said as he climbed in, referring to Richard Wiseman, her lover, who held the post of Surgeon to the King.

'Yes?' he asked coolly, hurt that she had only waylaid him to beg a favour.

'You must talk to him about the plague.'

Chaloner raised his eyebrows. 'I am sure he knows a lot more about it than I do.'

She glared at him. 'I do not want you to teach him about it. I want you to convince him not to risk himself by entering infected houses should it come. And you must also make him promise not to invent a cure.'

'I suspect that might be beyond even his lofty abilities,' said Chaloner soberly. 'There is no cure for the plague.'

Temperance's expression was wry. 'But there is money to be made in selling palliatives. However, as a man of integrity, Richard will want his to be effective, and I am afraid he will take it to a victim to see whether it works.'

'I should hope so! How else will he know if it is worth the money?'

'That is not the point, Thomas,' said Temperance irritably. 'I do not want him to die.'

She pulled out her pipe and began to puff furiously, filling the coach with fumes. They were still stationary, and with no breeze to dissipate the fug, the air soon turned poisonous. Chaloner started to open a window, but she stopped him.

'Tobacco is the best way to prevent infection. In fact, it is the only way to stay healthy.'

'Did Wiseman tell you that?'

'No, it is common knowledge. Richard has some lunatic notion that the plague is caused by worms, creatures so small that they cannot be seen by the naked eye.'

'I was just speaking to a physician who thought the same. Abner Coo.'

'Yes – he, Richard and a colleague called Dr Misick have devised this wild theory between them, although every other sensible person knows that a miasma is to blame.'

'Did you ever meet Coo?' asked Chaloner.

'Several times. A nicer man is difficult to imagine.'

'So everyone says, but he has just been shot.'

Temperance listened in horror as Chaloner recounted what had happened. 'Richard will be upset when he hears. He likes Coo. I must send him a message at once.'

She snapped her fingers, and one of the footmen instantly appeared to do her bidding. She gave him a brief report, then dispatched him to Chyrurgeons' Hall, after which she felt the dent in Chaloner's hat. 'And it was definitely Coo who was the target? Not you?'

Chaloner regarded her balefully, wishing she held him in higher regard. 'I have not been home long enough to warrant those sorts of attentions. It was certainly him they meant to kill.'

'Ask Richard or Dr Misick about him. They knew him better than I. Especially Misick. He is physician to the bankers, and can usually be found in and around Goldsmiths' Row. Where are you going, by the way? Now I have my own coach, I can take you there.'

'Chancery Lane,' replied Chaloner. 'To see John Thurloe.'

*

68

As it transpired, Chaloner would have made better time on foot, because London was in the grip of one of its 'stops' – traffic was often heavy on Cheapside, even late into the evening. A vehicle had broken a wheel by the Little Conduit, and coaches, hackney carriages and wagons were jammed nose to tail, none going anywhere until it was removed.

Chaloner begrudged the wasted time, although Temperance was content to lounge in smoky luxury, chatting about the club. Her patrons gossiped, especially when they were in their cups, and as some were members of government, the Church, various national committees and the Privy Council, they were party to a good deal of sensitive information. Thus Chaloner learned that the war was predicted to cost a good deal more than the two million pounds that had originally been anticipated, and that this, along with the reckless excesses of Colburn the gambler, had put the city's bankers in a tight spot.

'I know,' he said. 'Robin Shaw mentioned it earlier.'

'The man who sells music to the Court? He is a morose fellow, and I cannot imagine how Lettice puts up with him. However, they did teach me how to play "Green Sleeves" on the flageolet that I bought from them. I shall entertain you with it the next time you visit.'

'Oh,' said Chaloner, sincerely hoping she would forget.

'There is his shop.' Temperance pointed out of the window, reminding him that they had only travelled half the length of Cheapside since he had embarked. 'And the scruffy place next door is the home of that revolting Oxley family. Did Shaw tell you about their sewage?'

'Lettice mentioned an overflow from her neighbours' cesspit.' The conversation had taken a distinct nosedive,

69

and he searched for a way to bring it back to his investigations.

'It caused a terrible mess,' Temperance went on before he could think of one. 'Oxley is in Baron's trainband, which he thinks gives him the right to do whatever he likes. However, his wife is a whore, while his children should have been strangled at birth.'

'You do not like them, then.'

'No, I do not,' spat Temperance, then became aware that he was laughing at her. She scowled at him and fell into a sulk, although not for long. The sight of a carriage that was even more sumptuously appointed than her own prompted another bout of gossip.

'That is Backwell's coach. He is impossibly wealthy, but even *he* cannot give the King everything he wants for the war, so he has been obliged to sell his clients' debts to Taylor.'

'Yes,' said Chaloner drily. 'Hannah's was one of them.'

'Then I pity her. Taylor is a beast, and so are the men he hires to do his bidding.'

'The bankers should tell the King that they cannot meet his demands. It is unreasonable to expect them to pull money from thin air.'

Temperance smirked. 'They are afraid that if they do not give him what he wants, he will follow his father's example and help himself.'

'Impossible! A monarch seizing his subjects' assets would start another civil war.'

'On the contrary, everyone hates the goldsmiths and would love to see them broken. Indeed, it would make His Majesty the most popular man in the country. After all, would *you* give your life to defend the riches of wealthy financiers?'

70

Chaloner would not, especially after their dealings with Hannah. 'James Baron,' he said, turning to another matter. 'Have you ever met him?'

'Several times.' Temperance smiled. 'I know he is a lout, but I like him very much, and he has been nothing but charming to me. He visits the club on occasion, and although some of my patrons were wary at first, he soon won them around.'

'Do you know where he lives?'

'At the far end of Cheapside, near St Mary Woolchurch. He has a very nice house, more like the home of a respectable merchant than a felon. He has a beautiful but stupid wife named Frances, and two well-behaved children who are a world apart from the Oxley brats.'

She began to list the crimes that Baron was alleged to have committed – theft, extortion, fraud, burglary, robbery. As they were still on Cheapside, she was even able to point out some of his operatives: the crook-backed man was a counterfeiter, the fair-haired boy was a pick-pocket, while the pair in the grubby brown coats – whom Chaloner recognised as Gabb and Knowles –collected the Protection Tax.

'I would invite you to see *my* new curtains,' she said, after Chaloner had given her a brief account of the Earl's problem, 'but someone stole them last week. I have no idea how, because every door and window was locked. It was almost as if they disappeared into thin air.'

'My wife – my first wife, that is – put curtains in our house in Amsterdam,' recalled Chaloner, surprising himself with the confidence. He rarely spoke about Aletta. 'They were always full of soot and were a nuisance to wash. I do not think the fashion will last.'

71

'Perhaps, but they do look pretty. All the best houses have them, and to be without is considered passé, although I do not think I shall replace the ones at the club. They are a fire hazard when you have patrons who are careless with their pipes. I am surprised that Hannah has not invested in some, though. She is a lady of fashion and taste.'

'Please do not talk to her about it,' begged Chaloner. 'We cannot afford them.'

'Then take out a loan,' suggested Temperance. 'You dismiss such things as frippery, but appearances matter at Court, and Hannah might lose her post if she is seen as miserly or impecunious. She is not just being frivolous, you know.'

At that moment, they crawled past the broken coach, and both peered out of the window to look at it. It was illuminated by pitch torches, and to Chaloner, the damage looked deliberate, as though someone had taken a mallet to the spokes. The driver was struggling to replace them, working alone, because the footmen who should have been helping were involved in a furious fracas with a band of thickset, pugilistic louts. The argument was about Coo's murder, with each side accusing the other of being responsible.

'That carriage belongs to the Goldsmiths,' said Temperance, annoying Chaloner, who was trying to listen to the squabble. 'Their hall is in Baron's domain, but its members have decided not to pay the Protection Tax. I suppose their coach has just suffered the consequences.'

'There will be a fight,' predicted Chaloner, watching the footmen produce cudgels, cheered on by apprentices from their Company, who had been drawn to the trouble like moths to a flame.

'There he is,' said Temperance suddenly, lowering her voice. 'The King of Cheapside.'

Chaloner studied Baron with interest. The felon was tall and powerfully built, although the area around his middle was tending to fat. Even from a distance, he was a person who commanded attention, and when he spoke, people stopped bickering and listened.

'The pair standing behind him are his captains,' Temperance continued. 'The one with the big nose is Charles Doe, said to be wild, dim-witted and dangerous.'

Chaloner had met lots of men who fitted that description, but he could believe it of Doe, who was a ball of restless energy; his red face suggested he had been drinking.

'And the other?' he asked, looking at a small fellow whose shoulders seemed to be sewn to his ears, so that his head sank into his body like a tortoise's. His hair was his own, a thick brown mane that was swept directly back from his forehead to tumble impressively down his back. It formed a smooth roll at the front, and Chaloner could not imagine how it stayed in place. With egg white, perhaps.

'Francis Poachin,' replied Temperance. 'He runs the Feathers tavern, which is famous for its naked dancers.' She sounded disapproving, which was rich coming from a brothel-keeper. 'And there is Oxley. I might have known *he* would appear where there is trouble.'

Oxley might have been handsome were it not for the look of sullen resentment on features that had been allowed to grow dissipated. He had black hair and blue eyes, and brandished a stick that was longer and thicker than anyone else's. Chaloner was sorry for the Shaws – they seemed decent people and deserved better neighbours.

'That slimy Randal Taylor is here, too,' Temperance chattered on. 'He comes to the club sometimes, and I would refuse to let him in were it not for the fact that he always pays his bills on time. He is the middle son of Taylor the banker – the one who married Joan Wheler.'

'I met Joan today,' said Chaloner absently, looking to where she pointed. Randal was a puny, tow-haired individual who looked nothing like his charismatic sire.

'Ferret-face,' said Temperance nastily. 'She hitched herself to Randal with indecent haste, just to secure an alliance with his father. Of course, it was a shrewd decision. It has given her enormous power – more than most men.'

'Who will inherit the bank when Taylor dies?' asked Chaloner. 'Randal?'

'Evan, the eldest. By all accounts, Joan wanted to marry Taylor himself, but he was not in the market for another wife at the time, although word is that he now regrets turning her down. Then she asked for Evan, but he was already wed, so it had to be the next in line – namely Randal. She was stupid to have accepted him – she should have held out for Silas.'

'Silas?'

'The youngest of the Taylor boys. He is handsome, charming *and* single. Apparently, she is furious with herself for taking Randal before looking at Silas, but she was under pressure to secure a strong ally fast, lest Baron stole any more of her inheritance.'

'I served with a Silas Taylor in the army,' mused Chaloner, wondering if it could be the same man. '*He* was the son of a banker. He was also very interested in music.'

'And in killing Royalists, presumably,' remarked Temperance.

Chaloner veered away from that subject. 'He is an excellent violist, and composed airs—'

He jumped when there was a thump on the door, but it was only a ragged boy shoving a leaflet at them. It transpired to be one of Baron's semi-literate notices – the felon was taking advantage of the stop to engage in a little impromptu advertising.

Suddenly, the shouting outside reached a new phase of intensity, and Oxley drew a knife. It was the spark that both sides had been waiting for, and the quarrel quickly became a brawl. One apprentice lobbed a pot of oil with a burning cloth stuffed into its neck, which exploded on impact. As such items took time to prepare, it was clear that he had come expecting the situation to turn violent. It skittered beneath Temperance's carriage, shedding flames as it went. Terrified, her staff fled without a backwards glance, prudently stripping off their scarlet finery as they went.

'Tom!' shrieked Temperance, as smoke began to ooze up through the floor.

Chaloner flung open the door, and was obliged to draw his sword when Oxley ran towards him, aiming to trounce him before ransacking the vehicle. Chaloner drove him back with a wild slash, then pulled Temperance to safety. Others snatched at them as they hurried past, but half-heartedly, and it was clear that they were more interested in the coach.

He draped his coat around Temperance's shoulders to disguise her fine clothes, and she had had the sense to remove her costly wig. She was shaven-headed underneath, so he gave her his hat, and they beat a tortuous path through the frenzy of flailing fists, aiming for the nearest alley. It was not easy, but they managed eventually, after which he took her hand and led her home.

By the time Chaloner had delivered Temperance to the club, it was too late to visit Thurloe, who liked to retire early. He went home instead, where he found the house oddly quiet. The housekeeper had gone to Shoreditch to convalesce, while the footman, cook-maid and scullion were out. Hannah was still at Court, so the only person in was the elderly page – Gram – who grinned amiably when Chaloner walked into the kitchen.

Chaloner nodded coolly, knowing perfectly well that Gram was trying to ingratiate himself in the hope that he would not feature among the economies that would have to be made to resolve Hannah's debt problem.

'But I like it here,' the page objected, when Chaloner told him the ploy would not work.

Chaloner was sure he did. None of the servants worked very hard, but they still enjoyed regular meals, pleasant living quarters and a generous salary. 'I am sorry.'

'Not as sorry as me,' cried Gram. 'I have nowhere else to go.'

'You have no family?'

'All dead,' replied Gram. 'They perished to a man in the plague that swept through London the year that Good Queen Bess passed away.'

'But that was more than sixty years ago!' exclaimed Chaloner, feeling it should have been enough time for Gram to have either married and produced a family of his own or acquired some friends.

'So?' sniffed Gram. 'I still feel their loss keenly. But if you cannot pay me, you may have my services for free

– which is better than me starving in a Cheapside gutter.'

'Cheapside?' asked Chaloner, bemused. 'Why there?'

Gram shot him a lugubrious look. 'Because that is where I was born – and where I will die if you oust me.'

He proceeded to tell Chaloner the story of his life – a singularly uneventful one, as his way of dealing with the political and social upheavals that had occurred that century was to pretend they were not happening. The wars had touched him not at all, and the closest he had come to witnessing a significant incident was hearing the bells toll after the old king's execution.

He and Chaloner shared the remains of a pie and a jug of ale, after which Chaloner wrote a brief message to the Earl outlining his meagre discoveries, and asked Gram to take it to Clarendon House. Gram seized it with a pathetic eagerness to please, and disappeared into the night.

Chaloner went to bed and slept until Hannah arrived home, which she did just as the nightwatchman was calling the hour as three o'clock. She had been to a banquet, and wore a fabulous dress of green silk. It caught the colour of her eyes and accentuated her dainty figure, yet all Chaloner could wonder was how much it had cost.

'We need to discuss our predicament,' she said soberly, stepping out of it and laying it carefully on a chair. The only jewellery she wore was a necklace of pearls, which had belonged to her mother. 'Bab May was waylaid by Taylor's henchmen tonight, and only escaped a beating by giving them a beautiful gold hatpin in the shape of a ship.'

Chaloner sat up, rubbing his eyes. He had been enjoying an unusually deep sleep, and his wits were sluggish. 'Were they the same louts who came here?'

77

'I believe so. Bab's experience encouraged others to admit their difficulties, too – Lord Rochester and Sir Alan Brodrick are also being hounded by them.'

'I met Robin and Lettice Shaw yesterday.' Chaloner swallowed, feeling an unpleasant scratchiness at the back of his throat; he supposed he had been snoring. 'They told me that you bought a flageolet from them.'

Hannah pulled a disagreeable face. 'Do they still want to be paid? How tiresome! I bought it ages ago, when I was trying to impress you with my musical talents.'

Chaloner refrained from remarking that she was fortunate not to have driven him away. 'You also told them that I owned some alum mines.'

Hannah's expression grew decidedly furtive. 'They were going to withhold credit, but they knew your uncle, and *he* had mentioned the mines. So I made a few general observations about the venture, and it was hardly my fault that they concluded you were his heir.'

'You mean you deliberately misled them,' said Chaloner coolly.

Hannah came to sit next to him. 'Yes and no. Your uncle talked to me about Guisborough once, and he said the concern belonged to *all* the Chaloners.'

'Perhaps he did, but that does not make it true. And even if they were returned to my family, I would not be a beneficiary. I am the youngest son of a youngest son – too far removed to be in line for anything.'

'That is a pity,' sighed Hannah. 'We could do with a windfall. But you cannot castigate me for letting the Shaws believe what they wanted to hear – they were so keen to imagine me as the wife of a wealthy alum mine owner that it would have been churlish to disillusion them.'

Chaloner shot her an irritable glance, and told her to bring all the outstanding bills to the drawing room, where they began the depressing task of sorting through them. His temper was not improved by the breakfast she cooked, which comprised eggs fried to the consistency of rubber, heaped on a piece of bread from which she had not bothered to scrape the mould.

'We can extricate ourselves from this muddle,' he said eventually, sitting back and trying to ease the ache from his shoulders. 'But it will involve sacrifices.'

Hannah promptly burst into tears. She did not often cry, and it had the effect of making him feel guilty as well as disheartened. He rested his elbows on the table and scrubbed his face with his hands. His eyes were sore, and her cooking had exacerbated the rawness of his throat. He waited until her sobs had subsided – it did not occur to him that she might appreciate a hug or a few kindly words – before continuing.

'First, we must move out of this house. What do you say to an attic in Long Acre?'

'I would sooner die,' sniffed Hannah. She saw his dark expression. 'All right, we will leave our home, but not for an unfashionable location like Long Acre. I will ask at Court today. Someone may have rooms we can rent, perhaps in Cannon Row or Axe Yard.'

'Second, we must dismiss the servants. Can you find them posts elsewhere?'

She nodded, dabbing her eyes. 'The housekeeper has offered to take unpaid leave while she recovers from her illness, and the girls will be easy to place, as there is always a demand for cook-maids and scullions. The footman will be more difficult, because he is surly and has an aversion to work. And as for poor Gram . . .'

'Perhaps Temperance will take him, although I cannot imagine what he might do.'

'Temperance.' Hannah brightened. 'She is wealthy. Perhaps she will lend us—'

'No,' interrupted Chaloner firmly. 'We do not borrow from friends.'

There were more tears when he listed the possessions that would need to be sold, and he wished she had commissioned Lely to paint someone other than herself. No one would be interested in a portrait of a minor courtier, whereas one of the King or a famous noble might have been worth something. Unfortunately, although the outstanding pay he had collected from Clarendon House the previous day would allow him to disburse the baker, butcher, fishmonger, tailor and grocer, it would not begin to touch what they owed Taylor.

'Or Shaw,' he added. 'Where is that flageolet? I know it is dented, but Shaw still might agree to reduce the amount we owe if we give it back to him.'

'I threw it away. You did not appreciate my musical efforts, so I lost interest in it.'

He knew they would argue if they debated her casual approach to expensive belongings, so he let the matter drop. 'Are there any other debts that I should know about?'

She shook her head. 'The only truly pressing one is Taylor's – which would not have been a problem if Backwell had not sold it.'

Chaloner glanced at the figures he had scrawled on a piece of paper, and hoped Taylor would agree to wait until she had secured buyers for some of their belongings.

'You can dismiss the servants,' he said, feeling this was

an unpleasantness he did not have to endure. It had been her decision to hire them, so she could deal with their dismay when told they were no longer needed. Hannah eyed him balefully, but nodded assent.

'That Nicholas Colburn has a lot to answer for,' she said bitterly. 'He knew the heartache he would inflict on decent people with his profligacy, and he killed himself because he could not bear the shame. Horrid, selfish man!'

As Colburn was not the only one who had amassed debts, Chaloner thought she was a fine one to pass judgement.

Chapter 3

It was still dark as Chaloner trudged towards Lincoln's Inn, but he knew Thurloe would be awake. The hours around dawn were his friend's favourite time of day, a quiet period in which he could think and reflect without interruption. Generally speaking, Thurloe disliked his musings interrupted, but he always made an exception for Chaloner.

Thurloe had been Cromwell's sole Secretary of State, a post he had held concurrently with those of Spymaster General and Controller of the Post Office. There had been other titles and honours, too, but he had resigned them all when the Commonwealth had fallen. The King had bewailed the loss of so much expertise, but Thurloe had steadfastly declined to serve another regime. He now lived unobtrusively, dividing his time between Lincoln's Inn and his estates in Oxfordshire.

Lincoln's Inn was one of four foundations in London that licensed lawyers; Chaloner had been a student there himself briefly, after he had finished his degree at Cambridge. The spy crossed Dial Court, named for the sundial that always graced its centre – the current model had such a complex array of rings and discs that no one knew how to read it – and made his way to Chamber XIII, a suite of rooms on the top floor. He listened outside the door for a moment, and when there was only silence within, he tapped softly and opened it.

'Tom!' cried Thurloe, giving one of his rare smiles. He was slightly built with light brown hair and large blue eyes. His unimposing physique led some to believe him weak, but he had not survived the hurly-burly of interregnum politics by being bland and ineffective. There was a core of steel in Thurloe that had made him a formidable statesman. 'When did you return?'

'Yesterday.' Chaloner sat in one of the fireside chairs and looked around, aware of the comfortingly familiar aroma of woodsmoke, beeswax polish and the musty scent of old paper. The decor was sombre and heavy, with book-packed shelves and dark, substantial furniture. He had once found it oppressive, but had grown to appreciate its air of venerable solidity.

'Well, I am glad to see you safe,' said Thurloe, touching his shoulder in a self-conscious gesture of affection. The ex-Spymaster was not a demonstrative man, and it was often said that he had no friends. It was true to a degree – he knew a lot of people, but allowed few to grow close. Chaloner understood why: it did not do for spies to have too large a circle of confidants, and although Thurloe was no longer engaged in espionage, it was a difficult habit to break.

Knowing Thurloe would want a report on his travels, Chaloner told him about the feeble uprising in Hull. The ex-Spymaster liked to keep abreast of current affairs, partly because he was interested, but mostly because he was still hated by many Royalists, and staying informed allowed him to be one step ahead of those who itched to see his head on a pole outside Westminster Hall, next to Cromwell's.

'But it kept you out of London for a while,' he said, when Chaloner had finished, 'which was no bad thing after you crossed the Duke of Buckingham. He is still vexed with you, so you might want to avoid White Hall until he travels north himself.'

'Then let us hope he goes soon. I do not have time to play hide and seek with him.'

'Thank you for visiting Cromwell's wife and son on my behalf,' Thurloe went on. 'How was poor Elizabeth? I expected your missive to contain a little more detail, to be frank – a letter to a friend, not a terse memorandum to a spymaster.'

Chaloner struggled to think of what else he could add. Mrs Cromwell, who had once held the lofty title of Lady Protectress, was now just a tired, ageing widow with health problems. She had played no part in Commonwealth politics, and had never been comfortable with the role that Parliament had thrust upon her. She now lived quietly in the country with her favourite daughter, and spent her days wishing that the civil wars had never happened.

'She grieves for her husband,' he replied eventually. 'And probably will until she dies.'

Thurloe sighed sadly. 'Yes, she was devoted to Oliver. Anything else?'

Chaloner shook his head. 'She is as content as can be expected.'

'She is in reasonable spirits?' pressed Thurloe. 'Nothing has vexed her of late?'

'Well, she was irked when the cook put too many onions in his sausages.'

84

'You discussed baking with her?' demanded Thurloe sharply.

Chaloner was startled by the abrupt tone. 'Once or twice. It was difficult to find subjects that interested her, to be honest, and meals *are* the highlight of her day. What is this about?'

Thurloe picked up a booklet from the table. 'I am trying to ascertain whether she might have seen this nasty little epistle.'

Chaloner took it. It was not very long, and was entitled *The Court & Kitchin of Elizabeth, Commonly called Joan Cromwel, Wife of the late Usurper, Truly Described and Represented, and now Made Publick for General Satisfaction*. It comprised a Preface to the Reader, an Introduction, and then a lot of recipes, beginning with 'How to make a rare Dutch pudding'.

'Were her Dutch puddings any good?' he asked, wondering what he was supposed to say.

Thurloe shot him a baleful look. 'Take it with you and read it, then you will understand my concern. It is a vicious piece of invective against a harmless old lady who has never hurt a soul. It accuses her of niggardliness, greed and corruption.'

'Printed for Randal Taylor,' read Chaloner. He glanced up. 'Taylor the banker has a son named Randal. He married Dick Wheler's widow.'

'Yes.' Thurloe's expression was contemptuous. 'He fancies himself a writer, although it is a pity his talents do not match his aspirations. Walk with me in the garden, Tom. Even the thought of that loathsome worm makes me long for clean air.'

It was still not fully light, although it would not be long before the sun poked its fiery head above the horizon.

Pale pink clouds dappled the sky, promising a fine day to come, and birds were already singing in the Inn's plentiful trees and bushes.

'Did you know about the pamphlet when you asked me to visit Mrs Cromwell?' asked Chaloner, as they strolled along one of the Inn's neatly gravelled paths, past manicured rose beds and miniature hedges of lavender and thyme. 'Is that why you wanted a report on her well-being?'

Thurloe shook his head. 'The pamphlet appeared after you had left – I asked you to go because I heard she was in poor health and I was worried.' He made a moue of distaste. 'Randal should be ashamed of himself. Not only might his vicious musings distress a vulnerable widow, but mean-spirited Royalists crow that every word is true, while gallant Roundheads leap to defend her. There have been several quarrels over the thing already, especially along Cheapside.'

'Why?' Chaloner was puzzled. 'She was not like the wives of other heads of state, who are either loved or hated. Most folk have no opinion whatsoever of Mrs Cromwell, as she was virtually invisible. I do not see why an attack on her should incite discord.'

Thurloe eyed him lugubriously: he disliked disparaging remarks about the Lord Protector's family, regardless of whether or not they were true. 'Yes, such a disgusting piece of nonsense should *not* be taken seriously, but someone is using it as an excuse to stir up trouble. And there will be even more turmoil soon, because Randal is planning a sequel.'

'Then perhaps someone should suggest that he stays his hand.'

'My thoughts exactly. I would visit him myself, but a

86

request from the Commonwealth's ex-Secretary of State is likely to inflame him to even greater spite. Will you do it?'

'Of course. Where does he live?'

'And there lies the problem. There have been threats against his life by angry Roundheads, so he has gone into hiding. His kin claim they do not know where he is, but they may be lying.'

'I have to visit Taylor today anyway. I will ask after Randal at the same time.'

'Then be careful. Taylor has always been formidable, but the last few weeks have turned him into a despot.'

'Because of his alliance with the widow of Dick Wheler, which has united two extremely profitable businesses?'

'That is one reason. The second is that he is the current Master of the Goldsmiths' Company, and the third is that he was a Royalist during the Commonwealth so the King has exempted him from providing "donations" for the Dutch war. These combine to give him rather too much power, allowing him to expand at his colleagues' expense. He now controls London's purse strings, which is unfortunate, as he does it with a view to his own coffers, not the good of the city.'

'My father always told me never to trust bankers,' mused Chaloner. 'He kept his money in a box under the stairs. But then our house was raided by Royalists during the wars, and guess what they found? My family have struggled ever since, so I am not sure what to think about banks.'

'Under the stairs?' asked Thurloe incredulously. 'He should have buried it in the garden – mine is under that tree over there. But he was right to be wary of financiers. Even if they are honest, it still means putting faith in their judgement. And recent events have proved that they are as fallible as the rest of us.'

'You mean because they lent vast sums to Colburn the gambler?'

Thurloe nodded. 'They were greedy for the high interest he offered. It has ruined Angier, Hinton and Johnson, and more are likely to follow. Only the larger concerns, like Taylor, Vyner, Glosson and Backwell, have managed to weather the storm.'

'The Earl wants me to investigate the death of a spy named Georges DuPont,' said Chaloner, changing the subject. 'Have you heard of him?'

Thurloe shook his head. 'How did he die?'

'The plague.' Briefly, Chaloner outlined what little he knew about the Frenchman, finishing with the bold murder of Coo by two masked gunmen.

'Coo was killed because you were asking questions about DuPont?'

'I doubt it. DuPont died last Friday, and Coo would have been dispatched sooner if someone had wanted to silence him on the matter. I am not sure Coo had much to tell, anyway. I had the feeling that he knew about the disease, not the man.'

'He was loved for his kindness, and his death will cause much anger along Cheapside. The culprits must be found as soon as possible, before their vile act causes trouble.'

'Williamson agrees,' said Chaloner. 'And has ordered me to investigate.'

'Good,' said Thurloe. 'Although I imagine you will be keen to find the rogues anyway, given that they came close to killing you as well. I shall make a few enquiries on your behalf. I leave for Oxfordshire on Sunday, though, so I do not have much time.'

'You are going home?'

Thurloe nodded. 'The authorities are taking the threat of plague seriously, but Londoners have been regaled with rumours about it for so long that they are inclined to dismiss it. The city is no longer safe, and men with delicate constitutions, such as myself, must flee while we can.'

He had nothing of the kind, although he had convinced himself that he was in fragile health, and swallowed all manner of potions in search of one that would make him feel young again.

'Do you know a felon named James Baron?' asked Chaloner, watching him remove a bottle from his pocket and take a substantial gulp. A glimpse of the label revealed that it was *Bayhurst's Elixir, an Improved Antidote or Pectoral against the Plague.*

'I know *of* him,' replied Thurloe. 'When Wheler was murdered, the general consensus was that Baron did it. He certainly benefited, as now he controls a large part of Cheapside.'

At that moment, a plump man with a gap between his front teeth bustled up. It was Philip Starkey, the master chef who had run the kitchens when Cromwell had kept court at White Hall.

'It is very early in the day for visiting, Starkey,' said Thurloe coolly. He disliked interruptions to his morning stroll.

'I am sorry, Mr Thurloe,' cried Starkey, wringing his hands in consternation. 'But I am desperate and do not know where else to turn. It is about that slanderous claptrap penned by Randal Taylor. Have you seen it?'

'We were just discussing it, as a matter of fact,' replied Thurloe. 'It—'

'Did you read what it said about me?' The chef's red face was a mask of distress. 'That I am a drunkard, who had to be summoned before Cromwell to answer for stealing wine.'

'No one believes it,' said Thurloe soothingly. 'It is obviously a—'

'Yes, they *do*, and that is the problem, Mr Thurloe. I am tipped to be Master of the Company of Cooks in a year, and this sort of tale could see me passed over. You *must* make the villain issue a public apology. It is the only thing that will salvage my reputation now.'

'I am afraid that is well beyond my sway,' said Thurloe apologetically. 'The best we can do is persuade him not to publish a sequel.'

'A sequel?' squawked Starkey, appalled. 'But more slanderous remarks will ruin me for certain! I have borrowed money to open a cook-shop, and the venture will fail if people think I am a sot who cannot bake. Then I will default on my loan and . . . well, suffice to say that Banker Taylor is not gentle with those who cannot pay what they owe.'

'Why did you approach him for a loan in the first place?' asked Thurloe disapprovingly. 'You know he was a Royalist during the Commonwealth.'

'Because he is the only London goldsmith with cash to spare,' explained the cook tearfully. 'All the others are funding the war. Of course, I was offended when he demanded collateral.'

'Collateral?'

'The lovely crystal salt cellar that Mrs Cromwell gave me. He says he will keep it if I default, so I hope I do not, because I should hate to lose it. *Please* stop his despicable son from writing more scurrilous lies, Mr Thurloe.

If you do, I shall bake you a cake every week for a year.'

'Well, then,' drawled Thurloe. 'We had better see what we can do.'

As Chaloner left Lincoln's Inn, he began planning his day. His most pressing task was to visit Taylor, where he had three things to do: discuss Hannah's debt; find out what Taylor knew about Wheler's murder; and ask where Randal was hiding. Randal would probably refuse to keep his sequel to himself, so some form of coercion would have to be devised. Perhaps it could revolve around his recently acquired wife, who was another suspect in Wheler's death.

Once Chaloner had finished with the Taylors, he would have to tackle Baron, to secure the last two pairs of curtains and sever relations between him and Clarendon House. While he was there, he would question yet another suspect for Wheler's stabbing – Baron had moved suspiciously fast to seize the criminal side of Wheler's operation. Next on the list was DuPont: Long Acre had yielded nothing useful, so Chaloner would have to visit Bearbinder Lane, where the French spy had died. And finally, he had to find Coo's killers.

He crossed the bridge over the slimy streak of the Fleet River, then climbed Ludgate Hill towards the shabby splendour of St Paul's. The cathedral close was busy, business brisk in the stalls that huddled against its massive buttresses. He was assailed by a range of smells as he passed – incense, back in fashion after the Puritan ban; cakes from a tray balanced on a vendor's head; sewage spilling from a blocked drain; and a sweeter waft from the new grass growing over the graves in the churchyard.

He soon reached Goldsmiths' Row, a short but glorious jewel of a lane that ran between Bread and Friday Streets, parallel to and south of Cheapside. When he was a boy, his mother had taught him a rhyme about the beauty of this particular road, and as he walked along it, he understood why poets had been moved to wax lyrical. It was not quite as glittering as it had been in its Elizabethan heyday, but was still impressive – a line of extravagant houses, most plastered with gilt, interspersed with shops that sold some of the most expensive jewellery in the country.

Taylor's Bank was the largest and grandest of all, and bespoke old money and good taste. It comprised a large sales area at street level, leading to workshops and a sturdy vault below ground. The shop was opulent, with glass cases holding display after display of sparkling bijouterie – bracelets, necklaces, tiaras, chains of office. Many were works of art that would have taken months to create, and a glance into the workshop revealed artisans and their apprentices bent over benches, their faces taut with concentration.

Chaloner stated his purpose to a servant, and was conducted to the next floor, which had several offices for clerks and a large chamber for Taylor himself. This was sumptuously appointed, and silver-rimmed mirrors filled it with reflected light. The banker sat behind an ornately carved desk, while two men hovered behind him. One was a younger version of himself; the other was a black-garbed physician with the biggest wig Chaloner had ever seen – the extravagant curls not only fell well past its wearer's waist, but billowed out at the sides, so it appeared as though he was wearing a large sheep.

'Thank you, Misick,' Taylor was saying, as the medic

proffered a beaker containing medicine. 'I cannot afford to catch the pestilence when business is at such a critical juncture.'

Misick, thought Chaloner. Coo's colleague and *medicus* to the bankers, whom Temperance had recommended as a source of information on the murdered physician.

'One can never be too careful, Father,' said the younger man. His hair was brown where Taylor's was grey, and he looked strong and fit, yet he lacked his sire's charisma and his expression was obsequious. 'Those who do not take preventatives will certainly die.'

'It will not touch us,' Misick predicted confidently. 'How could it, when we all take a daily dose of my Plague Elixir – a potion that the Royal College of Physicians itself has endorsed?'

Taylor glanced up and seemed to notice Chaloner for the first time. 'Step away,' he ordered imperiously. 'I want a *private* word with my son Evan. Go on. You, too, Misick. *Back*, I say!'

It was hardly polite, and Chaloner was tempted to say so, but Misick grabbed his arm and drew him to the far side of the room, obviously unwilling to incur the great man's wrath. Chaloner tugged free, resenting the liberty, a movement that caused him to brush against the wig, which released a thick billow of white powder.

'It is a remedy against fleas,' Misick explained, while Chaloner coughed. 'Wigs are splendid inventions, and I would not be without mine for the world, but they do attract hordes of unwelcome visitors. Do you wear one? If so, I shall send you a packet. You will never have a problem with fleas, lice, ticks or nits ever again.'

Manfully, Chaloner resisted the urge to scratch, and instead took the opportunity to further one of his

93

enquiries. 'I am told you are friends with Abner Coo and Richard Wiseman.'

The physician's face clouded. 'I *was* friends with Coo, but the poor man was shot yesterday. And Surgeon Wiseman does not have friends, so perhaps "colleague" might be a better description of my relationship with him. Why? Do you know them, too?'

'I was with Coo when he was killed,' explained Chaloner, deciding not to mention the fact that Wiseman was *his* friend, and he considered him a good one. 'And I should like to see the culprits brought to justice.'

'Good!' declared Misick passionately. 'Coo was a fine man, and did not deserve to be gunned down in so terrible a manner.'

'Do you know who might have done it?'

'If I did, I would go after the villains myself. But unfortunately, Coo was willing to tend anyone in need, which meant he mingled with some very undesirable characters. He lived and worked on Cheapside, which is in the domain of a powerful criminal called Baron.'

'Could Baron have ordered the execution?'

Misick pondered. 'Probably not, because Coo physicked his trainband. However, I shall keep my ears open for gossip. What is your name, and where can you be reached?'

Chaloner told him, and as Taylor and his son were still deep in conversation, he turned to another matter. 'Did you know Dick Wheler?'

'Of course. Between you and me, he was not a very nice man. He paid Baron to collect unpaid debts, and was not fussy about how it was done.'

'So who might have killed *him*?'

'Where to start? His colleagues hated his haughty arrogance towards them—'

94

'Including Taylor?' interrupted Chaloner softly.

'Yes, along with Backwell, Vyner, Angier, Hinton and every other banker in the city. Then there were the clients he abused – a list that will run to several pages, and will include members of Court and the government as well as tradesmen, clerks and paupers. I applaud the sense of justice that drives you to hunt killers, Chaloner, but concentrate on Coo. He *deserves* it.'

'And Wheler does not?'

Misick sighed. 'I suppose even the wicked have a right to justice. But why wait until now to explore the matter? He died weeks ago.'

'I know,' said Chaloner heavily, heartily wishing his Earl would not burden him with such impractical assignments.

It was some time before the Master of the Goldsmiths' Company deigned to ask Chaloner his business, although the spy did not mind, because Misick kept him entertained with gossip while they waited. The physician was able to tell him nothing more to help with Coo, and he had never heard of DuPont, but he provided a detailed account of what had happened immediately after Wheler's murder – namely that Baron had moved within hours to seize the gambling dens and brothels, and that Joan had visited Taylor the very next day to discuss an alliance between their houses.

'It was a clever move on her part,' Misick said admiringly. 'Wheler left her very rich, but on her own, she lacked teeth. The alliance with Taylor's Bank has made her part of the most powerful financial body in the city.'

Chaloner recalled the hard-faced woman he had seen the previous afternoon, and thought she probably had enough 'teeth' for all the goldsmiths combined. 'So she and Taylor run it together?'

Misick's voice dropped to a whisper. 'Not yet, as Taylor is unused to sharing. But she is working quietly and diligently to take her rightful place. She is already indispensable – he rarely attends meetings without her at his side these days. She will succeed, of that I have no doubt.'

Eventually, Taylor beckoned Chaloner forward, and the spy again sensed that he was in the presence of a very powerful man. By contrast, Evan was a nonentity, and compensated for his lack of personality with an attitude of sullen aggression, which sat poorly with his boyish looks and made him seem like a petulant child, although he must have been well past forty.

'We have met before,' said Taylor, fixing Chaloner with bright brown eyes. 'Yesterday, on Cheapside. You were with Coo when he was shot, and almost shared his fate.'

'Villains!' muttered Evan, while Chaloner was surprised that Taylor should remember him when he had barely glanced in his direction. It warned him not to underestimate the man.

'Coo was a fine physician,' said Taylor soberly. 'He will be missed.'

'Who do you think did it?' asked Chaloner.

'Baron, probably,' replied Evan. 'He is the one with killers in his employ – I assume you are familiar with the criminal gang he calls his trainband? But he should watch himself, because one of those vile rogues might turn on *him*.'

'One might,' agreed Taylor. 'Just as one turned on poor Wheler.'

'So you think Wheler was killed by Baron or someone from his retinue?' probed Chaloner.

'It was not Baron's retinue at the time,' Taylor reminded him. 'It was Wheler's. However, I cannot begin to guess which of those villains summoned up the courage to dispatch him, so if you want to know, you will have to ask them yourself. However, if you discover that they are innocent, then some client he annoyed will be the culprit.'

'They are *our* clients now,' put in Evan. 'Joan brought them to us when she married Randal. However, I have not met any who look like assassins, Father.'

'You think you could tell, do you?' asked Taylor with a sneer that made his son bristle, although only behind his back. He turned back to Chaloner. 'And, of course, Wheler was also disliked by his fellow financiers.'

'Including you?' Chaloner tried not to flinch when Taylor's eyes bored into his own.

'No, I liked him,' the banker replied. 'He was not some chattering monkey, like Backwell, Vyner, Glosson and the others, but a man of steel. I admired his strength.'

When he turned to the papers on his desk, Chaloner began to gabble in the hope of keeping the discussion going. 'I am a friend of your son Silas. He and I served together in the New Model Army.'

'We do not mention my brother's politics,' said Evan curtly. 'We Taylors were Royalists in the wars and Royalists in the Commonwealth. Silas was an aberration.'

But Chaloner knew otherwise. Silas liked to drink, and had confided a number of family secrets when in his cups. One was that he was the Taylors' 'insurance', so they could claim to be supporters of Parliament should the need arise. The ploy had worked: Silas's courage during the conflict meant that Cromwell had given the

97

family the benefit of the doubt when he was in power, while they had reaped great rewards from the King at the Restoration.

'Silas was always the bravest of my three sons,' declared Taylor. 'So he was the perfect choice to enrol in an army – although only when it became clear which side was going to win, of course.'

It was a curious thing to admit, and Chaloner regarded him sharply. There was a thin film of sweat on Taylor's face, and was that a hint of wildness in the piercing brown eyes?

'We have always been Cavaliers, Father,' averred Evan firmly. 'We never—'

'Silas is Keeper of Stores at the Harwich shipyard now,' Taylor interrupted. He lowered his voice to a hoarse whisper, but there was something in his slightly manic expression that made Chaloner wonder if he was in complete control of his wits. 'Evan bought the post for him, on the grounds that there will be plenty of scope for taking bribes.'

'Not so,' countered Evan, although with a sickly smile that did much to suggest that Taylor was telling the truth. 'Silas is an honest man, like us. After all, no banker or public official can operate efficiently if he has a reputation for being corrupt.'

The last words were spoken pointedly, which caused Taylor to whip around and glare at him. 'Who are you calling corrupt?' he demanded.

'Not you,' gulped Evan. 'I—'

'Good.' Taylor turned to Chaloner again. 'Now, why did *you* come here today?'

'I know Randal, too,' lied Chaloner, sensing the interview would not last long once Taylor discovered that he was just another debtor, so aiming to learn as much as he could before he was ousted. 'I should like to see him again, to talk over old times. Where does he live?'

'We do not give out that sort of information,' said Evan sharply.

'Of course,' said Chaloner. 'But I should like to buy him a drink. Will you—'

'He has gone into hiding, on account of some nonsense he wrote about Cromwell's wife,' interrupted Taylor. 'There are people who would kill him for it, and while I have no great affection for the fool, I do not want him dead. But never mind him. Come and look at this.'

He indicated the chest that sat on his table. It was square, with sides about the length of his forearm, made of rosewood and inlaid with mother-of-pearl. He made no effort to open it, though, and only stroked it lovingly.

'It contains power,' he said with a peculiar leer, snatching it up suddenly and cradling it in his arms. 'The power of life and death. Have you ever seen anything like it?'

'Er . . . no,' replied Chaloner, when he saw the banker expected an answer.

'Plague,' Taylor hissed, leaning forward conspiratorially. 'I shall release it in the city one day, but the sickness will not claim me. I am taking the best preventatives money can buy.'

'Speaking of money, we should get down to business,' said Evan loudly, while Chaloner regarded the older man askance. Taylor was likely to land himself in trouble if he went around claiming that he had the wherewithal to smite London with a deadly disease.

'Business.' Taylor smiled rather predatorily as he set the box back on the table. 'Have you come to beg a loan or to repay a debt? You will forgive me for not knowing, but I have acquired a *lot* of new clients recently – some bought from my fellow bankers, others who came with Joan.'

'My wife borrowed from Backwell,' explained Chaloner, supposing it was time to attend his own affairs. 'A debt you then bought. I came to see how the matter might best be managed.'

Evan went to a pile of ledgers, where it took but a moment to locate Hannah's case. She had borrowed three thousand pounds at five per cent per annum. The White Hall clerks had removed twelve pounds and six shillings from her salary each month, which had then been taken directly to Backwell. She was to pay interest only for twenty years, after which the original sum would be due in full – she would raise it either from her savings or by selling the post to someone else. Chaloner stared at the figures, and calculated that by the end of two decades, Backwell would have earned enough interest to double his original investment.

Evan explained how things were now different. 'We charge *fifteen* per cent. If you do not like it, you must repay the original three thousand, plus the two months' interest that is currently outstanding, plus our severance fee, which is another five hundred. That makes three thousand, seven hundred and fifty pounds.'

No wonder so many people were in trouble, thought Chaloner, if that was the way Taylor's Bank conducted its business.

'It is perfectly legal,' said Taylor smugly. 'Ask the Lord Chancellor.'

'Perhaps so, but it is unethical.' Chaloner knew others would have said the same, and he was almost certainly wasting his breath, but he could not help himself. 'You will ruin your clients, and they will pay nothing at all if they are destitute.'

'Then we shall seize their assets,' said Evan smoothly. 'Such as your wife's post at Court, her clothes, jewels and any other possessions she might have. It sounds harsh, but it is the way such matters work. She should not have taken a loan if she could not repay it.'

'Oh, oh, oh!' cried Taylor, so loudly that Chaloner and Evan leapt in alarm. The banker shot to his feet, and pointed out of the window. 'Look! A cloud shaped like a *snake!*'

'So there is, Father,' said Evan, although Chaloner could not see one. 'But—'

The door flew open and Misick scurried in, long wig flying behind him. He glanced around quickly, then looked sheepish. 'Forgive me. I thought someone was calling for help.'

'There!' yelled Taylor excitedly. 'A serpent with three heads! It is a financial omen, and means the country will be crippled by three calamities: war, plague and the Colburn Crisis.'

'I am sure you are right,' said Misick soothingly, while Chaloner tried in vain to see what Taylor claimed to have spotted. 'I imagine all London will be talking about it tomorrow. But sit down now, and I shall mix you a soothing tonic.'

Evan had summoned henchmen while Misick had been talking, and Chaloner found himself bundled out of the office by three burly men. He could have fought free, but there was no point – the Taylors were not going to change the terms they had decided upon, and he had no choice but to pay what they demanded. It was a fortune, and he was not sure how it could be done – unless Hannah was willing to sell her Court post, of course, but he doubted that was an option.

Out on the stairs, Evan grabbed his wrist to speak in a low, menacing hiss. 'My father *did* see a three-headed snake, and if you claim otherwise, or even hint that he is losing his wits, the interest on your loan will rise to fifty per cent. Do I make myself clear?'

Chaloner wrenched away with more vigour than was necessary, and then it was Evan's arm held in a painful pinch. 'You do. But while we are exchanging pleasantries, let me say something to you. You will not send your louts to terrorise my wife again. If you have any questions, you will address them to me. Is *that* clear?'

Wincing, Evan nodded, so Chaloner released him and stalked out.

Chapter 4

Chaloner had learned little to further his enquiries into the deaths of Wheler and Coo, he had failed to learn where Randal was hiding, and his final words to Evan were more likely to exacerbate his financial difficulties than ease them. He had, however, spoken to Misick about Coo, and had questioned Taylor and Evan about Wheler's murder – although the discussion had failed to tell him whether they could be eliminated or bumped to the top of his list of suspects.

He pondered Taylor as he went. *Was* there something wrong with the banker's wits? Misick obviously thought so, because he had had a pre-prepared tonic to hand, while the rants about the box and the cloud were peculiar, to say the least. On the other hand, Taylor had been perfectly lucid when deliberating Hannah's debt, and had readily grasped the complex figures involved. Chaloner was still mulling the matter over when he heard his name called.

He was surprised by the depth of pleasure he experienced when he turned to see Richard Wiseman. Their friendship had developed slowly, because although Wiseman had quickly decided that Chaloner was worthy of *his* approbation, Chaloner had not liked the surgeon's arrogance, hauteur and condescension. Wiseman had persisted, though, and Chaloner had gradually come to appreciate the virtues beneath the irritating exterior: courage, an unwavering loyalty to those few he considered to be friends, and an integrity that was rare among courtiers.

Wiseman was an imposing figure in his trademark red. He never wore any other colour, and even his hair was auburn. He claimed it was to be instantly recognisable to the sick, but his detractors – and there were plenty of them – said it was to hide the blood he spilled in botched operations. Personally, Chaloner thought that Wiseman just liked to be noticed.

'Temperance told me you were home,' the surgeon said, pounding him rather vigorously on the back. He was a powerful man, and his comradely blows were enough to make Chaloner stagger. 'Although it does not seem to have taken you long to embroil yourself in trouble.'

'Which particular trouble is that?' asked Chaloner.

'Being in a carriage that was attacked in Cheapside,' replied Wiseman. 'Temperance told me how you saved her from an angry mob. She told me about Coo as well. It is not easy to remain compassionate when you see so much suffering, and *medici* become jaded with time. But Coo never did. He was the best of all of us.'

As he usually had scant time for his colleagues, this was praise indeed. It, more than anything else he had heard, told Chaloner that Coo must indeed have been an exceptional man.

'He was,' came a voice from behind them, and both turned to see Misick, his enormous wig undulating in the breeze. 'I shall miss him terribly.'

'I thought you would be with Taylor,' said Chaloner. 'Trying to restore his reason.'

'I was ordered out when I failed to agree that his three-headed snake was pink,' explained Misick. 'I have just suggested that Evan makes him lie down. The poor man works too hard, and it is lack of sleep that causes these odd delusions.'

'I know how he feels,' sighed Wiseman. 'I have scant time for rest myself these days. Not only do I have an ever-expanding practice, but I am working on a cure for the plague *and* I am Master of the Company of Barber–Surgeons.'

Chaloner knew this last fact as Wiseman mentioned it almost every time they met. He had been elected not because he was popular or the best man for the job, but because he was the only senior member who had not had a crack at the post, and his repeated rejection by his esteemed colleagues had become embarrassing.

'I do not suppose you know anything about a Frenchman named Georges DuPont, do you?' asked Chaloner hopefully. Misick had not, but perhaps Coo had discussed the case with Wiseman. 'Coo diagnosed him with the plague in Long Acre, but he managed to rise from his sickbed and walk to Bearbinder Lane, where he died.'

'I do, as a matter of fact,' replied Wiseman. 'Coo told me that he manifested symptoms that included griping in the guts, faltering speech, frenzy and blains rising all over the body. Plague tokens, in other words – swellings in the groin and armpits that turn black and pestilential with—'

'Actually, I meant something other than his symptoms,' interrupted Chaloner, loath to be reminded of what the sickness could do. 'Such as why he traipsed halfway across the city.'

105

'It was a question I put to Coo,' said Wiseman bleakly. 'But he had no answer. All I can tell you is that DuPont was selfish to have made such a journey. Most folk believe the disease is spread by a miasma, but it is actually caused by worms so tiny that they are carried in the breath and clothes of an infected person – which is why those exposed to it *must* stay in their houses.'

'Or they will pass it to healthy folk without realising what they are doing,' elaborated Misick, as if he imagined that Chaloner might not understand the implications. 'Yet there is no indication that DuPont shed these worms over anyone, Wiseman. The only cases – other than him – are confined to the St Giles rookery.'

Rookeries were slums, where the poor were packed into teetering tenements, sometimes twenty or thirty people to a room, and where disease was rife anyway.

'So far,' said Wiseman grimly. 'But I fear he will set the trend for others. I was told last night that most victims' families object to being shut up for forty days, and several have threatened to leave and go about their business.'

'They have,' sighed Misick, shaking his head in mystification at such foolery. 'So an hour ago, the government passed emergency measures to stop them – measures that will be enforced by Spymaster Williamson, who is the only one with troops at his fingertips since the army disbanded. I feel sorry for him. He has his hands full with the Dutch war, and it is unfair to ask him fight the spread of invisible worms as well.'

'Well, I hope he makes it a priority,' said Wiseman soberly. 'Or it will not matter if the Dutch win or lose, because we shall all be dead.'

*

According to Misick, the best place to catch Baron was the tavern named the Feathers, which was located on a dirty, insalubrious lane behind St Mary Woolchurch.

'Not that I have ever been, of course,' he said. 'I do not mingle with felons.'

'You mingle with Taylor,' said Wiseman drily. 'And he is the greatest rogue in the city.'

Misick raised his hands in a shrug. 'I owe Joan money, and she offered to write off the debt in exchange for my medical services. Refusal was not really an option.'

Chaloner left them debating the ethics of such an arrangement, and followed their directions to the Feathers, a building identifiable by the sign above its door depicting a woman wearing nothing but a strategically placed plume. Two thickset men stood guard outside, and he was obliged to pay an entry fee before he was allowed in.

Inside, the Feathers was dim. All the window shutters were closed, and its few lamps had been draped with red gauze for atmosphere. It reeked of cheap tobacco, and a trio of musicians played an unimaginatively improvised medley of popular songs. They were loud, which made talking difficult, but Chaloner doubted the clientele were there for conversation anyway – there was a dais at the front, on which scantily clad women cavorted; ogling men slipped coins into what remained of their clothing in the hope of persuading them to remove more.

Chaloner found a table and ordered wine from a lady who wore nothing but an apron. It was early for strong drink, but his throat was still raw, and he thought a sip of claret might do it good.

There was no sign of Baron, although Shaw's pugnacious neighbour was there with a group of rowdy men.

Oxley called something lewd to one dancer, but fell silent when another woman – a busty person with the jaded look of someone who lived hand to mouth – came to hover menacingly at his shoulder, after which there were a lot of jokes about the folly of whoring in front of one's wife. Eventually, she came to ask if Chaloner wanted some game pie.

'No, thank you,' replied Chaloner, knowing that 'game' in such establishments might mean virtually anything. 'But I would like to speak to Mr Baron.'

'I shall see if he is available,' she replied haughtily. 'But only if you take the pie. I made it myself, see, and everyone says that Emma Oxley's pies are the best on Cheapside.'

Chaloner nodded acceptance of the terms and she marched away. He hoped Baron would not be too long, because the music was giving him a headache. The food arrived, and he was obliged to eat it because Emma loomed over him, and made it clear that she was going nowhere until she had been complimented. It was much as he had feared – tough meat of indeterminate origin mixed with peas and onions in a glutinous sauce that appeared black in the murky light.

When it and Emma were gone, Chaloner sensed someone behind him, and glanced around to see the King of Cheapside flanked by his 'captains' – the big-nosed Doe and Poachin with his mane of swept-back hair. None looked friendly, and when Poachin and Doe perched on either side of him, they sat too close, aiming to intimidate.

'You wanted to talk to me,' said Baron, sitting opposite. 'Who are you?'

Chaloner introduced himself as an agent for the Earl,

and Baron's manner immediately changed. He grinned engagingly, and Chaloner understood why Temperance had found him charming – Baron possessed a magnetism that was far more attractive than Taylor's raw power.

'Why did you not say?' He clicked his fingers, and although the snap was inaudible above the music, Emma immediately appeared with better wine and clean goblets. 'Clarendon is my most valued client, God bless him. I am honoured to entertain any member of his household.'

Chaloner's heart sank. Baron was clearly delighted by the kudos accruing from having a member of the government among his customers, and was unlikely to appreciate being told not only that the association was at an end, but that he was no longer allowed to mention it. Chaloner forced a smile, and hoped he would at least manage to resolve one of his employer's concerns.

'Good, because his latest order has gone awry,' he said. 'He ordered nine pairs of curtains, but only seven have been delivered.'

'Really?' Baron was all shocked mystification. 'Doe, fetch my ledger, will you? We must settle this matter before any offence is taken. By either party.'

Chaloner stifled a sigh, suspecting he was about to be shown 'evidence' that the Earl was mistaken. He was not wrong. The ledger, in a surprisingly elegant hand, showed that two thousand, nine hundred pounds had been paid for seven pairs of curtains. Neve had endorsed the entry, although there was a suspicious smudge over the seven that made Chaloner suspect it had been altered after the upholder had signed. There was another discrepancy, too: the Earl had said they cost three thousand, so where was the other hundred?

'You are in error, I am afraid.' Baron's eyes were bright with triumph, although his face was grave. 'Seven pairs were ordered and seven have been delivered. Or are you saying that your Earl wants to buy two more?'

'No,' said Chaloner patiently. 'But there are nine windows in his Great Parlour, so it is unlikely that Neve made a mistake. It is—'

'Are you accusing us of cheating?' demanded Doe, gimlet-eyed.

'Of course he is not,' said Baron, gently chiding. 'We are just talking here.'

'Have another drink, Mr Chaloner,' said Poachin, then smiled coldly. 'Before you go.'

Chaloner wondered what to do as he sipped the wine. The Earl would not be happy until the remaining drapery was delivered, but it was clear that Baron was not going to provide them without additional payment. He fought down his irritation. He was an intelligencer of some repute, so why was he in a dingy tavern arguing about curtains? Neve should be sorting this matter out – *he* was the one employed to furnish Clarendon House. Then an idea came.

'We have a problem,' he began. 'Clarendon says you are the only one who can supply that particular colour.'

'Yes,' agreed Baron. 'My brother-in-law the linen-draper made them to order. Seven pairs.'

'So bugger off,' growled Doe. 'Before I break your legs.'

Chaloner shot him a contemptuous glance. Doe was a brute, whose solution to problems was to hit them. Poachin was cleverer, although Chaloner sensed that Baron trusted Doe more. Perhaps the felon was nervous of Poachin's greater intelligence.

'However, most things are available for a price,' said Poachin, raising a hand to his hair. The lotion applied to keep it in place had set it rigid, like a helmet. 'I am sure we can come to an arrangement.'

'I am sure we can,' agreed Chaloner smoothly. 'Especially if we understand that money is not the only currency. Recommendations can be worth a great deal more.'

'What are you saying?' demanded Doe irritably. 'Recommendations? We are not interested in those. We want good hard cash, or you can take your custom elsewhere.'

'Wait,' ordered Baron, as Chaloner took him at his word and stood. 'Explain, if you please.'

'Curtains are currently in vogue,' obliged Chaloner. 'And wealthy courtiers are prepared to pay well for good ones. If the Earl is satisfied, he will tell his friends about you.'

'In other words, if we give him two more pairs for free, he will send us new clients,' surmised Baron. 'It is a tempting offer and I admire your audacity, but your Earl is unpopular. He does not have enough friends to make this deal worth our while.'

'Nobles do not make these purchases themselves,' said Chaloner, risking a good deal by injecting a note of scorn into his voice. 'People like Neve do – upholders or trusted stewards, whose duty is to oversee such matters.'

Baron was thoughtful. 'And you are on good terms with these upholders and stewards?'

Chaloner nodded. 'The King's mistress is always eager to redecorate, while the Duke of Buckingham had a house-fire recently. And Lord Rochester is a man of fashion, as is Bab May.'

111

'They are also deeply in debt,' said Poachin, the intelligent one. 'They may want our wares, but they will be unable to pay for them.'

Chaloner smiled to conceal his exasperation: it was a valid point. 'They can always find money for luxuries. Ask anyone at White Hall.'

'How many additional customers can you promise?' asked Baron.

'Four,' replied Chaloner, hoping it would be possible. 'However, as you pointed out, my Earl is unpopular, so do not mention him to these new clients. It would be a pity if they took their custom elsewhere, just so as not to be associated with him at any level.'

Baron laughed. 'Very well, you have a bargain: four new clients in exchange for two pairs of curtains. You have my word on it, as God is my witness.'

There was nothing godly about the King of Cheapside, and Chaloner was left feeling as though he had just made a pact with the devil. Still, his plan should work: the Earl's enemies would not be able to condemn him for dealing with a criminal if they were doing it themselves. All Chaloner had to do now was persuade key members of their households to buy Baron's goods without them guessing what he was trying to do.

'Wheler,' he said, launching into another subject as Baron and his captains stood. 'He was killed in your domain, but I am told the murder remains unsolved. Does that not disturb you?'

'Dreadfully,' replied Baron blandly. 'I would have investigated myself, but Spymaster Williamson came to do it instead, although he met with no success, and I fear he has given up. Poor Wheler! It was a terrible crime, and I miss him very much.'

'We all do,' put in Doe. 'Although it was not nearly as grave a crime as the one against Coo, which has all Cheapside in an uproar. Coo was a *good* man – a saint, in fact.'

'And Wheler was not?' probed Chaloner.

Baron laughed, a genuine guffaw that had other patrons glancing over and smiling with him – he was audible even over the thumping music. 'Wheler never professed to be anything other than what he was,' he managed to gasp once he had his mirth under control. 'A banker.'

'And that says it all,' drawled Poachin.

There was no time like the present, so Chaloner decided to put his plan into action immediately. He walked to the King's Head tavern near White Hall, which was a favourite haunt of Lady Castlemaine's steward, and settled down to wait.

It was not long before his quarry appeared. Crispin Blow was a handsome fellow, hired more for his shapely legs and legendary skill in the bedchamber than for his business acumen. He was already drunk, so it was absurdly easy to convince him that Baron of Cheapside was the only place to go for superior upholstery at whole-sale prices. Blow was delighted by the tip, because his mistress had confided only the previous day that she wanted curtains in her boudoir.

One down, three to go, thought Chaloner, as he returned to Cheapside in the hope of waylaying Joan Taylor. Her new father-in-law had declined to reveal where Randal was hiding, so perhaps she would oblige. He was in luck, because she had been visiting the Shaws, and he was able to catch her between the door of their shop and her carriage.

113

Unlike Taylor, she did not recognise the elegantly clad courtier as the man in rough travelling clothes who had been shot at the previous day, so Chaloner introduced himself as an envoy of the Lord Chancellor and engaged her in conversation by congratulating her on her recent nuptials. Like many merchants, she was impressed by rank, and was more than happy to exchange pleasantries with someone from White Hall. Such was her arrogance that she did not once stop to wonder why a member of Clarendon's household should be interested in her.

'I was delighted to join the Taylor clan,' she said smugly. 'Although I would be happier if Randal did not write silly pamphlets that force him to go into hiding.'

'You mean his cook book?' asked Chaloner innocently.

'I mean his barbed denunciation of Mrs Cromwell,' she spat. 'I cannot imagine why he decided to pick on her. Why bother? She is nothing now.'

'Perhaps he knew she is unlikely to fight back,' suggested Chaloner, and before she could object to the inference that her new husband was a coward, he added, 'I should like to wish him happiness, too. Do you know where he might be found?'

'None of the family do – we thought it would be safer if he kept his whereabouts to himself. You will have to wait until the fuss has died down before giving him your felicitations.'

Chaloner had no idea whether to believe her. 'It must be upsetting to have him disappear when you have not been wed for long.'

Joan shrugged. 'I am too busy to pine. I have many duties and responsibilities, not just at Taylor's Bank, but

114

with the properties I inherited from my first husband.' She gestured behind her. 'Such as this one – the Shaws are my tenants.'

'Do you have more to do now than when Wheler was alive?'

Joan smiled. 'Oh, yes! Dick liked me to sit quietly at home, but my new family appreciates my worth and encourages me to stretch my wings. And not just because I brought them a fortune, but because I have innovative ideas about commerce. They are beginning to solicit my opinion in all the important decisions.'

'*Beginning* to solicit? You mean they do not—'

'It is only a matter of time before I am accepted as their equal,' she interrupted icily: his question had irked her. 'Now, if you will excuse me . . .'

Chaloner segued hastily to another subject. 'The Earl means to bring your husband's killer to justice. Can you tell me anything that might help?'

Joan grimaced. 'I have already reported all I know to Spymaster Williamson. Dick was walking up White Goat Wynd when he was waylaid by robbers. It was an opportunistic crime – a random attack by villains from the rookeries. I doubt Clarendon will solve it, although it is good of him to take an interest. Thank him for me, but tell him not to waste his time. Good day.'

She strode towards her carriage, leaving Chaloner to stare after her thoughtfully. She had certainly benefited from her husband's death, not only by inheriting his wealth, but with the opportunity to shine in the world of finance. Had she hired someone to dispatch him? Chaloner had no trouble believing her capable of such a thing.

*

115

Chaloner loitered in and around Cheapside for the rest of the day, asking questions about Joan, Wheler, Randal, Taylor's Bank and Coo, but learned nothing new. Eventually, he arrived at Bearbinder Lane, at the extreme eastern end of Cheapside. It was time to concentrate on DuPont.

The alley linked Cheapside with Walbrook Street, although few used it as a shortcut. Its narrow entrances were uninviting, and it was characterised by four- and five-storey tenements on either side, rendering it dark and dismal, like a canyon. There were one or two unlicensed alehouses, but most of the buildings were the kind of places that rented out single rooms to whole families, and were unkempt and dingy. Mildew crept across façades that never saw the sun, and the ground was unpleasantly sticky underfoot.

Chaloner started down it, but was stopped before he had taken many steps by the sight of a house being boarded up. Two men were nailing wooden planks across its ground-floor windows, while a third painted a large red cross on the door. He did not need to be told what was happening – plague measures were being implemented. He glanced up to see the residents clustered at an upstairs window, their faces strained and frightened. A 'watcher' – someone hired to make sure they did not escape – stood ready to begin his unenviable duties.

'Their maid has the plague,' he was explaining to the horrified neighbours. 'They must be kept inside now, lest they spread the disease to others – to you.'

'But they are healthy,' objected the brewer named Farrow. 'However, they will certainly sicken if they are locked in there with an infected scullion.'

'And they include father, mother, ten children,

116

grandmother, aunt and two more servants,' added a seamstress disapprovingly. 'You cannot condemn them all to death.'

'They are the Court's milliners,' added Farrow. 'But poor, because they have so many brats. If they had been rich, the authorities would have looked the other way – recorded that the maid has dropsy or spotted fever. It is always the same: one law for them and another for us.'

'We should not put up with it,' declared the seamstress. 'We must make a stand.'

She did not say how, but it was a sentiment that won the approval of the other onlookers, who jeered when the watcher tried again to explain the government's rationale. The scene reminded Chaloner painfully of his first wife, and suddenly all he wanted was to go home. DuPont could wait until morning.

Night was approaching as he trudged west, and he stopped at the Half Moon on the Strand for something to eat, doubting there would be much on offer at Tothill Street. When he saw the prices, he wondered if he should find somewhere else, but he was tired, hungry and his throat hurt, so he stayed. He ordered something called 'a Turkish dish of meat', which sounded more palatable than stewed udders or eel pie, which were the alternatives. It transpired to be one of the most delicious things he had ever tasted – thin slices of beef wrapped in bacon and then simmered with rice, onions and spices. He complimented the landlord.

'It is a recipe from *The Court & Kitchin*,' the man confided. 'Although it galls me to admit it. This is a Royalist establishment, see, and I bought that book because I hate Roundheads and wanted to learn some nasty secrets about Mrs Cromwell. But that bit was dull, so I looked at the recipes instead. And they are all excellent.'

'Really?' asked Chaloner, surprised.

'I would not have minded living in White Hall myself if she had been running the kitchen,' the landlord went on. 'Such skill and imagination!'

Chaloner had never seen any indication that Mrs Cromwell was a good cook, and she had certainly not tried her hand when he had been in Northamptonshire, but he said nothing. He nodded a farewell to the landlord, and was just passing the New Exchange when he saw the Earl's private carriage disgorging his employer, Lady Clarendon and a gaggle of chattering ladies. Chaloner kept walking, but Lady Clarendon spotted him and called him over.

'Thank you, Thomas,' she said, as he escorted her up the steps to the front door. She smiled rather girlishly. 'My friends and I are going on a foray for bargains.'

The New Exchange, a building that was at least half a century old, boasted upwards of two hundred shops, all catering to the wealthier end of the market. It was the last place to find bargains, and Chaloner suspected his master was in for a very expensive evening. The other ladies hurried after her, forming a chirruping cluster, all bustling skirts and excited voices. The Earl watched with an expression of gloomy resignation, then turned to Chaloner.

'Have you learned what happened to DuPont?'

'He died of the plague.' Chaloner had included this in the letter he had sent to Clarendon House with Gram the previous evening, but confirmation that his missives were routinely ignored came in the Earl's shocked response.

118

'*What?* The plague is on Cheapside now?'

'In Bearbinder Lane. Two cases so far, including DuPont's.'

'Do not put yourself at risk again,' ordered the Earl, but even as Chaloner looked at him in astonishment for the uncharacteristic display of concern, he added, 'I do not want you bringing it to Clarendon House. Now, what about my curtains?'

'The only way to ensure Baron's silence about your association with him is to furnish him with some new customers. I think I have given him Lady Castlemaine, and I shall see about Buckingham and a few others tomorrow. He will provide the remaining drapery in return.'

A slow, vengeful smile spread across the Earl's face. 'Lord, that is sly! My enemies cannot condemn me for dealing with a felon if they are doing it themselves. You really are a devious rogue, Chaloner, and I am glad you are not working against me. I should be impeached in days!'

Chaloner was not entirely sure this was meant as a compliment. 'Yes, sir.'

'Accompany me,' instructed the Earl, eyeing the shops with considerable trepidation. 'The company of another man might make this excursion bearable.'

Inside, the New Exchange comprised a large piazza with a covered walkway, and the stalls were in two tiers around the edges; standing sentinel above them were life-sized statues of past monarchs. It was a place to be seen as much as to buy, and the ambitious navy clerk, Samuel Pepys, was among the glittering throng. Pepys only ever acknowledged Chaloner when he thought it would be worth his while, and being in the company of an earl was enough to bring the clerk scurrying over. He almost swooned with delight when the Earl touched his head in an affectionate manner and praised his work with the Tangier Committee.

'Damn!' breathed the Earl suddenly, grabbing Chaloner's arm and pulling him away. 'Taylor and his friends are here. I do not like the way he has bought debts from the other bankers and called them in. He has put my poor friend Bishop Morley in a terrible position.'

'Yes, you mentioned it yesterday.' Chaloner was disappointed but not surprised that Randal was not among the throng that clustered obsequiously at the financier's heels.

'And look at Joan,' the Earl went on cattily. '*She* certainly landed on her feet when her husband died. Of course, she paid a high price for her alliance with the Taylors – namely marriage to the insipid Randal. Still, he is better than his older brother Evan, who is frightened of his father and bullies everyone else in revenge. He—'

He stopped talking and donned a patently false smile when Taylor saw him and came to exchange greetings. The Master of the Goldsmiths had Joan on one arm, and his rosewood box under the other. Evan was behind them, along with several other financiers, most of whom the Earl addressed by name – Vyner, Glosson, Backwell. The Shaws were there, too, and Chaloner recalled that Backwell had invited the couple out for anchovies and shopping.

'This is the man who aims to look into Dick's murder,' Joan told Taylor, indicating Chaloner with a rather contemptuous flick of her hand.

120

'On my orders,' put in the Earl. 'It is a crime that should be solved.'

'It should,' agreed Taylor. 'However, Williamson could not do it, and too much time has passed for you to succeed where he failed. Concentrate on your personal finances instead. Have you considered investing in commodities with a high market liquidity?'

There followed an extremely tedious conversation with Joan playing no small part. She had not exaggerated when she had boasted about her commercial acumen – she knew a great deal about the matter in question and was not afraid to express her opinions. Taylor's eyes glowed in admiration, but then he started in surprise and pointed at a nearby shop.

'There is a stoat in that confectionery,' he declared, cutting abruptly into her analysis of graduated dividend yields. 'It is eating all the comfits.'

Everyone turned, but all Chaloner could see was Joan's startled reflection in the window. Taylor grabbed the Earl's hand and towed him towards it, muttering darkly about the known fondness of all mustelines for any form of sugar. His colleagues followed, careful to conceal their bemused glances, but before Chaloner could rescue his employer, he found his way barred by Evan. He could have shoved past the man, but was curious to know what he wanted.

'I hope you will not forget our little conversation earlier,' Evan said softly. 'Utter one word about my father's . . . eccentricities, and you will find yourself in deeper debt than ever.'

Chaloner almost laughed, given what Taylor had just done in front of a member of the Privy Council and London's most prominent financiers. He glanced towards them. Taylor was scowling, but his angry expression lifted when Backwell announced in an artificially bright voice that he had just seen the stoat devour a honey-coated almond. The other bankers nodded sycophantically, all afraid of contradicting the Master of the Goldsmiths. Did Taylor know it, Chaloner wondered, and was seeing how far he could push them before one had the courage to challenge him?

'He is tired, not mad,' Evan was saying. 'He should not have worked today, and it is a pity that he insisted on joining Backwell this evening. He should have had an early—'

He was interrupted by an equine bray and his jaw dropped in horror when he realised the sound had come from his sire. Taylor pawed the floor with one foot and neighed again, while the other bankers regarded him in alarm and the Earl's eyes went wide with astonishment. Taylor finished his display and glared around imperiously. Most shrank from the basilisk gaze. Then Joan took his arm and distracted him by pointing out some prettily decorated cakes in the shop window.

'We should enjoy them while we can,' remarked Taylor, and suddenly he was the picture of normality. 'It will be difficult to import sugar once the war gains momentum.'

There was an audible sigh of relief from the company when it seemed the peculiar interlude was at an end. Chaloner started towards the Earl a second time, but was intercepted by someone else. This time it was Backwell, who was holding two coins in his hand, which he stroked lovingly. The Shaws were with him.

'Lettice tells me that you are Tom Chaloner,' said Backwell pleasantly. 'I thought you looked familiar when we met yesterday. You must be kin to my old friend, the

122

Member of Parliament for Scarborough. I see the likeness in your eyes.'

'My uncle,' said Chaloner, heartily wishing his kinsman had kept a lower profile. Loved or hated, he had made an indelible impression on those he encountered, and Chaloner was frequently accosted by people with something to say about him.

'He was a great man,' averred Backwell. He lowered his voice. '*He* understood the beauty of money, and I did a great deal of business with him when I was financial advisor to Cromwell. I am sorry he died – especially as he promised to give me some shares in his family's alum mines.'

'Chaloner's wife offered us the same,' said Shaw, adding pointedly, 'in the event of her not being able to pay for the flageolet she bought.'

'Hold out for the alum,' advised Backwell. 'It is an excellent venture and will make you rich. Is that not so, Chaloner?' He continued before Chaloner could reply. 'Tell Shaw where you can be contacted, and I shall invite you to my next soirée. They are lovely occasions, and we always devote plenty of time to discussing money. You always enjoy them, do you not, Shaw?'

'Oh, yes,' said Shaw, heavily sarcastic, and it was probably fortunate that Backwell's attention was caught at that moment by Joan dropping her reticule. Coins spilled out of the little bag, and the banker was one of several men who raced to help her retrieve them.

'I would keep your whereabouts secret, if I were you, Chaloner,' said Shaw sourly. 'Or you will find yourself compelled to attend occasions like this – overcooked fish and stilted conversation, followed by a shopping expedition where you will be permitted to watch wealthy folk

123

buy things that they do not need at obscenely inflated prices.'

'Mr Backwell is trying to be nice, Robin,' said Lettice chidingly. 'And he extends his largesse not just to us, but to Mr Meynell, Mr Hinton, the wives of Mr Johnson and Mr Angier . . .'

She nodded towards a despondent gaggle who stood apart from those who formed the glittering horde around the confectioner's stall. Their clothes were of good quality, but not the height of fashion – folk who had been rich but who had fallen on hard times. They looked uncomfortable and resentful, and Chaloner suspected that they had not wanted to be included in the foray any more than Shaw, but had dared not refuse.

'The *widows* of Johnson and Angier,' corrected Shaw. 'Johnson died of broken wits in Bedlam, while Angier killed himself. Both were destroyed by the Colburn Crisis.'

'They should have done what we did, and opened a different kind of business,' said Lettice. 'We may not be rich, but I warrant we have better lives.'

'Our neighbours being the only fly in the ointment,' sighed Shaw. 'I am sure they tip extra water into their cesspit to ensure their filth keeps overflowing into our cellar. Damn them!'

'But Joan has hired builders to remedy the problem,' said Lettice, glancing to where the lady in question was addressing her father-in-law in softly soothing tones. 'We shall soon be all clean and fragrant again.' She turned to Chaloner. 'You had better give us your details. Mr Backwell loves to entertain, and he was fond of your uncle. He will certainly want you at his next occasion.'

'You will regret it,' warned Shaw.

'Oh, fie! You loved the time when the King's Private Musick came to entertain us, as it gave you the chance to hear the best violists in the country.'

It was enough to convince Chaloner, who was willing to endure a great deal for the sake of his muse. Moreover, there was always the possibility that an invitation to hobnob with Backwell and his friends would provide him with an opportunity to further his investigations.

Chapter 5

The next day was clear and bright, although Chaloner was in no condition to appreciate it. He woke with a sore throat, a blocked nose and the urge to cough. He fought it, because it would disturb Hannah, and he had no wish to deal with the sour temper that always assailed her first thing in the morning. Her mood on waking was so different from her mien during the rest of the day that he had once taken her to Surgeon Wiseman, sure there was something wrong with her.

He glanced at her as she slumbered next to him, and wondered again what had possessed him to marry her. They had nothing in common and disagreed over the most basic of things. He supposed he loved her, although he had never been very good at analysing his feelings, let alone expressing them, a failing that had become more pronounced as he had grown older. He also did not understand hers, which was a sight more dangerous.

Unbidden, his first wife's face swam into his mind. Theirs had been a whirlwind romance, but even at the time he had known that their passion for each other was unlikely to have lasted had she lived. He had always tried to resist comparing Hannah to Aletta, for the simple reason that Aletta had been dead for more than a decade and he had forgotten any annoying habits she might have had, while Hannah's tended to plague him on a daily basis. Then Hannah shifted in her sleep, bringing him back to the here and now, and he winced. What sort of husband was he to be gazing at one wife while thinking of another?

To take his mind off the conflicting emotions he always experienced when he pondered his marriages, he turned his mind to what he had to do that day: find Randal, provide Baron with three more customers, investigate the murders of Wheler and Coo, and explore the business with DuPont. He would also have to give notice to his landlord in Long Acre, as the attic refuge was no longer a luxury he could afford. He would be sorry to lose it, and sighed without thinking, which irritated his throat. He began to cough and Hannah's eyes flew open.

'Do not hack over me,' she snapped, covering her mouth and nose with the blanket. 'I do not want to catch your cold.'

'Is that what it is?' he asked, startled to find his voice a full octave lower than normal.

'Yes – there are a lot of them around at the moment. Still, better that than the plague. Do not look so wretched, Tom. Surely you have had a cold before?'

Chaloner supposed he must have done, although he could not recall ever suffering a more unpleasant collection of symptoms. He had always been blessed with robust good health, and disliked feeling so low. His wits were muddy, there was a nagging ache behind his eyes, and even breathing hurt his inflamed throat.

'It will be gone in a few days,' said Hannah, dropping the waspish tone and adopting a kinder one. He regarded

127

her warily, suspicious of sympathy at an hour when she was usually either asleep or simmering with bad temper. 'Rest, and drink plenty of honey-water.'

She began to get up, chatting amiably, and he was beginning to wonder if she was unwell herself when it occurred to him that she was making an effort to be cordial because she felt guilty about the debt. As well she might, he thought sullenly, because it would not be *her* carted off to gaol if they could not pay, given that he was responsible for such matters in the eyes of the law.

'Peter Newton, that bald Gentleman Usher, is dead,' she told him. 'He hanged himself.'

'I am sorry to hear it,' said Chaloner, struggling to recall if he had ever met the man.

'Debts,' said Hannah, not looking at him. 'But his were far greater than ours, and he decided that he could never repay what he had borrowed, so he put a rope around his neck and jumped off the Holbein Gate. You will not consider such a solution, will you, Tom? It is quite unnecessary – we will manage, even if we have to sell everything we own.'

'Did he owe money to Taylor?' asked Chaloner, wondering if the hapless Newton had not killed himself at all, but had been dispatched by the banker's henchmen as a warning to others.

'Yes, and to Vyner and Hinton, although Hinton is ruined now, so he is irrelevant. Poor Newton even gave up the emeralds he inherited from his grandmother.'

'Did you write references for the servants?' asked Chaloner, supposing they should discuss their own situation rather than pawing over someone else's. 'And look for a smaller house?'

'The number of insolvent courtiers increases by the day,' Hannah chattered on, ignoring his questions. 'Lady Castlemaine is in the greatest trouble, because she likes to play cards. She is easily distracted by anyone who flirts with her, so she forgets to concentrate and loses a lot.'

With a pang, Chaloner wondered if it had been kind to encourage the Lady's steward to buy goods from Baron, who was unlikely to be very patient with outstanding bills. Then he reminded himself that the King's sharp-tongued mistress had done his Earl a great deal of cruel and unnecessary harm. A run-in with Baron might teach her the importance of compassion.

'The poor Duke has had some of his debts recalled, too,' Hannah went on. She referred to Buckingham, for whom she had formed a rather unfathomable attachment. 'That is why he was so keen to discover the Philosopher's Stone earlier in the year – to save himself by turning lead into gold. It is a pity you ruined his experiments. Did you hear about the Howards, by the way?'

'The Earl of Carlisle's family?'

'No, silly! The milliners from Bearbinder Lane. You must know them, as no one at Court would wear hats made by anyone else. Well, their house was shut up yesterday. Parents, children, elderly relatives and servants, all locked in with a sick maid. It makes me cold to think of it.'

'I saw it being—'

'It is Backwell's fault,' blurted Hannah. 'The situation with my debt, I mean. Everything worked perfectly until he sold it. I would *never* have borrowed money if I had known that he would sell my loan to Taylor. Taylor is a pig, who has even made things difficult for George Morley, and *he* is a bishop!'

'The servants,' prompted Chaloner, feeling they had skirted the matter quite long enough. 'I assume you have told them that they must look for other positions?'

Hannah looked away. 'I could not bring myself to do it. I was hoping that perhaps you . . .'

When Chaloner entered his dressing room, it was to find smart clothes laid out for him, beautifully pressed and starched. The shirt smelled of lavender and sage, herbs used not only to give laundry a pleasant aroma, but to repel moths, lice and fleas. There was also hot water and equipment put ready for shaving. As the servants did not usually bother to pamper him, he could only assume they were trying – belatedly, as far as he was concerned – to make themselves agreeable.

He washed and shaved quickly, noting as he did so that his travel-stained clothes had been laundered and his boots buffed to an impressive shine. Someone had even polished his sword, which now gleamed rather artificially. He walked down the stairs, and was surprised to be intercepted by Nan the cook-maid, who was evidently in charge now that the housekeeper had decanted to the country to regain her health.

'Would you like some breakfast, sir?' she asked with a bobbing curtsy. 'There is smoked pork and eggs, and I rose very early to bake you an eel pie with oysters. I followed one of Mrs Cromwell's recipes, because I know you are partial to Parliamentarian food.'

Chaloner did not particularly like eels or oysters, and the combination sounded unappealing. Moreover, such elaborate fare was more likely to be popular with the hedonists at White Hall than the Commonwealth's abstemious Puritans.

'You have read *The Court & Kitchin*?' he asked.

Anxiety flashed across Nan's face. 'Only the recipes, sir, as I thought I could make them for you. I did not read the preliminary remarks.'

Chaloner imagined she had. He wondered if he should let her fête him with a sumptuous breakfast and then tell her that she and her cronies were dismissed, but decency won out. 'I need to talk to all the servants as soon as possible.'

'It is not convenient,' said Nan, in a transparent attempt to postpone the inevitable. 'Everyone is busy with the many tasks necessary for running a household of this size.'

'I am sure.' Chaloner took a step towards the kitchen, but she grabbed his arm.

'You cannot oust us just because you are in debt,' she hissed, unctuous servility evaporating. 'It would not be fair, and the mistress swore that we would not suffer.'

'It was not in her power to make such a promise,' said Chaloner, wishing Hannah had not seen fit to hire them in the first place. 'And we have no choice.'

'Yes, you do.' Nan turned tearful, and Chaloner wondered why he felt guilty. It was not his extravagance that had brought them to this pass, and Nan, surly, rude and disagreeable, had never made the slightest effort to win his good graces. 'You could keep us if you wanted.'

He pulled away from her and strode towards the kitchen, flinging open the door before she could stop him. The servants were not busy at all. Jacob the footman was by the fire drinking ale, the scullion was fast asleep in the corner, while Gram the page was cleaning his nails with one of the dinner knives. The aforementioned pie was stamped with the name of the cook-shop from which it had been bought, and most had already been eaten.

131

'We are resting briefly after working frantically since first light,' declared Jacob, leaping to his feet. Gram shoved the dinner knife out of sight, and the scullion slipped under the table, where she pretended to be scrubbing the floor. 'We have been—'

'Stop,' commanded Chaloner. 'I appreciate that you are reluctant to abandon such a comfortable existence, but I am afraid we can keep you no longer.'

'You cannot get rid of us,' said Jacob defiantly. 'We know things about you and your wife, and you do not want us gossiping. We are staying on, and nothing will change.'

'That's right,' averred Nan. 'Jacob and Gram hail from Cheapside and have friends in Baron's trainband. Even you must have heard what *they* do to folk who annoy them. If you dismiss us, they will come here and . . .'

She faltered when Chaloner whipped around to glare at her, not about to stand meekly while she threatened him in his own house. He controlled his temper with difficulty.

'Hannah will try to find you posts elsewhere. You may stay here until they start.'

It was more consideration than most employers would show, and while he felt they did not deserve it, he did not want to toss them out if they had nowhere to go. He had been poor too often himself to inflict that sort of misery on anyone else.

'Discharge us, and we will tell everyone about your debts,' warned the scullion, her small face full of spite as she emerged from under the table to stand with her fellows. Only Gram held back. 'And we shall inform all London that your uncle was a king-killer and that you were once a Roundhead spy.'

Chaloner shrugged. 'Go ahead. Those are not secrets.'

'Then we will say that Hannah is the Duke of Buckingham's whore,' declared Nan, eyes flashing. 'And that he visited her here every night when you were away.'

Had Nan been a man, Chaloner would have punched her. 'You can try,' he said, ice in his voice. 'But bear in mind that no one will hire you ever again if you reveal yourselves to be the sort of people who slander former employers.'

'We are not going,' snarled Jacob, fists clenching at his side. 'My cousin is married to Doe's niece, and Doe is Baron's favourite captain. Moreover, Gram taught Doe how to . . .'

He trailed off, and from Gram's agonised expression, Chaloner judged that whatever skill had been passed on was either illegal, unethical or unpleasant, and definitely something the elderly page would have preferred kept quiet. Jacob's obvious irritation at the slip suggested that he also knew the claim was unlikely to strengthen their argument.

'I know this is inconvenient,' said Chaloner. 'And we are sorry, but—'

'Do not bother to find us other posts,' interrupted Jacob coldly. 'I have no intention of working my fingers to the bone in another household. I shall go back to Cheapside, where Baron will find a use for my talents. Indeed, I shall go today, and you can do your own chores.'

He turned and stalked towards his bedchamber to pack, leaving Chaloner wryly amused that the footman should baulk at the prospect of a job where he might actually have to do what he was being paid for. All injured indignation, the two women followed his example, and began tossing their belongings into bags. Chaloner stopped the scullion from including one of his coats and Hannah's silver ladle, but was disinclined to do battle for two pots, a set of brushes and a milk jug.

'You will regret this,' vowed Nan, shouldering past him roughly enough to make him stagger. 'I swear it on my life.'

Jacob looked as though he would like to jostle Chaloner, too, but changed his mind at the last minute. It was a wise decision: the spy might overlook an assault by a cook-maid, but a footman was another matter altogether. The scullion was next through the door, although not before she had shoved a brass poker up her sleeve. She turned to spit at Chaloner when she was sure she was far enough away not to be caught in the event of a chase.

'That went well,' remarked Hannah, emerging from the shadows. Chaloner felt a flash of irritation that she should have been watching but had not come to support him. 'Who is this terrifying Baron they kept mentioning? He is not the linen-draper who is going to supply Lady Castlemaine's new curtains, is he?'

'Please,' came a quiet voice before Chaloner could answer, and they saw that Gram had not followed the others. 'Jacob has family on Cheapside, while the girls will get work in Mr Starkey's new bakery. But I have nowhere else to go.'

'Tom is going to secure you a post in Hercules' Pillars Alley,' said Hannah. 'You can stay here until it is all arranged, but I am afraid we cannot pay you.'

'You have not paid me in weeks anyway,' shrugged Gram. 'So what is different?'

The house where Chaloner rented an attic was in the middle of Long Acre. It was a nondescript building,

134

neither overly shabby nor particularly smart, and he was sorry he could no longer afford it. It had been a useful refuge in the past, and he would miss having a place where no one minded his viol. Landlord Lamb nodded glumly when Chaloner informed him that he was moving out.

'You are the second this week. Is it because you fear the plague?'

'No,' replied Chaloner. 'It is because of—'

'That damn DuPont,' Lamb went on bitterly. 'Why could he not have died quietly, instead of attracting attention by trailing across half the city?'

'That is a good question.'

'Poor Mr Grey is ruined,' Lamb went on. 'He owns the house where DuPont became sick, and all his tenants have vanished lest the authorities order the place shut up with them inside. I do not blame them. Who can afford to be locked away for forty days? They would starve!'

'The parish will provide food.'

'Bread, cheese and herrings,' spat Lamb in disdain. 'But who can live without beer and sausages? And what about a fellow's livelihood? Being kept from business for the best part of seven weeks will kill it dead. Of course, most of Grey's residents were thieves, so I suppose we would not miss *them* plying their trade.'

'DuPont was a criminal?' Here was something new.

'Well, put it this way, Grey does not rent to angels. You should ask him about DuPont. I imagine he will have stories to tell.'

'I have heard that DuPont was a spy. Could it be true?'

'DuPont?' asked Lamb, startled. 'I would not have thought so. He had friends in St Giles.'

135

Chaloner raised his eyebrows. 'And that precludes him from being an intelligencer?'

'Of course! What spymaster would hire someone who chooses to loiter in that sort of place?'

Chaloner climbed the stairs to his attic for the last time, but it contained very little that belonged to him. The furniture was Lamb's, and the only thing of value was his viol – a better instrument than the one that lived in the cupboard under the stairs in Tothill Street. He pulled off the cover and ran his fingers over its silky wood. Then, because he felt like it, he began to play.

His skill with and love of the viol had once led him to dream of becoming a professional musician, but his family had considered it an unworthy occupation for a gentleman. They had not been particularly impressed by espionage either, and would have prevented it had Thurloe not convinced them that it was an honourable way to serve his country. Chaloner winced as he imagined his parents' dismay if they could see him now – chasing undelivered curtains and investigating murders.

His gloomy mood caused him to bow sad, tragic airs by Lawes and Dowland, but gradually his spirits lifted, and he launched into lighter pieces by Ferrabosco. As always, he became lost in the music, so it was a shock when he glanced out of the window to see that it was nearing noon. He packed his remaining belongings and set them ready to be sent to Tothill Street. He paid the outstanding rent from his rapidly dwindling supply of money, and thanked Lamb for his kindness.

'I shall miss that viol,' sighed Lamb. 'So will the coach-spring maker next door, and he could do with something to cheer him up. He borrowed heavily to expand his business, but few folk want carriages in the present

136

financial climate, and he cannot repay his loan. He spends all his time hiding from his bankers – damned leeches!'

Chaloner walked to the grubby tenement where DuPont had lived, and this time the landlord was home. Grey was a man who matched his name. He was drab in every respect, from his pewter-coloured hair and watery eyes to his dirty clothes and pallid skin. He sniffed mournfully when Chaloner asked about DuPont, and indicated that the spy was to enter his lair. The inside of the house was worse than the outside, and reeked of burned cabbage and dirty feet.

'There is only me here now,' he said glumly. 'So if you want a room, I got plenty spare.'

'I shall bear it in mind,' said Chaloner, sincerely hoping he and Hannah would not be reduced to accepting. 'Now, what can you tell me about Georges DuPont?'

'Why do you want to know?' asked Grey suspiciously.

'Because Spymaster Williamson charged me to find out.'

'Christ! I heard rumours that DuPont was an intelligencer, but I dismissed them as nonsense. Clearly, I should not have done, given that his death has attracted the government's interest.'

'Why did you not believe the tales?'

'Because he did not move in the right circles. He was always disappearing into the St Giles rookery, for a start, and nothing ever happens in there that is interesting enough for espionage.'

'Where in St Giles did he go? And who did he meet?'

'He never told me, but you could ask his friend Everard. Of course, I have no idea where he lives either, but he has a purple nose. That might help you track him down.'

'Why? Is it an unusually large one? Or an odd shape?'

137

Grey shook his head. 'No, it is quite normal. Just a different colour to most.'

Chaloner suppressed a sigh: he doubted that snippet of information was going to prove very useful. He moved on. 'What can you tell me about DuPont's death?'

Grey looked furtive. 'Well, it was not the plague – it was some other kind of fever.'

'That is not what Dr Coo says.'

Grey's expression darkened with anger. 'For a saint, he had a very loose tongue. He should have kept quiet, like I asked. Then my tenants would not have moved out, leaving me all alone with debts to pay.'

Chaloner was beginning to think he was wasting his time. He asked to see DuPont's room, and followed Grey up stairs that needed to be negotiated with care, as several had rotted away.

'He did not use his quarters here very often,' the landlord said as they went. 'He must have had another place elsewhere. Probably Bearbinder Lane, given that is where he died.'

'I understand he was a criminal.' Grey opened his mouth to deny it, but Chaloner raised his hand. 'No lies, please – unless you would rather explain yourself to Williamson?'

'God, no!' blurted Grey. 'Very well, then. DuPont was a thief, although I do not know any more than that. We never discussed it – wise rogues keep their doings to themselves, and DuPont was good at what he did.'

'How do you know he was good if you never talked about it?'

'Because he was often flush with cash, as talented felons always are. Of course, he never kept it very long. He liked playing cards, see.'

138

'You leased him a room, even though you knew he was dishonest?'

Grey twisted around to glare rather defiantly. 'Even crooks have to sleep somewhere, and their rent money is as good as anyone else's.'

They arrived at the top floor, where he opened a door to reveal a dismal chamber. There were patches of mould on the walls, and one window shutter was so badly warped that the chamber might as well have been open to the elements. The bed was a mess of rumpled covers, a pair of boots lay in a corner where they had been tossed, and a half-eaten meal was on the table. A glance told Chaloner that nothing had been touched since DuPont had left, probably because no one wanted to risk infection.

'He took nothing with him when he went?' he asked, stepping inside reluctantly.

'A bag, but I did not see what he put in it. Dr Coo had already diagnosed the plague—' Grey stopped speaking abruptly when he realised that he had just contradicted his earlier claim. He shot a sly glance at Chaloner, who tactfully pretended not to have noticed. 'I stood here in the doorway, and asked where he was going. He said he had business in Bearbinder Lane.'

'What kind of business?'

'He did not tell me, but he had entertained a visitor not long before, and I think it might have had something to do with him.'

'Who was it? His friend Everard?'

'No – someone smaller. But he was wearing one of those plague-masks, so I never saw his face, and there is not much I can tell you about the rest of his clothes, except that they were good quality without being showy. Yet there was one thing . . .'

139

'Yes?' prompted Chaloner.

'It will sound odd, but he hissed under his breath. I think he was nervous.'

As well he might be, thought Chaloner, if he was in company with a man who had a deadly and contagious disease. 'Is there anything else?'

'Well, there was a jingle when DuPont hefted the bag over his shoulder, and I know the sound of shillings clattering together when I hear it.'

'You think this hissing man gave him money?'

Grey nodded. 'Because I had asked DuPont for the rent earlier that morning, and he said he did not have a penny to his name. He could have been lying, but I do not think so. He never went anywhere else that day, so he could only have got the coins from his hissing guest.'

Chaloner began a systematic search of the room. It was unpleasant, but his diligence paid off with the discovery of a bundle of papers cunningly concealed inside the seat of a chair. There were seventeen in all, and each comprised a single sentence. He read a few randomly: *ten the sun in wood, eagle in bear twelve, three swan in bread*, none of which meant anything to him whatsoever. All were signed *your Father in Cheepsyde*.

He stared at them. Were they evidence that DuPont *was* a spy? He supposed they must be, although instinct and experience told him that the missives were too short to contain any useful intelligence. He gazed at them for a long time, but no answers came and eventually he gave up. Perhaps someone in Bearbinder Lane would know.

It was not a particularly long walk from Long Acre to Cheapside, but Chaloner felt lethargic, and wished he

140

could afford a hackney carriage. The fresh air had done nothing to sharpen his wits, and his sore throat was not helped by the fact that the sooty air made him cough. He had also left home with nothing to eat. He bought a meat pastry from a street vendor, but it was soggy, salty and dripping with fat. He swallowed as much as he could bear, then tossed the remainder away, where a stray dog took one sniff and shot him a reproachful look.

He reached Fleet Street, and was trudging wearily along it when a familiar aroma assailed his nostrils, one powerful enough to be detected even with a cold. It came from the Rainbow Coffee House. He brightened. Perhaps a dish of coffee would serve to rouse him.

The Rainbow had the distinction of being one of London's oldest coffee houses – its owner James Farr claimed it was second only to Bowman's in Cornhill. It stood at the point where Fleet Street narrowed to accommodate the inconvenient Temple Bar, a gate that had probably once been effective at excluding undesirables from the city, but that was now a nuisance to traffic and pedestrians alike. There was always pushing and shoving to get through it, and Farr did well out of those who needed a reviving draught after the experience.

Chaloner opened the door and entered. He did not know why he liked the Rainbow. It reeked of burned beans and cheap tobacco, its patrons were opinionated bigots, and its coffee was terrible, although it did have the distinction of being considerably stronger than anything that could be bought elsewhere. He declined to sweeten it with sugar – as a silent and meaningless protest against a trade he felt was immoral – which rendered Farr's brews virtually undrinkable.

141

As was their habit, the regulars had gathered at a table by the window. Besides Farr, who was mean-spirited and parochial, there was Fabian Stedman, a young printer who seemed to spend most of his working hours in the Rainbow, and who held such radically Royalist convictions that Chaloner sometimes wondered if he was a government spy, hired to entrap anyone who disagreed with him. Then there was Sam Speed, a bookseller who only sold texts that were seditious, obscene or controversial, along with medicines to help the reader recover from the shock afterwards.

As usual, they were bickering about the contents of the government's latest newsbook, specifically a report about the declaration of war that had been read out recently in Bristol. Apparently, the city worthies had been too busy to do it sooner, and had been reprimanded by the Privy Council for their tardiness. To make amends, they had put on a splendid display with a whole chorus of trumpets and a show of drawn swords.

'But everyone there knew we were at war anyway,' Farr was saying. 'It is a port, and such places will be invaded first when the Dutch attack, so they have been preparing for months.'

'That is not the point,' argued Stedman. 'His Majesty took the time to write that proclamation, so the least Bristol's mayor could do was have it read out.'

'The King did not write it,' averred Speed scornfully. 'One of his clerks did. He would never be sufficiently sober for such a task. Or he would spot a woman that he would rather—'

'That is treason!' cried Stedman outraged. 'How dare you malign His Majesty!'

'Did you hear about that coffin-shaped cloud over Hampstead?' interrupted Farr conversationally. 'It was

142

said to glow purple before exploding into a thousand pieces. It means that a great disaster will soon befall our city.'

It was as if Chaloner had never been away – these were the exact same matters that were being aired back in February. Perhaps it was the Rainbow's constancy that attracted him to its smuggy interior, given that stability was a feature sadly lacking from the rest of his life. Speed would always denigrate the current regime, Stedman would leap to defend it, and Farr would change the subject as and when he pleased. And it was never long before someone reported a celestial omen that was held to be a portent of doom.

'What news?' asked Farr, voicing the traditional coffee-house greeting as he turned to see Chaloner standing behind him. 'And where have you been? You disappeared without a word, and we all thought you must have died.'

'Of the plague,' elaborated Speed darkly. 'Sent by the Dutch to demoralise us and make sure they win the war. There have now been twenty cases in the St Giles rookery.'

'And two near Cheapside,' added Stedman. As usual, they were more interested in talking than listening, which suited Chaloner perfectly. 'I have taken up smoking, which is the only way to combat the miasmas that carry pestilential diseases.'

To underline his point, he puffed a prodigious amount of it into the already thick air.

'I have better remedies than that,' said Speed, reaching for a bag at his side. 'First, there is Red Snake Electuary at three and six a pint.' He slapped a bottle on the table. 'Then there are Bayhurst's Lozenges and—'

'You should not use too much tobacco, Stedman,' said Farr, interrupting what promised to be a lengthy list. 'It is

143

toxic. Did you not hear about the experiment conducted by the gentlemen of the Royal Society? They acquired some tobacco oil from Florence, and it killed a cat and a hen.'

'The Royal Society is always dispatching some hapless creature in the name of science,' said Speed disapprovingly. 'I cannot say I like it.'

Nor did Chaloner, who had always been partial to cats and birds.

'Have you heard that the Dutch landed troops in northern Scotland last night?' asked Farr, dropping his voice to a fearful whisper. 'Word is that they will be in London later today.'

'That cannot be true,' stated Chaloner, surprised that anyone should believe such an outlandish claim. 'No army can march that fast. And no messenger either.'

'I am only repeating what I was told,' said Farr huffily, and Chaloner recalled that the coffee-house owner's sense of geography had never been good.

'I hope you have all bought *The Court & Kitchin*,' said Speed affably. 'If not, I have plenty for sale. It is well worth a browse, although I recommend a dose of Goddard's Drops before you start. Some of Mrs Cromwell's recipes are deeply disturbing.'

Chaloner still had Thurloe's copy in his pocket, so he pulled it out and leafed through it. 'Stewed collops of beef, almond tart, cheese-cake, barley broth,' he read aloud. 'These are not disturbing at all. My mother used to make them.'

Too late, it occurred to him that this might be taken as an admission of a Parliamentarian past, and he wished he had not spoken. Fortunately, Farr came to his rescue.

'So did mine, and they were very nice. No medicinal draughts are needed for those, Speed.'

The bookseller snatched the pamphlet from Chaloner's hand, and found the page he wanted. 'Then what about *this* section, telling people to pickle cucumbers?' he demanded, stabbing at the words with an indignant forefinger. 'We all know that cucumbers are poisonous. And then there is marrow pudding' – he made it sound distinctly sinister by lowering his voice and speaking in a hiss – 'which she had for her breakfast every day. And still does.'

Chaloner could not help himself. 'Actually, she has a little bread and a lightly poached egg.'

'How do you know?' demanded Stedman, eyes narrowing.

'I heard it in a coffee house,' lied Chaloner.

'Then it must be true,' asserted Farr. 'Although I am sorry to learn that you took your custom elsewhere. Have we done something to offend you?'

'He is tired of Speed trying to sell him remedies every time he appears,' said Stedman sulkily, sparing Chaloner the need to invent an excuse.

'Have you heard about the new comet?' asked Farr, off on a tangent again.

'It is the same one that we saw in November,' scoffed Stedman. 'A bright, white thing with a long tail. It must have gone all round the Earth, and come back for a second look.'

'I doubt they are sentient,' said Speed coolly. 'And it is *not* the same anyway. The recent one is not as bright.'

'Then there was the purple mist with the leprous spots,' Farr went on, cutting across whatever Stedman started to say. 'All are signs that the plague is coming. As Speed says, the Dutch have sent it over deliberately.'

145

'There was another omen, too,' said Speed soberly. 'Taylor the banker saw a three-headed serpent in the sky, and claims that each face represented a different financial disaster: the war, the Colburn Crisis and the plague.'

'How can the plague be a financial disaster?' asked Stedman.

'Is it not obvious?' said the bookseller. 'Labourers will die, so there will be no one to supply us with food and fuel, which means industry will grind to a halt. The wealthy will flee for their lives, so no one will buy what few goods *are* available. And we shall not be able to export cloth, leather and glassware, so there will be no money coming into the country.'

'We cannot export them anyway,' shrugged Farr. 'Because of the Dutch, who sink or seize any ships that belong to our merchants.'

'Speaking of the Dutch, did you hear what they did in Guinea?' asked Stedman. 'They invaded one of our ports, took fifteen hundred people – men, women and children – tied them back to back and tossed them into the sea.'

Chaloner started to say that no African outpost had that many settlers, so the tale was almost certainly apocryphal, but Stedman was getting into his stride, and Chaloner did not have the energy to argue. He shoved Randal's pamphlet back in his pocket, finished his coffee and left, aware that the others were so engrossed in their debate that they did not notice.

The coffee had done nothing to dispel Chaloner's lethargy, and he was still thick-headed as he threaded through the maze of alleys surrounding St Paul's Cathedral to emerge on Cheapside. Thus when someone flew out of the porch of St Michael's church and raced towards him, he was slow in dropping his hand to the hilt of his sword. If it had been a person with evil intent, rather than Neve, he might have been in trouble.

'I have been looking everywhere for you,' the upholder snapped irritably. 'Where have you been? The Earl told me that you would be on Cheapside today, but I thought you would have arrived a lot sooner than this.'

Chaloner was not in the mood to be scolded, especially by an interior designer. 'Do you have a message for me?' he asked coolly, biting back a more acerbic response.

Neve regarded him suspiciously. 'Do you have a sickness? Your voice sounds very odd.'

'Yes, I do,' said Chaloner sourly. 'A cold.'

Neve covered his face with his sleeve, so his next words were difficult to understand. 'The Earl sent me to say that he wants his last curtains *urgently*. The other seven pairs look very nice now they are up, so getting the rest is more important than whatever else you are doing. He is worried that an outbreak of plague will prevent them from being made, and he hates the thought of waiting for months. He wants you to approach Baron today.'

'His compassion is duly noted,' muttered Chaloner.

'What?' Neve cocked his head, but made no attempt to move closer. 'Speak up.'

'Tell him I will do it at once.'

'Good, because he said you cannot have any more of your salary until they are delivered. I tried to tell him it was unfair, but he would not listen. You know how he is.'

Chaloner did. 'Was there anything else?'

'Yes. He is very concerned about the fact that the Frenchman – DuPont – died of plague and wants you to find out exactly when and where he caught it.'

Chaloner regarded him sharply. The Earl's orders had been to stay away from such areas, and he was sure he had not changed his mind about protecting Clarendon House – which meant that Neve was lying. And Chaloner knew why.

'It is *you* who is eager to know, because *you* are the "mutual acquaintance" who introduced DuPont to the Earl,' he surmised. 'The person who told him that DuPont had information to sell. Bearbinder Lane is not far from the Feathers, where you would have gone to deal with Baron about the drapery.'

'No!' gulped Neve, although his furtive eyes told the truth. 'I did treat with Baron in the Feathers, as it is where he conducts all his business, but . . .' He tailed off when he saw Chaloner's scepticism, and sagged. 'Damn!'

'Why the secrecy? Putting the Earl in touch with a potentially useful source of intelligence is not a crime.'

'No,' acknowledged Neve. 'But it is distasteful, and I am an upholder, not a spy. However, when DuPont told me that he had important news to hawk, I thought I had better do something about it. If you had been here, I would have put the matter in your hands, but you were in Hull, so I was forced to go directly to the Earl.'

'What kind of "news"?'

'He had intercepted reports from Dutch agents in London, but he died before he could pass any of them on. He and the Earl had agreed a price, and he was going to bring them to Clarendon House, but he never came. The Earl asked me to find out why, and I learned in the Feathers that he was dead – although no one said

148

it was the plague. I assumed enemy spies had killed him.'

Chaloner thought about the messages in his pocket. Could they be what DuPont had intended to peddle? They were not in Dutch – or even French – and Chaloner had already decided that they were too short to contain anything important. Perhaps DuPont's death had prevented the Earl from wasting his money.

'Did you know he was a felon?' he asked.

Neve shook his head. 'But it does not surprise me. He was an unsavoury fellow, which is why I was loath to become involved in the first place. Yet the war is balanced on a knife-edge, and I am not qualified to judge who will be useful and who will not. The only thing . . .'

'Yes?' asked Chaloner, when the upholder hesitated.

'It is probably nothing, but when he was first trying to convince me that he was worth taking seriously, he said something about Onions at the Well.'

'What does that mean?'

Neve shrugged. 'He nodded and winked, but I did not like to express my ignorance by telling him that I had no idea what he was talking about. So I nodded and winked back.'

'Did he mention a friend called Everard?'

'Not to me, but we never spoke for long. To be frank, I found his company repellent.'

All of a sudden, he grabbed Chaloner's arm and dragged him into a nearby alehouse, an insalubrious place that reeked of unwashed bodies and spilled drink. Chaloner could have resisted, but the upholder looked frightened, so he allowed himself to be bundled out of sight. Neve peered nervously out of the window.

'Those three men,' the upholder whispered. 'They are Taylor's villains.'

Chaloner glanced into the street, and saw the same trio who had terrorised Hannah. One was limping, presumably as a result of being stabbed during the subsequent skirmish. 'You owe Taylor money, too?'

Neve nodded. 'I had to borrow from Vyner to start my business, but he sold the debt to Taylor, and I do not want to be accosted in the street by those louts. Did you hear what happened to Sir George Carteret?'

Chaloner shook his head. 'Who is he?'

'The Treasurer of the Navy. They cornered him on the Strand and cut off all his jewelled buttons with a knife. They were pretty baubles, too – thirty of them, each with a diamond and rubies set in gold, valued at forty shillings each.'

'His buttons were worth sixty pounds?' asked Chaloner, stunned.

'Yes, and they looked lovely on his coat. But I had better go. Some new paintings are arriving at Clarendon House today, and I should be on hand to receive them.'

Chaloner headed for the Feathers, supposing he had better do as he was told and enquire after the Earl's curtains – and while he was there, he would ask about DuPont – but he was barely past the Little Conduit when he ran into trouble. Evan appeared next to him. He tried to move away, but liveried henchmen materialised on his other side and hemmed him in. He cursed the cold that numbed his wits, because he would not have been caught in such a position had he been himself.

'I am glad we met,' said Evan softly. 'Father has decided

that it is time you paid off some of the money you owe, and he wants to discuss it. I would have given you longer, personally, but he is in charge, so you had better come. Now, if you would not mind.'

Chaloner did mind, but suspected resistance would be used as an excuse for violence, and he did not feel up to a brawl. He nodded obligingly and began to walk at Evan's side, alert for a chance to escape. Unfortunately, the guards were used to people objecting to where they were being taken, and were careful to ensure that no opportunity arose.

'The tale of my father's three-headed snake is all over the city today,' said Evan smugly, as they went. 'No one will believe you now if you say he was mistaken. Indeed, others claim to have seen it, too. It has become a fact, not a story.'

Chaloner could only suppose that either the 'witnesses' aimed to curry favour by pretending to have seen what had not been there, or Evan had paid them to lie, to protect his father's credibility. He understood why: no one would want a man who suffered from delusions to be in charge of the city's fiscal well-being.

They arrived at Goldsmiths' Row, where Chaloner was escorted straight up the stairs to Taylor's office. The banker had his rosewood box on his knees, and appeared to be crooning to it. The henchmen took up station by the door – not so close that they would be able to hear the discussion between banker and client, but certainly near enough to act should there be trouble. Joan was there, too, her ferret face proud and haughty above a new dress that was adorned with six diamond and ruby buttons. Chaloner wondered what had happened to the other twenty-four.

'You again,' she said coolly. 'I hope you are not wasting your time with my first husband's murder. It will never be solved, as I told you, and I would rather he was left in peace. Indeed, recalling that terrible night is distressing, so I shall not speak of it with you again.'

'Quite right,' nodded Evan. 'If the Lord Chancellor wants to do something useful, tell him to pay his retainers' debts. You, Neve, Kipps, Edgeman – you all owe us a fortune.'

'My box,' announced Taylor suddenly. 'It contains all I need to defeat the Three Horsemen of the Apocalypse – the ones in the Book of Revelation.'

'*Four* Horsemen,' corrected Chaloner, then staggered when Evan delivered a warning thump from behind. He whipped around fast, but thought better of hitting Evan back when he saw that one of the guards held a handgun, while the others fingered daggers and knives.

Taylor seemed unaware of the hostility that crackled in the air around him. 'The Bible miscounted,' he declared. 'There are three. I saw them when you were last here, Chaloner.'

'You saw a snake with three heads, Father,' Evan reminded him. 'As did many folk.'

Taylor scowled furiously. 'How dare you contradict me! I saw the Three Horsemen: plague, death and war. There will be no famine, because we shall be able to eat the corpses of the—'

'Chaloner has come to pay the money he owes,' interrupted Joan briskly. 'Where is the ledger? Or have you already calculated what you want from him?'

Taylor grinned, an abrupt change of mood that caused Evan to shoot Joan a worried glance. The banker coughed, took a sip from a bottle labelled *The Duchess of*

152

Kent's Plague Water, then looked up, his dark eyes blazing acquisitively.

'I want three pounds a week,' he said, and suddenly he did not seem mad at all. 'Ten shillings every day. Except Sunday, when I shall be in church. I shall take the first instalment now. Do you have it, or shall we visit your house to see what might suffice in lieu of specie?'

Chaloner did have ten shillings, but parting with it would leave him virtually penniless, and he had just been told that he could not draw more pay until the Earl had his curtains. However, he was heavily outnumbered, and suspected they would have the money from him anyway, so he handed it over, deciding to keep his dignity intact. Taylor counted it greedily.

'Thank you. Come again at the same time tomorrow.'

Evan opened the door to indicate that the interview was at an end, and Chaloner was about to step through it when someone else arrived. It was Silas, the youngest of the Taylor sons. He was a bluff, hearty fellow with sandy hair and a ready smile. Unlike Evan, he had considerable presence, and had been a popular commander during the wars, although Chaloner had liked him mostly because he was a talented composer and music had been an important diversion during a time when so much else had been bleak and harrowing. Silas stopped dead in his tracks, then his face broke into a wide grin of delight.

'Tom Chaloner! What are you doing here?'

'You know him?' asked Evan suspiciously.

Silas flung a comradely arm around Chaloner's shoulders. 'We fought in several skirmishes together after our families enrolled us to fight for Cromwell.' Then he pretended to look hangdog. 'But I misspeak. No one

153

admits these days that they hedged their bets during the wars by having a foot in both camps.'

Chaloner's clan had been Parliamentarian through and through, and there had been no hedging of bets with them, but he made no effort to say so. Evan grimaced his annoyance at his brother's remarks, while Taylor frowned, almost as if he was trying to recall who Silas was.

'We never—' began Evan irritably, but Silas interrupted.

'It is *good* to see you, Tom!' He turned to his father. 'He and I shared many a bold adventure. We were ambushed once near Newbury, and I was knocked sense-less and tossed in a raging river. He risked his life to fish me out.'

The 'ambush' had been a prank by a group of their friends, and Silas had been drunk. He had fallen in a brook, and Chaloner had indeed pulled him out, although the water had only been knee deep, and the only danger had been getting wet.

'Then we owe you our gratitude,' said Taylor, although Evan remained pointedly silent, and Chaloner sensed there was no love lost between the brothers. 'Perhaps you will accept a biscuit as a reward. Joan bakes them for me every day, because they are my favourite.'

Silas's eyebrows shot up in astonishment to learn that his life was only worth a pastry, while Evan grinned tauntingly. Chaloner took a cake from the proffered plate, and recognised it as one from a cook-shop on Fleet Street. Joan shot him a threatening glare, an expression that was quickly masked when Silas looked at her. She simpered, and Chaloner saw she was smitten with his old friend.

'Randal is a lucky man,' Silas told her gallantly. 'A wife who is pretty, intelligent *and* can cook.' Joan inclined her head graciously, but Silas had turned back to Chaloner before she could respond further. 'Do you still play the viol?'

Chaloner nodded. 'Yes, whenever I can.'

'Excellent! I also dabble in music.' He spoke modestly, because even the great Henry Lawes had praised Silas's compositions. 'And I am holding a soirée on Friday, so you must come. Are you married? Yes? Bring your wife. What does she play?'

'She prefers to listen,' said Chaloner, unwilling to admit to having a spouse who had stooped to learning the flageolet. And if that were not bad enough, she had not even paid for it.

'Then you should not have wed her,' said Silas, quite seriously. 'Or do you have servants who can accommodate you by the parlour fire of an evening?'

'No,' replied Chaloner shortly, although the cosy image reminded him of his very happy childhood in Buckinghamshire, where music had been an integral part of family life.

'I suppose you have been forced to dismiss them because you are in debt to Taylor's Bank,' said Silas heavily. He had always been astute. 'Well, I think—'

'Stay out of it, Silas,' warned Evan. 'Go back to Harwich, and be thankful that I was willing to buy you a post that keeps you out of mischief.'

Silas glanced at his father, who was talking to his box. He frowned, but Evan hastily stepped in front of the desk, shielding their sire from view. Silas threw up his hands in surrender, and turned to Joan instead.

'I need a word with your husband, sister,' he said, positively oozing charm. 'He borrowed my lute a couple of months ago, and I want it back. I know he is hiding

155

because of the trouble he caused with his silly pamphlet, but this is important. Where is he?'

'I wish I knew,' replied Joan with a sultry smile. 'But he refuses to confide. However, you might try the Green Dragon – it is one of his favourite haunts.'

Chaloner listened with interest: he had seen Randal near that very tavern when Temperance had given him a lift along Cheapside.

'Joan!' hissed Evan angrily. 'What are you—'

'Silas is family,' interrupted Joan crisply. 'He has a right to speak to Randal if he likes.'

'Chaloner is not, though,' countered Evan. 'He is a client, and has asked after Randal before. He could be a Parliamentarian sympathiser for all you know, itching to avenge himself on the man who maligned his Lady Protectress.'

Joan regarded him coolly. 'If he is, then I am sure my brave Randal can look after himself.'

'The Green Dragon,' mused Taylor, not taking his eyes off the box. 'That big, flashy inn. I go there myself sometimes, but it is always full of debtors. I shall blow them all up one day.'

'Blow them up?' echoed Silas in bafflement. 'I would not recommend that, Father. How will they pay what they owe you if they are dead?'

Taylor's reply was lost to Chaloner, because Evan had bundled him towards the door.

'Bring ten shillings tomorrow,' Evan said coldly. 'Or else.'

'Or else what?' asked Chaloner loudly, aware that Silas was listening, and aiming to make Evan back down. But Evan only sneered, first at Chaloner and then at his brother.

'Or else we will break your neck. And do not think your friendship with Silas will save you.'

'Steady on, Evan,' objected Silas angrily. 'Tom is one of my—'

'Shut up, Silas,' snarled Evan. 'And do not come here again. We are too busy to bother with your damned lutes. Go back to Harwich and play with your ships.'

'I need fifty pounds,' said Silas, not moving. 'To buy cannon for the *Plymouth*.'

Evan opened his mouth to refuse, but Taylor made them both jump by speaking close behind them. 'Get it for him, Evan. It is our patriotic duty to help the navy. Moreover, obliging with the occasional donation will make it more difficult for the King to request bigger sums.'

It was a shrewd strategy, and left Chaloner more uncertain than ever about the enigma that was Rich Taylor.

Chapter 6

Once out in Goldsmiths' Row, Chaloner waited for Silas to emerge, delighted by the prospect of renewing a friendship with a man he had liked and admired. True, they had not met since the wars had ended almost fourteen years ago, but Silas seemed much the same – jovial, energetic and fiercely devoted to his muse.

Chaloner leaned against a wall and looked around. There were groups of clients outside each great banking house, all kept in line by liveried guards, although the gaggle that clustered around Taylor's was different from the rest. His petitioners comprised folk who had the frightened, bewildered look of people for whom life had gone awry, whereas the other banks were beset by depositors demanding the return of their money.

'Of course you may have it,' one of Vyner's clerks was assuring a particularly agitated customer. 'But it is company policy not to release large sums all at once. Our city is rife with crime, and we are mindful of your safety – it is unwise to strut around loaded down with cash.'

'*You* are the criminals,' cried the saver, distressed. 'You steal from those who trust you – I heard the tale in my coffee house this morning, so I want my money and I want it *now*!'

'The tale is a lie,' replied the clerk superiorly. 'And you may have your capital whenever you wish, as long as you keep your withdrawals to within the limits set out in the agreement you signed. These rules are in place to protect you, as your interests are our prime concern.'

Chaloner laughed at that notion, then turned to see that Silas had also been listening.

'Vyner, Backwell and the others *cannot* return their depositors' money,' Silas explained softly, so that no one else would hear. 'If they did, they would have nothing to give the King for the war. Thank God my father is excluded from the royal demand for "donations".'

'He is lucky, but it is a pity he does not share his good fortune with his clients.' Chaloner pointed to the disconsolate rabble outside Taylor's door. 'His greed is ruining lives.'

Silas grimaced. 'I did suggest he show some mercy, but he said such silly sentimentality is why I was packed off to Harwich – a place where my radical views can do no harm.'

'He is the fool, Silas,' said Chaloner soberly. 'There is a rumour that his friend Wheler was killed by a disgruntled customer, and if your father continues in this vein, he might suffer a similar fate.'

Silas indicated the liveried guards. 'They will protect him – he pays them so generously that he has their complete and undying loyalty. The other bankers have followed his example and recruited reliable old soldiers of their own.' He began to walk towards Cheapside. 'Take no notice of Evan, by the way: he is all bark and no bite. My father should never have made him heir to the family business – he is not up to the mark.'

159

'Who should it be then? You?'

Silas grinned impishly. 'Of course. It is only a matter of time before Father realises his first-born is no good, while he has already dismissed Randal as worthless. The day will come when he will *beg* me to step in and save the day.'

'Unless Joan steps in first.'

Silas rubbed his chin thoughtfully. 'Yes, she could be a threat to my plans.' Then he laughed boyishly. 'But she adores me, so I shall offer her my person in exchange for a clear run at my goals. It will make a cuckold of Randal, but who cares?'

'You had better not return to Harwich, then. Your father does not seem entirely well to me, and you might have to put your schemes into action sooner than you think.'

'Oh, he is all right,' declared Silas with a dismissive wave of his hand. 'He is probably just recovering from the shock of seeing that serpent in the sky.'

'There was no serpent. I was with him when he claimed to have seen it, and it was a figment of his imagination. He also thought he saw a stoat in the New Exchange – eating sweetmeats.'

Silas laughed again. 'He was just enjoying himself at your expense. But where are you going now? Do you have time for an ale with an old friend?'

'In the Feathers?' asked Chaloner, aiming to further his investigations and enjoy Silas's company at the same time.

Silas blinked. 'Really? It is terribly seedy.'

He shrugged when Chaloner began to walk there, and fell into step at his side, chatting amiably about old times. They reached the Feathers, where Chaloner was

160

surprised but pleased when they were ushered inside without being asked for an admission fee. They were also supplied with free ale, and this time Emma did not insist on selling her nasty pies. But best of all, when Silas winced at the racket the musicians were making, someone suggested that it was time they took a break, and blessed silence fell.

'My apologies,' said Oxley, all greasy servility when Chaloner asked if Baron was available. 'He is not here at the moment, but you are welcome to wait until he returns, although we do not know when that might be. Is there anything I can fetch you in the meantime? More wine? Some French cheese? A clean whore?'

'As I doubt all this fawning is for my benefit,' said Chaloner to Silas when the henchman had gone, 'I can only assume that it is you they aim to impress. Why? Because of your father?'

Silas chuckled. 'He would never set foot in a place like this. They pander to me because I play the occasional game of cards here, and I tip generously. I cannot abide Oxley, though. He loves money too much to be loyal to any master, and if I were Baron, I would get rid of him. But never mind that rogue. Why did *you* want to come here?'

Chaloner saw no reason not to tell him about DuPont. Silas listened intently until he had finished, then flicked his fingers at the staff. They sidled over nervously, reminding Chaloner that while Silas might be bluff and amiable to his friends, he could be formidable to minions.

'Ask your questions, Tom,' he said, eyeing the rabble sternly. 'They will be *truthfully* answered.'

'Yes, DuPont was a regular here,' said one, when Chaloner told them what he wanted to know. 'But we never met any Everard, and we have no idea about onions or wells.'

Chaloner pressed them further, but it soon became clear that while DuPont had spent a considerable amount of time in the Feathers, no one knew much about him. However, none seemed surprised to hear that he might have offered to sell information about the Dutch.

'Spies,' said the drummer in rank distaste. 'I might have known a fellow like him would dabble in murk. It is a good thing he is dead, because you never know what side vermin like that are on – they profess to be friendly, but then they betray you.'

'Well, there you are, Tom,' said Silas, amused. 'The real truth about intelligencers.'

There was no more to be learned, so Chaloner led the way outside, blinking in the brightness of the day after the subterranean atmosphere of the tavern.

'Now where?' asked Silas amiably. 'Or may I choose this time?'

'Bearbinder Lane,' replied Chaloner. 'Where DuPont died.'

'You cannot – it is closed with the plague. Come, walk with me and I will show you. A maid became ill last night, and the authorities have shut it off until the searcher has issued her verdict.'

Searchers were poor and usually elderly women who were paid to look at the sick and dying, to determine what was wrong with them. They had no medical training, so their diagnoses tended to be hit-and-miss. Moreover, many were not averse to being bribed, so often gave false reports to spare a house from being shut up.

Silas paused by the Great Conduit, his face a mask of

disapproval. 'My God! Look at those brats. They are Oxley's spawn, and will hang unless he takes them in hand.'

He pointed to a boy and a girl in their mid teens. The boy was flinging mud at passers-by, and when his victims stopped to remonstrate, the girl picked their pockets.

'That house,' said Chaloner, nodding to a glorious jewel of architecture that stood proudly between some very drab neighbours. It had recently been refurbished, and bespoke unlimited wealth. 'Who lives there? A banker?'

'James Baron,' replied Silas. 'He did well for himself when he seized the criminal half of Wheler's empire. Joan was livid, of course, as she wanted it for herself.'

'Then your family must have been relieved that she was thwarted. Running pickpockets and a protection tax are hardly activities that respectable financiers should condone.'

Silas roared with laughter. 'You would never make a businessman, Tom – too ingenuous by half. My father will make money any way he can, and he was as disappointed as Joan to lose the shadier side of Wheler's operation.'

The door to Baron's house opened at that moment, and the King of Cheapside himself stepped out. There was a woman at his side, a slim, pretty blonde dressed in clothes designed to accentuate her fine figure. A boy and a girl of roughly the same age as Oxley's offspring trotted demurely at her side, while behind them were Doe and Poachin. The family stood in an expectant huddle, then broke into cries of delight when a servant appeared with a horse.

'Caesar,' said Silas, watching. 'The nag, I mean. It was Wheler's, but Baron loves it and so do his family. I cannot imagine why – it is a wretched old thing.'

163

Chaloner was inclined to agree, and doubted if Caesar had ever been worthy of its lofty name. It was sway-backed, its tail was set too high and its chest was too narrow. However, it had a good nature, and nuzzled affectionately at the family when they came to pet it. Baron's hard eyes softened and Chaloner saw that Silas was right: the felon did love the animal. Meanwhile, Doe hissed his impatience at the delay, while Poachin was more difficult to read.

'Shall we pay our respects?' asked Silas. 'I rather like Baron. It is not easy to foil Joan, and I am all admiration for any man who succeeds.'

He set off across the road without waiting for a reply, but Chaloner did not mind. Meeting Baron was one of the reasons why he had gone to the Feathers, after all.

'You left the card table last night without settling your debt,' snarled Doe when Silas reached the little party, thrusting his large nose aggressively forward. 'You owe—'

'Stop!' snapped Baron, holding up a beefy hand. 'You know we do not discuss business in front of Frances.'

Doe opened his mouth to argue, but the words died in his throat when a fierce expression suffused Baron's face. He closed it quickly, and Poachin smirked to see his fellow captain in trouble. Baron glared a moment longer, then beckoned to his family, who tore their attention from Caesar with obvious reluctance, and came to bob and curtsy.

'God has blessed me and Frances with these two fine children,' he said, obviously proud of their pretty manners. 'We are about to go shopping for more Turpentine Pills.'

'Very wise,' said Silas. 'They are excellent for colic and other digestive perils, and there is evidence that they also prevent the plague.'

164

'They do,' averred Baron. 'We have been taking them ever since we heard about the first case in St Giles back in February.' He turned to his wife. 'Here is some money, chicken. Buy yourself a nice ribbon while I talk to these gentlemen. I shall join you when I have finished.'

'She will spend it on apples for Caesar,' piped the boy, while Chaloner reflected that Hannah would be livid if he used such patronising tones on her – and with good cause. He could only assume that either Frances was very patient or very stupid. 'He adores apples.'

Baron beamed at them both. 'He heard you! Look at the way he paws the ground! Run along now, before he grows impatient. Poachin will go with you.'

'I would rather stay with—' began Poachin, but stopped when Baron turned a glare of such malignancy on him that he blanched. It was Doe's turn to gloat.

'You can buy more alum for your hair,' he said, sober-faced, although his eyes were bright with malicious glee. 'Frances will advise you, I am sure.'

'Alum?' asked Chaloner warily.

'It is the only thing that will hold,' explained Poachin, attempting to show that he was unfazed by Baron's scowl with a show of amiable chattiness. 'Most folk use egg white, but that has a tendency to dissolve in wet weather. An alum-based lotion, on the other hand, lasts all day.'

'Bugger off, then,' said Doe. 'Or you may find the barber has sold out.'

Poachin turned to offer Frances his arm, but thrilled by her husband's generosity, she and the children had already skipped away, leaving him scampering to catch up. There was a happy innocence about the trio, and Chaloner wondered how long it would last – it was only a matter of time before one of them came to understand the truth about how Baron made his living.

'Our money, Silas,' said Doe, the moment the family were out of earshot. 'Where is it?'

'I was just coming to deliver it,' said Silas, handing him the purse containing the fifty pounds for *Plymouth*'s cannon. Chaloner struggled to keep his expression blank. Was the ship to put to without them then? 'When is the next game?'

'Tonight,' replied Doe, removing a few coins, but passing the lion's share to Baron. 'Same place, same time, same rules.'

'Excellent,' beamed Silas. 'I shall look forward to winning it back.' He turned to Chaloner. 'Join us. It sounds as though you need a windfall.'

Chaloner did, but was not so rash as to believe that gambling was the way to do it. He murmured a polite refusal, then addressed Baron. 'My Earl has asked me to collect his curtains today. When will they be ready?'

Baron put a heavy arm around his shoulders. 'I understand his impatience, but he has not yet fulfilled his end of the bargain. Lady Castlemaine ordered brocade drapery for her bedroom today, and there is talk of more, but she is only one customer. You promised four.'

'And you will have them,' promised Chaloner. 'But perhaps you will show good faith by—'

'Four clients,' interrupted Baron firmly. 'And the curtains are his, as God is my witness.'

Chaloner could see there was no point arguing, so indicated weary acquiescence. Baron clapped him on the back, then regaled him with a list of the best places to buy Turpentine Pills and the kind of apples that were most favoured by horses.

'Caesar might not look like much,' he confided, lowering his voice as if he feared the remark might be heard by the beast in question, 'but he has a lovely nature, and the face of an angel. Do you not agree?'

Chaloner nodded cautiously, not daring to look at Silas in case he laughed. 'I understand he was Wheler's.'

'The loveliest creature in his stables! Unfortunately, Joan inherited him, and we are negotiating for ownership. Do you have any advice, Silas? She is your sister-in-law, after all.'

'Just bear in mind that she will cheat you,' replied Silas. 'It is a pity she knows you care for the animal, because that will drive up the price. You did not dispatch Wheler to lay hold of it, did you? She told me last night that you did.'

'She has a wicked tongue on her,' said Baron, while Chaloner noted that he had not denied the charge. 'She probably started the rumour that I sent assassins to kill Coo as well.'

'I heard that tale in the market today,' said Doe. He did not look at Baron, leaving Chaloner wondering whether there might be some truth to the claim. 'People are angry about his murder.'

'They are angry about many things,' sighed Baron. 'Coo, greedy bankers, the new plague measures. It is not easy being King of Cheapside, and I cannot imagine how His Majesty manages an entire country. Perhaps I should ask his advice.'

Silas released a sharp guffaw. 'He would demand your head if you did! But we have kept you from Caesar quite long enough. Good day, Baron.'

Chaloner watched the two felons saunter away. Baron was a ruthless and inflexible rogue, but he was a lot more personable than Joan, and Chaloner found himself hoping that Baron would not transpire to be Wheler's killer, as it would be a good deal more satisfying if Joan were the culprit.

'What will happen to *Plymouth*?' he asked. 'Or will she sail to war unarmed?'

Silas chuckled. 'Backwell bought and paid for her cannon weeks ago.'

'You lied to your father and Evan?' asked Chaloner, startled.

'Why not? They forced me to join the New Model Army *and* take a dull job in Harwich, so they owe me something, and I will win the money back sooner or later. Perhaps even tonight. But here we are at Bearbinder Lane, and there seems to be trouble.'

There was indeed trouble. As Silas had reported, Bearbinder Lane was closed, and a watcher had been stationed at the entrance to prevent anyone from coming or going. A crowd had gathered there, and virtually every person present was muttering resentfully. The watcher was obviously terrified, and gripped his cudgel tightly.

'We *know* the Howard maid is sick,' said Farrow the brewer. Chaloner noticed several other familiar faces in the crowd, including the laundress who had been hired to scrub Coo's blood from his doorstep. 'But why seal off the whole lane?'

'You know why!' shouted the laundress before the watcher could answer. 'Because its residents are poor. This would not be happening if it were Goldsmiths' Row.'

'Yes, it would,' argued the watcher, although he did not look convinced and neither were the onlookers. He was a scrawny fellow with bad teeth and oily skin, who

168

was probably not being paid enough to do battle with hostile mobs. 'There have been three cases here now – DuPont, the Howard maid and Mother Sage. This is the *plague*, you know. We cannot risk—'

'Mother Sage has dropsy, not plague,' shouted Farrow. 'Is that not so, Widow Porteous?'

'It is,' agreed the laundress. 'I visited her myself. It is not the plague.'

'Oh, and you are a searcher, are you?' demanded the watcher archly.

'I do not need to be a searcher,' flashed Widow Porteous. 'I know dropsy when I see it.'

The watcher shrugged. 'Then the lane will be re-opened. However, until I hear otherwise, it must be kept closed. For your own safety.'

'When do you expect the searcher to tell you her findings?' asked Chaloner, supposing that exploring DuPont's lodgings would have to wait until the lane was declared safe.

'Not today. She needs to see if buboes appear, which can take a while.'

'I need a drink,' said Silas, backing away hastily. 'All this talk of plague is very disturbing.'

'At the Green Dragon?' suggested Chaloner. 'You can get your lute back, and I can advise Randal about the perils of producing a sequel to *The Court & Kitchin*.'

Silas grimaced. 'I cannot imagine what possessed him to pick on poor Mrs Cromwell. What harm has she ever done?'

'Parliamentarian sentiments, Silas? I cannot see your family approving of that.'

Silas shrugged. 'Then they should not have enrolled me in the New Model Army. However, there are some who have not forgotten that a Taylor served under Cromwell, so I suppose Randal aims to make the family's loyalties clear. Yet it seems shabby to do it by ridiculing an old lady.'

Chaloner agreed. 'What does Randal do for a living – when he is not penning contentious pamphlets and hiding from angry republicans?'

Silas grinned. 'He is a professional husband.'

Chaloner blinked. 'A what?'

'Father needed some fast capital once, so Randal offered to marry an elderly dowager – in return for a handsome allowance, of course. The crone passed away a few weeks later, so he repeated the arrangement with a second ancient. Then *she* died, and Joan came along . . .'

'So Randal does nothing except make widows happy?'

'I do not think their happiness features in the arrangement. He says what is necessary in church, then leaves them to their own devices. He spends his time writing and cooking, although he has no talent for either, as you will know if you have read *The Court & Kitchin*.'

Chaloner did not like the sound of Randal. 'My Earl has charged me to look into Wheler's murder. Obviously, Baron, your father and Joan are on my list of suspects, but your remarks tell me that Randal should join them there. How big an allowance did he win by wedding Joan?'

'Oh, a huge one,' replied Silas carelessly. 'Randal does not sell himself cheap. However, you should have a lot more than four suspects. Wheler was hated by the people who worked for him, the people who owed him money, and the people he forced to pay him Protection Tax.'

'Baron forces them to pay Protection Tax, too.'

'Yes, but he actually provides the promised service, and his rates are far more reasonable. However, I am afraid your Earl is going to be disappointed, because Spymaster Williamson did his damnedest to solve that murder, and he failed. I doubt you will achieve what he could not.'

They had not walked far along Cheapside when Silas suggested visiting the music shop so he could show off his latest published work and had crossed the road before Chaloner could protest about the wasted time. Lettice was outside, sweeping muck from her doorstep.

'I cannot bear to be indoors,' she confided. 'The Oxleys are having one of their rows.'

As soon as they stepped across the threshold, Chaloner understood what she meant. A screaming quarrel was under way in the house next door, the voices so loud that every word was audible. The spat was about whose turn it was to fetch water. A sharp crack followed by a lot of wailing indicated that someone had been slapped.

'They are dreadful people,' said Lettice unhappily. 'The boy killed my cat last week, and had the temerity to shake its little body at me over the wall. He is a horrid child, and so is his sister. But never mind them. Allow me to apologise for the mess. We have workmen in the cellar.'

'Ah, yes,' said Silas, wrinkling his nose in distaste. 'Your charming neighbours arranged for their cesspit to over-flow into your basement.'

Lettice smiled. 'Thank you for persuading Joan to begin repairs, Silas. We could not have afforded it ourselves, and you will appreciate that it is not nice living with such a stench.'

171

Silas waved a deprecating hand. 'All I did was remind her of her responsibilities.'

'*We* reminded her and she ignored us,' said Shaw, hearing the last remark as he emerged from the cellar. 'But it is an expensive undertaking, so I understand why she baulked – the entire floor must be raised, so that any spillages will stay where they originate, and not encroach on our territory. Come, let me show you.'

Chaloner had better – and more pleasant – things to do, but Hannah owed them money, so he supposed the least he could do was feign an interest in their affairs. He followed them down some steps to a cavernous basement of unusual depth, which provided the perfect repository for next-door's spare sewage.

To remedy the problem, workmen were filling the bottom half of the room with a muddy cement, a malodorous mixture of mortar, rubble and silt, all mixed with the noxious slops provided by the Oxleys. However, as the cellar was enormous, this was no mean undertaking, and many tons of material would be required before it was completed.

'What is the scaffolding for?' asked Chaloner politely, when Shaw turned in expectation of interested remarks. Silas's face was a mask of distaste, so he was clearly going to make no sensible contribution to the discussion.

'It marks where the new floor will be,' explained Shaw. 'Obviously, such a large volume of mortar will take weeks to set, so the walkway that runs around all four sides will allow us access to this room until the cement is hard enough to walk on.'

A plump, jolly-faced man bustled up. Shaw introduced him as Yaile, the foreman, who was equally eager to discuss details of the project.

'It would be dangerous to step on it while it is still molten. It is like quicksand – you would disappear without a trace.' He grinned in ghoulish glee. 'And there would not be so much as a ripple left on the surface to indicate where you had been.'

'Do you have any corpses to dispose of, Tom?' murmured Silas in Chaloner's ear. 'If so, here is a godsent opportunity.'

'But it is not just a case of hurling mortar in at random,' Yaile went on, blithely oblivious of the fact that neither Chaloner nor Silas were very interested. 'Oh, no. To get a proper finish, it needs to be mixed and poured by the *ton*, not by the bucket-load.'

He pointed to where an enormous leather bag was suspended from the roof. It bulged with the many pails of sludge that had been emptied into it, and water oozed through its sides.

'Is it ready?' asked Shaw, more animated than usual. 'Can you give a demonstration?'

With palpable pride, Yaile yanked on a lever. The bag began to tip, and a mass of sloppy muck cascaded downwards. As soon as it was empty, Yaile's labourers began to smooth the surface with specially designed tools.

'And now we fill the bag again,' he said happily. 'By the time it is ready, the previous load will have settled, and we shall repeat the process. We shall continue until the mortar is ten feet deep and level with the scaffolding.'

Silas's eyes were glazed with boredom. 'Lord! Is that the time? I shall just show Tom my latest composition, and then we must be on our way. I have an appointment with Backwell.' He showed them several silver shillings. 'I borrowed these from him last night, and if I do not return them soon, he will send out a search party.'

Lettice giggled as she led the way back to the shop. 'He might! It is common knowledge that he would sell his mother if someone offered him a shiny coin.'

Shaw pulled Silas's music from a shelf, and Chaloner tuned out the chatter around him as the notes soared through his mind. By the time he had finished scanning the piece, Shaw had turned to more gloomy topics of conversation.

'Have you heard about Bearbinder Lane? It is closed until a searcher decides whether Mother Sage has the plague, although it is probably just another attack of her dropsy, poor soul.'

'It would not be closed if Cromwell were still in power,' declared Yaile, who had followed them out of the cellar in the hope of explaining his clever contraption in more detail. 'And he would not have done such a terrible thing to the Howard family either – sixteen healthy souls shut away with a sick maid. Have you had news of them?'

'Only that the maid died today,' reported Lettice. 'I cannot believe what is happening to those poor people! Mr Howard made me a hat only last week. Indeed, I may even have been his last customer, given that his house was boarded up not long after I had gone to collect it.'

'If he or any of his family die, it will be sheer bloody murder,' stated Yaile angrily. 'They should be allowed out now the lass is dead.'

'I think it would be wiser to wait,' said Lettice reasonably. 'The authorities are right to take serious measures against an outbreak.'

'Then why is Essex House not closed up?' demanded Yaile. 'One of *its* maids took sick at the same time, but the grand Earl is not locked in.'

174

'Lord! Such sombre talk!' cried Silas. 'I am beginning to wish I had not come!'

The Green Dragon was spacious, pleasant and airy. It was also crowded, but unfortunately, Randal was not among the noisy throng. Silas ordered a jug of ale, and Chaloner was glad when the taverner, a plump, greasy, sweating individual named Ned Hanson, declared it was on the house, as he had very little money left – and less than he should have done, because he had bought Silas's music to assuage his guilt over the forty pounds Hannah owed the Shaws.

'Hanson is in debt to my father,' said Silas, to explain the landlord's generosity. 'And he hopes I will put in a good word for him. I might. I like this tavern, and should not like to see it closed on my family's account.'

He turned the conversation to music, and Chaloner soon forgot both his cold and his investigations as they talked, only realising how much time had passed when Hanson brought them a meal of bread and roasted meat. He knew he should leave and do some work, but he was hungry, so he lingered, enjoying Silas's easy banter, and had just finished eating when Shaw and Lettice arrived.

'A quartet!' cried Silas, and promptly demanded the use of a private room. They were given one that was clean, quiet and smelled of the herbs that were springing to life in the garden outside. A bee buzzed among the blossoms, and a blackbird trilled from a tree in the next yard.

Lettice entertained Chaloner and Silas with conversation while her husband went to fetch two viols from his shop, but soon ran out of interesting things to say, and confined herself instead to naming all those courtiers

175

who bought music from her shop. Chaloner was unimpressed when Silas made an excuse to disappear, leaving him to listen to the dull monologue alone.

Bored, he went to stare out of the window and was surprised to see Backwell lurking behind a bush in the garden – and even more surprised to see Silas join him there a few moments later. Both glanced around furtively as they held a low-voiced conversation, so it was clear they did not want to be observed. At first, Chaloner assumed that Silas was just returning the coins he said he had borrowed, but no money changed hands. The spy strained his ears to listen to them, but all he could hear was Lettice's inconsequential gabble.

'Do you know Backwell well?' he asked, when his friend eventually returned.

Silas gave one of his rakish grins. 'Not at all. He is a dry old stick, so I leave him to the likes of my father and Joan.'

'But I just saw you talking to him,' said Chaloner, disliking the lie.

'You mean in the garden? You saw us, did you? Well, do not tell anyone – it would do my reputation as a man of verve no good whatsoever. Ah, here is Shaw at last. And he has brought songs by Gibbons. Excellent! Which of these viols will you have, Tom?'

Chaloner tried to pursue the discussion about Backwell, but Silas raised a hand for silence while they tuned their instruments, and by the time they had finished, Lettice and Shaw were ready to sing. Silas began playing at once, forcing Chaloner to scramble to catch his place. Lettice giggled once during a rest, but Silas silenced her with a glance, and it did not happen again. The remainder of the piece was blissful, and when it was over, Chaloner did not care about what had transpired in the garden.

They played until the light faded, at which point Silas called for a lamp, and they continued until Lettice declared herself too tired for more. Chaloner was sorry, even though his own fingers were sore from the exercise, and took his leave reluctantly.

Cheapside was busy. Every tavern, alehouse and eatery was doing a roaring trade, and the atmosphere was light and relaxed, as often happened on warm evenings. There was some trouble at the Standard, where Puritans brandishing Randal's pamphlet yelled abuse at a few Cavaliers, but trainband men appeared and the fracas was soon quelled.

Chaloner walked to Baron's house, then stood in the shadows of St Mary Woolchurch opposite, thinking that if the King of Cheapside refused to give him the curtains, he would just have to take them. It was not stealing, as the Earl had paid for them, and his only concern was that they might be too heavy for him to carry. He found a comfortable place to wedge himself, and settled down to wait.

Lamps burned inside the house, and he could see Baron on the ground floor, lounging in a throne-like chair while people came and went. Most brought money, which was accepted with polite grace; some did not, and were bundled away to be dealt with by his charmless captains. Hours passed, and the bellman was calling two o'clock before the lamps in Baron's mansion were finally doused. Only one remained, and Chaloner crept forward to see Baron, Doe and Poachin counting money at a table.

He waited again, and eventually saw a shadow pass across an upstairs window – Baron joining his wife in bed. Chaloner began to prowl, and soon discovered that the felon was very mindful of his security. Not only were there substantial locks on all the doors, but the window shutters had been carefully sealed, and the grounds were patrolled by vigilant guards.

But Chaloner had made a career out of breaking into places that wanted to keep people out, and it did not take him long to identify a window that was weaker than the rest. Meanwhile, the sentries had settled into a routine, so it was easy to predict when they would next appear.

Moving with utmost care, he used his knife to prise open the shutter. He scrambled through it just as the guards reappeared, both engaged in a low-voiced conversation about a house that had been shut up by the authorities. Their voices were sharp with indignation as they agreed that the baby was suffering from colic, not the plague, but its parents had not had the funds to encourage the searcher to concur.

Chaloner lit a candle and began his search, noting that Baron felt sufficiently safe to have left all his money in a pile on the table. He tiptoed on, passing through any number of handsomely furnished rooms. There was nothing of interest on the ground floor, so he descended to the cellar. Curtains – including some exceptionally ugly ones with embroidered roses – were piled neatly on tables, along with tapestries, rugs and the kind of hangings that went around four-poster beds. Unfortunately, none were red with gold thread. Then he heard a noise behind him, and whipped around to see Baron standing there, watching him.

Chaloner doused the candle quickly, aware of the felon surging forward to lay hold of him. He jigged around the man, but Baron managed to snag his sleeve. He punched his way free and ran, but Baron started to yell, and suddenly the house was full of trainband men.

178

Chaloner aimed for the stairs, knowing instinctively that his best option was to escape over the roof, but Baron's son blocked his route – the lad was pale but resolute as he gripped a wooden sword in hands that shook. It would be easy to knock him down, but Chaloner was not in the habit of hurting children, so he ran back down the stairs and fought a brisk but brief battle with the men by the front door. They were unprepared for the ferocity of his attack, and were quickly defeated.

He would have escaped handily if it had been a normal door. Unluckily, it was not only locked, but secured with three bolts and two bars. It was too much, and although Chaloner defeated the lock and the bolts, he was still struggling with the bars when Doe appeared. The captain launched himself forward with such force that Chaloner was knocked clean off his feet. Before he could scramble upright, Doe was on him, screaming furiously as he delivered a frenzy of kicks and punches.

Chaloner was not sure what happened next. Doe was still trying to batter him, but his blows either missed or lacked force, and he risked a glance upwards to see Poachin holding his fellow captain off. Then more of the trainband arrived and Chaloner was hauled roughly to his feet. Doe howled at Poachin to let him go, and there was no question that he aimed to kill the intruder with his bare hands.

'Stop,' came a commanding voice from the doorway. It was Baron, rubbing his jaw where one of Chaloner's wild clouts had struck home. 'I want to talk to him.'

A sly expression crossed Poachin's face and he released Doe, who was far too enraged to hear orders. He surged forward, ignoring Baron's bellow to desist. Chaloner braced himself, but the trainband reacted quickly and intercepted Doe before he reached his target. Doe fought tooth and nail until Baron gripped a handful of his hair, yanked his head back and whispered in his ear. It had no effect at first, but the stream of low words gradually began to calm him.

Only when Doe nodded to say that he had his temper under control did Baron let him go. He shook himself like a dog, while the King of Cheapside shot Poachin a glance that was none too friendly – the attempt to see Doe disgrace himself had misfired. Then Baron turned his attention to Chaloner.

'What are you doing in my house?' His voice was soft, but Chaloner knew he was in serious trouble. The trainband comprised the kind of men who would not only turn a blind eye to murder, but who were probably also experienced at disposing of inconvenient corpses. Chaloner noticed Oxley among them, eyes bright at the prospect of violence.

'Looking for the Earl of Clarendon's curtains,' he replied with as much swagger as he could muster. If he was going to be summarily dispatched, then he was certainly not about to give them the satisfaction of showing fear.

Baron stared at him for a moment, then burst out laughing. The trainband joined in, albeit nervously. 'And you expect me to believe that?'

Chaloner nodded. 'He will not pay my salary until they are delivered, and my wife is in debt with Taylor, who is inflexible about repayment.'

'That might be true,' said Poachin to Baron. 'Half the Court owes money to Taylor, while Neve told me that Clarendon often abuses his staff.'

'Leave us,' Baron ordered his trainband.

They trooped out obediently. Poachin drew a handgun, evidently as uneasy in Chaloner's company as Chaloner was in Doe's, who he was sure was still not fully in command of his rage – the younger captain jigged from foot to foot, fingering a dagger he had pulled from his belt and hissing between his teeth.

'Did you see any curtains that caught your fancy?' asked Baron mildly.

'No,' replied Chaloner. 'They must be red and gold, colours you do not seem to have.'

'They are being made by my brother-in-law the linen-draper,' said Baron smoothly. 'As I told you earlier, you can have them when you have given me four wealthy clients.'

'I am going to check the parlour,' snarled Doe. 'And if I find one penny missing—'

'I watched him in the parlour,' interrupted Baron, a claim Chaloner found unnerving. 'He barely glanced at our money.'

'We should kill him anyway,' said Doe, tossing the blade from hand to hand. 'For his audacity.'

'No,' countered Baron. 'For three reasons. First, because he is telling the truth; second, because no one has ever invaded my house before and I am impressed; and third, because he could have escaped up the stairs, but he chose another route to avoid harming my son.'

'That is a good point – no one *has* broached our security before,' said Doe, apparently deciding that points one and three were irrelevant. He glared at Chaloner. 'Tell us how you did it.'

Chaloner saw no reason not to oblige. It could not make his predicament worse than it was already, with

Poachin's gun cocked and ready, and Doe clearly itching to stab him. As he spoke, he let his own knife from his sleeve slip into his hand – they would not find him an easy kill. There was silence when he finished speaking.

'Work for me,' said Baron eventually. 'I could use a man with your talents.'

Chaloner was startled – this was not an outcome he had anticipated. 'I already have an employer, thank you.'

'One who withholds your salary on a whim,' scoffed Baron. 'You would not suffer that sort of indignity with me, and you will earn more than enough to settle up with Taylor.'

'It is a tempting offer,' hedged Chaloner, suspecting his family would disown him if he went to work for a criminal, while Hannah would die of shame. Or should he accept, just to escape Baron's house in one piece? He could always go into hiding afterwards. 'I will consider it.'

'Do,' said Baron. 'Your Earl may not be in a position to keep you much longer. That monstrous Dunkirk House will be his undoing, and when he falls, you will fall with him.'

'Yes,' sighed Chaloner. 'I know.'

'I control all Cheapside, from the Poultry to St Michael's,' Baron went on. 'Seven churches, fifteen taverns, three coffee houses, forty-one shops, a hundred and eighty-three houses and twenty-two alehouses. All pay Protection Tax, which equals a lot of money.'

'We also own seven houses in Bearbinder Lane,' added Doe. 'Tenements, which we lease to the working poor. It is all extremely lucrative.'

'Bearbinder Lane,' mused Chaloner. 'I went there earlier, but it was closed.'

182

'It is not closed now,' said Baron. 'Mother Sage does not have the plague, just dropsy, thanks be to God.'

'Are you sure?' asked Chaloner, watching him closely, and wondering whether the searcher had been paid for a verdict that would keep the tenements open and working. 'Because her neighbour DuPont definitely died of the plague. Dr Coo told me so, before he was murdered.'

The trio exchanged glances that were difficult to interpret. 'We did not know that,' said Baron eventually. 'Was he certain?'

Chaloner nodded. 'Quite certain.'

'Do you think someone shot Coo so he would not be in a position to enlighten you?' asked Poachin, addressing Baron. 'There must be some reason why the poor man was so viciously gunned down.'

Baron shook his head. 'If Coo had wanted to talk, he had plenty of time to do it. In fact, the question we should ask is: why did he *not* come to us with this information? I would have been grateful for it.'

'He was very absent-minded,' said Doe.

'I will find his killer,' said Baron, his eyes boring into Chaloner's. 'And then I shall dispense my own justice. Coo was a good man – kind to my family and my trainband. Moreover, I do not appreciate murder committed in my territory without my permission.'

Chaloner took that to mean that he did not mind it committed if his consent was sought first, and that there was probably a price attached. 'What about DuPont – did you know him?'

'Why all these questions?' demanded Poachin suspiciously. 'I do not like it.'

'*I* do not mind discussing DuPont with a potential

183

employee,' smirked Baron. 'He was French, and very charming. Women found him irresistible.'

'They will not think so now,' said Doe with an evil snigger. 'He was shoved in the ground so fast that the priest barely had time to recite the committal. And now we know why.'

'We should have been told,' said Poachin worriedly. 'Not knowing these things makes us look weak.'

'Why do you think he walked across the city when he was carrying such a deadly disease?' asked Chaloner, tending to agree. 'He might have infected dozens of people along the way – people in *your* domain.'

Alarm flared in Baron's eyes, although it was quickly masked. 'Well, if he did bring the plague to Bearbinder Lane, it is under control now. The Howard house is safely shut up, the searcher diagnosed Mother Sage with a different fever, and any deadly miasma DuPont might have brought from Long Acre will have dissipated. We are safe.'

'Coo did not believe that plague is spread by a miasma,' said Chaloner. 'He thought it is transmitted by tiny worms, which may still be in DuPont's house waiting to—'

'Rubbish,' interrupted Doe. 'Everyone knows it is carried in a stinking mist, and this talk of worms is a nonsense, designed to frighten the gullible.'

'Why would Coo want to do that?' asked Baron quietly.

Doe shrugged. 'Who knows the thoughts of saints? However, *we* need not worry about the plague – not with all the Turpentine Pills we have been swallowing.'

'Pah!' spat Poachin. 'They are not nearly as good as Red Snake Electuary. And every time *I* experience a worrying symptom, I put a dried toad on my chest.'

'I shall use Mithridatum if I catch the plague,' Baron informed them confidentially. 'It has fifty-four separate ingredients, and with that number, how can it not be an effective cure? It is expensive, but no price is too high for the lives of me and my family.'

'And your friends,' said Poachin with an odd glance.

'Oh, yes,' said Baron flatly. 'And my friends.' Then he eyed Chaloner warily. 'Are you sure *you* do not have the disease? Your voice was not so husky yesterday.'

'It is terror that makes him hoarse,' declared Doe snidely. 'But what shall we do with him? We can hardly let him go.'

'Why not?' asked Baron. 'I want him to consider my offer of employment. There is always room in my retinue for men who respect my children and do not steal my money.'

Chapter 7

Chaloner woke the next day feeling wretched. His nose was blocked, his eyes were gritty, his throat was sore, and the first thing he did was sneeze four times in quick succession, vigorously enough to wake Hannah.

'Perhaps you should stay in bed,' she said, trying hard to sound sympathetic, although he could tell it was an effort not to let her morning temper prevail and give him a piece of her mind for disturbing her. 'Gram will look after you. Poor Gram. I wish we could keep him. Did you talk to Temperance about taking him in? I cannot imagine what use he will be to her, though. He is so *old*.'

'That did not stop you from hiring him,' Chaloner pointed out.

Hannah scowled, but remembered that she was in the wrong over their finances, so struggled to smile. Then she attempted to distract him with Court gossip, particularly chatter that was pertinent to her own situation and gave credence to her belief that she was a victim.

'Do you remember Lady Carnegie – the woman who passed the Duke of York that shameful pox? Well, she borrowed nine hundred pounds from Backwell, but under Taylor it became *twelve* hundred in less than a month.'

'I cannot hear properly,' said Chaloner. He shook his head and blew his nose, but his ears remained plugged. Worse, his eyes were watery, so his vision was blurred, and his mouth felt as though it was full of cotton. How was he supposed to catch killers and hunt down curtains when half his senses did not work?

'I could name a host of others with similar financial problems,' Hannah went on. 'And to make matters worse, the two million pounds voted by Parliament for the war is unlikely to be enough, so the bankers must provide more – which means the burden will fall on us, their clients. Men who wanted to fight are now saying that we should have exercised restraint. You were right all along.'

'What have you done about the house?' rasped Chaloner, unwilling to be mollified. 'Have you found somewhere smaller to live?'

'Not yet – virtually everyone at Court is trying to do the same, so it may take a while. You must be patient, Tom.'

'Try telling Taylor that,' retorted Chaloner. 'And speaking of Taylor, do you have ten shillings? He wants it today, so you had better take it to him.'

'I cannot – the Queen is entertaining the French ambassador, and she needs me with her. Besides, I only have five shillings, and as Taylor will be vexed by the shortfall, you had better go instead. He is less likely to frighten you than me.'

'And less likely to trounce you,' muttered Chaloner, although he took the proffered coins.

'Do you remember me telling you about the Howard family? The milliners, who were shut up in their house on Bearbinder Lane with a sick maid? Well, word came late last night that they are all dead – mother, father, children, elderly relatives and servants. Seventeen people, all gone.'

If the pestilence spread, thought Chaloner grimly, such stories would become distressingly familiar. Had DuPont given the disease to the hapless maid? Baron had said that women had found him charming, so perhaps she had stopped to exchange greetings with him on his final, fatal journey. And as all the victims were unlikely to have breathed their last at the same time, he could only suppose that some were already dead when he and Silas had been at Bearbinder Lane the previous day, but the news had been suppressed by the survivors in the desperate hope that they might be allowed out to live another day.

'If the plague takes hold, will you stay in London or will you leave?' he asked.

'I have not thought about it. Why?'

Chaloner swallowed hard, uncomfortable as always about revealing his private feelings. 'Because my first wife . . . well, I should not like to lose another.'

'I suppose that is your way of saying that you love me, although why you find it so difficult to utter those three small words is beyond me. Do you realise you have never once said it?'

'No,' replied Chaloner. He wished his wits were sharper. 'I mean yes.'

'I see,' said Hannah, although there was a flash of amusement in her eyes, and he suspected she had enjoyed baiting him. 'Shall I cook you breakfast? I begged eggs of some description – pigeon, perhaps – from the palace kitchen yesterday, and Gram found a cabbage.'

It sounded most unappealing, but she was insistent, and he did not have the energy to argue. She ran downstairs in her nightshift, while he rifled through his clothes in search of coins. He found another shilling, several pennies and five coffee-house tokens – small change was notoriously rare in London, so coffee-house owners produced their own, which comprised discs of metal or leather stamped with their names. They were accepted in lieu of money in many places.

He walked down the stairs, trying to summon the strength to face whatever was responsible for the foul smell that was emanating from the kitchen. He opened the door to be met by billowing smoke. Coughing, he hurried to open a window, although Hannah did not seem to have noticed anything amiss.

'Here,' she said, presenting him with a plate that contained something that was charred on the outside and oozed raw egg from the middle. Hunks of cabbage stalk were visible, along with hard black balls that transpired to be burned cobnuts.

'Christ God!' he muttered.

'Eat up,' said Hannah proudly. 'You will not feel better unless you have plenty of good, healthy food inside you.'

'No,' agreed Chaloner ambiguously.

A shape materialised through the smog, and Gram appeared. 'That looks nice,' he remarked, eyeing Chaloner's plate hopefully. 'Is there any spare?'

Chaloner seized the opportunity to offload most of it, and was astonished when the page devoured the lot with every appearance of enjoyment.

'Thank you, Hannah,' said Chaloner, when the last singed crumb had disappeared and Gram sat back with a sigh of contentment. 'I have never had a breakfast quite like it.'

Hannah beamed. 'Perhaps we should do it every day.'

*

Chaloner's first port of call was Clarendon House, to update the Earl on his progress. It was still early, but he knew his employer would be awake because it was Thursday, the day when the Privy Council met. Being conscientious, the Earl rose before dawn to prepare, although it was a waste of time, as no one listened to what he had to say anyway.

'We shall discuss the current financial situation today,' he said, when Chaloner arrived to find him at his desk. 'Namely what will happen if the banks collapse and we cannot fund the war. Why did they have to choose now for a crisis? And how have they contrived to make themselves so unpopular? *Everyone* hates them.'

Chaloner agreed. 'Debtors, the poor, depositors . . . and there are rumours that they are dishonest. However, part of the crisis came about because the King ordered them to donate a lot of money at very short notice—'

'Do not blame him for the trouble, Chaloner,' said the Earl sharply. 'If they had not been so eager to make a profit from their investors by lending what had been deposited, they would have had more cash in their coffers. Of course, it is the investors who worry us most. Do you know what happens when they lose confidence in the places that store their money?'

'Not really, sir.'

'They demand it back, and when a lot of them do it, the banks cannot cope – they default, which frightens other depositors into making hasty withdrawals, and the whole foundation collapses. It was a "run" that destroyed Angier and Hinton recently. And if we want an example in history, then just look at tulips.'

Chaloner recalled what Shaw had told him. 'Bulbs once fetched very high prices.'

The Earl nodded. 'I dabbled myself, although I had the sense to withdraw before the market crashed. It caused economic chaos, and we do not want the same thing to happen again.'

'Taylor will not be destroyed by a run,' predicted Chaloner wryly. 'He will simply refuse to give his investors their money, and none will be bold enough to press him.'

'Yes, but he is part of the problem. While the other banks wobble, he grows stronger, and we are uneasy that one man has so much power. Backwell and Vyner might be greedy, but they are essentially decent. Taylor is not.'

'No,' agreed Chaloner.

'Although I did see Backwell enjoy a very animated discussion with *Silas* Taylor the other day. Both were staunch Parliamentarians, so I hope they are not plotting insurrection.'

Chaloner blinked. 'Is there a reason to suppose they might?'

The Earl flapped a plump hand. 'It was a joke, Chaloner – a jest because it was odd to see a banker and a Keeper of Stores so deep in conversation. They were probably chatting about music.'

Chaloner was sure they had not been talking about music in the Green Dragon's garden the previous evening, and hoped his old friend was not about to do anything reckless.

'When did you see them, sir?'

The plump fingers were waved again. 'I cannot recall. A week ago, perhaps? But never mind them. What did you come to report?'

He wrinkled his nose in distaste when Chaloner told what he had learned about DuPont and Wheler, and repeated his order to stay away from anywhere that might harbour the plague. 'Which includes Bearbinder Lane *and* St Giles. This "Onions at the Well" business is a nonsense, and you should forget about it. Now what about my curtains?'

'They are not in Baron's house. He says they are still being made.'

'Well, tell him to hurry up,' ordered the Earl irritably. 'I want the matter concluded as soon as possible. Is there anything else? If not, will you send Neve to see me? I want to discuss buying another Lely.'

'Would you like one of Hannah?' asked Chaloner hopefully.

The Earl regarded him lugubriously. 'I only collect portraits of princes or bishops, thank you. I do not think Lely shines as well when he paints ladies.'

Chaloner hoped no one else thought the same, or they would never sell the thing. 'Incidentally, I know Neve was the "mutual acquaintance" who put you in touch with DuPont.'

The Earl gaped at him. 'How did you find that out? Lord! I hope he does not think that *I* told you.'

'It would have saved time if you had.' Chaloner tried not to sound recriminatory, but did not succeed. 'And danger – I could have learned far sooner that DuPont had died of the plague.'

'He swore me to secrecy. And he is the best upholder in London, so I had no choice but to accede to his request. I cannot afford to lose him.'

Feeling the need for Thurloe's wise counsel, Chaloner began to walk to Lincoln's Inn. He stopped at the Rainbow en route to down a dish of Farr's best, but declined to be drawn into a heated debate about bankers, as he was already bored with the subject.

'A great sea-battle was fought against the Dutch yesterday,' said Farr, trying to interest him in something else. 'The guns were heard rumbling all day. *Royal Katherine* was involved and Captain Teddeman's legs were shot off. Damn those butter-eaters! They aim to invade us and steal all our money.'

'You sound like Backwell,' said Speed, deftly turning the subject back to economics. Chaloner blew on his coffee, to cool it so he could drink up and leave. '*He* worships lucre, too.'

'He does,' nodded Stedman. 'And he hates the fact that he and his fellows are being forced to fund the war, even though it is his patriotic duty.'

'He is a greedy villain,' declared Farr. 'Like all bankers – rapacious parasites, who suck the wealth from others to make themselves rich.'

'There was a fierce quarrel in my shop yesterday,' reported Speed gleefully. 'Over *The Court & Kitchin*. I love it when a book makes an impact, as it is good for sales. Copies are flying off my shelves. Have you read it yet, Chaloner?'

'Inflaming trouble between Royalists and Roundheads is nothing to be proud of,' said Farr sternly, before Chaloner could admit that he had not. 'You should be ashamed of yourself.'

Chaloner left when Speed began to defend himself in a hectoring voice that was sure to annoy the others. He had hoped the coffee would perk him up, but it only made his heart pound and his head ache more than ever. He trudged lethargically along Fleet Street, the morsel of cabbage omelette that he had forced himself to

193

swallow lying so heavily in his stomach that he was glad he had not eaten more. He coughed when he turned into Chancery Lane, as several bonfires had been lit, all loaded with damp twigs to make them smoke.

'Spymaster Williamson's orders,' a soldier explained when Chaloner asked what was going on. The lower half of his face was covered with a scarf, and a dried toad hung around his neck. 'The fumes combat dangerous miasmas, see, and a woman was took ill here yesterday. It was probably a fainting sickness, but he says we cannot be too careful.'

'He is right.' Chaloner wondered why the Spymaster should have been discussing such a matter with minions.

'He is in charge of implementing the city's anti-plague measures now,' the soldier went on. 'He hires watchers and searchers, sees the streets are washed, arranges for fires to be lit, and ensures the victims are locked up before they infect the rest of us. Listen! Did you hear that?'

'What? The donkey braying? Or the pie-seller swearing?'

'The bell! It is the second time it has tolled today. It means someone has died.'

'People die every day,' Chaloner pointed out. 'And bells toll. It does not mean the plague—'

He stopped to sneeze, and the soldier backed away in horror. Then a bell began to chime in a different part of the city, and Chaloner listened uneasily. Would *he* start to notice them now, even though it was inevitable that people would pass away on a daily basis in a city of three hundred thousand inhabitants? He had never paid them much heed before, blending as they did into the usual hubbub of London's streets.

Chaloner arrived at Chamber XIII to find preparations

194

for the ex-Spymaster's departure well under way. Clothes sat in neatly folded piles, and a travelling trunk was already half filled with books, papers and gifts for the children.

'My colleagues here at Lincoln's Inn think I am leaving because I fear a Dutch invasion,' said Thurloe, tearing up the government's latest newsbook and using the shreds to pack a glass vase. 'But the rumour that they are in Scotland is a canard. Moreover, there was no sea-battle yesterday. *Royal Katherine* has not yet left port, and Captain Teddeman is still in possession of both his legs. The "gunfire" people claim to have heard was thunder. After all, the weather is unusually mild.'

Chaloner sat down and helped himself to Thurloe's breakfast, which was a good deal more palatable than his own, although there was very little of it – the ex-Spymaster was abstemious.

'On the other hand,' Thurloe went on, 'the plague terrifies me. Unfortunately, it does not terrify others, and there was trouble on Cheapside yesterday over the measures taken to contain it – they are considered too harsh. Fools! Do they *want* it to kill them?'

'My wife's maid brought it to our house in Amsterdam,' confided Chaloner. He did not normally discuss that terrible time, and supposed his cold was lowering his defences. 'Aletta and my baby caught it because they were locked in with her, as did three more servants, two neighbours and a friend. I am sure some would have lived had they been allowed out.'

'Perhaps.' Thurloe's voice was kind. 'Or they may have spread the infection to others.'

Chaloner changed the subject, unwilling to dwell on it. 'I still have not found Randal, but I will try again today. I know which tavern he frequents.'

195

'Good,' said Thurloe. 'Now tell me about Hannah's obligations to Taylor. I sense that is the matter giving you the most cause for concern.'

Thurloe had read him correctly, because Chaloner was indeed anxious about the way the debt was spiralling out of control. 'He wants more than we can give him, and the Earl has stopped my pay until I can arrange for two pairs of curtains to be delivered.'

Thurloe rolled his eyes. 'Your master has some very strange priorities.'

'Hannah is not the only one in trouble. Others include Bab May, Will Chiffinch, Peter Newton who killed himself over it, Sir George Carteret who was stripped of his jewelled buttons, Lord Rochester, Prince Rupert, Lady Carnegie and the Bishop of Winchester.'

'The government should pass a law forbidding usurious rates of interest,' said Thurloe sourly. 'Cromwell would never have permitted such greedy opportunism.'

'They dare not upset the bankers, as they need them to finance the war.'

'I sense disaster in the air, Tom. No streets will run with blood, nothing will explode, sink, burn or collapse, but people will be ruined and the usual scapegoats will take the blame – Catholics, Quakers, foreigners. And supporters of the old regime.'

Chaloner stared at him. 'Do you think *you* might be accused?'

'It is possible. Perhaps you should consider leaving, too, because I sense that London will be a very bad place to live before much more time has passed.'

At Thurloe's insistence, Chaloner went to the Green Dragon to look for Randal immediately upon leaving

Lincoln's Inn. Without Silas to attract free ale, he was obliged to pay for a drink, as no landlord appreciated customers who occupied seats without buying. What he was served was sour and weak, but he took a tentative mouthful anyway, wondering how long he could make it last before he was obliged to order a refill.

While he waited for Randal to appear, he listened to the buzz of conversation around him. He learned that the tale about the fifteen hundred drowned Britons was exposed as a lie, fabricated by a Swede for the attention it would bring. But that was old news, and the latest was that the Dutch fleet had been sighted off Yarmouth – invasion was imminent. Any sane Londoner should know that the Dutch would never risk attacking the capital, but several jittery merchants raced off to withdraw their money from the banks anyway, leading Chaloner to wonder whether the Earl might be right to fear a run.

There was also talk about *The Court & Kitchin*, and an ill-natured row it had sparked on Friday Street not an hour ago. Supposing he had better read the thing to see what all the fuss was about, Chaloner took it from his pocket.

It comprised three parts: the recipes, which seemed perfectly wholesome to him; a Preface to the Reader; and an Introduction that comprised a wordy and tedious rant spangled with quotes in Latin and references to classical mythology. Most was arrant nonsense, and he was surprised a printer had agreed to produce it – personally, he would have been embarrassed to have his business associated with such a peculiar and incomprehensible piece.

That thought gave him an idea, and he turned to the title page, where he read that it had been published by

197

Thos Milbourn in St Martin le Grand. He frowned. Thomas Milbourn had printed Baron's advertisements, too. He pulled Baron's card from his pocket and compared it to the book, where idiosyncrasies in the typesetting showed they were from the same press. He could almost see St Martin le Grand from where he sat, so he abandoned the remains of his ale and went there at once, thinking that Milbourn might know where Randal was living.

Unfortunately, he arrived to find that the premises had been gutted by fire. The inferno had been recent, because none of the wreckage had been cleared away, although the charred wood was cold. A man from the house opposite saw him looking, and came to talk.

'No one knows what happened,' he said. 'We just woke a few nights ago to see the place in flames. Poor Milbourn has not been seen since, so he must have been inside. Of course, I know who was responsible – Roundheads.'

'Why them?' asked Chaloner, a little defensively.

'Because of that pamphlet about Mrs Cromwell. They would rather lynch the author, of course, but he is in hiding, so they picked on the printer instead.'

Chaloner walked back to the Green Dragon in an anxious frame of mind. *The Court & Kitchin* had been published weeks ago, yet feelings still ran high, so what would happen if Randal did produce a sequel? Clearly, Thurloe was right to be concerned.

When he reached the tavern, the dregs of his ale were where he had left them, so he sipped them while he perused the rest of Randal's tirade. It was petty and spiteful, claiming that Cromwell would have been a glutton were it not for his wife's *sordid frugality and thrifty baseness*, and that she was *a hundred times fitter for a barn than a palace*. She was accused of accepting bribes and the spoils of war, yet baulked at the cost of a personal carriage, so used ones confiscated from Royalists. Randal also scoffed that she sat by while custard was lobbed by guests at her daughter's wedding, and that she kept three cows in St James's Park so she would not have to pay for butter.

Its sly poison made Chaloner determined to talk to its author, but although he waited in the Green Dragon all day, Randal did not appear. Exasperated, he abandoned his vigil, and decided to see what could be learned from DuPont's lodgings in Bearbinder Lane instead. The Earl had ordered him to stay away from the place, but Chaloner needed clues if he was to get to the bottom of the Frenchman's death. He had no choice but to take the risk.

Outside, the sun bathed the city in the soft, gold light of a fine spring evening, and the scent of warm manure was in the air. As usual, Cheapside was busy, and Chaloner started uneasily when he passed St Mary le Bow and its bells began to chime, but then he relaxed. It was not the tenor tolling for a death, but all six bells beginning a series of sequences known as 'change ringing', which was becoming popular for weddings. The groom was waiting in the porch, and Chaloner hoped the lad's pale, sweaty face derived from nerves, not the start of a fatal fever.

Beyond the church was a commotion, and he approached to see two houses with red crosses on their doors and watchers stationed outside. Small crowds had gathered around each, calling encouragement to the

199

people who leaned out of the upstairs windows. Every so often, someone would dart forward for mischief, and the spectators would hoot and jeer when the watcher was obliged to chase them back.

'My boy has a griping in the guts,' shouted an angry man from one house. 'We should not be locked in. We are bakers – our business will be ruined if we are gone for forty days.'

'The searcher said it was plague,' countered the watcher, fingering his sword uneasily. 'And Mr Williamson gave orders that—'

'And my baby is only teething,' interrupted a woman from next door. 'Look!'

She brandished the hapless tot out of the window. He howled in lusty alarm, and it was clear that there was very little wrong with him.

'Plague rages in the homes of the rich, though,' yelled a spectator. It was the loutish Oxley, and while he spoke, his daughter was busily picking the pocket of the man next to her, while his son lobbed pebbles at the watchers. 'Yet *they* are not locked away.'

'Do you mean Essex House?' asked one watcher. 'Because that was spotted fever.'

'It was the plague,' countered Oxley. 'And two victims are already in their graves.'

The watchers tried to deny it, but Oxley overrode them with a lot of bombast that had the crowd bawling indignant agreement. Then reinforcements arrived in the form of Williamson's soldiers. The mood of the onlookers grew uglier, and the situation might have turned violent had Baron and his trainband not appeared. A few sharp words from the King of Cheapside sent most of the protesters slinking away, while Oxley was taken to one side, and whatever was murmured in his ear had him nodding sullen acquiescence.

Chaloner walked on, and saw a number of residents scrubbing the ground outside their houses, while more of Williamson's men supervised. Others set about lighting bonfires that filled the street with a thick white haze. He reached Bearbinder Lane, and this time there was no watcher to prevent people from using it. Brewer Farrow, who never seemed to do anything other than loiter around being a malcontent, saw him eyeing it warily.

'It is safe now,' he declared. 'Mother Sage just has dropsy – the searcher said so.'

'Are you happy with her verdict?' asked Chaloner. 'Bearing in mind that if she was bribed to lie, your whole family might catch a terrible disease?'

'She was not bribed – it is the truth,' said Farrow crossly. 'There is no plague here.'

'Then what about DuPont and the Howards? DuPont was diagnosed by a physician, while no other sickness is likely to have killed seventeen people in so short a space of time.'

'Those are isolated cases. The danger is past.' Farrow smirked. 'The Spymaster would love to close off Cheapside as he did this lane, given that his searchers have shut up more than three houses there, but he cannot – he does not have enough soldiers to patrol all the ways in and out.'

'Then God help us all,' said Chaloner soberly, appalled that such a grave situation should be seen in terms of a battle of wills with Williamson.

He pushed past the brewer and entered Bearbinder Lane. It was narrow, mean and squalid, and its towering tenements were so close together that they met overhead.

201

It was also deserted, and he strongly suspected that its residents had fled before the authorities could change their minds and close it again. Eventually, he identified DuPont's house – it was the one next to Howard's. However, while the milliner's home had been carefully boarded up, nothing had been done to DuPont's. He could only suppose that, as it was one of Baron's 'lucrative concerns', the felon had arranged for it to be left alone. Between it and the Howard home was a hanging sign with a childishly depicted picture of an eagle, and Chaloner had the sudden melancholy thought that the youthful artist was probably one of the dead.

He looked around carefully to ensure no one was looking, then picked DuPont's lock. It was easier than it should have been, and he was inside in a trice. He closed the door behind him, then listened intently for any indication that the house was still occupied, although his catarrh-blocked ears rendered the exercise somewhat futile.

He began to explore. Each room had been stripped bare, and nothing but the odd scrap of food or crumpled piece of paper showed that anyone had ever lived there. He did not blame the occupants for leaving, but sincerely hoped they had not taken the disease with them.

He had just reached the third floor when he saw a shadow on the landing below: someone was coming up the stairs towards him. He hid behind a door, and the moment a head poked around it, he pounced, to find himself holding a puny child whose age was impossible to guess. The lad was uncommunicative at first, then became cheerfully garrulous when Chaloner gave him a ribbon he had in his pocket. His name was Noll, and he had known that someone had broken in, because there was a damp footprint on the doorstep. He had come to find out why.

'Where is everyone?' Chaloner was more inclined to ask questions than answer them.

'Gone away,' chirruped Noll. 'Except the landlord, who is probably upstairs. They ran off after DuPont died, but the landlord can't disappear, because he runs this house for Mr Baron. Mr Baron don't like folk disappearing on him, see.'

'What can you tell me about DuPont?'

'He was foreign and spoke funny, but only some of the time. He sounded like us when he was drunk. I didn't like him much. He was oily, like old grease, and he was always surrounded by girls. He liked cockfighting and cards.'

Chaloner thought about the messages he had found in Long Acre. 'Did his father live here?'

Noll regarded him askance. 'Course not! DuPont was French, so his sire will be in France. It stands to reason, see.' He looked pleased with himself for his incisive logic.

'Then is there anyone else he might have called father?'

'Yes,' replied Noll brightly. 'Top floor.'

'The landlord?'

Noll nodded. 'Mr Fatherton. His curbers call him Father.'

'His what?'

'Curbers. You know: a curb is a hook, and curbers use hooks to pull stuff through other people's windows.' Chaloner must have continued to look blank, because the lad added with some asperity, 'Thieves. Father tells them where and when to work, and they give everything they get to Mr Baron, who is in charge of this area.'

'Ah, yes,' said Chaloner. 'I heard that DuPont was a criminal.'

'Like you and me,' said Noll with a wink, a misunder-standing that explained his willingness to chat. 'You are a napper – although not a very good one, or you would have picked a better place than this to rob – and I am a nip. Everyone else who lived here was a curber.'

Chaloner did not know what a nip did, but guessed it was something to do with filching purses – the boy had the sharp, darting mien of the professional pickpocket. He thought again about the notes he had found in Long Acre, and the knowledge that Fatherton told his felons where and when to strike, along with the sign hanging outside, allowed him to make sense of them at last. Indeed, the explanation was so obvious that he was disgusted he had not seen it sooner.

'"Ten the sun in wood",' he recited. 'It means that DuPont had to be at the Sign of the Sun in Wood Street at ten o'clock, while "three swan in bread" means a house by the Sign of the Swan in Bread Street should be raided at three o'clock.'

The notes were not coded messages from Dutch intel-ligencers to their spymasters, and he felt a small glow of satisfaction that his scepticism on that front had been justified.

'That sounds right.' Noll beamed happily. 'Ten and three are times when owners tend to be asleep, and the house by the Sun on Wood Street is an especially nice one. The curbers did that a couple of weeks ago, and got some lovely stuff.'

'Onions at the Well. Does that mean anything to you?'

Noll's small face creased into a frown of concentration, but then he shook his head. 'There are no onions or wells around here. That is not one of Mr Fatherton's instructions.'

Chaloner climbed to the top floor, the boy chattering at his heels. He knocked, but there was no reply, so he tried the door. It was unlocked and swung open to reveal yet another abandoned room, only this one had a body in the middle. Chaloner approached and turned it over carefully with his foot. It was the man who had sneezed over him in Coo's house.

'Mr Fatherton!' exclaimed Noll. 'No wonder no one has seen him today!'

Stomach churning, Chaloner looked for plague tokens, and was relieved to find none. The cause of death was obvious, however: Fatherton had been shot in the head.

Chaloner sent Noll to fetch a constable, then stared at the body. Why had Fatherton been killed? Because he knew something about DuPont that the culprit wanted kept quiet, perhaps something involving the plague? Or was the disease irrelevant, and the reason revolved around the way DuPont had made his living, either his work as a spy or a criminal?

Chaloner knelt to inspect the fatal wound. It was unusually small, even for a handgun, and he had seen another just like it three days ago – on Coo. He rubbed his chin thoughtfully. If the physician and Fatherton had been killed with the same weapon, then it was likely that they had been shot by the same assailant. Until then, he had been inclined to view Coo's death as separate from the peculiar circumstances surrounding DuPont's final hours, but now he was not so sure.

He began to search the Frenchman's rooms, hurrying to finish before Noll returned with help. There were two chambers. The first was spacious, but completely empty. The second was a pantry containing a table, a stool, and a shelf on which rested a threadbare blanket and a sack of dried peas. A smattering of rat droppings lay on the bag, old and grey, which led Chaloner to surmise that it had not been opened in some time. Then he reconsidered: the sack looked slightly newer than the scats . . .

He emptied it on the floor, wincing when a spring trap dropped out that would certainly have broken his fingers. Right at the bottom was a package. He unwrapped it carefully. It contained promissory notes from several different bankers – promissory notes were issued to people who deposited money, and were thus a kind of receipt. The ones in his hands were made out to Robert Howard, and represented a fortune.

Clearly, DuPont had 'curbed' them from the Howard house next door – one of Fatherton's letters had read *the eagle in bear twelve*, meaning that the house at the Sign of the Eagle in Bearbinder Street was to be raided at midnight – but why had he kept them? They were no good to anyone, as they could only be redeemed by Howard himself – bankers remembered who deposited large sums of money, so even talented imposters were unlikely to succeed in using promissory notes to make withdrawals.

Chaloner was still pondering his discovery when he heard a creak on the stairs. He shoved the notes in his pocket, and called out a greeting, assuming it was Noll with the constable. But he was answered only by silence. Suspicious, he drew a knife and slipped behind the door to wait. Nothing happened, and he was beginning to wonder whether he had imagined the sound when the door flew inwards with such force that he suffered a painful crack on the nose and was fortunate not to stab himself.

While he reeled, a man darted in, and although

Chaloner's eyes were watering furiously, instinct warned him that the fellow had a gun. He threw himself to one side just as the weapon discharged with an almighty bang that deprived him of his hearing completely. As he lay on the floor, he was vaguely aware of the door being slammed.

He staggered to his feet, still deaf, and coughed as the acrid stench of smoke seared his nostrils. What was burning? The house or one of the government's anti-plague bonfires? He staggered to the door, only to find it blocked from the outside, and it was several minutes before he managed to prise it open – at which point he discovered that the hall outside was well and truly ablaze. He closed it quickly and hurried to the window. It had been nailed shut. He glanced back at the door, and saw smoke begin to ooze under it.

Chaloner had been in many desperate situations during his career in espionage, but this was one of the more serious. Yet he had been trained to think rationally in dire circumstances, and he was soon reviewing his predicament dispassionately. He grabbed the stool from the pantry, smashed it against the wall, and used a leg to lever away first one window slat and then another until he had opened a hole large enough to lean through.

Far below was a dingy yard, shared with the Howard house. It contained a pig, which was trotting around in agitation, frightened by the crackle of flames. Smoke poured from each of the four floors beneath Chaloner's, showing that fires had been set there, too – and the tenement was old, made of wood, and tinder-dry. There was no question that it would quickly become an inferno, and might even spread to the neighbouring properties and beyond.

He coughed again as fumes belched upwards. The door was already smouldering, and it would not be long before it burned through completely, at which point the fire, greedy for air, would explode into the room like a bomb. He needed to get out fast. He ran back to the pantry, snatched the blanket from the shelf, and sliced it into shreds with his knife. Then he began knotting them together, acutely aware that the door was charring at an alarmingly rapid rate. His hearing cleared just enough to let him detect the sinister roar of flames on the other side. He was going to be too late!

He dragged the table to the window, then tied one end of his blanket-rope around it before tossing the rest over the sill. It snaked downwards, but his eyes were streaming far too much to tell if it was long enough. He squeezed through the hole after it, and took a firm hold. It stretched alarmingly when he put his weight on it, and he dropped several sickening feet when the table flipped upwards before becoming jammed against the shutter.

Flames spurted through the window, and he knew there was no time to hesitate. He descended hand over hand as fast as he could, past the fourth floor, the third, the second. Then his rope burned through, sending him plummeting downwards in a shower of sparks.

He might have been seriously injured, but there was a compost heap below, which broke his fall. Even so, he landed hard enough to jolt the leg that had been injured by an exploding cannon during the wars. He lay there, pain washing over him, then forced himself to roll away when the remnants of the shutter began to drop. They missed him by inches. He scrambled upright and hobbled to the far side of the yard, trying not to trip over the terrified pig.

The yard had two doors. One led to DuPont's house, which was belching flames and was clearly not an option for escape. The other was Howard's, which had been barred from the inside. More burning wreckage hurtled down, and a quick glance told him that DuPont's building was on the brink of collapse, at which point he would be buried under hot rubble.

He could see the bar through a gap in Howard's door, so he took his sword and began to lever it upwards. His first attempt failed and so did his second. More smouldering timber fell, and the pig battered his legs, squealing its distress. Stoically, he ignored it all. His third try had the bar dropping away, and he flung the door open in relief.

The pig was through it first, and as it seemed to know where it was going, Chaloner followed it along a dirty corridor to another door – not the front one, which had been nailed shut by the authorities, but one at the side of the house. The animal turned and regarded him beseechingly, so he unfastened the latch. Out went the pig, along a narrow alley, and suddenly they were on Cheapside. The pig trotted away without a backwards glance.

Almost being incinerated had not been a pleasant experience, and Chaloner's knees were rubbery as he peered around the corner at a gathering ring of spectators – fires were one of London's greatest hazards and they always attracted attention. His lame leg throbbed, his throat was raw, his eyes stung, he still could not hear properly and his nose was sore from its encounter with the door. He wanted to go home and lie down, but whoever had set the fire was almost certainly watching, and Chaloner wanted answers. He forced himself to mingle.

Baron's trainband had arrived to fight the blaze. They did not waste time on Fatherton's house or the Howard residence, but concentrated on the buildings to either side, a battle they were winning so handily that Chaloner could not but help wonder whether they had been ready for it. Ladders, leather buckets and fire-hooks were plied with impressive efficiency, while so much water was available for dousing that Chaloner grew more suspicious still.

A pack of grubby children was nearby, and a bright flash of green ribbon in the fist of one showed that Noll was among them. The boy saw Chaloner at the same time, and his eyes went wide with astonishment before he turned to dart away. Chaloner did not try to follow, and could only suppose that the brat had reported his message to someone other than the constable, someone who had decided to eliminate Fatherton's body, the scene of the crime and its discoverer in one fell swoop.

Chaloner stepped back into the shadows and scanned the milling spectators. Oxley and his family stood near the front, drinking ale from leather flasks, clearly of the opinion that an inferno was fine entertainment. They cackled their delight as flames flew high into the sky – it was now dusk, and the cascading sparks were bright against it.

'I am going to look at the corpses when they are pulled out,' the boy was declaring with ghoulish relish. 'I cannot wait to see them!'

His sister shot him a disdainful look; she had not wasted time in idle gawping, and held three stolen purses. Oxley saw them, and made a lunge, but she ducked away with an obscene gesture before aiming for a merchant, her eyes fixed unblinkingly on the fellow's pockets.

Chaloner watched in distaste. Had *they* set the fire?

And if so, had it been of their own volition or on Baron's orders? He glanced around, certain the King of Cheapside would be among the onlookers, and sure enough, Baron was a short distance away. His captains were with him, and he had one beefy arm draped around Doe's shoulders while Poachin watched enviously. He turned suddenly and his eyes locked with Chaloner's. His face was devoid of expression, so the spy had no idea whether he was surprised to see him alive. He went to see if he could find out.

'Quite a sight,' said Baron, nodding at the flames. 'But it will not spread. My men have it under control, God be praised.'

'It could have been worse,' said Poachin. His hair had been freshly dressed, and every strand was perfectly placed. 'Fortunately, it happened when all the tenants had left or are dead, so both places were empty.'

'What about the landlord?' asked Chaloner, watching intently for guilty glances. He was wasting his time – there was not so much as a flicker from any of the three.

'Fatherton?' Doe scratched his big nose. 'I doubt he lingered once the flames took hold.'

'How do you think it started?'

Poachin shrugged. 'These are old houses, made of wood, and the weather has been unusually dry. It was an accident waiting to happen.'

'They are no great loss,' added Baron. 'They should have been demolished years ago, and a fire means we can build something better in their place. But you sound hoarse today, Chaloner. Perhaps you should go home and rest. I shall keep you in my prayers.'

'Thank you,' said Chaloner. 'But first I must speak to Milbourn, the printer who produced your advertisements.

Unfortunately, *his* house burned down, too. Do you know what happened?'

'He died in the inferno,' replied Doe. He sighed theatrically. 'Poor man.'

'He was late with his Protection Tax,' added Poachin. 'And it is not unusual for people to suffer mishaps when they fail to provide what they owe.'

'Not Milbourn,' said Baron sharply. 'He agreed to print my advertisement cards free of charge, so we exempted him.'

Poachin's expression darkened. 'Did you? You mentioned nothing to me.'

'Doe made the arrangements,' said Baron, while the younger man regarded Poachin with a sly smirk. 'I told him to let you know.'

'It must have slipped my mind,' said Doe carelessly, then addressed Chaloner. 'We know other printers, and can introduce you to them for a price. What do you want produced?'

'Promissory notes,' replied Chaloner, to gauge their reactions. But again it was hopeless – they were far too wily to incriminate themselves with flickers of unease.

'That would be illegal: only bankers can issue those,' said Baron. 'Have you thought any more about my offer of employment, by the way? It will not remain on the table for ever.'

Chaloner smiled to disguise his frustration. 'I need to discuss it with my wife.'

Baron blinked. 'I love Frances more than life itself, but I would never consult her on a matter of business. She is a woman.'

'So is mine,' said Chaloner. 'And she has opinions.'

Baron regarded him pityingly. 'I suppose we cannot

all have perfect spouses. My Frances is one in a million, and there are very few like her.'

'There are very few like Hannah, too,' said Chaloner, thinking of his breakfast.

Baron and his men were not the only familiar faces among the crowd. There was a house on Cheapside, opposite the entrance to Bearbinder Lane, with three large upper-floor windows that afforded excellent views of the drama. Taylor was at the first one; he leaned out, watching the flames with an eager intensity, while Dr Misick hovered anxiously behind him. Backwell stood at the middle window, talking to Silas. The third housed Joan, Evan and five or six other wealthy bankers; Joan was holding forth, while the men listened with rapt attention.

Chaloner learned from Poachin, who was more readily disposed to chat than Baron and Doe, that the building had belonged to Angier, the goldsmith who had committed suicide when his bank had failed. Ownership had subsequently fallen to Taylor. Chaloner was about to go and see whether eavesdropping was possible – he was particularly interested in what Silas and Backwell were saying to each other – when he heard his name called. It was Shaw and Lettice.

'I am glad we met,' said Shaw tightly. 'It will save me a journey. I am afraid we must press you for the money your wife owes. Forty pounds.'

'It is Mr Oxley's fault,' explained Lettice apologetically. 'He has bought a terribly fierce dog, which keeps jumping into our garden, and we need to buy a taller fence to keep it out.'

'We told Joan, but she says she is already spending a fortune on the cellar and cannot afford more.' Shaw scowled as he glanced up at the sharp-faced woman in the window, but then turned from angry to agitated as he blurted, 'Our latrine is in the garden – we cannot use it as long as that vile beast is on the loose!'

'But Mr Oxley declines to tether it,' added Lettice. 'I am sure he bought it for spite – when our cellar is finished, his sewage will stay in his own house, which he considers an imposition.'

'I love our shop,' sighed Shaw. 'Selling music to appreciative courtiers is a delight, but sometimes I wish I were still a banker. The cost of a fence would not have bothered us, then.'

'The cost of a physician for our baby would not have bothered us either,' whispered Lettice. 'We could have summoned Dr Misick, and he would have saved her.'

'It is no good thinking like that,' said Shaw gruffly. 'It will send you mad.'

Tears glittered in Lettice's eyes before she took a breath and pulled herself together. 'We hate to ask for money, Mr Chaloner, but the dog leaves us no choice.'

'Does the Protection Tax not cover this sort of thing?' asked Chaloner, the first time he had been able to insert a word into the conversation.

Shaw grimaced. 'Oxley is Baron's minion, so I doubt *he* will be sympathetic. I suppose we could poison the beast – the dog, I mean, not Baron – but I would not know how.' Then he brightened. 'Unless you would oblige? Then we would not need to erect a palisade, and you could have a reprieve on your wife's debt.'

'No,' cried Lettice, shocked. 'It is hardly the dog's fault.'

'Oxley will probably sell it anyway, once we have bought the fence,' said Shaw acidly.

'Leave it to me,' said Chaloner, silently cursing Hannah

214

for putting him in such a position. He saw Lettice's dismay, and smiled to reassure her. 'There are more ways to be rid of annoying animals than killing them.'

He resumed his walk to Angier's house, but had not gone far before he felt something dig into his side. He started to jerk away, but an arm went around his neck and the blade jabbed harder. He was disgusted with himself. Someone had just tried to incinerate him, and he should have known to be vigilant. He could only suppose that his cold was robbing him of his wits, because he was not normally careless.

'Mr Taylor wants to see you,' whispered a soft voice in his ear. 'Now.'

The knife and arm remained in place until Chaloner was inside Angier's house, after which he was bundled up the stairs and shoved roughly into the room in which the bankers were watching the fire. He could have escaped at any point – no single henchman was a match for him – but his 'captor' was taking him where he wanted to go, so he let the man believe he was in control.

'Of course, this blaze concerns me,' Taylor told him when he arrived, as though continuing a conversation they had been having before. 'The wind is blowing towards Goldsmiths' Row, where my Plague Box is kept. I knew I should have brought it with me.'

'Your what?' asked Chaloner, aware that Evan was grimacing irritably, while the other bankers and Silas regarded Taylor askance. He wished his wits were sharper: his question had been stupid, given that the box had featured large in previous discussions with Taylor.

'My Plague Box,' repeated Taylor. 'It contains worms and other items of equal importance – jewels, cloth and

215

the like. I should never have let it out of my sight, and I shall not do it again, no matter what my firstborn advises.' He scowled at Evan.

'It is heavy, Father,' said Evan patiently. 'And you have not been well.'

'Not well?' Taylor drew himself up to his full height, and his eyes darkened dangerously. He looked deranged, and Chaloner wondered if he would follow the hapless Johnson to Bedlam. 'How can I be unwell when Joan has hired Misick to tend me? And he is doing a splendid job. He gave me a dose of Red Snake Electuary with my Plague Elixir today, and I have never felt better.'

'My Plague Elixir does promote good health,' averred Misick. 'While all the best people take Red Snake Electuary, too, including myself.'

'Poachin swears by it,' said Chaloner slyly. 'So you are in good company indeed.'

Evan stepped forward angrily, but Silas was suddenly at Chaloner's side, and as his younger brother was stronger and heavier, Evan thought better of doing anything reckless.

'Of course, the plague will never harm me,' Taylor went on, 'because I control it. It never does anything without asking me first. For example, I told it to kill Howard and—'

'Ten shillings, Chaloner,' interrupted Evan loudly. 'It is due today, if you recall.'

'Ten shillings!' breathed Backwell, his eyes shining as he came to join the discussion. 'Ten lovely, shiny coins. Would you like me to count them for you?'

Perhaps all bankers were insane, thought Chaloner, eyeing him warily.

'I will give you the plague if you do not pay up,'

216

warned Taylor. He raised his forefinger and began muttering what sounded like an incantation. Chaloner struggled to stop himself, but it was no use. He sneezed, and Taylor hopped from foot to foot in excitement. 'See? See? I can do it even without my Plague Box!'

'Chaloner does not have the plague,' said Joan quickly, as several of the company edged towards the door. 'It is an old debtors' trick – a ruse to escape without paying.'

The bankers did not look convinced, and when Taylor's finger started to come up a second time, they backed away in consternation. Evan tugged his father's arm in an effort to make him desist, but Taylor flung him away with a bellow of rage. Evan lost his balance and fell, but scrambled hastily to his feet and dusted himself off, laughing falsely to disguise his mortification.

'Father and I love to wrestle,' he blustered. 'We have such japes! Is that not true, Joan?'

'He does not wrestle with me,' replied Joan haughtily. 'Although we have excellent *verbal* battles over collateralised debt obligations and share capital.'

'I cannot imagine he wins,' gushed Vyner. 'Not against you.'

'I am Master of the Goldsmiths' Company,' stated Taylor coldly, and suddenly he did not seem lunatic at all, but angry. 'I was elected on the basis of my superior knowledge and ability, and no one defeats me in a debate, not even Joan. Now, did you mention more debts to sell me, Glosson? Good. Come to my office, if you please.'

He aimed for the door, Joan and Glosson scurrying after him. Evan remained and resumed his efforts to convince the other financiers that his father's eccentricity derived from a desire to amuse himself.

'It did not look as though he was jesting to me,' said Vyner worriedly. 'Are you sure he is well? You must understand our concern, Evan – there are already rumours about our probity, and we cannot have it said that the Master of our Company is insane into the bargain. We should have a run for certain!'

'He is *not* insane,' insisted Evan. 'Buying your debts is hard work and he is exhausted. But he considers it his patriotic duty to take these tiresome clients off your hands, as he is keen to ensure that His Majesty will have enough cash to pay for the war.'

'His motive is personal profit, not patriotism,' countered Vyner sharply. 'He is making a fortune from the customers we have been obliged to pass him. However, we shall sell him no more if he is mad. It would be unethical.'

The others murmured agreement, although Chaloner suspected that the real reason for their sudden attack of morals was that they were jealous of the money Taylor was making – money that could have been theirs.

'Well, you need not worry,' said Misick, picking cinders from his wig. 'As his physician, I would know if he had lost his wits. He has not, and any oddness is a result of overwork.'

Vyner shot him a glance that was full of disbelieving disdain before aiming for the door. His cronies followed, and Evan hurried after them, still bleating excuses. It was not long before the room was empty except for Backwell and Silas. Backwell returned to the window to watch the fire, while Silas sauntered to a table and poured himself more wine. Chaloner joined Backwell, realising with a surge of relief that Taylor had forgotten to take his ten shillings.

218

'Your uncle always said that Taylor was unstable,' murmured Backwell, speaking softly so Silas would not hear. 'I never believed him, but now I see he was right. Taylor is unhinged.'

'Then perhaps you should elect someone else as Master of the Goldsmiths' Company. He is causing much bad feeling with his unscrupulous tactics – bad feeling that reflects poorly on the rest of you.'

Backwell sighed. 'It is not that easy, and he is still the best fellow for the task, lunatic or not. These are uneasy times, Chaloner, and we need a strong leader. Even your uncle was in awe of Taylor, and he was a very difficult man to daunt.'

'I am glad he is not alive to see what you did to my wife,' said Chaloner acidly. 'Selling her debt to a man who sends louts to her house to threaten her.'

Backwell would not meet his eyes. 'I did not realise the connection. She took that loan before she married you, so the name on my books was Hannah Cotton. I did ask Taylor to be gentle with my old customers, but he said they are no longer my concern.'

'You are a man of principle,' said Chaloner, although he had no idea whether it was true. 'You must be appalled by what Taylor is doing. If you were Master, you could put an end to it, and restore your Company's good name.'

Backwell smiled. 'It is good of you to say so, but I cannot stand for election, even if my colleagues did agree to oust the current incumbent. I am too busy with the war.'

When Backwell had gone, Chaloner took the opportunity to ask Silas what he and the banker had been discussing with such seriousness in the middle window not long before.

'The war,' replied Silas shortly. 'I imagine you do the same with your friends. As Keeper of Stores for a ship-yard, you will appreciate that it is a matter I view with some concern.'

'Backwell is your friend? I thought you said he was dull, and that being seen in his company would adversely affect your fun-loving reputation.'

'Oh, it would,' grinned Silas. 'Which is why I usually meet him in shadowy places. But I have some news for you about Everard – DuPont's crony. I have found him.'

'How?' asked Chaloner suspiciously.

Silas flung an arm around his shoulders. 'Do not look so wary! Backwell happened to mention him in a conversation – Everard is one of the little bankers destroyed by the Colburn Crisis, and he has recently taken lodgings on Cheapside. Shall we visit him together? Now?'

Alarm bells were ringing in Chaloner's head, but he was shaken, bruised and far from well, so he ignored them. Indeed, he even began to relax in his old friend's company, feeling he was probably a good deal safer with Silas than on his own, while instinct told him that he would be wasting his time by lingering longer at the scene of the fire anyway. They left Angier's house and began to walk west, eventually reaching a small, tatty cottage near the Standard.

'Everard was forced to move here when his bank failed,' said Silas, regarding it in distaste. 'Quite a downward slide from Goldsmiths' Row.'

The ruined financier was a sad, wan man who did indeed have a purple nose. He gestured that Chaloner and Silas were to enter his home, then conducted them to a room that contained nothing except a chair.

'Even this meagre dwelling will be sold next week,' he said, slumping down on it. 'And I shall go to live in the country with my mother. I shall not be sorry. These last few weeks have been a dreadful ordeal, and if your father had not bought most of my clients, Silas, I would be rotting in debtors' gaol.'

'We understand you knew a man named DuPont,' began Chaloner quickly, loath to dwell on what happened to those who could not pay what they owed.

'Yes – we met in the Feathers,' replied Everard. 'An insalubrious place, I know, but I happen to like dancing girls. The Feathers' lasses loved DuPont, and whenever I sat with him, they paid me much attention, too. Naturally, I went out of my way to encourage him to my side.'

'Yet the tavern's staff claim not to know you,' remarked Chaloner.

'I used a false name to stop my mother from finding out,' explained Everard with the ghost of a smile. 'She does not approve of that sort of place.'

'DuPont was a spy. Did he discuss that work with you?'

'A little. He told me that he planned to acquire certain documents from Dutch merchants who live in the city, although he never explained how.'

'By sticking a hook through their windows and fishing them out,' supplied Chaloner.

Everard blinked his surprise. 'Really? Lord! The talents of some people! Anyway, once he had them, he was going to sell them to the government. He knew one of the Lord Chancellor's retainers, and arrangements had been made.'

'Does the term Onions at the Well mean anything to you?'

Everard shrugged. 'I heard him say it a couple of times, but I have no idea what it meant. However, it may

221

have had something to do with the St Giles rookery – we were walking past it once, and he talked about onions and wells before disappearing into it.'

'There, Tom,' said Silas in satisfaction, once they were out on Cheapside again. 'All you have to do is visit this rookery, and you will have all the answers you need.'

Unfortunately, Everard's testimony was not as useful as Silas believed, as the area was vast and Chaloner doubted he could just stroll in and find what he was looking for. Moreover, most cases of plague were there, so it was a risky place to be. He supposed Silas had forgotten the outbreak, because he was sure his friend would not have recommended that he go there otherwise.

As it was on his way home, Chaloner decided to deal with Oxley's dog, so walked to the lane that ran along the back of the henchman's house. He soon understood why Shaw and Lettice did not want it in their garden. It was a squat, bull-chested bitch of an unusual silvery grey, which set up a furious barking when he scrambled up the wall to look. No one came to investigate, so he supposed the Oxleys were still watching the fire. The beast wore a collar with her name painted in large white letters, and he was not surprised to learn that she went by the appellation of Slasher.

He looked down at her while he considered his options. He could easily lob a knife and be rid of the problem permanently, but he suspected that Oxley would just buy another. Moreover, as Lettice had said, the situation was hardly Slasher's fault. Then he happened to glance across the lane. The house opposite belonged to a butcher, whose distinctive cart was parked in the yard. Chaloner smiled as a solution began to form in his mind.

It was not easy to lasso Slasher with his belt, especially when she was so determined to bite him, but he managed eventually. He hauled her up, and wrapped his coat around her head before she could do him any damage. Plunging her world into darkness served to quieten her somewhat, which allowed him to climb the butcher's wall with her slung over his shoulder.

The cart was packed with goods ready for delivery the following morning. Chaloner gently placed Slasher inside it and removed his coat and belt. She shook herself furiously and released an angry snarl, but then her brain registered the delicious aroma of raw meat. Her eyes lit up, and she gave an excited yip before pitching in to the delights around her.

A light went on in the butcher's bedroom, and Chaloner had only just scrambled back over the wall before the door to the yard was flung open and the man appeared with a cleaver. Slasher broke off from her repast just long enough to chase him back inside, then returned to her meal. It was clear that she was going to enjoy a very pleasant interlude until Oxley came to reclaim her.

Chaloner grinned as he walked away, brushing dog hairs from his coat. Devouring the contents of a butcher's cart was rather more serious than preventing neighbours from using their latrine, and Oxley would be liable for costs. He doubted Slasher would be in residence on Cheapside much longer, but fierce dogs had their price, so Oxley would sell her. She would live to see another day, the butcher would be reimbursed, and the Shaws would have safe access to their garden. In fact, everyone would benefit except Oxley, which was exactly how it should be.

He emerged on Cheapside, but had not gone far before a carriage drew up beside him. It bore the arms of the

Company of Barber–Surgeons, and Wiseman was inside. Chaloner knew Misick was with him, because part of the physician's massive wig was poking through the window – either that, or Wiseman was transporting a sheep.

'You have the Cheapside cold,' noted Wiseman when he heard Chaloner's gravelly voice. 'Several of my patients have come down with it, and two have been shut up in their houses because the damn-fool searchers cannot distinguish between common ailments and the plague. Unless the victim happens to be wealthy, of course, in which case they are open to suggestion.'

'It is a sorry state of affairs,' sighed Misick. 'How is your remedy coming along, Wiseman? My Plague Elixir is selling so fast that I can barely keep up with the demand for it.'

Wiseman shot him a resentful glance, indicating that his own efforts in that area were less than satisfactory, for which Chaloner was grateful – he had not forgotten that Temperance had charged him to prevent the surgeon from testing it on a victim.

'Speaking of the plague,' he said to Misick, 'did you mention your worm theory to Taylor? There must be some reason why he seems to think that he has some in his box.'

'I thought it might serve to make him reflect on the frailty of life and render him a little kinder,' replied Misick defensively. 'I did not anticipate that he would harbour notions of collecting them up with a view to annihilating London.'

'The man should be in Bedlam,' declared Wiseman, who knew all about that place, as he had installed his wife there. 'But I am in the mood for company. Come to Chyrurgeons' Hall for dinner, both of you. My cook is making liver pudding.'

It occurred to Chaloner that it was rash to eat liver with Wiseman when there were pickled human ones in the jars in his laboratory, but he had eaten nothing since breakfast and was hungry. He climbed into the carriage, and began to cough when Misick lit a pipe.

'Plague worms hate smoke,' the physician informed him, waving a hand in an effort to see his companions through the fug. 'And so do the ones that cause colds, so inhale as deeply as you can. Tobacco is an excellent tonic for congested lungs.'

'Colds are not caused by worms,' stated Wiseman dogmatically. 'They come from changes in the weather. Chaloner caught one because it is cooler here than in Hull.'

Chaloner did not have the energy for the argument that would ensue if he informed them that London was milder than Yorkshire had been, so he held his tongue. Wiseman continued to pontificate until they arrived at Chyrurgeons' Hall, a large precinct near the London Wall dominated by its curiously shaped Anatomy Theatre. The Master's quarters were above the dining hall, and comprised a suite of beautiful rooms that afforded fine views of the surrounding rooftops.

Chaloner had always found it unsettling that Wiseman's servants were missing various body parts. The cook had one arm, the groom had lost an eye, and the footman was missing a leg. He had never liked to ask whether they had been relieved of them by the surgeon, and he sincerely hoped the absent bits were not among the items displayed in the laboratory.

All three fussed around their employer and his guests, plying them with great slabs of liver pudding, while Wiseman gleefully listed all the ingredients that had

225

gone into it – lungs, thymus, skin, ears, eyelids and liver. Chaloner was glad that his cold prevented him from having functional taste buds. Eventually, Misick left, saying he had patients to see.

'We shall stand guard tonight, sir,' said the footman, once he had seen the physician out. He was wearing the kind of armour that had been donned by the less well protected members of the Royalist army during the civil wars. The groom was similarly attired. 'We shall sleep in the hall downstairs, and no one will enter without us seeing.'

'Why?' asked Wiseman, bemused. 'And watch where you are waving that sword, man! It almost took my head off.'

'Because of the thieves. A number of folk have been burgled around here of late, but no one knows how the villains do it, because all the victims' doors and windows are locked. Yet a lot of stuff has gone missing.'

'It has,' agreed Wiseman. 'Temperance lost some curtains a couple of weeks ago. I do not hold with them personally, but she insisted on buying me some.'

He gestured to his windows, where fine lengths of green material hung. They clashed with the scarlet decor in the rest of the room, so it was no surprise that he had not taken to them. When the servants had gone, he talked about the plague measures that Williamson was implementing. Chaloner began to drowse, lulled by the droning voice and the comforting crackle of the fire in the hearth. But he snapped into alertness when one sentence penetrated his consciousness.

'What?'

'I said the reason that I was on Cheapside this evening was because I had a patient who lived in the house that

226

burned down – Fatherton, whom I inherited from Coo. He summoned me a couple of days ago, because he thought he might have the plague.'

'And did he?' asked Chaloner uneasily, remembering the sneeze.

'No, it was a heavy cold, but I thought I had better make sure, so I went to see him again this evening. When I arrived, the house was ablaze, and Misick, who had been listening to gossip among the spectators, says that Fatherton was inside.'

'He was,' said Chaloner, but did not elaborate.

The surgeon regarded him thoughtfully. 'Did you catch your sickness from him? No, do not tell me. I prefer to remain in blissful ignorance where your antics are concerned. However, you should watch yourself if you intend to lurk around Bearbinder Lane. It lies in James Baron's domain, and even I am wary of annoying *him.*'

'Really? Why?'

'Because he is a cunning and dangerous criminal, who indulges in all manner of dishonest activities, although he has never been caught. His captains and trainband have sworn oaths of fealty, you see, and would rather die than betray him.'

Chaloner coughed and then sneezed.

'You need an early night,' declared Wiseman. 'So you had better stay here. You can have the laboratory. It is the room furthest away from my bedchamber, and I do not want you keeping me awake with your snoring.'

'I do not snore,' objected Chaloner indignantly. 'And that laboratory reeks.'

Not to mention the horrors that sat on the shelves, he thought, which were hardly conducive to restful repose.

'Everyone snores with a cold. And you cannot breathe through your nose anyway, so reeks are immaterial.' Then Wiseman brightened. 'I have devised a certain mixture that I believe will alleviate the symptoms you are suffering, although I have not tested it on anyone yet. I do not suppose you . . .'

'No,' said Chaloner firmly.

Chapter 8

It was still dark outside when Chaloner was woken the next day by Wiseman moving about in the next room. He was tempted to go back to sleep, but the surgeon was making a peculiar scratching sound, which was annoying enough to keep him awake.

He rose and dressed in silence so as not to alarm the servants standing guard in the hall downstairs. He opened the laboratory door, but immediately heard the soft rasp of Wiseman's breathing from the bedchamber opposite. Thus it was not the surgeon rustling about in the parlour. Curious, Chaloner crept towards the sound. The room was in darkness, but Chyrurgeons' Hall kept plenty of lamps burning in its grounds, so some light drifted in from outside.

Someone was standing outside the window, but as the Master's quarters were on the top floor, no one should have been there, especially at such an hour. Chaloner edged closer to see that a pane of glass had been removed, and a long stick with a hook on the end was thrust through the resulting hole. The implement inched across the table to snag a silver goblet, which was then deftly manoeuvred towards the window.

So here was a curber in action, thought Chaloner with interest, watching the cup disappear through the gap. Doubtless the pane would be replaced when the thief had finished, leaving nothing to show how the crime had been committed – both Wiseman's groom and Temperance had commented on burglaries carried out with no sign of forced entry.

Within moments, the hook reappeared to snag one of Wiseman's curtains. The material was pulled carefully through the hole, after which a few sharp tugs were enough to dislodge it from the fastenings that held it up. Chaloner was tempted to yank it back again, knowing what a fright it would give the culprit, but decided it would be better to catch the fellow instead. He ran lightly down the stairs to alert the servants, but they were fast asleep on the floor, and an empty wine jug suggested they would not be easy to rouse. He did not waste time trying.

He opened the door, and peered out to see that the thief had brought an accomplice – a second man stood beneath the window to catch what was pilfered and put it in a sack. The curber himself clung precariously to the ivy that grew up the wall. Chaloner tiptoed forward, but his nose began to tickle and he knew he was going to sneeze. He held his breath and clamped both hands over his face, but to no avail. It was a stifled sound, but the two men heard it anyway.

The accomplice fled. Chaloner tore after him, and brought him down with a flying tackle. When the fellow drew a knife, Chaloner stunned him with a punch. Then he leapt up to confront the curber, who had already scrambled down the ivy and was coming towards him. The fellow held a pair of handguns – almost certainly stolen, as such items were far too expensive to be bought legally by common criminals.

Chaloner dived behind a tree, and saw the flash of the weapon igniting in the darkness, followed a split second later by the cracking report. He heard running footsteps, and peered around the trunk to see both felons aiming for the gate. The curber whipped around to fire his second dag at Chaloner. He missed again, but not by much.

As the pistols were now harmless until they could be reloaded, Chaloner raced forward, but the Chyrurgeons' Hall porter, appalled by the sound of gunfire in his domain, hurtled out of his lodge and lunged at him with such vigour that both went tumbling into the vegetable plots. By the time the misunderstanding had been corrected, the real culprits had escaped and lamps were bobbing all over the precinct as residents came to see what was going on. Wiseman was among them, clad rather bizarrely in a long red mantua with a matching nightcap.

'What are you doing, Chaloner?' he asked suspiciously, his robe billowing around him so that the spy was put in mind of an angry Old Testament prophet.

'Saving your curtains.' Chaloner pointed to where the sack had been abandoned, and briefly explained what had happened.

'The scoundrels!' cried a surgeon named Knight. 'How dare they invade our home!'

'They will not do it again,' vowed Wiseman. 'Our students will patrol it from now on.' He glared at the porter. 'And our guards will be more vigilant.'

He stalked back to his quarters, pausing only to grab the sack. When he reached his parlour, he upended it to

231

discover that it held not only one of his curtains and the goblet, but a bag containing medicine, a valuable vase and a selection of clothing.

'And this is what Fatherton did?' he asked. 'You said last night that he was a curber. Or rather, that he directed crews of curbers and nips, telling them where to go and when.'

Chaloner nodded. 'But we cannot blame him for raiding you. He is dead.'

'Yes, but Baron is not. It did not take *him* long to recruit a replacement, did it! Yet it is a pity you rescued this curtain, because now I shall have to put it back up, and I have never liked green – it reminds me of bile. The ones Temperance bought for the club were much nicer. Red with a hint of gold. Very smart.'

'Red and gold?' asked Chaloner sharply. 'How many did she have?'

'Well, the club has seven windows along the front, so she had seven pairs. Why?'

'Because the Earl's Great Parlour has nine windows that are roughly the same size, and his curtains – two pairs short – were delivered after hers went missing. He bought them from Baron.'

Wiseman gazed at him. 'So did she. Do you think they were the same ones?'

'It would explain why Baron declines to deliver the last part of the order – it does not exist.'

'The Earl will not be pleased when you tell him that he has been decorating Clarendon House with stolen property,' predicted Wiseman. 'Rather you than me.'

It was still dark, but neither Chaloner nor Wiseman felt like going back to sleep, so the surgeon roused his servants

232

and told them to make his breakfast. The groom and footman had dozed right through the rumpus, even the gunshots. Thus they were sheepish as they took his order – boiled eggs, smoked pork, toasted bread, eel pie, leftover liver pudding and an apple.

'They were very quiet,' said the footman resentfully, balancing precariously on one leg, because he had forgotten where he had left his crutches. 'We never heard a thing.'

'Like mice,' added the groom, producing an apple from about his grimy person and handing it to his master with an ingratiating smile. 'Very *silent* mice.'

'Rogues!' spat Wiseman when they had gone. 'They were drunk on my wine, and *that* is why they heard nothing.' He turned his attention to the apple. 'These are good for you. I eat one every day, and it keeps me in excellent health. I should hate to be in a position where I am obliged to call a surgeon. I would not let one of those near me with a feather, let alone a sharp implement.'

He continued to denigrate his colleagues while he performed the peculiar ritual of stone-lifting that he undertook each morning. His muscles bulged under his mantua, and Chaloner pitied his patients. They would be powerless to resist once he had decided upon a course of treatment, and he was not a gentle man.

When the rest of the meal arrived, Wiseman set to with heartening enthusiasm. Chaloner might have been eating paper for all he could taste through his cold, but he took everything Wiseman passed him on the grounds that it would save him buying something later with his dwindling funds. Then there was a knock on the door and the footman hopped back in.

233

'Mr Taylor of Goldsmiths' Row dropped a box on his toe last night,' he reported. 'And now he is in great pain. Dr Misick asks if you will go at once, because surgery is needed.'

'Very well,' said Wiseman. 'Bring me my clothes. The red ones.'

As all his clothes were red, Chaloner expected the footman to query the order, but the fellow left obediently, apparently knowing exactly what was required.

'I love being Surgeon to the Person and Master of the Company of Barber–Surgeons,' grinned Wiseman. 'It means I am summoned by all manner of wealthy and influential people –Taylor is one of the richest men in London, although I cannot say I like him.'

'No,' agreed Chaloner. 'When you are there, assess whether he is losing his reason.'

'Oh, I am fairly sure he is. But come with me. You will see him when he is vulnerable, and even the biggest tyrants turn coward in the presence of their *medicus*.'

'It is a tempting offer, but I owe him money.' Chaloner told him about Hannah's loan.

'He will not demand anything if you are with me. Indeed, he may even agree to renegotiate the debt – I am rather good at getting people to do what I want just before painful procedures.'

'Is that ethical?'

'As ethical as Taylor abusing his clients,' Wiseman shot back.

Chaloner had a lot to do that day: take Temperance to Clarendon House to look at the Earl's curtains; make more enquiries along Cheapside about the deaths of DuPont, Coo, Fatherton and Wheler; learn who had tried to burn him alive; and find Randal. But Hannah's predicament weighed heavily on his mind and it would be a relief to have the interest reduced to a more reasonable level. When the surgeon had dressed in scarlet long-coat with matching breeches, crimson hat and black boots with red heels, Chaloner followed him down the stairs and out through the gate, feeling the plan was worth a try.

Dawn was breaking, and carts were rumbling in from the surrounding countryside, bringing produce for London's ever-hungry stomach – onions, cheese, butter, eggs, beer and milk. Street vendors were also arriving, slouching towards their patches with trays of cakes, pies, flowers, vegetables and herbs. A clean breeze had been blowing from the west, carrying the scent of blossom, but it was quickly masked by soot as thousands of sea-coal fires were lit across the city.

When they reached Cheapside, two more houses had red crosses on the doors, each with an uneasy watcher stationed outside. The affected buildings were the poorer kind of tenement, and there was a good deal of resentment from passers-by, who claimed the inmates were suffering from quinsy, not the plague. One or two apprentices even fingered daggers, as if considering an attack to free those imprisoned within. Tension was thick in the air, especially when a bell began to toll to announce that someone had died.

'I know forty days is a long time to be incarcerated,' murmured Wiseman, watching a crowd begin to gather outside one house to yell abuse at the hapless guard, 'but how else will we stop the disease? People are not taking the threat as seriously as they should.'

'Can you blame them, when the rich are allowed to buy different verdicts?' asked Chaloner. 'And if you do not believe me, look over there.'

A crude message had been daubed on the door of one mansion, claiming that plague was within, but a few pieces of silver could turn it into spotted fever.

'These double standards will have the city in uproar,' sighed Wiseman. 'Although that will not matter if the plague comes. Nothing will.'

At Goldsmiths' Row, a maid was waiting to escort Wiseman to Taylor's bedside, and made no demur when the surgeon informed him that Chaloner was there to assist. They followed her up the stairs to the top floor, where Chaloner stopped in astonishment: the hall outside Taylor's chamber thronged with hushed-voiced well-wishers. They included not only members of the Gold-smiths' Company, but wealthy merchants, clerics and even one or two courtiers. Oxley was there, too, standing out like a sore thumb in his rough clothes. Chaloner could only suppose he had been charged to represent the King of Cheapside.

'I thought Taylor had hurt his toe,' Chaloner whispered. 'But he must be on his deathbed.'

The surgeon, inured to such scenes, was more interested in his surroundings. The floor was covered in silk rugs, and the ceiling had bosses picked out with gold leaf. The walls were panelled in ebony, although they were mostly invisible beneath the many paintings that hung there.

'Look at them,' he breathed. 'Portraits by Samuel Cooper and Lely, and of such subjects – Lady Castlemaine, Lord Rochester, George Carteret, Prince Rupert, Will Chiffinch, Bab May . . .'

'All people who owe him money,' remarked Chaloner. 'Taylor must have taken them in lieu of payment, along with their hatpins and jewelled buttons.'

He turned as Evan approached, pale and rumpled, as though he had spent a difficult night. Even so, avarice gleamed in his eyes.

'Good,' he said. 'You have come to pay us our thirty shillings.'

'Twenty,' corrected Chaloner. 'Ten from yesterday and ten for today.'

'*Twenty* from yesterday: there is a penalty for being late. Well? Where is it?'

Chaloner sneezed, and was gratified when Evan backed away.

'You shall have your money, Evan,' said Wiseman, 'the moment you have paid *us* for our visit here today. However, quality costs – I am the King's personal surgeon, and my services do not come cheap. Neither do Chaloner's, and he has graciously agreed to be my assistant this morning. I hope you have plenty of cash to hand.'

'We are a bank,' retorted Evan. 'Of course we have cash. However, we will not be overcharged by a jumped-up—'

'I never overcharge,' asserted Wiseman icily. 'I merely set a fee that is commensurate with my abilities. Come, Chaloner. Let us see what we can do for our patient. It is unethical to chatter out here while he is desperate for the relief that only we can provide.'

He sailed through the door before Evan could take issue, Chaloner at his heels. Taylor was sitting on the bed, his face crumpled in agony. He hugged his box with one hand and his toe with the other, vigorously resisting the efforts of Silas and Joan to make him lie back. Misick, who was mixing a remedy on a bench near the window, heaved a sigh of relief when he saw Wiseman.

'Let me put your chest on the table, Father,' Silas was begging. 'You will hurt yourself if you grip it so hard. I am not sure it should be in bed with you anyway, not if it contains what you say.'

Taylor clutched it harder. 'My Plague Box contains the fate of all London, and I am its guardian,' he hissed dangerously. 'Gold and silver, worms and miasmas.'

'Yes,' said Silas gently. 'But let me help you with the burden. It is too much for one man.'

'You mean to steal it,' cried Taylor. 'You have hated me ever since I packed you off to the wars to fight for Cromwell.'

'I do not hate you. I am merely concerned that—'

'You have been plotting with Backwell to overthrow me,' interrupted Taylor. 'Oh, yes! I have seen the two of you muttering together when you think no one is looking.'

'We discuss the war,' said Silas shortly, beginning to be irked. 'Now, the surgeon is here. Give me the box, so he can tend you.'

He made a grab for it, but Taylor released a howl of such anger and distress that Silas started back in alarm.

'Leave him be, Silas,' warned Misick. 'Let Wiseman do it.'

'It should not have been necessary to summon a surgeon,' said Joan, her small face hard and unfriendly. '*You* should have made him better, Misick. We pay you enough.'

'You pay me nothing,' Misick reminded her with quiet dignity. 'I render my services for free, in exchange for you writing off the money I borrowed from your husband.'

'Yes, and you have the better end of the bargain,' snapped Joan nastily. 'Infinitely better, given that you call in someone else whenever there is a problem. At our expense.'

'I have done it once,' countered Misick, stung. 'For a *surgical* problem. Or would you have me attempt a procedure for which I am not qualified?'

'No,' conceded Joan, and rubbed her eyes tiredly. 'Forgive me, Dr Misick. It has been a long night and—'

'Enough babble,' ordered Wiseman curtly. 'Tell me what happened.'

'Silas tried to steal the Plague Box, and it fell on Father's foot during the ensuing struggle,' obliged Evan. 'It is his fault that—'

'I was not *stealing* it,' interrupted Silas irritably. 'He told me that it contains plague worms, which is not the sort of thing anyone should be toting around. Of course I tried to wrest it away from him. So would any loving son.'

'*I* love him, which is why I would never risk anything that might harm him,' said Evan haughtily. 'You, on the other hand—'

'I acted for his own good,' flashed Silas angrily. 'Anyone can see he is witless.'

'I am not witless,' said Taylor.

Everyone turned to look at him, startled by the quiet reason in his voice: he sounded astonished, even hurt, that anyone should consider him anything other than a rational being. He set the box on the bedside table and folded his hands in his lap, the very picture of lucidity. 'And if my temper has been short, it is because of this agonising pain. Well, Wiseman? Are you just going to stand there like some great crimson ape, or are you going to amputate?'

'Father, I was only—' began Silas, disconcerted by his sire's sudden lucidity.

'You are worse than Randal,' said Taylor coolly. 'He is worthless, too, with his silly book that has set Royalists

239

and Parliamentarians at each others' throats. How does he expect commerce to thrive when the city is in such turmoil?'

'He aims to publish a sequel,' interposed Chaloner, seizing the opportunity to discuss it, 'which will cause even more trouble. Tell me where he is hiding and I will persuade him to stop.'

'We have already told you that we have no idea,' said Joan sharply. 'I wish we did, because I would order him to desist myself.'

'I should never have let him marry you,' murmured Taylor, looking up at her affectionately. 'You are far too good for him. I should have taken you myself.'

Joan said nothing, but it was clear that she thought the same. She shot Silas a rather longing look, too, but he was telling Wiseman how his father had come to be injured and did not notice.

In essence, he and Taylor had grappled for the box, which had fallen in such a way that one corner had landed square on Taylor's unprotected big toe. Blood had pooled beneath the nail, and increasing pressure was causing the discomfort.

'It is a serious case,' averred Wiseman, reaching into his bag and laying out an array of gruesome-looking implements. 'It is a good thing you called me, Misick. There is only one man in London who can bring about a happy outcome, and that is me.'

He spoke with such arrogant authority that no one dared argue, and all watched in appalled fascination as he began heating a metal probe in the flame of a candle. Silas promptly abandoned his father's bedside and retreated to the far side of the room, although Joan was made of sterner stuff and held her father-in-law's hand, whispering words of comfort. Chaloner joined Silas, unwilling to witness anything grisly if it could be avoided.

'Are you sure you have not seen Randal?' he whispered. 'We really do need to warn him against publishing another pamphlet.'

'I have not seen him in weeks,' Silas muttered back. 'He might even be dead for all I know. However, if he is, Joan is the first person I shall question about his murder. Are you still coming to my soirée tonight, by the way? I can promise you some excellent music. Well, as long as you do not sing – you sound like an old saw. Rough night, was it?'

Chaloner had forgotten his friend's invitation, but saw no reason not to accept. After all, the Earl was not paying him, so could hardly complain about him taking an evening off. Misick overheard, and came to join them.

'You should cancel it, Silas,' he said. 'Your father will not be well enough to attend.'

'I doubt he will mind staying at home – he does not like music anyway.' Silas's voice turned acerbic. 'I am sure Evan will keep him company.'

'Few bankers *do* appreciate music,' said Misick, tactfully ignoring the last part. 'Perhaps the sound of clinking coins destroys their ability to listen to anything else. Vyner, Glosson, Hinton – none knows his Gibbons from his Playford. And as for Wheler . . .'

'He was incapable of carrying even the simplest of tunes,' agreed Silas. 'No wonder Joan did not spend long mourning him. Imagine a life without music!'

Chaloner shuddered.

'He had lung-rot,' added Misick, 'and would have been dead by now, even if someone had not stuck a knife in his chest.'

'Coo mentioned his illness,' recalled Chaloner. 'Can we assume that his killer was someone who did not know? After all, why commit murder when it is unnecessary?'

'Perhaps the culprit could not wait,' suggested Silas. 'Personally, I always thought it was Joan. After all, look at her now – wealthy in her own right and married into the strongest banking dynasty in London. She was nothing but a housewife when she was wed to Wheler.'

'Joan is no killer,' breathed Misick, shocked. 'And not stupid either, to take such a risk when she would have been a widow within a few weeks anyway.'

'Much can happen in a few weeks,' countered Silas. 'Wheler might have changed his will, my father might have refused an alliance, Wheler's increasing incapacity might have damaged his business. Joan is not a woman to sit back and let fate decide.'

Wiseman interrupted at that point with a demand for Chaloner's help. Chaloner wanted to refuse but he could hardly claim to be Wiseman's assistant if he skulked squeamishly in the background. Reluctantly, he gripped the banker's foot, then forced himself to watch as the surgeon directed the now red-hot probe towards the afflicted digit. There was a hiss, followed by a spurting pop as the trapped blood escaped. Taylor, who had been lying with his eyes squeezed tightly closed, sat up in astonishment.

'The pain has gone!' he cried. 'It is as though it was never there. I am completely cured!'

'Of course,' said Wiseman smugly. 'I am a master of my profession.'

'He is,' agreed Misick. 'I would not have summoned him otherwise. Now drink this potion.'

'He does not need poppy juice,' said Wiseman sharply.

He pointed to a bottle on the table. 'And certainly not if he has been taking Venice Treacle. They do not mix well.'

'This is not poppy juice, it is my Plague Elixir,' explained Misick, removing a tendril of his wig that had plopped into the cup. He glanced at Chaloner. 'To prevent my patient from catching whatever *he* has.'

'In that case, give him double.' Wiseman turned to Taylor. 'Now we shall discuss the small matter of remuneration.'

Chaloner expected trouble when the surgeon named an outrageous sum, but Taylor was too grateful to quibble, and indicated that Evan should pay. Evan baulked, though, so Wiseman fixed him with one of his imperious glares.

'I am Master of the Company of Barber–Surgeons and Surgeon to the Person. I do not haggle – I tell you my price and you pay. And my assistant will have the same.'

'Just for holding a leg?' demanded Evan, outraged. 'No! You cannot—'

'Perhaps we can compromise,' interposed Joan quickly, when Taylor's expression darkened at the notion that Evan should haggle over the cost of his well-being. 'Chaloner will waive his fee, and we will forget the thirty shillings he owes.'

'You will forget *forty* shillings,' argued Wiseman, much to Joan's irritation. Evan folded his arms and scowled at the floor like a petulant child. 'Because he will pay nothing tomorrow either, and the day after is Sunday, so the next instalment will not be due until Monday. Agreed?'

'You drive a hard bargain. I like that in a man.' Taylor smiled at Joan. 'Or a woman.'

'And now I must go,' said Wiseman, aiming for the door, red coat-tails flying importantly behind him. 'There are dozens more customers in desperate need of my services, and I cannot waste time listening to your effusions of gratitude, no matter how richly I might deserve them.'

In the corridor outside, people jostled forward to demand news of the patient's condition. Wiseman described how he had saved Taylor's life, and although everyone professed to be delighted, Chaloner was sure few were sincere. Then Silas emerged and went to talk to Backwell, who was standing with the Shaws. Chaloner edged towards them. The crowded room was as good a place as any to eavesdrop, and Vyner's bulk provided a convenient screen – the portly banker was engrossed in a newsbook, and had no idea of the service he was providing.

'. . . off the coin presses yesterday,' Backwell was saying as he brandished a new shilling. 'See how it glitters? I intend to show it to your father later. His spirits will soar at the sight, and any residual debility will vanish like mist in the sun.'

'Perhaps you should offer it as a cure for plague,' suggested Shaw. His face was grave, but amusement glinted in his eyes, and Lettice began to giggle.

'Perhaps I should,' agreed Backwell seriously. 'The reason people die is because they lose hope. But no one will do that if they know a few of *these* beauties are waiting for them to recover.'

'There is no need for you to linger,' said Silas to the Shaws. 'You are not bankers, so you have no need to visit ailing colleagues, and I am sure you have better things to do. Such as selling my music to as many courtiers as you can.'

244

Shaw's expression was wry. 'You know Joan is our landlord, and we cannot afford to annoy her, so we thought it politic to come and show our faces. But if the crisis is over . . .'

'This one is,' said Backwell, looking at Silas. 'But there is a rumour that another will befall us on Tuesday. I heard it from Howard the milliner – before he died, obviously – but it must be true, because it has been repeated to me by several customers since.'

'What sort of something?' Silas cast an irritable glance at the music-sellers, and it was clear that he wished they would leave so he could talk to Backwell alone. But the couple missed the look and continued to loiter.

'One that will serve us "greedy bankers" right, apparently,' replied Backwell worriedly.

'Another run?' asked Silas sharply. 'Like the one precipitated by the Colburn Crisis? That would be disastrous! Not even the larger banks will survive a second emergency.'

Backwell was pale. 'I know, so let us hope it is something else.'

Shaw eyed him reproachfully. 'If it is a run, you only have yourself to blame. You caused much distress by selling your debtors. One was so upset by a visit from Taylor's henchmen that she refuses to eat, while two others lie in suicides' graves.'

Backwell became defensive. 'On the contrary, *I* am the victim – my customers abused my soft-heartedness for years, and I should have taken a firmer hand ages ago. Take Howard, for example. He earned a good wage selling hats at Court, but he told me he was poor, because he had ten children. I believed him and treated him gently. But do you know the truth?'

245

'No,' replied Shaw cautiously.

'He was a gamester! He played in Baron's gambling dens, and *that* is why he never had any money. He had been taking advantage of my kindness for years.'

'Are you sure?' asked Lettice doubtfully. 'He always seemed so nice.' She gestured to her hat, a fancy creation with too many feathers in it for Chaloner's liking – he preferred to see them on birds, where they belonged. 'He made me this last week, and chatted with such happiness about his newest child . . . I do not see him as a gambler.'

'Well, he was,' said Backwell sourly. 'He owed money to lots of people, including poor Dr Coo. In fact, perhaps *he* shot Coo, in order to avoid paying his bills.'

'He would never have done such a thing!' cried Lettice, shocked. 'It is far more likely to have been a ruffian from Baron's trainband. They are an unruly horde.'

'I doubt Baron would have allowed that,' said Silas. 'He was grateful to Coo for tending his minions when they were sick or injured.'

'Perhaps it was done without Baron's knowledge,' suggested Shaw. 'He does not seem to have the control he enjoyed a few days ago. His authority is slipping.'

'Pity,' sighed Silas. 'I rather like him.'

'Most people do,' said Shaw. 'But he is a felon with a penchant for the property of others, and he is not averse to using violent means to get it. Charming he might be, but it is a dangerous charm, and you should be wary of it.'

'Then I shall,' said Silas lightly. 'But there is really no need for you two to waste any more of your time here. I shall tell Joan that you came. Goodbye.'

Thus dismissed, the Shaws had no choice but to take their leave. Chaloner peered around Vyner and watched Backwell and Silas embark on a discussion that was too low for him to hear. Then Silas glanced up and looked directly at him.

'Join us, Tom,' he called. 'I am sure you have plenty of useful thoughts on asset turnovers.'

'Excellent!' beamed Backwell. 'Although I hope they are more sensible than his uncle's.'

There was no more to be learned from Taylor's house, and Chaloner was more than happy to leave. He started to walk up White Goat Wynd, recalling that it was here that Wheler had been stabbed. The lane was deeply shadowed, and he saw it would be easy for a killer to hide there unseen, especially at night. It was also the kind of place that common thieves might haunt – an alley with plenty of hiding places that was used by wealthy pedestrians. If Chaloner had been a robber, White Goat Wynd would certainly be high on his list of hunting grounds.

He whipped around suddenly when he heard a sound behind him, but it was only Silas.

'I have been working on your behalf yet again, Tom,' his old comrade said genially. 'Although I did not want to tell you so in front of Backwell. These are uncertain times, and I have learned to be wary of everyone.'

'So have I,' said Chaloner, bemused by Silas's eagerness to help him.

'I was in the Feathers last night, and got talking to a rogue named Watkin, who knew DuPont. Watkin will wake with a sore head this morning, because I plied him with enough ale to float a ship. But it paid off – he told me the whereabouts of a Dutch spy!'

'How is he party to such information?' asked Chaloner sceptically.

'Because he and DuPont curbed the villain's house together, and DuPont snagged some of his secret documents. It was these that he planned to sell to your Earl, apparently – intelligence reports. Shall we go there now? The spy lives at the Sign of the Swan on Bread Street.'

'"Three swan in bread",' quoted Chaloner. 'Fatherton certainly sent DuPont that way.'

The Sign of the Swan was halfway up Bread Street, and they soon found the house in question. Its windows were either boarded over or broken, anti-Dutch slogans were daubed on its walls, and excrement had been smeared on the door. It was a long time before their knock was answered, and they were permitted inside only because Chaloner was able to speak Dutch. They were an elderly importer of Chinese porcelain named Jan Meer and his wife. Both were terrified.

'We are trapped here,' Meer gulped, ashen-faced. He used English out of courtesy to Silas. 'We did not have enough money to buy passage across the Channel when war first broke out, so we had to stay until we had sold all our belongings. But thieves came and stole every last penny of what we had managed to raise, leaving us stranded . . .'

'Other than the money, a few clothes and some letters, the only thing left in the house was the curtains,' added his wife, gesturing to the room in which they stood, from which even the door handles and latches had been removed. 'We had arranged to take them to Mr Baron the following day, but the burglars got them first. They were pretty things, too – patterned with roses.'

So that was how Fatherton had known where to send his curbers, thought Chaloner, recalling those particular items in Baron's cellar. Meer had gone to the King of Cheapside in panicky desperation, and Baron had

248

responded by arranging to steal what he had offered to buy, along with all the couple's painstakingly amassed coins for a journey home.

'The villains even took the messages we had written to our children,' Meer went on tearfully. 'The ones we hoped would reach them one day, should anything terrible happen to us here . . .'

'Were they in Dutch?' asked Chaloner.

Meer blinked. 'Of course. Would you write to *your* children in a foreign language?'

'They are not spies,' declared Silas, once he and Chaloner were outside again. 'They are just people caught in the wrong place at the wrong time. I shall arrange for them to take a ship to France today. I know a fisherman who will oblige.'

'Good,' said Chaloner. 'And I agree – documents stolen from Meer are unlikely to help with the war. However, I doubt letters from one house would have been enough to send DuPont flying to the Earl with offers of secret intelligence. He must have burgled other Dutchmen, too.'

'Then I had better visit the Feathers again, to see what might be learned from DuPont's other cronies.' Silas held up his hand before Chaloner could speak. 'No, you cannot join me – they will not talk to Clarendon's envoy. I, however, am popular there.'

'Perhaps so,' said Chaloner. 'But—'

'You are concerned for my well-being,' said Silas, draping a comradely arm over Chaloner's shoulders. 'Well, do not be. Common criminals are no match for the Keeper of Stores at the Harwich Shipyard, and I am delighted to serve my country by thwarting Dutch spies.'

Silas's safety had not crossed Chaloner's mind – his friend was more than capable of looking after himself

– and his reservations arose from the fact that he was baffled by Silas's determination to help him. Then he shook himself. He had been a spy for too long, and should learn not to react to every offer of help with instant suspicion. He nodded his thanks, and they parted ways.

It was mid-morning by the time Chaloner had finished with Silas, and the streets were busy, but he knew one place where business would just be winding down. He started to walk towards Hercules' Pillars Alley, then saw a familiar red figure striding along ahead of him. He ran to catch up.

'Being with those bankers has made me feel unclean,' confided Wiseman. 'And although many important patients clamour for my services, I feel the need for some decent company first – Temperance and her lasses.'

Chaloner supposed the financiers must have galled Wiseman indeed if he felt obliged to cleanse himself with whores. 'I am going there, too – to ask about her curtains.'

Most of the guests had gone by the time they arrived, and judging from the state of the lingerers who were being packed into carriages, it had been another night of rollicking good fun.

'You cannot come in,' said the doorman when he saw Chaloner. 'We are closing.'

He had never liked the spy, and getting past him was invariably a trial. His name was Preacher Hill, and he loved working at the club, because the timing of his duties left him free to harangue people about the perils of sin during the afternoons. He genuinely failed to see that working in a brothel meant he was not in a strong position to criticise the morals of others.

'He is with me,' said Wiseman. 'But stand back – he has a cold.'

Chaloner sneezed obligingly, and when Hill shied away, he took the opportunity to sidle past. Hill could have followed, but evidently decided it was not worth the risk to his health, as he turned to help an emerging patron into a hackney carriage instead. Inside, Temperance rushed to give Wiseman a hug, but held out a hand to tell Chaloner to keep his distance.

'And stay away from the girls,' she instructed sternly. 'We cannot have them snuffling all over the clients.'

Her helpmeet, the formidable Maude, was more sympathetic. She whisked Chaloner to the kitchen, where she and Wiseman argued about what should go in a tonic. While they quarrelled, Chaloner helped himself to a piece of beef pie – Temperance's cook was one of the best in London, and the spy could always find a corner for Monsieur Bonnefon's wares.

'From *The Court & Kitchin*?' he asked. The mercurial Bonnefon spoke a bizarre combination of Latin, French and Spanish, and Chaloner was one of few people who could communicate with him.

'I do not serve English muck here,' replied Bonnefon archly, then gave a Gallic shrug. 'Although Mrs Cromwell is the person to convince me otherwise. She has some excellent and innovative ideas.'

When the discussion between Maude and Wiseman grew heated – and he did not want to be used as an experiment to see whose remedy was more effective – Chaloner went to the parlour, where Temperance was chatting to the last of her guests, who comprised a prominent churchman, three members of parliament and two of the more dissipated rakes from Court. Someone else was there, too: Randal Taylor. Chaloner stepped towards him, but Temperance grabbed his arm.

'No, Tom,' she warned. 'Randal might be a maggot, but he is a customer – one who pays his bills promptly. Do not pester him here.'

Chaloner nodded demurely, waited until she was distracted by the politicians, then advanced on his quarry. Randal was a miserable specimen. His clothes were stained and rumpled, and his skin had an unhealthy pallor that resulted from too many pipes, drinks and late nights. Chaloner was not surprised that his family did not seem to have much time for him.

'Your book,' he said, getting straight to the point before Temperance could come and stop him. 'The one about Mrs Cromwell.'

'It has caused quite a stir,' grinned Randal, peering at him through bloodshot eyes, 'which is excellent for sales. I have sold hundreds of copies, although I cannot say I like a lot of venomous old Roundheads trying to kill me. I have had to go into hiding, you know.'

Chaloner did. 'I have just seen your wife. She wants a word with you.'

'Dear Joan,' slurred Randal. 'Well, she can wait, because I am not dancing attendance on her. She is a shrew, and makes no bones about the fact that she would rather have had Silas or my father instead. Have you read my book, by the way?'

Chaloner nodded. 'And I have a few questions. How do you *know* that Mrs Cromwell eats marrow pudding for breakfast? And who told you that her cook Starkey was always drunk?'

'I never reveal my sources,' replied Randal loftily. Then he smirked again. 'Just wait until you see my sequel. It will set London *aflame*, and good riddance. I hate this city.'

252

'Then live somewhere else, but do not publish your book. If you do, there will—'

'Temperance!' Randal screeched, so loudly that Chaloner almost jumped out of his skin. 'This man is threatening me! Get him away from me before I take my custom elsewhere.'

Temperance swooped down like an avenging angel, and Randal took the opportunity to scuttle through the front door. Chaloner tried to go after him, but Temperance blocked his way. He could have knocked her aside, but not without hurting her, which he had no wish to do.

'I told you to leave him be,' she shouted angrily. 'How dare you ignore me!'

'Easy, dearest,' cooed Wiseman, who had hurried from the kitchen when he had heard raised voices. 'What has poor Chaloner done this time?'

'Upset Randal Taylor. Probably over that stupid book.'

'All I did was ask him not to publish another,' said Chaloner tiredly. 'I do not suppose you know where he lives, do you? He is in hiding, but—'

'I would not share such information with you if I did!' declared Temperance curtly. 'He is a customer, and thus entitled to my protection.'

'Just tell me one thing,' persisted Chaloner. 'How much did you pay for the curtains that were stolen? The ones you bought from Baron?'

'Curtains?' echoed Temperance, wrong-footed by the question. She shook her head in bemusement. 'Why in God's name would you want to know that?'

'How much?'

'Two thousand pounds. I was delighted with them at first, as the red and gold went perfectly with my new wallpaper. Unfortunately, they were a fire hazard, so perhaps their theft was a blessing in disguise. We shall stick with shutters from now on.'

'I think they might be hanging in Clarendon House.'

Temperance gaped at him. 'You mean your *Earl* stole them from me? Lord! Who would have thought it of an upright prig like him!'

'Of course he did not steal them,' said Chaloner irritably. 'He bought them in good faith from Baron, whose curbers probably reclaimed them from you when the Earl asked for some of the same colour. Will you come to Clarendon House to look?'

'No,' replied Temperance shortly. 'I am too tired – last night was unusually taxing. Come for me tomorrow morning instead, and we shall do it then. Incidentally, I meant to tell you the other day that Hannah visited me a couple of weeks ago. She wanted to borrow some money.'

Chaloner winced. 'How much do we owe you?'

'Nothing – I had just bought five beds, so I did not have any spare cash to give her. She was disappointed, and said you would be vexed if you ever learned about the perilous state of your household finances. She was trying to sort them out before you came home.'

'Raising new debts was hardly the best way to go about it,' said Chaloner sourly.

'Yes and no,' replied Temperance, her voice kinder than he would have expected. '*I* would not have charged her interest.'

Chaloner went to White Hall next, to try and persuade more of the Earl's enemies to buy goods from a man who would cheat them. He aimed for the Spares Gallery, a room so named because the King deposited duplicate

254

or unwanted pieces of art there. It was used by minor courtiers as a kind of common room, and Chaloner was pleased when he saw a number of suitable victims.

He stood in the shadows listening to the chatter that swirled around him. There was a rumour, gloatingly reported, that there would soon be a heavy tax on anyone who had supported Parliament during the wars. This was not news, as Chaloner's family could attest, but the tale would alarm those who had managed to talk their way out of it so far – men like the bankers, who had sided with Cromwell but who now declared themselves to be Royalists.

Another group was discussing the murders of Wheler and Coo, and how they continued to cause strife along Cheapside. The plague was also a popular topic of conversation, with most courtiers of the opinion that the poor objected to the measures devised to control the disease for no reason other than pure cussedness.

Two of the Earl's most bitter enemies, Bab May and Will Chiffinch, were standing near the wine bemoaning their debts. As far as they were concerned, the tailors, vintners, grocers and others who provided them with goods had no right to demand what they were owed. They were also vexed with the bankers for insisting that some of the massive sums they had borrowed be repaid – if not in cash, then in kind.

'Taylor took my ship-shaped hatpin when I could not produce a hundred pounds,' May grumbled. 'The one made of pearl with gold mast and rigging. I love it dearly, but I doubt I shall ever be able to redeem it.'

'Well, Taylor told *me* that I owe more than the rest of Court put together,' said Chiffinch. 'I had to appease him with that jewelled scent bottle the French ambassador gave me. But of course I have debts! Keeping the King supplied with whores does not come cheap.'

'Taylor is not himself these days,' whispered May. 'In fact, I think he is mad.'

'When I went to pay him yesterday, he told me that he keeps the plague in a box on his desk.' Chiffinch shuddered. 'It was nonsense, yet it frightened the life out of me.'

They wandered away, and Chaloner was just aiming for Lord Shaftesbury's Chief Usher, a silly, pompous man who was easy to manipulate, when he was intercepted by Philip Starkey.

'Should you be here?' asked Chaloner, wondering whether it was wise to be seen conversing with Cromwell's old cook in the centre of Royalist power.

'I have been commissioned to oversee the King's banquet tonight,' replied Starkey. 'You seem startled. Do you not believe me capable?'

'I thought you were a Parliamentarian.'

'I was,' replied Starkey. 'But now I am a Cavalier. What has Thurloe done about Randal Taylor? I notice that his vile pamphlet is still being sold by the dozen.'

'We are working on it,' said Chaloner, loath to admit that his efforts to reason with the author had been cut short. 'And Randal will have to find another publisher for his sequel – Milbourn is probably dead, incinerated when his workshop burned down.'

'What a shame,' said Starkey, so smugly that Chaloner found himself wondering whether the cook knew more about the matter than was innocent. 'But perhaps his fate will warn other printers to be a little more discerning about what they produce.'

He had strutted away before Chaloner could question

him about the fire, although it was perhaps just as well – the Spares Gallery was not the place for such an interview.

Chaloner composed his features into a scowl, and slouched towards the wine. He poured himself a generous goblet, and leaned against the wall, knowing his uncharacteristic display of bad temper would attract attention. It did, and Shaftesbury's man, a fellow named Innes, came to make a sneering remark.

'What is the matter, Chaloner? Has your Earl threatened to dismiss you again?'

'So what if he has?' growled Chaloner.

Innes grinned. 'What did you do this time? Track mud on his new carpets? Refer to his mansion as Dunkirk House? Or, God forbid, swear in his lofty presence?'

'I found a linen-draper who offers the best prices in London,' replied Chaloner, affecting indignation. 'But just because Baron turned a blind eye to me making a small profit . . .'

'You mean you charged a commission?' asked Innes, intrigued.

'A very modest one.' Chaloner was aware that Lord Arlington's secretary and Rochester's clerk were listening. 'But the Earl thinks that constitutes theft, and refuses to have anything to do with the arrangements I made.'

'And you need the money, of course,' said Innes tauntingly. 'To pay off your debts. It must be a blow to work for a man with such foolish principles.'

He strode away, and was promptly intercepted by Arlington and Rochester's retainers. Chaloner left the Spares Gallery pleased with himself: all three were notoriously corrupt, and would leap at the chance to earn a backhander by dealing with Baron. Moreover, Chaloner

257

had just made the public statement that his Earl would never buy anything from dubious sources, thus forestalling any accusations that might come later. He had killed two birds with one stone.

He spent the rest of what felt like a very long day asking questions along Cheapside, but learned little of use. He did discover the name of Baron's linen-draper brother-in-law, and visited the shop to see if any red and gold curtains were being made. Unfortunately, the man refused to talk to him, and there were too many apprentices around to make burglary a practical option.

He saw the King of Cheapside shortly afterwards, riding proudly through his domain on Caesar, his captains trotting at his heels. Baron rode with all the elegance of a ploughboy, while Doe and Poachin looked foolish as they hurried along in his wake. Poachin made light of the spectacle he was making, but Doe scowled, clearly judging it an affront to his dignity.

'Baron had better enjoy it while he can,' Chaloner heard a butcher tell a crony. 'Because that horse belongs to Wheler's widow, and she wants it back. She hired lawyers to draw up official documents, and she plans to reclaim the beast tomorrow.'

'It is an act of spite on her part,' remarked the friend. 'Because Baron took so much of her inheritance before she protected it by marrying a Taylor. She aims to wound.'

Chaloner gave up on his enquiries as evening approached, and trudged home to change for Silas's party. As he was tired and out of sorts, he stopped for a dish of Farr's powerful coffee en route, in the hope that it would restore his vitality. He entered the Rainbow's fuggy warmth to find a very different scene from the one he was used to. It was virtually empty, and with his customers gone, Farr was reduced to reading a newsbook. Chaloner soon understood what was amiss: Williamson was there.

Chaloner started to back out, but the Spymaster had glanced up when the door was opened, and had seen him.

'Chaloner! There you are. Come and join me, if you please. We have much to discuss.'

Farr's eyes were wide with astonishment that one of his customers should be known to such a man, and Chaloner wondered if he would now have to find another coffee house: the other patrons might shun him if they thought he hobnobbed with spymasters. Reluctantly, he went to sit at Williamson's table, afraid that if he declined, the Spymaster might bray something else that would damage his reputation. He sneezed several times as he did so.

'A cold,' he explained, seeing Williamson's immediate alarm. 'Probably.'

Williamson placed a handkerchief over his nose. 'Then do not give it to me. I cannot afford to be laid low when I am so busy. What have you learned about DuPont? I expected to hear from you before now – spying is a serious business, you know.'

Chaloner supposed he had been remiss not to keep Williamson informed. 'I did not want to waste your time,' he hedged. 'All I have discovered is that DuPont was a professional thief who planned to curb documents from Dutch intelligencers in London.'

'Which intelligencers?' demanded Williamson. 'I want their names.'

'I do not have them yet. Nor do I know why he went from Long Acre to Bearbinder Lane, although he had a masked and hissing visitor shortly before he left, who gave him money. Does "Onions at the Well" mean anything to you? Perhaps in connection to St Giles?'

Williamson shook his head, and Chaloner was about to add more when he became aware of a shadow easing towards them. The knife in his sleeve dropped neatly into the palm of his hand, and he clutched it even harder when he recognised John Swaddell, whom Williamson referred to as his clerk, but who everyone knew was really an assassin.

Swaddell was dressed in his trademark black, the only exception being a white falling band – the square of linen fastened around his neck like a bib. Chaloner wore one, too, but his had lace as a sop to fashion. Swaddell's had none, which gave him the look of a Puritan, although he was not a religious man. He had restless dark eyes, lank black hair, and was one of the most dangerous men in London. He came to perch on Chaloner's other side.

'It is good of you to investigate DuPont,' he said, thus proving that he had been eavesdropping. 'However, we have another small problem that you can help us resolve.'

Chaloner imagined they had rather more than one, given Williamson's burgeoning responsibilities.

'You have probably heard about the murder of Dick Wheler,' said Williamson. He grimaced. 'And that I failed to identify the killer. However, that is not strictly true. I *did* find the culprit – I am certain it was Baron. Unfortunately, proving it was another matter.'

'Baron benefited hugely from Wheler's death,' elaborated Swaddell. 'He assumed control of Wheler's burglars, gambling dens, the Protection Tax . . . He probably killed Coo, too.'

'Then arrest him,' suggested Chaloner.

'We did,' said Williamson sourly. 'But without evidence, I was forced to let him go.'

Chaloner stirred the thick, gritty sludge that Farr claimed was coffee. 'Why would Baron kill Coo? The man physicked members of his trainband. And his family.'

'Which is what he wants everyone to think,' said Williamson. 'Yet something odd is unfolding on Cheapside. Wheler, DuPont, Coo, Fatherton – all dead in peculiar circumstances.'

'Yes,' agreed Chaloner. 'But these matters are trivial compared to the other challenges that face you, and I cannot imagine why you are wasting your time with them.'

'They are not trivial,' snapped Williamson. He winced – his voice had been loud, and Farr had looked up from his reading. He lowered it to a confidential whisper. 'They are not trivial, because I fear they will result in another run on the banks – a major one this time.'

Chaloner blinked. '*What?* How can the—'

'Cheapside,' interrupted Williamson harshly. 'It is all happening in and around *Cheapside*, which is where the goldsmiths live. The worst thing that could happen now is a second run, and we are a hairsbreadth away from it.'

'Worse than the plague or war?' asked Chaloner.

'Of course! We cannot fight either without money. But so much is going wrong. First, there was Colburn, who did irreparable damage with his reckless gambling. Then there was Wheler's murder, which had all manner of repercussions – not least that a felon now runs Cheapside . . .'

'Wheler would have died anyway,' said Chaloner. 'He had lung-rot.'

'We know,' said Swaddell sourly. 'We aimed to destroy his illegal empire the moment he breathed his last – he was too powerful to tackle when he was alive – but his murder deprived us of the chance. And now it is Baron who is too powerful to depose.'

'And to top it all, Cheapside's residents are being difficult over the plague measures,' finished Williamson. 'Which is beyond belief, when it is them we are trying to protect.'

'They are being difficult about Randal Taylor's pamphlet, too,' Swaddell reminded him. 'There was a near-riot over it last night. Then there are these rumours about Tuesday . . .'

'What rumours?' asked Chaloner.

'That something terrible will happen,' explained Swaddell. 'But no one seems to know what, which makes it rather tough to prevent. So we are here to make you an offer. One you will like.'

'We know about your financial difficulties,' said Williamson, oily again. 'We also know that you will never repay Taylor with what you earn from the Earl. So, I have a proposition: help us for a few days, and I shall ensure that your debt is discharged.'

'How?' asked Chaloner suspiciously. 'I owe three thousand, seven hundred and forty-eight pounds. Or I did – Taylor's interest rates are so outrageous that it may have doubled by now. Do you have that sort of money to spare?'

'No, but there are other ways of doing business,' replied Williamson. 'You do not need to know details. Suffice to say that your slate will be wiped clean.'

'Right,' said Chaloner, suspecting nothing of the kind would happen. Yet could he afford to ignore the chance that it might? 'And what must I do in return?'

'Two things. First, find out what is going on in Cheapside, and if there is some dire event planned for Tuesday, help us stop it. And second, gather evidence that will allow us to charge Baron with Wheler's murder.'

Chaloner was puzzled. 'You must have spies who can do it.'

'Actually, we do not. They are all busy with the war, and the government keeps cutting my budget, so I am not in a position to hire more. But you and I have combined forces in the past to good effect, so why not collaborate again?'

'We can do something else for you as well,' added Swaddell, when Chaloner continued to hesitate. 'I was in the Spares Gallery when you spun that yarn about Baron. You want them to do business with him, so they will not be in a position to condemn your Earl for doing likewise.'

Chaloner sincerely hoped no one else had seen through his ploy, or he might have done his employer a serious disservice. He also disliked the fact that he had been monitored without his knowledge. Was he losing his edge – that tasks like chasing curtains were blunting the skills he had so painstakingly acquired during a decade of real espionage?

'Work with us, and I shall spread the word further still,' Swaddell went on. 'To lords Seymour or Southampton, for example. Well? What do you say? Will you accept our offer?'

Chaloner stood. 'I will think about it.'

'Fine,' said Williamson, although irritation flashed in his eyes. 'But do not wait too long. I have a bad feeling

263

about Cheapside, and unless we act soon, it might be too late – for all of us.'

'I do not like Cheapside,' said Hannah, looking around in distaste as she and Chaloner walked to the rooms that Silas had hired for his party – a pleasant tavern near the Standard. 'Jacob and Gram grew up here, and they have told me some dreadful stories about it.'

'What stories?' asked Chaloner. He had forgotten the servants' association with the place.

'Murder, theft, extortion. And that is just the felons – you should hear what the bankers do.'

Chaloner laughed, then saw that she was in earnest. 'Why? What do they do?'

'The same, only on a larger scale. And *that* place is sinister,' she said, pointing to where the Standard loomed out of the darkness. 'Do you see that balcony at the top? Well, Puritan fanatics used to climb up there, and howl to everyone that Cromwell was a saint.'

'He was, compared to bankers,' murmured Chaloner, although he did not need Hannah to remind him of the zealous speech-makers who had haunted London during the Protectorate.

The tavern had been sumptuously decorated for the occasion, and there was plenty of food and drink. The guests were an eclectic mix of courtiers, financiers, musicians and local worthies. Baron was evidently included in the latter category, because he stood by the fireplace with his wife and his captains. His party was clearly thrilled to be part of the glittering company, although they valiantly strove to conceal it.

Another guest was Alan Brodrick, the Earl of Clarendon's cousin. He was a notorious debauchee, although his prim kinsman steadfastly refused to believe anything bad about him. However, he was also a connoisseur of good music, which meant that Chaloner was able to overlook his many faults and talk to him.

'Baron owns this tavern,' whispered Brodrick. 'So I imagine Silas got a discount by inviting him to join us tonight. Go and talk to him – he is very amusing for a commoner, although I cannot say I like his henchmen. The one with the peculiar hairstyle just told me that he uses alum to keep his mop in place, as if he imagines I might like to emulate it!'

'Will there be music tonight?' asked Chaloner, cutting to the chase.

'There had better be, or I am leaving. I have more pleasant things to do than demean myself in company with bankers. Especially *that* one.'

Brodrick nodded to the other side of the room, where Chaloner saw that Taylor had declined the opportunity for an early night and was glad-handing his son's guests. He carried his box under his arm, which he kept patting fondly. Joan and Evan were at his heels, and they exchanged nervous glances whenever he opened his mouth, while Misick lurked nearby with a bag that was no doubt full of soothing tonics lest Taylor suffered another of his turns.

'Why especially him?' asked Chaloner.

'Because he is not a gentleman,' replied Brodrick stiffly. 'I did not mind doing business with Backwell, who is a decent soul, but Taylor is a brute.'

Chaloner agreed, and if the music proved to be lacking, he would make an excuse to slip away early, too. Hannah would not mind – Taylor had homed in on her, baring his teeth in a grin that was probably meant to be paternal, but instead was unpleasantly insincere and vaguely menacing.

He retreated to the shadows and watched the other guests interact. The different factions had little in common, and miscommunications were rife, especially when Baron and his coterie were involved. Chaloner struggled not to laugh when a maid offered Doe a delicacy from the tray she carried – he thanked her politely and took the whole platter. It was silver, so when all the food had been eaten, he wiped it on a tablecloth and slipped it down the back of his breeches.

'You want your portrait done by a lily?' Frances was asking the portly Vyner. She had overdressed for the occasion, and looked like a courtesan. 'My husband knows an artist, and I am sure he can get you a very good price. He will set you by whatever flower you choose.'

'By *Lely*,' corrected Vyner. 'The King's Principal Painter in Ordinary.'

'Our man is not ordinary,' averred Frances with a bright smile. 'He is very good. In fact, he did me next to Caesar.'

'Julius or Augustus?' asked Vyner drolly, although classical witticisms were lost on Frances, whose only response was to flutter her eyelashes in a desperate attempt to distract him from noticing that she had no clue what he was talking about.

Suddenly, the hair rose on the back of Chaloner's neck, as it often did when he was in danger. He tensed, and saw with alarm that Baron was looking directly at him. He was disconcerted, as he prided himself on being invisible at such occasions. Unwilling to be accused of spying, he went to exchange pleasantries.

'The Earl of Shaftesbury bought a carpet from us today,' said Poachin. His peculiar hair had set as hard as iron, and Chaloner wondered how much alum had been used. 'And he says he will have some table-linen, too. Another two customers, and your Earl will win his curtains.'

'But pestering my brother-in-law will not expedite matters,' said Baron. His voice was soft, but held unmistakeable irritation. 'In fact, it shows a disturbing lack of trust.'

'Very disturbing,' agreed Doe, but he had been at the wine and was in an ebullient mood, so his menacing scowl dissolved quickly into a proud grin. 'What do you think of my clothes?'

He had contrived to dress in an outfit that was identical to Baron's, even down to the ill-fitting wig. Baron patted his shoulder, flattered, although Chaloner would have been mortified.

'I heard today that something terrible will happen on Cheapside next Tuesday,' Chaloner said, aiming to see what they knew about the rumour. 'It is true?'

'Who knows what the future holds?' replied Baron with a shrug. 'It is all in the hands of God, so we must put our trust in Him to keep us safe.'

A quartet began to play at that point, so he hurried over to Frances and led her in a jig around the room, while Poachin and Doe clapped in time to the music. It was not a dancing or clapping sort of occasion, and the other guests gawped at their gaucheness. Chaloner could not bear to watch, so went to stand near where Taylor was holding court in the next chamber.

The banker had acquired a sycophantic audience, and was giving his opinion about liquidity ratios, asset turnovers and net profit. He sounded as sane as any other man of commerce, and the only hint of oddness was the box under his arm. Joan added observations that had the other financiers in the throng murmuring appreciatively. Misick came to talk to Chaloner.

'He is not well enough to be out really,' he whispered, absently picking a lock of wig out of the syllabub he was eating and sucking it clean. 'I wish he had agreed to stay home and rest.'

'He seems all right to me,' said Chaloner. 'Less lunatic than usual.'

Misick frowned. 'He is not a lunatic, he is afflicted with the eccentricity of genius. And I was actually thinking about his poor toe, which remains sore after Wiseman's ministrations. Still, I have dosed him with my Plague Elixir, so—'

'Chaloner,' interrupted Evan, his loud voice making both men turn. 'The pearls your wife is wearing – my father wants them.'

'I am sure he does,' said Chaloner icily, 'but you agreed to demand no more money until Monday.'

'They will serve to help pay off the *capital*, not the interest,' said Evan. 'Those are two separate and distinct issues. And besides, debtors do not dictate terms to my father. He—'

Chaloner took a step towards him. He could be intimidating when he was angry, and he was angry now – not just that Evan should try to take the only keepsake Hannah had from her mother, but that he was graceless enough to do it at a social function. Evan blanched and scurried away.

'I really dislike him,' confided Misick. 'He has none of his father's charm, but all his greed. And speaking of greed, here comes another banker – Backwell.'

'I have been counting money all day,' announced

268

Backwell with a contented sigh. 'So many lovely, *lovely* coins . . .'

'I see,' said Chaloner, not sure how else to respond to such a bizarre declaration. 'Did Silas assist you? You seem to spend a lot of time with him these days.'

'We discuss the war,' said Backwell airily. 'We are both afraid of the spiralling costs. The King should have restrained himself, because the conflict will beggar us all. Hah! There is Hinton. You must excuse me while I go to commiserate with him. He declared himself bankrupt today.'

He bowed and hurried away. Chaloner watched him go, wondering what it was about conversations between Silas and Backwell that always set alarm bells ringing in his mind. There was no reason why the pair should not discuss the war, yet he was certain that Backwell had just lied to him. He started to follow, aiming to have the truth, but bumped into Shaw and Lettice, who had been given the task of handing out sheets of music. A quick glance at the notes, and all else flew from Chaloner's mind. It was a motet in ten parts, with some very intriguing harmonies.

'Silas wrote it,' said Lettice with a giggle. 'We cannot wait to hear it performed.'

Silas had been talking in a low voice to Poachin, but he abandoned the discussion when he heard his name and came to join them.

'Baron is a fine bass by all accounts,' he murmured, 'but he cannot read music, so I have enlisted Poachin's help in persuading him against volunteering for a solo.'

Chaloner frowned: it had not looked like that sort of conversation to him. But Lettice was addressing him, so he was forced to give his attention to her.

'Thank you for ridding us of Slasher,' she said. 'The butcher was incandescent with rage, and Mr Oxley must pay him compensation. The dog has now been sold.'

'You can pay us the forty pounds next year if you like,' said Shaw generously. 'It may help you, as Silas tells us that you are heavily in debt to his father. We know what it is like to be broken financially, and would not inflict it on anyone. Imagine how we would feel if you chose the same path as poor Colburn – suicide.'

'*Poor* Colburn?' asked Silas archly. 'He was a rogue, who knowingly destroyed others just so he could enjoy himself at the card tables. Do not waste your sympathy on him.'

'He was a friend,' said Shaw sharply. 'One of few who stood by me after the Tulip Bubble.'

'This is gloomy talk,' said Lettice. She smiled at Chaloner. 'Hannah was just telling us about your alum mines again. They sound very interesting, and I should love to visit them, but I doubt I shall ever make such a journey. The north is a wild and dangerous place, by all accounts, and I am not as young as I was . . .'

Chaloner wished he had reminded Hannah to put the record straight with them that evening, and started to explain the position again, but an impatient gesture from Silas sent them scurrying away to distribute more music.

'Meer and his wife are safely away,' said Silas in a low voice. 'I saw them off myself. They should reach France by the morning, and I gave them money to travel by coach the rest of the way. Or rather Evan did. I raided his funds when he was not looking.'

'I knew I should not have come tonight,' declared Brodrick furiously, storming up before Chaloner could respond. 'Your wretched brother has just deprived me of my Genovese watch.'

Silas raised his eyebrows. 'How crass. Shall I ask for it back?'

'No,' said Brodrick sullenly. 'He will only take it away again tomorrow, at which point he might demand something else, too, as interest. Damn him for an ungentlemanly villain!'

'Well, let us soothe our ragged tempers with music,' said Silas. 'Chaloner, will you take a viol?'

Chaloner would always take a viol, so the rest of the evening passed very pleasantly indeed.

Chapter 9

The next day, Saturday, dawned clear and bright, but Chaloner was unimpressed to find that his cold was still with him. Would the thing never go? He had enjoyed the music the previous night, but felt he would have performed better had his ears not been plugged, his nose blocked and his throat sore, while sneezing and coughing had been a nuisance, particularly during one adagio. Worse, he had not been able to sing, which meant that Silas had been one part short for his motet so it had not been performed.

He dressed and went to the kitchen, where he found Gram hacking at a grey, rubbery slab with a knife. It was week-old oatmeal, but Chaloner ate the slice he was offered anyway.

'I understand you were born and bred on Cheapside,' he said. 'Did you know Dick Wheler?'

'Of course not! I do not demean myself by consorting with bankers. And he was a nasty piece, anyway – not a man I would want as a friend. He was stabbed, you know.'

Chaloner did. 'Have you heard any rumours about who might have done it?'

'Plenty. But the one I favour is that the culprit was a customer who objected to his rough tactics – Wheler bullied dozens of folk every day. And now the Taylor clan is following in his footsteps. Personally, I think too much money sends men insane, so perhaps it is just as well that you are destitute, sir. You would not want to be like them.'

'No,' agreed Chaloner, although he thought there was probably a happy medium on the scale between obscene wealth and looming debt. 'So you do not believe that Baron killed Wheler?'

'He might have done, I suppose. But so might Taylor, who also gained from Wheler's death. Or Joan. In fact, there are lots of people who wanted him dead, so I hope you do not intend to solve the case. You will not succeed, and you will make dangerous enemies in the process.'

That was an occupational hazard in Chaloner's line of work, and he had learned not to worry about it. 'What do you think of Baron?' he asked.

Gram pondered the question. 'A curious man. He is charming, kind to his family and loves animals – horses in particular. But woe betide anyone who crosses him. Then he is a monster.'

'What else?'

'He is ambitious and greedy, and even has his tentacles in White Hall. I escorted the mistress there yesterday and heard people talking: Buckingham, Shaftesbury, Rochester *and* Arlington have either bought stuff from him already, or have arranged to put in an order today.'

Good, thought Chaloner. That made five new customers with Lady Castlemaine, and if Swaddell did what he promised, there might be even more. Baron would have to fulfil his end of the bargain now. He nodded his thanks to Gram for the 'breakfast' and left.

He reviewed his investigations as he walked. The negatives were that he had failed to convince Randal not to publish a second book; he still did not know who had murdered Wheler, Coo and Fatherton; and he had no idea what dire event was planned for Tuesday. On the positive side, the last two pairs of curtains should be delivered soon; he had taken steps to distance his Earl from Baron; and he had worked out how DuPont had aimed to gather intelligence.

He reached Cheapside just as the tenor bell of St Michael's Church began a dreary toll to mark the death of a man in his forties. Two more houses had been shut up, but the watchers were no longer lone men toting swords and cudgels – they were squads of grizzled veterans armed with muskets. Small gaggles of people clustered around each, howling abuse.

'My uncle had a stoppage in the stomach,' shouted a woman from the attic of one building. 'He had been suffering from it for weeks. Ask anyone. It was *not* the plague.'

The watchers took no notice, but there was a sudden flurry of activity at the window, and something was levered out. It was a body, which landed with a crunch that made everyone shy away in alarm.

'Examine it!' she screeched. 'Then you will see.'

The watchers did not oblige, but one onlooker – the laundress, Widow Porteous – stepped forward and pulled off the sheet. Even Chaloner, from his safe distance, could see a notable absence of plague tokens, and wondered whether the authorities might have been over-hasty.

'A stoppage of the stomach,' Widow Porteous announced, wiping her forehead with the back of her hand. It was shiny with sweat. 'This is no case of plague.'

274

'Then take it up with Williamson,' said the chief watcher, staring stoically ahead so he would not have to meet anyone's eyes. 'We are just following orders.'

There was a chorus of jeers, but the soldiers were armed and the hecklers were not, so there was little that could be done. The mob was, however, thoroughly bad-tempered, and the plague was not the only subject that was cause for dissent. An argument had broken out over Randal's pamphlet, while a fist-fight was in progress over Coo's murder – someone had accused Baron of the crime, and members of his trainband had taken umbrage.

Chaloner left them to it and walked to Baron's house, wanting the matter of the Earl's curtains resolved as soon as possible so he could be reinstated on the payroll. The door was answered by Frances, who began to chat happily about the 'pretty jigs' played at Silas's soirée the previous evening. Chaloner bristled: it was no way to refer to Lawes, Gibbons and Dumont. Then he reminded himself that here was a woman who had danced a reel to Dowland.

She took him to a parlour, where her children were at their lessons. Then the peace was shattered by a sudden roar of rage from the yard below. Chaloner joined her and the children at the window to see what had elicited it.

Joan was there with a party of Taylor's henchmen and a lawyer. The cry had come from Baron, who was standing with his horse. With a wail of dismay, Frances raced towards the door, the children at her heels, and all three appeared in the yard a moment later to cluster protectively around the nag. Chaloner opened the window so he could hear what was being said.

'I am offering you a *good* price,' Baron was snarling. 'Why will you not take it?'

275

'Because I am disinclined to sell,' replied Joan loftily. 'Now step aside.'

'No!' cried Baron. 'You do not want Caesar. You are punishing me because you think you should be in charge of business here. You—'

'That horse is lawfully mine,' interrupted Joan coldly. 'I inherited it, and if you do not believe me, this gentleman has a copy of my late husband's will.'

The lawyer stepped forward, but Baron waved him away, and there followed as distressing a scene as Chaloner had ever witnessed. Joan refused to negotiate, and sly references to the speed with which Baron had installed himself as King of Cheapside explained exactly why she had struck where he was vulnerable. The children and Frances wept as Caesar was led away, but Baron waved his trainband back when they started to intervene. It was a wise decision: they were heavily outnumbered and Taylor's men had guns.

'There,' said Joan in satisfaction. 'Our business is done. Good day to you.'

She strode out, head held high, leaving Chaloner thinking that if she was shot or stabbed in the next few days, he would not have far to look for the culprit. She was a fool to enrage such a dangerous man, and he wondered whether it was her idea or Taylor's. Regardless, the dark expression on Baron's face told him the incident was unlikely to be forgotten or forgiven.

It was some time before Baron appeared in the parlour. His eyes were red, and the fury that oozed from him in waves reminded Chaloner to be on his guard – he did not want to pay the price for Joan's spite. Doe and Poachin obviously thought the same, as they kept their distance.

276

A fourth man was with them, and Chaloner recoiled in surprise. It was Jacob, his erstwhile footman.

'You dismissed your staff, so I took him on,' said Doe. His tone was triumphant, as if he imagined he had somehow scored a victory over the spy. Chaloner suspected that both men were in for an unpleasant surprise – one when he learned he had hired an inveterate sluggard, and the other when he realised he was employed by a man who expected him to work.

'Come to my office,' instructed Baron curtly. 'I do not do business in this room.'

He led the way, Doe and Poachin at his heels, while Chaloner and Jacob brought up the rear.

'Are you sure this is a good idea?' Chaloner whispered, feeling obliged to warn the footman against the path he had elected to take. 'You are—'

'You ousted me,' said Jacob coldly. 'I had no choice but to throw myself on Doe's mercy.'

'Hannah will ask at Court whether there are vacancies in—'

'Do not bother. But I will have my revenge, Chaloner. I shall tell your wife's fine friends about her frolics with the Duke of Buckingham.'

Chaloner declined to be provoked into a fight in a place where it was likely to see him trounced – or worse – and treated the remark to the contempt it deserved by ignoring it. Jacob was a fool for running to Doe, but if he would not to listen to good advice, then there was nothing Chaloner could do about it.

They reached Baron's office at the same time as two men carrying sacks and long poles, and it did not take a genius to see that here were a pair of curbers bringing spoils to their masters. Poachin made an impatient noise at the back of his throat and bundled them away before they could say anything incriminating. Baron smiled coldly.

'My commercial interests are diverse,' he said, and Chaloner had the feeling that he was being challenged – that both knew stolen goods had just been paraded, and Baron was defying him to do anything about it. 'God has been good to me. In business, at least. He let me down rather in the matter of Caesar. I shall have to have a word with Him later.'

'I have supplied you with the requisite number of new customers,' said Chaloner, declining to comment on Baron's relationship with the Almighty. 'Where are the Earl's curtains?'

'New customers,' mused Baron, tapping his chin. 'Who, exactly?'

'Lady Castlemaine and lords Rochester, Shaftesbury, Arlington and Buckingham,' replied Chaloner briskly. 'Seymour and Southampton will soon follow – almost twice as many as stipulated in our agreement.'

'Their servants have opened negotiations certainly, but no coins have yet changed hands.'

If Baron intended to wait for money before honouring the agreement, the Earl might never see his goods, thought Chaloner in alarm. Those particular courtiers never settled bills promptly.

'I have every faith in your ability to collect what you are owed,' he said, forcing a smile. 'And now it is time for you to keep your promise.'

There was a flash of something unreadable in Baron's eyes, while Doe tensed, ready to spring forward with his fists, and Poachin fingered the knife in his belt. Chaloner saw he should have been more circumspect. Then Baron laughed, and clapped a friendly arm around his shoulders. Chaloner sneezed, and he removed it quickly.

'You *should* work for me,' he said. 'I could do with a man like you.'

'No!' objected Jacob. He gulped when Baron whipped around to glare at him. 'I mean you do not want him in your retinue, sir. He has a reputation for insolence.'

'Then I would kill him,' said Baron, and laughed again. Chaloner had no idea if he was joking. Then the felon gestured to where food had been left to keep warm over the fire. 'Eat with me, Chaloner. My wife is an excellent cook, and has prepared a mash of eggs with smoked pork and onions. Leave us, Jacob. You, too, Poachin.'

Doe smugly took a seat at the table, and behind Baron's back, Poachin's eyes blazed with envy. He did not move for a moment, but stamped out when Baron swivelled around to look questioningly at him. Doe began to pass around spoons and knives, while Baron brought the pot from the hearth. It might have been a homely scene, if Chaloner's dining companions had not been two very dangerous criminals.

'Is this a recipe from *The Court & Kitchin*?' asked Chaloner, once they were seated and Baron had filled their bowls.

'Certainly not!' declared Baron. 'It was political claptrap that tore our country apart for the best part of twenty years, and I want no more of it. God does not approve of needless discord.'

'Poor Milbourn,' sighed Doe. 'He did not deserve such a terrible fate. Poachin—'

'But accidents happen,' interrupted Baron smoothly. His expression hardened. 'Even to lofty ladies like Joan Taylor, who cheat honest men of their horses.'

'Or envoys of the Lord Chancellor,' added Doe.

'Speaking of the Earl, he has asked me to learn more about DuPont,' said Chaloner. 'He—'

'But you already know about him,' interrupted Baron, eyes narrowing. 'It was you who told us, if you recall – he died of the plague, God rest his soul.'

'Clarendon is more interested in his life than his death,' explained Chaloner. 'Especially the fact that he was a curber – one who planned to dabble in espionage by stealing documents from Dutchmen living in London.'

'Is that so?' said Baron flatly. 'Well, well.'

'I imagine Fatherton knew.' Chaloner looked pointedly at two long hooks that were propped in the corner. 'At least, it was Fatherton who told DuPont where and when to steal.'

'Then it is a pity that neither is here to enlighten us,' sighed Baron. 'Fatherton has not been seen for several days, and he is believed to have perished in the Bearbinder Lane fire. He may even have started it, the silly fellow.'

Chaloner wanted to press the matter further, but sensed he would be wasting his time – Baron was far too old a hand at interrogations to be tricked or cajoled into a confession. He stood. 'Give me the Earl's curtains, and I shall be on my way.'

'They are not finished yet,' replied Baron. 'But sit down and have some more eggs, then tell me about that musical implement you sawed away at last night. Did I hear it called a *vile*?'

It was later than agreed, but Chaloner went to Hercules' Pillars Alley next, to collect Temperance and take her to Clarendon House. She thought he had forgotten, and groaned wearily when he walked into the kitchen, where she was sharing a pipe and a pot of strong coffee with Maude. The air was so thick with fug that it made him cough, although both assured him that there was nothing better for a cold than a few lungfuls of good Virginia tobacco.

'We shall have to walk, though,' warned Chaloner, as Temperance heaved her bulk out of the chair; he wondered if she would make it all the way to Piccadilly, as she rarely left the club and was unused to exercise. 'I do not have enough money for a hackney.'

Temperance grimaced. 'You certainly know how to impress a girl, Tom. We shall take my personal carriage then. The horses could do with a run.'

'No!' gulped Chaloner, horrified. He would lose his post if the Earl saw the lewd coat-of-arms emblazoned on the side.

'Yes!' countered Temperance, adamant. 'I am *not* going on foot. It is a long way and I am tired. Besides, I like riding in it, and I do not have the opportunity very often.'

'Perhaps that is just as well, given what happened when you took it along Cheapside,' remarked Chaloner. 'We were lucky to escape in one piece.'

Temperance pouted. 'I shall not go there again. Those rioting thieves would have stripped it bare if Mr Baron had not recognised it and arranged for it to be sent back to me. But Fleet Street and the Strand do not seethe with unrest, so there is no need to fear for your safety.'

'It was not *my* safety that worried me—' But Chaloner was speaking to thin air, as she had already hurried away to issue orders to her grooms.

It was some time before the coach was ready as it had to be backed out of its shed, the horses had to be hitched up, and the servants had to don their uniforms. Chaloner

281

chafed at the delay, sure he could have walked there and back twice during the time it took to prepare it all. While they waited, he persuaded Temperance to give Gram a job in the kitchen, although she yielded reluctantly, not liking the notion of a septuagenarian scullery boy.

'Smoke, Tom,' she ordered, once they were in the carriage and it was making its stately way westwards. She handed him a pipe. 'To keep the plague at bay.'

Chaloner obliged, although her tobacco was unusually pungent and irritated his sore throat. The atmosphere soon became thick with two of them puffing.

'I hope no one sees me,' said Temperance, although Chaloner thought there was little chance of that – *he* could barely make her out and she was sitting next to him. 'What would my patrons think if I was spotted entering the home of that villain?'

But despite her sour words, she was in a good mood that day, because Lord Rochester had asked her to a private party. She was not often included in such invitations, and was delighted.

'He is up to his ears in debt,' she confided. 'And Taylor has threatened to seize his art collection if he does not pay, but Rochester cannot abide bankers, and does not see why they should interfere with his social life. He has decided to ignore Taylor and have his soirée anyway.'

'Good for him,' remarked Chaloner absently, wondering how he would confront Baron if the curtains in the Great Parlour did transpire to be Temperance's. The King of Cheapside was unlikely to make it easy for him.

They arrived to find Clarendon House in a frenzy of activity. Two Bernini sculptures were being delivered, along with a consignment of wallpaper. However, work

282

stopped when Temperance appeared, and Chaloner saw her reputation had gone before her – the female servants treated her with icy disdain, while the men hastened to fawn over her. Neve was particularly unctuous, and insisted on taking her to inspect the curtains himself.

The upholder conducted her up the back stairs – while he was eager to win her good graces, even he dared not take her on a route where they might meet the Earl – and into the Great Parlour. It was a room of impressive proportion, complete with marble pillars and a fabulously ornate ceiling. Chaloner was not surprised that his employer wanted the remaining curtains, as they really did go very well with his expensive rugs.

'Yes, those are mine,' said Temperance, giving the drapery a brief inspection. 'And if you want proof, there is a burn on one where it met Buckingham's pipe, and a brown stain on another where there was a mishap involving a fricassee.'

Neve rummaged through the material to reveal first one mark and then the other. 'What a pity,' he said uncomfortably. 'The Earl will be mortified.'

Chaloner was sure he would. He returned Temperance to the kitchen and left her in the solicitous care of three admiring footmen, two valets and a butler, then took the upholder aside.

'How much did Baron charge for them?' he asked.

Neve's expression turned shifty. 'Three thousand pounds.'

'His ledger read two thousand nine hundred, and he had no reason to set it down wrongly. You have effectively stolen a hundred pounds from our employer.'

Neve opened his mouth to deny the accusation, but Chaloner fixed him with a steely glare, and the upholder's indignation dissolved into bleating excuses. 'I am in debt, which you of all people should understand. Besides, it was a good price, even with my commission. No other linen-draper charges so little.'

'And now we know why: what he sells does not belong to him. It was not a good price, anyway – Temperance paid two thousand pounds for seven pairs, but you gave two thousand nine hundred for nine. You let Baron cheat you, and you cheated the Earl.'

Neve looked ready to cry. 'I *had* to! I borrowed heavily to start my upholding business, but it has never been as profitable as I hoped. Backwell's rates were good, but he sold my debt to Taylor . . . And Clarendon nags me incessantly about the last curtains. My life has been a living hell for weeks.'

'He never stopped my pay, did he?' said Chaloner coldly. 'That was a lie, designed to make me confront Baron more quickly, so that the Earl would stop pestering you.'

Neve had the grace to blush. 'I was desperate. And my commission was only a hundred pounds anyway. The Earl spends twice that amount every day on fripperies. He will not miss it.'

'It is not about the money.' Chaloner was exasperated. 'Do you not know what will happen if word gets out that Clarendon House is furnished with stolen goods? His enemies will use it to impeach him, and he will lose his post as Lord Chancellor – or worse.'

'Nonsense! He will just deny knowing that they came from the club. I certainly had no idea.'

'But you must have guessed their provenance was dubious,' persisted Chaloner, 'given Baron's reputation as a felon.'

Neve rubbed a weary hand over his eyes, and much

284

of the defensive bluster went out of him. 'Will you tell him?'

'That the curtains are stolen? Yes, of course, so he can decide what to do about them.'

'And my commission?'

'He is likely to find out anyway, so I recommend that you confess. It will not be pleasant, but at least you will have a chance to explain yourself. He admires your work, so perhaps he will overlook the matter.'

'I cannot own up to such a thing!' cried Neve, appalled. 'He will tell everyone that I am dishonest, and no client would ever trust me again.'

'But you *are* dishonest.'

'That is not the point. I would rather resign.'

'Then resign. You have until tomorrow to do it, because that is when I will tell him what has happened. And do not glower at me. It is your own fault that you are in this predicament.'

Feeling soiled by the encounter, Chaloner went to My Lord's Lobby. The Earl was at his costly Venetian desk, surrounded by papers of state, although he must have been distracted by the workmen who were noisily installing his latest acquisitions in the hallway outside.

'What is wrong with your voice?' demanded the Earl suspiciously. 'Have you been in any plaguey areas? I thought I told you to stay away from them.'

'Too much pipe smoke,' lied Chaloner, unwilling to admit to a cold lest the Earl caught one and held him accountable.

'So what is the news about my curtains?'

'Not good, I am afraid, sir. The ones hanging in your house belong to the gentlemen's club on Hercules' Pillars

285

Alley. They were stolen specifically so that Baron could sell them to you.'

The Earl regarded him in horror. '*Stolen?* No! I have bills of receipt from the linen-draper that Baron commissioned to make them for me. His name and place of business are written on the bottom.' He rummaged about on his desk. 'Here they are.'

'Forgeries, sir,' said Chaloner, although he had to admit that they were very good ones. 'Jan Meer at Sign of the Swan in Bread Street is a Dutch porcelain-seller, not a linen-draper.'

The Earl was ashen. 'Lord! And they were pilfered from a brothel? Tell Neve to take them down at once! Christ God! What shall I do if the whores find out and assume that *I* am the thief?'

'They will not, sir.' Then Chaloner reconsidered. Temperance did not like the Earl, and would love a tale that showed him in a less than favourable light. For her, it would be a joke, but it would do the Earl immeasurable harm. He supposed he would have to beg her discretion. 'I shall arrange for Baron's arrest today.'

'No!' squeaked the Earl. 'That would entail me being called as a witness in a criminal case, and then the whole story would come out. There is only one way to ensure he is not in a position to harm me – by proving he killed Wheler. How are you proceeding with that?'

'Spymaster Williamson also thinks he is responsible,' hedged Chaloner, unwilling to admit that he had made no headway on that front.

'Yes!' hissed the Earl, his face hardening. 'Work with Williamson, and see about putting a noose around Baron's neck as soon as you can.'

'Williamson wants my help with another matter, too.

286

There are rumours that something will happen on Cheapside this Tuesday, and he fears that it might precipitate a run on the banks.'

'Then help him stop it!' cried the Earl, aghast. 'We cannot risk fiscal chaos when we need money for the war. And speaking of the war, what have you learned about my would-be spy, other than the fact that he died of the plague?'

'Just that his idea of intelligence-gathering was to shove a hook through the windows of Dutchmen and see what he could snag.' As the Earl clearly thought this was a perfectly reasonable thing to do, Chaloner hastened to explain. 'Good spies do not leave sensitive documents lying around in the open, so DuPont could never have supplied you with anything useful.'

'Oh,' said the Earl deflated. 'I suppose not.'

'I spoke to one of his targets, but it was a case of mistaken identity, and I suspect we will find the same is true of the others, too. I have someone looking for them as we speak.' Assuming Silas was doing what he promised, of course.

'Do you think DuPont took the plague to Cheapside?'

'I am not sure the plague *is* on Cheapside. It probably killed the Howard family, but the other "cases" are likely to be something else. Unfortunately, houses are being shut up anyway – unless their occupants can afford to bribe the searchers.'

'I was afraid that might happen. I shall raise the matter with the Privy Council, although I cannot see sensible solutions emerging from that direction. My colleagues' main concern about an outbreak is whether the Court will have more fun in Oxford or Salisbury.'

'What will you do, sir? Stay or go?'

'I do not want to leave my lovely house,' said the Earl, looking around fondly. 'But I shall have to follow the King. I cannot have my detractors running the country without me. They would have us declaring war on more innocent nations.'

The interview over, Chaloner went to collect Temperance. She was surrounded by manly admirers, and was reluctant to leave.

'Will you not present me to the Earl, Tom?' she simpered, to a chorus of amused titters.

'You will have a better time with us,' she was assured fervently by Kipps.

'I know it is a liberty,' said Chaloner, once he and Temperance were in her coach, clattering back along Piccadilly, 'but would you mind not telling anyone that your curtains are currently hanging in the Earl's Great Parlour?'

'Yes, I would,' said Temperance, pulling out her pipe and beginning to create another anti-plague miasma. 'It will make a tremendous tale to tell my patrons. They will love it.'

'They will,' acknowledged Chaloner. 'But it will do him terrible harm.'

'So what? If the shoe were on the other foot, would he spare me?'

It was a valid point, because the Earl would not hesitate to condemn a woman who had followed Temperance's career choices. 'But if he falls, I will lose my post. And I have debts . . .'

'You presume too much on our friendship, Thomas!' cried Temperance angrily. 'First, you beg me to take some ancient page because you cannot afford to keep him. Then you drag me to the home of a man I despise.

288

And now you demand my silence on a matter that will afford my customers a good deal of innocent amusement. Is there anything else you want of me?'

'It will not be *innocent* amusement, Temperance. It is—'

'I will do it,' interrupted Temperance sullenly. 'But the next time I want a favour, you had better be ready to oblige, no matter what it transpires to be.'

The Earl had given Chaloner some letters to deliver to White Hall, and Temperance insisted on dropping him there, not for his convenience, but for the delight of taking her personal carriage inside the palace. He was quick to alight and disappear, disliking the attention the vehicle immediately attracted. He handed his letters to the clerks, then went to the Queen's apartments, to see whether Hannah had managed to sell their belongings and find them a cheaper place to live.

'I sold the furniture and took the money to Taylor,' she said, leading him to a small chamber where they could talk. 'But he says we still owe him four thousand pounds, although I *swear* I only borrowed three from Backwell. The Duke thinks we will never pay it off, because Taylor will just keep raising the threshold.'

'The Duke may be right,' said Chaloner gloomily.

'In desperation, I offered Taylor our Lely,' she went on, 'but he said it is virtually worthless, because it is only of me.'

Chaloner was stunned Taylor should have made such a hurtful remark. 'That was ungentlemanly.'

'Yes, it was. He might be Master of the Goldsmiths' Company, but he has much to learn about manners. Anyway, I took the portrait back to Lely and asked if he would put someone else's face on it instead. I think he was offended. Regardless, he refused.' Hannah looked away and Chaloner saw the sparkle of tears. 'Taylor declined the painting, but he accepted my pearls.'

Chaloner's heart went out to her. 'Perhaps we can buy them back one day.'

Hannah attempted a smile, although it was one without hope. 'That would be nice. Yet my sorrow gained us one thing – the Queen saw me crying later, and wheedled the tale out of me. She has arranged for her equerry to take our house. We move out tomorrow.'

'Good. And tell Gram to go to Temperance – she will give him work.'

'She is a kind lady,' sniffed Hannah. 'Are you sure she cannot lend us some money? I would far rather be in her debt than Taylor's. Or Shaw's for that matter. At Silas's soirée, he indelicately reminded me that I forgot to pay for that flageolet. I expect such vulgarity from bankers, but he is music-seller to the Court!'

'But a banker once.' Chaloner shot her a dour look. 'And please do not tell him any more lies about the alum mines. It is unfair.'

'I cannot help myself. He and Lettice are such ridiculous people.' She saw Chaloner's disapproving expression. 'I will put matters straight when I next see them. Of course, that is unlikely to be very soon . . . However, I must go; I left the Queen with Brodrick, but her English has improved recently, so she understands a lot more of what people say to her.'

She hurried away before Chaloner could ask what manner of conversation the Earl's rakish cousin liked to hold with Her Majesty. He walked back through the palace bowed down with worry. Buckingham was right: Taylor *would* keep raising the threshold of the debt, as that was how usurers worked, and he and Hannah might never be free of the man. His thoughts snapped back to the present when someone touched his shoulder. It was Williamson, who reared away in alarm when Chaloner whipped around with a dagger. Swaddell hastily stepped between them.

'What have you decided about my offer?' asked Williamson, once he had regained his composure.

Much as he disliked the notion of working for the Spymaster, Chaloner knew he had no choice. And if Williamson reneged or Taylor refused to relent? He pushed that possibility from his mind – he did not want even to consider it. 'I will do as you ask,' he said quietly.

Williamson's eyes narrowed in suspicion. 'And your conditions?'

Chaloner had not expected to be allowed to stipulate any, so he hastened to list a few. 'That you eliminate *all* Hannah's debts, but especially the one with Taylor. Permanently.'

'Yes, yes,' said Williamson impatiently. 'That is already understood. We have also made a start on that other business – one of my clerks recommended Baron to Lord Lauderdale, who has opened negotiations for a set of bed hangings. But is there anything else?'

Chaloner was tempted to ask for a post with the intelligence services – one that would see him sent overseas where he could return to the work at which he excelled – but there was always a danger that Williamson would avenge himself by giving him especially dangerous assignments. He settled for a more practical request instead.

'That if anything happens to me, you will look after Hannah. She might need a protector.'

'Done,' said Williamson promptly. 'And here are *my* terms. You will report to me and only to me. And you and Swaddell will combine forces to—'

'No!' Chaloner did not want an assassin for a partner. 'I always work alone.'

'Not this time – there is too much at stake. That is the deal, Chaloner. Take it or leave it. However, it is in both our interests to cooperate, so I hope you will be amenable.'

Chaloner glanced at Swaddell's bland face, but could not read whether the assassin objected as much as he did. He inclined his head, and the Spymaster smirked his triumph.

'Good. I suggest you begin by visiting Baron. At once, if you would not mind.'

Williamson had the luxury of a private coach to take him back to his lair in the Palace of Westminster, but Chaloner and Swaddell were faced with a lengthy walk to Cheapside. Swaddell suggested a hackney carriage, but Chaloner demurred – he could not pay his share, and was loath to put himself in the assassin's debt.

'I know what you think of me,' said Swaddell as they trudged along the Strand. Chaloner sincerely hoped not – they could hardly be expected to work together if he did. 'And you are wrong.'

'I am?'

'I might have dispatched the odd worthless rogue in the past, but there were always good reasons – patriotic reasons. However, Baron and his rabble kill without compunction, and they murder good men as well as fellow criminals.'

'What good men?'

'Abner Coo.' Swaddell looked away. 'He helped me

292

when I was attacked in the Fleet rookery last year. He took me in and repaired me, even though I was disguised in rags at the time, and as far as he was concerned, he would never be disbursed for his trouble. He was a fine person, and I liked him.'

'So did I,' admitted Chaloner.

'So although I also prefer to work alone, you represent my best chance of making Baron pay for Coo's murder. I am prepared to set my prejudices aside in the interests of justice, and I hope you will do the same.'

'Do you have any actual evidence that Baron killed Coo?'

'If we did, we would have arrested him already. But I feel his guilt in my very bones. You must know what I mean.'

Chaloner did, but in this case his hunch told him that Baron was innocent. 'Then why not eliminate him? I am sure you have plenty of experience on that front.'

Swaddell shot him a doleful look. 'Why do people have such a poor opinion of assassins? We do not dispatch just anyone, you know. We have rules and standards. And I would much rather see him convicted in a court of law.'

Chaloner was not sure what to make of that claim. 'Do your bones tell you whether he has murdered anyone other than Coo?'

'Well, Fatherton and DuPont were criminals who worked for him, while he would not be King of Cheapside if Wheler had not been stabbed. *Four* suspicious deaths, all within a few weeks of each other. It cannot be coincidence.'

'Perhaps not, but there are plenty more suspects for Wheler's demise – an angry client, Joan, the Taylor clan . . .'

293

'Yes,' acknowledged Swaddell, 'but Baron remains the most likely culprit, and I have learned not to overlook the obvious.'

He was silent for a while, then stepped suddenly into Maidenhead Alley, a dank ribbon of muck and weeds that was rarely used because it was a dead end. He beckoned Chaloner to follow. Common sense told Chaloner to stay on the Strand, but a ridiculous sense of bravado drove him into the lane's shadowy depths – he hated the notion that Swaddell might think he was afraid. All his senses were on high alert, and his hand rested on the hilt of his sword.

Very slowly, Swaddell reached for the dagger he carried in his belt and touched the blade to the tip of his forefinger. A bead of blood appeared at once, testament to its sharpness. Then he handed it to Chaloner, handle first.

'If our blood mingles, we will be bound by duty and honour. You will know that you can trust me, and I shall know that I can trust you.'

Chaloner regarded the small blob with rank suspicion. 'We used to do this in the army, but with rather more conviction – proper cuts, not pinpricks.'

Swaddell shrugged. 'Call me girlish if you will, but I have an aversion to hurting myself. Besides, the ritual does not call for great gouts of blood. A drop will suffice.'

'Is this really necessary?'

Swaddell looked him straight in the eye and held his gaze, the first time he had ever done so. 'Yes, for both our sakes. You will not betray an oath and neither will I.'

Chaloner had no idea whether that was true of Swaddell, but he would definitely not be able to trust the man if he refused, so he took the proffered knife and pricked his thumb. The moment it was done, the assassin grasped his hand and pushed both nicks together, holding them tight.

'I swear, by all that is holy, that we are now brothers,' he intoned. 'I will protect you to the utmost of my ability, and I will never do you harm. Now you say it.'

Chaloner obliged, although he added the caveat 'until the end of the investigation', unwilling to be tied to a truce for longer than was absolutely necessary.

'There,' said Swaddell, sheathing the weapon with satisfaction. 'It is done. Now neither of us needs fear a sly knife in the back.'

The very fact that he should have mentioned such a possibility made Chaloner wonder whether the oath was as sacred as Swaddell wanted him to believe.

Chapter 10

Chaloner was not sure if it was an act, but Swaddell seemed more easy in his company once they emerged from the alley and resumed their walk to Cheapside. The assassin began to chatter in a way he had not done before, confiding that he had never married because he was afraid of what he might do if his wife proved unfaithful, and that he too had an uncle, evidently the black sheep of the family, who had fought for Parliament during the wars.

'I am sorry about your financial difficulties,' he said, eventually deciding he had talked enough about himself. 'Well, it is fortunate for Williamson, as it gave him a lever to encourage you to help us, but no man should be in debt to another. It makes him vulnerable.'

'I know,' said Chaloner drily.

'Of course, you are not the only one. Half the Court owes money to the goldsmiths. Taylor is the least patient with defaulters – when payments are missed, he demands heirlooms instead.'

'Yes,' said Chaloner, thinking about Hannah's precious pearls.

'He had a hatpin from May, a jewelled scent bottle from Chiffinch, a Genovese watch from Brodrick . . . the list is endless.'

'I am surprised Williamson does not rein him in. Taylor's claims on his clients' debts might be legal, but his methods of collecting them are not.'

Swaddell gave a short bark of laughter. 'We have tried, believe me. For example, when we heard how Carteret was robbed of his buttons we offered to prosecute the culprits, but he told us it had never happened – he did not have the courage to challenge Taylor. No one does.'

'Because Taylor would avenge himself by raising the interest on their loans,' explained Chaloner, aware that *he* would not trust the legal system to see justice done either.

'Partly, but also because they cannot afford to be exposed as paupers. All courtiers rely on credit, and grocers, coal merchants, glovers, tailors, lacemakers and brewers would never deal with them again if they knew the real state of their finances. And that would do no one any good.'

Chaloner shook his head in disgust, and almost voiced what Thurloe would have said – that it would never have happened in Cromwell's day. He stopped himself in time, suspecting that the assassin would not appreciate being regaled with Parliamentarian sentiments.

'Have you learned any more about what might be planned for Tuesday?' he asked. He saw Swaddell's face immediately go blank, and sighed his irritation. Their so-called truce had not lasted long. 'If we are to work together, then we need to share information. Otherwise, we might as well pursue our enquiries separately.'

Swaddell inclined his head. 'Forgive me. Like you, I am unused to talking freely about my work. The rumour about Tuesday came to us via a Court milliner named Howard.'

'He told Backwell, too,' recalled Chaloner. 'But he is a dead Court milliner now. He was among the first to be put into quarantine with the plague, and died with his entire household.'

'Yes, which was unfortunate. You see, he was a gambler, and to offset his losses at the card tables, he did certain favours for Baron. When we found out, we offered him a choice: prison or passing us information. He chose the latter, and his death is a bitter blow.'

Chaloner stared at him. 'So he might not have died of the plague at all? He and his family might have been murdered to put an end to this arrangement?'

'It is tempting to say yes, and have Baron charged with the deaths of seventeen people. But the truth is that their maid really did catch the disease, and she carried it into their house.'

'What favours did Howard do for Baron?' asked Chaloner, wondering what an impoverished milliner could provide that the felon would want. 'Make him free hats?'

'He was a forger of some renown, so he provided Baron with counterfeit documents – mostly bills of receipt, so that stolen goods could be passed off as legitimate.'

Like the ones the Earl had been given, thought Chaloner. 'I do not suppose he replicated promissory notes, did he?'

'He might have done,' replied Swaddell warily. 'Why?'

Chaloner pulled out the ones he had found in DuPont's room. 'Could these be his work?'

298

Swaddell stopped walking to study them. 'Yes, I recognise the ink and the paper. Foolish man! He could never have cashed these – bankers remember who deposits large sums of money.'

'He must have been desperate,' said Chaloner, wondering how many others had been driven to frantic measures in an attempt to pay their debts.

Swaddell put the documents in his pocket. 'I shall take these to Williamson, although he will ask how you came to have them.'

Chaloner saw no reason to lie. 'I found them in DuPont's lodgings in Bearbinder Lane. He must have stolen them from Howard's house – which I know he raided, because I found a note from Fatherton, ordering him to do so.'

Swaddell nodded slowly. 'Howard mentioned an attack by curbers, so you are probably right. However, none of this helps us understand what is planned for Tuesday.'

They walked in silence through the alleys that radiated out from St Paul's, then entered the cathedral itself – the route they had taken meant it was quicker to cut through the building than fight past the busy stalls outside. It was hazy with the smoke of candles, which caught the sunlight that streamed through its windows. As always, Chaloner was struck by the contrast between the ethereal splendour of its soaring pillars and vaulted ceiling, and the tawdry booths that had been erected in its aisles.

It rang with sound, being a market as much as a place of devotion, and while the vendors were supposed to confine themselves to religious paraphernalia, sellers of secular books, purveyors of food and even basket-makers had set up shop. There were animals, too – cats in search of mice, dogs, a monkey and even a parrot, while sparrows and pigeons fluttered overhead.

'That crack was not there when I was here last,' remarked Chaloner, gazing upwards.

Swaddell tutted. 'The place is falling about our ears, but London would not be London without it. I hope the King does not order it demolished, so that Christopher Wren can build something else in its place. I do not like the look of his designs.'

Nor did Chaloner, although he could not bring himself to say so – he did not want the assassin to think they had something in common. They exited the cathedral, and began to walk down an alley that would take them to Cheapside. It was deserted except for three men coming from the opposite direction. Chaloner glanced absently at them, then stopped dead in his tracks: they were the trio who had visited Tothill Street and intimidated Hannah; one still limped from being stabbed in the leg. He glanced behind him. Two more men blocked the only other way out.

'You might want to leave,' he told Swaddell. 'I doubt this is going to be friendly.'

Swaddell shot him a hurt look. 'I have just sworn an oath to protect you. However, we are in luck, because I happen to know the leader of this little rabble. His name is Joliffe, and our paths have crossed before. Leave him to me.'

'Piss off, Swaddell,' growled Joliffe as the assassin approached. 'This does not concern you.'

'I am afraid it does,' replied Swaddell. 'Chaloner is a colleague and I do not abandon those. You are the one who should disappear, as I doubt you want Williamson vexed with you.'

'Williamson holds no sway here,' said Joliffe contemptuously. He turned to Chaloner. 'Mr Taylor wants more of the capital on your wife's loan – what she gave him earlier is not enough. So either pay or we shall get it from her.' He leered. 'Perhaps we will get something else from her, too.'

There was a blur of movement as Swaddell hurtled forward, and two of the five reeled away with cries of agony before they could so much as think of reaching for a weapon. Joliffe's reactions were quicker. He whipped out a cutlass and launched himself at the assassin, leaving his two remaining cronies to deal with Chaloner.

The ensuing skirmish was dirty and brutal, but did not last long. Nursing a slashed arm, Joliffe backed away, then fled. Two were able to follow, but the pair who had been injured in Swaddell's initial attack could only lie on the ground, groaning.

'No,' snapped Chaloner, lunging forward to stop the assassin from cutting their throats. Swaddell punched away from him, and there was a flash of something dark and very unpleasant in his eyes, although it was quickly masked.

'I swore an oath to protect you,' he said tightly. 'They insulted your wife. They should pay.'

'Joliffe insulted her and he has gone. We cannot afford a war with Taylor – we do not want to add to our troubles by encouraging vengeful henchmen to slip knives in our ribs.'

Swaddell grinned rather diabolically. 'No? I always find it adds a certain spice to life.'

The Feathers really was a seedy place, thought Chaloner, as he entered it with Swaddell at his side. The floor was sticky underfoot, and the whole place reeked of smoke, sweat, burned fat and spilled ale. The lamps were not quite dim enough to disguise the decrepitude of the furnishings or the shabbiness of the clientele. The half-naked women gyrating on the dais had a worn and weary look about them, and the band made noise rather than music.

'You are not dead yet, then,' said Poachin, making Chaloner jump by speaking in his ear. 'The last time we met, I thought you might have the plague.'

'No one need worry about the plague in here,' said Swaddell, looking around in distaste. 'Not with all these tobacco fumes.'

Poachin inclined his head, as if he had been given a compliment. 'The safety of our customers is ever our first concern. Of course, if your government had its way, all Cheapside taverns would be closed. Unless they cater to the wealthy, of course, in which case they would be left open to trade as they please.'

'The plague measures apply to everyone,' averred Swaddell. 'Rich *and* poor.'

Poachin laughed harshly. 'Liar! They are Williamson's way of attacking Baron's business interests – by depriving him of customers. Or maybe he just does not like Cheapside, because its people are not afraid to say what they think about corrupt and greedy bankers.'

'Here is a curious alliance – the minions of Clarendon and Williamson together,' remarked Baron as he emerged from the fug with Doe, Oxley and Jacob at his heels. He regarded Chaloner with exaggerated disappointment. 'I expected better of you, especially after my offer.'

'What offer?' asked Swaddell suspiciously.

'The same as the one I made you,' replied Baron smoothly. 'A place in my service.'

'Which I did not accept,' said Swaddell, rather quickly. 'I am happy where I am.'

'Of course you are,' said Baron evenly. 'But perhaps you would state your purpose here and leave – your presence is making our customers uneasy.'

It was true: several patrons had made themselves scarce when the assassin had arrived.

'There have been too many deaths near Cheapside of late,' began Swaddell. 'Wheler, Coo, DuPont, Fatherton, Milbourn, the Howard household. Naturally, we are concerned.'

'So are we,' said Baron. 'But we have no more to tell you now than when you were last in here asking about them.'

'Wheler,' said Swaddell with a reptilian smile. 'You may like to know that our enquiries have continued apace, and we have made some excellent progress.'

'Good,' replied Baron, although Chaloner thought Poachin looked uneasy. Doe leaned against the wall and folded his arms in an attitude of boredom. 'I miss him, God rest his soul.'

'Do you?' asked Swaddell. 'His death has allowed you to grow very powerful.'

'Yes,' acknowledged Baron. 'But that does not mean I had anything to do with his murder.'

'You can tell us *nothing* to help solve these crimes?' pressed Swaddell.

'No,' replied Baron. 'Although that should not trouble you, given that you just claimed you are making excellent progress.'

'There is a rumour that something terrible will happen on Tuesday,' said Swaddell, turning to another matter. 'What will it be, do you think? Another fire? More deaths?'

303

'Those sound like acts of God,' said Baron. 'And although I claim a close association with the Almighty, I am not party to all His plans.'

'I thought you ran Cheapside,' said Swaddell. 'Yet much goes on without your say-so.'

Doe reached for his dagger. 'Are you questioning our—'

'Our visitors mean no offence,' interrupted Baron, resting his hand on the younger man's shoulder. He smiled, although there was a hard glint in his eyes: Swaddell's remark had rankled. 'But perhaps it is time they left.'

'Just one more question,' said Chaloner, resisting when Jacob attempted to manoeuvre him towards the door. 'Why did DuPont come to Bearbinder Lane to die? You must have tried to find out, given that his journey put the people under your protection at serious risk.'

'Perhaps what you should ask is: why was he in Long Acre?' Doe grinned tauntingly.

'Meaning what?' demanded Chaloner.

'Meaning nothing,' said Poachin quickly. 'And now if there is nothing else . . .'

Chaloner stood his ground. 'I learned something disturbing about my Earl's curtains today. They are stolen property – removed from Hercules' Pillars Alley by curbers.'

'Impossible,' said Baron, meeting his eyes evenly. 'Or are you accusing me of providing your master with pilfered goods?'

'He had better not be,' snarled Doe, fingering the knife.

'They were identified by burns and stains,' persisted Chaloner. 'Seven pairs were stolen from Temperance North's club, and seven pairs were delivered to Clarendon House.'

304

Baron's expression was sly. 'Then arrest me. Or is your master loath to bear witness against me in a court of law? After all, he will not want it said that his fine new mansion has been furnished with items filched from a brothel.'

Baron was astute, thought Chaloner, to have anticipated the Earl so well.

The rest of the morning and the first half of the afternoon was an even greater waste of time than the interview with Baron. Chaloner and Swaddell trawled Cheapside talking to anyone who would pass the time of day with them, but learned nothing useful. At three o'clock, Swaddell went to report to Williamson, leaving Chaloner to his own devices. A bell was tolling when the spy passed St Mary le Bow, announcing the death of a mother and a child whose ages were the same as his first family. It disturbed him more than he would have expected, and he ducked into Shaw's shop in the hope that a few minutes' browsing would jolt him from his despondency.

'Grace Rugley and her baby,' Shaw was telling a customer, whose vast wig could belong to no one other than Misick. 'They died this morning. The neighbours say it was childbed fever, not the plague, but the house is shut up anyway. Chaloner! Do come in.'

The shop was quiet, but there was a lot of noise emanating from the cellar, where work was continuing to deprive Oxley of a convenient overflow for his cesspit. Muddy footprints trailed across the floor, and Lettice was on her hands and knees trying to scrub them off.

'Mr Yaile only needs to fill his big leather bucket eight more times,' she reported, 'and the work will be complete. Thank heavens! He is a nice man, but all this dirt . . .'

'Of course, it takes an age to load the contraption,' grumbled Shaw. 'So he will be here until at least Wednesday. I am heartily sick of the disruption.'

They all leapt in alarm at the sound of smashing glass. Chaloner's first thought was that Yaile was the culprit, but a ball bounced across the floor, and he saw Oxley's brats through the broken window, laughing gleefully. They made obscene gestures when he went to inspect the damage, and it was clear that an apology was not on the cards, let alone an offer to pay for repairs.

'I doubt you will find a glazier to mend it,' said Misick sympathetically. 'They are reluctant to visit Cheapside at the moment, lest they catch the plague.'

'Them and our patrons,' said Shaw glumly. 'Courtiers do not come here now, and this morning we were asked to stay away from White Hall until the danger is past. We are losing custom hand over fist.'

'Well,' said Lettice in an attempt to cheer, 'if the glaziers will not visit us, then at least we will not have to pay them. You can nail some wood over the hole instead.'

'Then do it quickly,' advised Misick. 'Or you will lose everything to curbers.'

Lettice smiled. 'Fortunately, those do not operate around here – it is one of the things covered by the Protection Tax.'

'Is wilful destruction by Oxley's little cherubs covered by the Tax as well?' asked Chaloner.

'I doubt it,' sighed Shaw. 'And there is no point asking Oxley to pay. He will refuse.'

'Not if I do it,' said Chaloner.

'Oh, Lord!' gulped Lettice. 'If you coerce him, we shall know no peace at all. Please let the matter go, Mr Chaloner. Better one broken pane than twenty.'

'Much as I should love to see you trounce the fellow, Lettice is right,' agreed Shaw. 'You may make him pay this once, but we shall lose in the long run. Indeed, I imagine this is revenge for Slasher. He knows we did not let her out, as we had alibis for the "crime", but he suspects we were behind it.'

'It is a sorry state of affairs,' said Misick. 'So how about a little music to raise our spirits? I composed a piece for four voices last night, and I should love to hear it performed.'

'Oh, yes!' Lettice clapped her hands in delight before turning to Chaloner. 'We would ask you to join us, but you are hoarse, so we shall commandeer Mr Yaile instead.'

Loath to be excluded, Chaloner offered to accompany them on the virginals. He was not as good a keyboard player as he was a violist, but he was certainly able to manage the simple chords that Misick had written. Moreover, Yaile transpired to be an unusually pure alto, while Misick was a rich bass who complimented Shaw's tenor. With Lettice on the top line, the voices were perfectly balanced, and Chaloner soon forgot the ache of sadness for his first family, his disquiet about working with Swaddell, and his irritation over the Oxleys' anti-social antics.

They were interrupted when the door opened and Taylor strode in. Chaloner tensed, anticipating either another demand for money or a vengeful tirade about Joliffe, but the banker only stalked to the middle of the room, where he stood looking around in haughty disdain, his Plague Box under his arm. The force of his personality was almost palpable, but it was a dangerous, unsteady power, and nothing like Silas's sunny charm or even Baron's coarse charisma. Chaloner looked for Joan or Evan, but the banker appeared to be alone. Misick started towards him, but a glare from his patient stopped him dead in his tracks.

'I have never liked this house,' Taylor declared. 'It belonged to Wheler – the man Baron murdered. Now it is Joan's, but perhaps I shall encourage her to sell it. It smells of sewage.'

'Do you have evidence that Baron killed Wheler?' asked Shaw. 'Because if so, you must inform Spymaster Williamson. He will—'

'My plague worms told me,' said Taylor, eyes blazing manically. 'Baron enticed Wheler to White Goat Wynd, and thrust a knife between his ribs.'

He grabbed a quill from a table, and demonstrated by lunging at Shaw, who cowered away in alarm. Then he began to dance with it, feinting first at the shelves and then at a viol.

'*Punta riversa!*' he shouted gleefully. 'Not even the King can fence as well as I.'

'Where were you when Wheler died?' Chaloner asked, in the hope that questioning him while he was in the grip of one of his turns would shake loose a clue.

'At home,' replied the banker, then whipped around to address Lettice. 'I am *very* fond of Joan, you know. She is too good for Randal, and I wish I had wed her myself. I would have done if I had known what an excellent financier she is.'

'Oh,' said Lettice, blinking her confusion at the confidence. 'How nice. Is she—'

'Plague worms,' interrupted Taylor in a low hiss. He tapped the box. 'This is full of them, and I could destroy London just by opening the lid. But I shall not do it . . . yet.'

'Good,' said Misick, advancing cautiously. 'Shall we go home now? It is not—'

'It is safe with me,' declared Taylor, hugging the box with one hand and waving the feather with the other. 'But no one else can be trusted, not even Joan. She does not understand, although she is a lovely lass.'

'Does not understand what?' asked Chaloner.

'Evil,' replied Taylor, eyes blazing again. 'It is always with me. I carry it in my box and in my heart. It is a black blight that will eat us all.'

Lettice shrieked when he dropped the feather, reached into his belt and pulled out a handgun. Misick dived behind a bookcase, Shaw stood rooted to the spot in terror, and Chaloner ducked through the cellar door. The knife from his sleeve dropped into his hand, ready to lob if Taylor looked as though he was going to shoot someone.

'Please put it down,' begged Misick from his hiding place. 'And we will send for—'

'I cannot abide earwigs,' declared Taylor, before pointing the gun at the ceiling and pulling the trigger. Lettice screamed again as plaster showered down, while Misick whimpered his fear and Shaw looked as though he might faint from fright.

Then the front door flew open, and Evan stood there, Joan at his heels. Both were breathing hard, and there was a veritable army of henchmen behind them.

'There you are, Father.' Evan assessed the scene quickly, including the fact that the gun was spent and so posed no further danger. 'Teasing Joan's tenants. You really are impish these days.'

'Prosperity,' declared Taylor, tucking the box under his arm and stalking out, pausing only to hand the useless dag to Joan. She took it warily. 'It is all that matters.'

'He loves a good riddle,' said Evan with a feeble smile, signalling to the henchmen to hurry after his sire. Then he approached Chaloner and lowered his voice. 'And do not think we will overlook what you did to Joliffe. Indeed, I have already repaid you with a nasty surprise.'

'What—' Chaloner began, but Taylor began haranguing a group of bemused apprentices, obliging Evan to race outside and stop him.

'You should not let him rove about on his own,' Misick was saying sternly to Joan. 'He needs rest, not the opportunity to hare up and down Cheapside with a loaded pistol.'

Joan regarded him coolly. 'He is Evan's responsibility, not mine. I am too busy trying to ensure that business does not suffer while he is . . . unsettled.'

Misick shot her a reproachful glance before hurrying after his patient, pulling a tonic from his bag as he went. Joan followed more sedately, although only after she had glanced around the shop in a proprietary manner, as if to ensure that her tenants were looking after it properly.

'Heavens!' gulped Lettice, glancing up at the hole in the ceiling. 'And to think that he is Master of the Goldsmiths' Company, and holds the financial future of London in his hands.'

'He is only a lunatic half the time, according to Misick,' said Shaw, mopping his brow with a hand that shook. 'Poor Joan. She cannot know from one moment to the next whether his fiscal decisions are brilliantly intelligent or dangerously insane.'

Chaloner left the music shop unsettled both by the knowledge that the country's economy was in the hands of a part-time madman and by the prospect of being ambushed by the 'nasty surprise' that Evan had arranged. But there was nothing he could do about it, so he sold one of his daggers and used the money to buy drinks for anyone willing to talk to him about his investigations. By the time he ran into Landlord Lamb in the Green Dragon, he was tired, frustrated and far from sober.

'You should go home,' advised Lamb. 'No good will come of excessive drinking. But I am glad we met as it happens, because I have something to tell you. You asked after DuPont when we last spoke. Well, I have since learned his real name. A chap from St Giles mentioned it in my coffee house yesterday. Georges DuPont was really George Bridge, and he hailed from Chelsey, not Paris.'

'*Pont* does mean bridge in French,' mused Chaloner, struggling to concentrate through his alcoholic fog. He remembered what the boy Noll had said in Bearbinder Lane: that DuPont's accent tended to disappear when he was in his cups. 'So he was an imposter?'

'More liar than imposter, apparently – he did it to make himself seem more interesting. It worked, because women loved him, and fell at his feet by the cartload.'

'Did he speak French?' asked Chaloner.

Lamb nodded, then surprised Chaloner by switching to it himself. 'Like a native, which is why he could carry off his deception with such aplomb.'

Chaloner reeled towards Tothill Street, trying to remember when he had last had so much to drink. He did not let himself become inebriated very often, as it left him vulnerable, and the sane part of his mind told him that it had been a stupid thing to do in the middle of an investigation, especially given Evan's earlier threat.

311

Fortunately, there were no sly attacks in the dark, and he reached home unmolested.

He stepped inside his house to find it devoid of furnishings – although the Lely still hung splendidly over the fireplace – and his footsteps echoed hollowly as he tottered along the hall to the kitchen. Hannah was there, sitting on the floor with a pile of papers. She leapt to her feet and rushed towards him, hugging him so fiercely that it almost sent both of them flying.

'What is the matter?' He was not usually greeted so effusively.

'Evan,' she sniffed. 'He told our other creditors that we have no money, and they came here in a pack, all shouting and angry. Gram had gone to see Temperance, so I was alone. They forced their way inside and—'

'Did they hurt you?' asked Chaloner anxiously, supposing this was Evan's 'nasty surprise'.

'No, but they frightened me half to death.'

Chaloner was tempted to storm to Goldsmiths' Row and demand satisfaction with pistols at dawn, but Evan was unlikely to accept such a challenge, and all it would achieve was letting Evan know that his spiteful scheme had worked. He took a deep breath to calm himself.

'What other creditors? I thought your only serious debt was to Taylor.'

Hannah looked away. 'There are a few that I have not liked to mention . . . But I spoke to them before you came home from Hull, and they said they did not mind waiting. However, I suspect Evan invented some lie about us defaulting, so when I could not give them money when they demanded it today, they took what little furniture I had kept back, most of our clothes, the utensils from the kitchen . . .'

'But not the Lely?' Chaloner stared up at it. In the gloom, its subject looked deranged with her wild hair and oddly shining eyes. Perhaps they had considered it too frightening.

'No one seems to want it, although I cannot imagine why. I am told it is a good likeness.'

'They do not appreciate its quality,' said Chaloner gallantly.

Hannah sniffed again. 'Evan is a pig. He accosted Winfred Wells – the courtier who looks like a sheep – and effectively *stole* an onyx cameo of Queen Elizabeth. In broad daylight! And even the Duke has creditors hounding him. He said he has never known anything like it, and feels that the common people do not respect the aristocracy as they once did.'

'Well, these hedonistic courtiers only have themselves to blame,' said Chaloner, a Parliamentarian notion he would never have voiced had he been sober.

For once, Hannah did not argue, and he was suddenly gripped by the conviction that she had not yet told him the worst of it. He waited, and eventually she blurted, 'They took your viols.'

He stared at her, while the cold hand of dread gripped his heart. '*What?*'

'I think it was the lacemaker, but I cannot be certain.' Hannah gestured to the papers on the floor. 'Some of the mob left a note of what they took, but others just came to loot. And there is no receipt for the viols.'

Chaloner felt weak at the knees, and looked for a chair to sit on, but there was none.

Hannah put her arms around him. 'We will get them back, Tom. And we move out of this house tomorrow. That will save a lot of money.'

Chaloner regarded her uneasily. 'We are not going to live with the Duke, are we?'

Hannah's smile was wan. 'He offered, but his finances are not much better than ours. I plan to sleep in the Queen's apartments until this business is over, but obviously you cannot join me there, so you are going to stay with our housekeeper in Shoreditch. It is all arranged.'

'Crikey,' breathed Chaloner.

'It is kind of her, because she does not like you. But she says she will not see you homeless.'

Chaloner took a deep breath, fighting an almost overwhelming urge to smash something – it was perhaps fortunate that there was nothing to hand except the Lely, which was too high to reach. He would never forgive Evan for organising the invasion, but worse, he was not sure whether he would ever forgive Hannah. Then there was a knock on the door, and Gram walked in.

'How was Hercules' Pillars Alley?' asked Hannah, clearly grateful for the interruption.

Gram was all offended indignation. 'You probably do not know this, miss, but that particular building is a brothel.' He lowered his voice to a shocked hiss. 'A *bawdy house*!'

'Temperance calls it a gentleman's club,' said Hannah.

'She can call it what she likes,' sniffed Gram primly, 'but it is full of loose women and the kind of fellow who does not deserve to be called a gentleman. I would sooner starve than work in a place like that.'

'Then you *will* starve,' said Chaloner, irked by the ingratitude. It had not been easy to persuade Temperance to take him, and he felt the page had no right to be choosy.

'Look on the bright side, Gram,' said Hannah kindly. 'She takes very good care of her staff.'

314

'I shall never know,' declared Gram haughtily. 'Because I am *not* working there. My mother would turn in her grave.'

'I shall ask whether the Duke has anything for you,' said Hannah, not very hopefully.

'Thank you.' Gram softened as he looked at Chaloner. 'I did something for you today, sir –I asked questions about the villains who stole your viols. They went to a shop on Foster Lane, where the things were exchanged for cash. You can go there and get them back.'

'Not with a few shillings and some coffee-house tokens,' said Chaloner bitterly.

Gram winked. 'There are more ways of getting stuff than paying for it, and I have a lot of experience in such matters. You have been good to me, and I should like to return the favour.'

So Gram was a thief, thought Chaloner. Perhaps he had decided he was too old for climbing through windows and scrambling down chimneys, so had retired to a more respectable profession. It was a pity that life as a page had not worked out. However, while it was tempting to reclaim his viols by sly means, Chaloner was disinclined to add burglary to his list of things to do. Large musical instruments were not jewels or money, and it would not be easy to spirit them away without being seen. Moreover, if they were the only items missing, it would be obvious who had taken them.

'We shall go tonight,' determined Gram, ignoring Chaloner's weary shake of the head. 'We could be there and back again before you know it.'

'Can you get my best blue dress at the same time?' asked Hannah hopefully. 'And perhaps the clock? And a chair or two would be nice.'

315

'Of course,' said Gram airily. 'We can steal a cart to put it all in. I know where one is usually left, and the three of us could pull it easy.'

'No,' said Chaloner, afraid they might actually do it. 'We would end up in prison.'

'So?' countered Gram. 'At least we would get fed.'

Chaloner was unwilling to stay in Tothill Street when there was nothing to eat, nowhere to sit, and no wood for a fire. He mumbled something about business for the Earl, and left Hannah and Gram making wild plans to redeem their losses by crime. Fortunately, neither was inclined to put their schemes into action that night, and he hoped the cold light of morning would remind them that she was unlikely to continue as lady-in-waiting to the Queen if she was caught stealing.

He wandered aimlessly, the loss of his instruments a dull ache in his heart. He found himself back on Cheapside, but had no desire to pursue his enquiries in the taverns and alehouses he passed. He met Silas near White Goat Wynd, and although he was not usually in the habit of unloading his problems on friends, he could not help himself. Silas listened gravely until the sad tale was told, then escorted him into the Bull's Head near the Standard, where the landlord obligingly provided ale – Taylor apparently owned that tavern, too, because there was no question of Silas paying for it.

'Do you want an accomplice when you raid the shop, Tom? Obviously, it would be better to buy the viols back legally, but as neither of us has any money . . . I feel responsible, given that it was my brother who precipitated all this nonsense.'

'Your father,' corrected Chaloner, knowing he should

316

not have more to drink, but too depressed to be sensible. 'Your *mad* father.'

'He does seem out of sorts. I will try to reason with him again, although he was furious the last time I attempted it, and threatened to disinherit me – which would be irksome, given that I do not want to be Keeper of Stores for the rest of my life, and a legacy is the only way I shall escape.'

He changed the subject before Chaloner could ask what else he saw himself doing, and began to talk about his next soirée. Then they drank more ale, and Chaloner stared morosely out of the window at the Standard.

It was busy, because it was the end of the day, and tradesmen had gathered there to sell off their remaining wares. Fountains and wells were good places for such activities, as locals needed to collect water for washing and cooking, so there was always a ready supply of customers. Chaloner watched a farmer offload two plaits of onions to a pinch-faced housewife, and frowned as something began to scratch at the back of his mind. Then the answer came like a lightning bolt, and he slammed his hand on the table in understanding.

'Onions at the Well! DuPont – George Bridge – told Neve that he had his information from Onions at the Well, and Everard thought it had something to do with St Giles. The answer is obvious now I think about it! DuPont met an onion-seller by a watering hole in that parish. How many wells are there in the area? Six? Eight?'

'One.' Silas shrugged at Chaloner's startled expression. 'It is a slum, Tom. No one cares about its residents' health or comfort. Where are you going?'

'St Giles,' replied Chaloner, making for the door.

317

'Are you sure you should? Rumour is that it is full of the plague.'

It was a risk, but following the lead allowed Chaloner to forget the heartache of losing his viols, and he was determined to see where it took him. However, he made no objection when Silas fell into step at his side, and they walked in silence through the darkening streets.

The St Giles rookery was a mass of filthy hovels and tenements near one of the finest churches in London, rebuilt forty years before by a wealthy noblewoman. There were more recent graves in its cemetery than there should have been, and Chaloner looked away when a sombre procession emerged and aimed for a newly dug hole.

'Plague,' whispered Silas. 'God help us.'

Entering the rookery was not easy. Williamson's soldiers had been charged to minimise comings and goings, and were taking their duties seriously. Chaloner and Silas were reduced to hiding in the back of a cart, but once they were inside, it did not take them long to locate the area's one and only source of fresh water.

It was noisy, busy and smelly, with vendors desperate to sell the last of their wares before people went home. Some were so pushy that spats broke out, and the atmosphere was tense and unfriendly. A few discreet enquiries took them to the man they were looking for – a disreputable villain who was disliked for his violent temper and refusal to let other purveyors of vegetables hawk their goods on 'his' patch. He was known only as Onions, and fought furiously when Chaloner and Silas manhandled him down a lane so they could talk undisturbed.

'I think you *will* chat to us,' said Silas mildly, once Onions' objections had petered into a furious silence. He took a knife from his belt and inspected its blade. 'It would be rash to refuse.'

'DuPont,' began Chaloner. 'Or should I say George Bridge? He was going to sell intelligence about the Dutch to my employer, the Earl of Clarendon.'

Relief suffused Onions' face. 'Is that why you are here? Thank God! I thought you were . . . never mind. If you are Clarendon's men, you will have come for these. But they will cost you.'

He held out a sheaf of letters. They were in Dutch, and a quick glance through them told Chaloner that they were the missives written by Meer and his wife to their children.

'Four shillings each.' Onions glanced around uneasily. 'But you cannot tell anyone you got them from me, or I am a dead man. They are reports on the Hollanders' fleet.'

'How do you know?' asked Chaloner.

Onions tapped the side of his nose. 'I learned Dutch when I was in the navy.'

'Then you will understand that they are nothing of the kind,' said Chaloner in that language. 'Do you have any more "reports" or is this it?'

Onions' blank look told him all he needed to know. He repeated the question in English.

'I can get more,' said Onions eagerly. 'Like DuPont, I know where all the foreigners live. But you have to keep my name out of it.'

'Who are you afraid of?' asked Chaloner, watching the man glance around fearfully again.

'No one,' lied Onions. 'Well? Do we have a deal? But do not try to cheat me, because DuPont was *my* man, and I know exactly what prices he agreed with Clarendon.'

319

'How can you be sure which Dutchmen are spies?' pressed Chaloner. 'They might be innocent citizens trapped on the wrong side of the Channel.'

'I just know,' declared Onions. 'And I can snag whatever is within easy reach of a window – I am every bit as good with a hook as DuPont was. You will not regret treating with me, I promise. However, there is one condition: you have to come here to collect these reports, because I am not going to the Feathers again.'

'Why not?' asked Silas. 'It is a little shabby, I grant you, but—'

'Because dangerous types haunt it,' interrupted Onions. 'I went there with the news that DuPont was sick. I thought Baron would be pleased that I was looking out for one of his curbers, but . . . well, suffice to say that I shall not be going *there* again.'

'Is that why Coo visited DuPont in Long Acre?' asked Chaloner. 'Because you told Baron, and he sent his tame physician on an errand of mercy?'

Onions nodded. 'But DuPont should never have gone to Bearbinder Lane after the physician had left. He might have lived if he had stayed home to rest.'

'He had the plague,' said Silas. 'So I doubt it.'

Onions' eyes widened in alarm. 'The plague? No! It was just a falling sickness. Of course, he did spend the previous night with the whores in the Crown tavern, and several of them are dead of the pestilence . . .'

He could be persuaded to say no more, and Chaloner took some satisfaction in informing him that his services would not be required for the war effort.

Chaloner felt cheated as he and Silas left the rookery, annoyed that he had expended so much time and energy tracking down what transpired to be nothing more than petty profiteers. He should have listened to Lamb and Grey: they had said that no one who frequented St Giles would have much of interest to report, and they had been right. Moreover, DuPont had virtually told Neve that the scheme was a fiddle, but the upholder had not understood the 'nods and winks' – he had only nodded and winked back. It was obvious why DuPont had approached Neve, of course: he knew the upholder to be corrupt for the simple reason that he had chosen to do business with Baron the felon.

Silas was also disgusted. 'I thought I was doing something vital to our nation's security, but it transpires to be a grubby little plot to swindle Clarendon. Do you do this kind of thing often, Tom? I cannot imagine your family are impressed.'

He made his excuses to part company shortly afterwards, still muttering his displeasure. Chaloner roamed restlessly, and when he reached Fleet Street, he saw a cart on which a hastily wrapped body had been loaded. He did not want to walk past it, so he ducked down Hercules' Pillars Alley to visit the club. Preacher Hill started to refuse him entry, but stood aside with a gulp when he saw the dark expression on the spy's face. The club was not as busy as usual, and Maude explained that there was a case of plague further down the lane, so regular patrons were afraid to come.

'But I know the searcher,' she went on. 'She is a drunken sot, and it is not plague at all. Her incompetence has condemned a family to forty days of isolation – and us to losing customers. I shall have strong words to say when I next see her.'

'Perhaps it should be physicians who decide,' suggested Chaloner. 'Like Coo.'

'Dr Coo,' said Maude, with a sudden smile. 'He treated

321

my bunions, and was a lovely man. The villain who shot him deserves to hang. What kind of person pulls out a handgun and—'

'The handgun!' exclaimed Chaloner, jumping up so suddenly that claret spilled all down his coat and breeches.

Maude regarded him suspiciously. 'What about it?'

'I saw it quite clearly, and tracing it may lead me to Coo's killer. I meant to ask the gunsmiths on St Martin's Lane, but it slipped my mind – which was stupid, as it represents a good line of enquiry. I will do it first thing in the morning.'

'It is Sunday tomorrow,' Maude reminded him. 'They will be closed.'

'Not these gunsmiths.'

Maude regarded him soberly for a moment, then reached into her bodice and produced a polished stone on a chain – it was a cabochon, also known as a carbuncle, and was thought to have special powers. 'This is an almandine garnet, and will not only keep you safe from plague, bad dreams and poison, but will also prevent melancholy. And you seem sad today.'

Chaloner was careless with jewellery and would almost certainly lose it. He had enough to worry about without risking the wrath of a formidable matriarch, so he refused it, but Maude was insistent.

'Wear it around your neck, inside your shirt,' she ordered. 'You may return it when you have solved Dr Coo's murder.'

Chaloner was too tired and drunk to do battle, and resignedly did as she ordered. When she left him to return to her duties, he wandered into the parlour and listened to the patrons grumbling about their bankers. They had also heard about a looming disaster for Tuesday, although no one seemed to know what form it might take.

322

When the subject turned to the King's latest amour, he went to hear the musicians who were playing in the ante-chamber, which did nothing to improve his temper as it made him long for his own viols. He drank more wine, but it sat badly with the ale he had swallowed earlier, so he decided he had better leave before he made himself sick.

Outside, he aimed for Lincoln's Inn, entering that great foundation through a little-used gate at the back, so as to avoid disturbing the night-porter. He lurched across Dial Court, and although he tried to tread softly as he climbed the stairs, Thurloe was waiting with a gun in his hand when he reached Chamber XIII.

'I think you had better sit down,' said the ex-Spymaster drily, when Chaloner tried to lean on the doorjamb and missed. 'And tell me how I can help.'

'I am past salvation this time,' said Chaloner bitterly. 'Williamson has blackmailed me into working for him with Swaddell as a partner; I am expected to live with our housekeeper in Shoreditch; and some of Hannah's debts have been settled with my viols, although we still owe Taylor's Bank a fortune.'

'Your viols?' asked Thurloe, immediately under-standing the worst of it. 'I am sure we can buy them back again. I have some money that—'

'No,' interrupted Chaloner shortly. 'I am not borrowing anything else, especially from friends. Perhaps I should ask Baron for lessons in curbing, so I can learn how to steal.'

'You do not need lessons. You were very good at it when you worked for me.'

'Documents and letters. I never stole jewels or money. Or viols.'

'I am glad to hear it,' said Thurloe. 'It would have been most unethical. But I think you had better stay here

323

tonight – you should not be roaming about the city in that state. I shall fetch you a blanket, and you can sleep by the fire. Enjoy it while you can, because this will be my last night in the city for a while – I leave at first light. Do you have anything to report before I go?'

'I tried to talk to Randal, but he would not listen. I think he will publish his sequel, because he is delighted by the trouble the first one has caused. Its controversial nature means it has sold extremely well, and has probably earned him a fortune.'

'Then you must stop him by fair means or foul,' ordered Thurloe. 'I will not see the widow of my poor old friend maligned a second time.'

Chapter 11

When he awoke the next day, Chaloner was immediately aware of a cold, sinking feeling in the pit of his stomach. It took him a moment to recall why, but then everything came crashing back – his viols had gone. He tried to think about his investigations, but he was queasy from the amount he had drunk the previous night, and could not concentrate. He was, however, aware of a hard knot of resentment against Hannah, Taylor and Evan. He tried to ignore it, but the feeling persisted, so he was surly company when Thurloe emerged from his bedchamber looking fresh, neat and sprightly in his travelling clothes.

Thurloe rang a bell, and a servant brought his idea of a hearty breakfast – thin slivers of bread and meat, a boiled egg cut into sixths, and a dozen raisins. Yet even this was more than Chaloner felt like eating, and he only picked at the elegant morsels that were passed his way. While he did so, he told Thurloe all that he had learned since they had last met – his report the previous night had been too terse and disjointed to count as a proper briefing.

'So,' concluded Thurloe, 'you still need to warn Randal against publishing his sequel; you have made no headway into the deaths of Wheler, Coo and Fatherton; you have determined that DuPont was no spy but you do not know why he staggered to Cheapside—'

'He had a visitor shortly before he left Long Acre,' put in Chaloner, a little defensively, 'one who wore a plague mask, hissed and gave him money.'

'—you have no idea who burned Fatherton's house or Milbourn's printworks; and your Earl is unlikely to have his remaining curtains.'

'He does not want them now he knows the others were stolen from the club. But it all pales into insignificance when compared to what else is in the offing – war, plague, economic collapse and a disaster scheduled for two days hence.'

'This poor city,' said Thurloe softly. 'Sometimes I wish I were Secretary of State again, because this would not have happened under Cromwell.'

'And how would he have prevented an outbreak of plague?' asked Chaloner acidly.

'By deploying his army to implement the necessary precautions. That is the beauty of a military dictatorship, Thomas – the instant availability of armed enforcement. Williamson's so-called troops are a pale imitation of the real thing. But time is passing, and I shall miss my coach if I dally much longer. You will not give up on speaking to Randal, will you?'

Chaloner shook his head. 'Swaddell might help. He knows how to persuade people to his point of view.'

'No,' said Thurloe sharply. 'I do not want Randal killed, just stopped. Try going to your coffee house and cornering Fabian Stedman. He is a printer with Royalist leanings – perhaps he will know where Randal is hiding.'

Chaloner nodded. 'And if that fails, I shall whisk Evan

326

down a dark alley, put a knife to his throat and ask *him* for answers.'

'Do not waste your time, Tom. He does not know. I spoke to him myself yesterday.'

'Do you think he told you the truth?'

'Yes – he is not clever enough to deceive me.'

Chaloner stood. 'But first, I need to ask the Trulocke brothers about the gun that killed Coo.'

'They are away until tomorrow,' said Thurloe, 'but there is much you can be doing in the interim. Speak to Stedman first, then go to Southwark.'

'Why there?'

'Because I have learned that one of Fatherton's tenants in Bearbinder Lane was a pewterer named Kelke, who now resides with his fiancée. I do not have a precise location, but she lives near the Bear Garden. Perhaps he will know who killed his landlord.'

Thurloe's coach left from Holborn, so Chaloner accompanied him there, and experienced a sharp pang of loss as the vehicle rattled away in the gathering light of the new day. The ex-Spymaster might be gone for weeks, and he would miss his calm friendship and practical advice.

When the carriage was out of sight, Chaloner went to nearby St Andrew's Church, where worshippers were gathering for their Sunday devotions. He was not a particularly devout man, but records were kept of those who did not put in an appearance at the weekly services, and he had no desire to be branded a dissenter. He watched the verger write his name in the attendance book, then slipped out through the vestry when no one was looking.

He walked down Fetter Lane, noting that it had been washed during the night in the hope of thwarting the plague. Two of Williamson's soldiers had been charged to supervise the operation, but they and the labourers were standing in a friendly cluster, smoking, so Chaloner wondered how well it had been done. By contrast, Fleet Street was too wide and busy to be scoured, so bonfires had been lit to fumigate it instead.

He entered the Rainbow coughing and sat at his usual table, but those already there immediately eased away from him.

'Fire,' he managed to croak. 'Not the plague.'

'It is not the hacking that bothers us,' said Speed the bookseller, very coldly. 'It is the fact that you are on intimate terms with Spymaster Williamson. Farr told us how he came in here and greeted you like an old friend.'

'He is not a friend, believe me,' muttered Chaloner.

'He must be the most unpopular man in London,' said Farr. 'His plague measures are detested by rich and poor alike; he has failed to gather proper intelligence for the Dutch war; he never caught Wheler's killer; and he lets bankers ride roughshod over everyone. Including members of Court and the government.'

Chaloner was tempted to say that it was hardly a spymaster's job to contain financiers, and that while Williamson had been charged to implement the plague measures, he had not devised them himself. But he held his tongue, unwilling to defend 'the most unpopular man in London'.

'The situation with the goldsmiths *is* disgraceful,' agreed Stedman. 'The rogues will beggar us all if they have their way.'

Farr grinned maliciously. 'I had my revenge on Williamson for foisting his oily presence on us on Friday. I served him lukewarm coffee and told him there was no sugar. But Chaloner did something even better.'

'I did?' asked Chaloner uneasily.

'You gave him a cold, and he is now confined to his bed. It serves him right! I lost a lot of business that day, and several of my regulars have declined to return lest he appears uninvited a second time. He has no business imposing himself on decent establishments.'

The conversation moved on to omens at that point, and Chaloner sipped his coffee. It was cold and tasted of soot. Was Farr trying to drive him away, too? As Stedman was looking bored with a subject that had been aired so many times before, Chaloner took the opportunity to question him.

'Did you know Thomas Milbourn, the printer who published *The Court & Kitchin* and who was burned to death when his shop was set alight?'

'Yes, but he is not dead.' Stedman lowered his voice. 'He is staying at the Green Dragon on Cheapside – incognito, lest there are Roundheads who want to finish the job. I saw him last night.'

Chaloner blinked, startled by the fact that Stedman should so casually provide information that he had been struggling to acquire for a week. But such was the life of an intelligencer.

Chaloner had agreed to meet Swaddell outside the Rainbow at ten o'clock, but that was a good two hours hence, so he determined to put the intervening time to good use by following up on what Stedman had told him. He walked towards the Green Dragon briskly, crossing the filthy Fleet River, which was even more noxious that day as there had been no serious rain for days and its fetid banks were exposed. Then he climbed Ludgate Hill to cut through St Paul's.

The cathedral choir was singing an anthem by Palestrina, so he stopped to listen. He was not the only one – Misick, Shaw and Lettice were also standing in rapt appreciation, all three in their Sunday best. Misick's wig had been brushed and powdered, so it was bushier than usual, and his white flea powder coated not only his clothes, but those of his companions.

'Albertus Bryne will play the organ soon,' Shaw told Chaloner, once the singing had finished. 'He has velvet fingers, and his recitals are a delight.'

'Join us,' invited Lettice. 'It is sure to be a treat, and you look as though you need some restorative music. You seem unwell.'

Chaloner could not bring himself to mention his viols, even though he was sure that the music-sellers were among the few who would understand.

'He only has a cold,' said Misick, in the callously unsympathetic manner adopted by many *medici* towards the sufferings of their patients. 'Cheer up, Chaloner. It could be worse – at least you do not have the plague. Unlike the Oxley family.'

'Emma became sick last night,' elaborated Shaw, 'and their house was shut up this morning.'

'It is a terrible thing,' said Lettice softly. 'We took them food last night, and Mr Oxley had to take it by lowering a rope through an upstairs window.'

'Is it really plague?' asked Chaloner. 'Not something else?'

'It really is,' said Misick soberly. 'I examined Emma myself.'

'Did you?' Chaloner took a step away.

'From a safe distance – it is irresponsible to invite trouble, even though my Plague Elixir will protect me. However, I saw the buboes quite clearly from the door.'

330

'Oxley is terrified,' said Shaw. He tried to keep the gloat from his voice, but did not quite succeed. 'He wanted to abandon his family in order to save himself.'

'He is not a very nice man,' whispered Lettice. 'His poor children . . .'

'Bryne is starting,' said Misick suddenly. 'Hush! No talking now.'

They craned forward eagerly, leaving Chaloner wishing he could stay and listen with them, especially when the first strains of a particularly fine fantasia by Scheidemann began to echo through the nave. Reluctantly, he turned and headed for the exit, although the melody filled his mind long after he could no longer hear the organ.

Since Chaloner's last visit to the Green Dragon, enormous braziers had been installed in every room, which produced great clouds of plague-repelling smoke. He had no idea what was being burned in them, but he was not the only one coughing, so he hoped they were doing some good. There were also sacks of medicinal herbs hanging from the rafters, which represented something of a hazard to customers, who were obliged to duck and weave their way through them.

Chaloner exchanged his coffee tokens for a jug of buttered ale, and engaged Landlord Hanson in conversation. Hanson was suspicious when Chaloner asked after Milbourn, but caved in almost eagerly when spun a yarn about the printer being owed five shillings.

'He has not paid his rent yet,' Hanson said to explain himself. 'I took him in as a favour to Randal, whose father owns this tavern, but I did not agree to do it for nothing. He is over there.'

Milbourn was huddled so deeply into the shadows that

he was virtually invisible. He was smoking a pipe, and Chaloner had an impression of heavy eyebrows and a weak chin.

'Poor man,' said Hanson. 'He is not only hunted by Roundheads, but by the banks – he borrowed heavily to start his business, but now his workshop is destroyed, he cannot repay them.'

Chaloner might have felt more sympathy had Milbourn not printed a pamphlet that slandered a helpless old lady. He was about to go and question the man when a remark from Hanson snagged his attention.

'What?'

'I said Milbourn is not the only one who lost all in a fire. Old Fatherton has also not been seen since his tenement burned down, and although Baron's trainband swear the house was empty, there are many who suspect he was inside.'

'You knew Fatherton?'

'He came here for a drink occasionally. I always noticed, because he was a thief, and I had to watch him lest he picked my regulars' pockets. He came the day before the fire.'

'Alone?'

'No, with two other men, but they kept their hats on, so I never saw their faces, although I can tell you that one reeked of onions. He was nothing, though, and it was the third who was in charge. I could tell by the way the other two bowed and scraped to him. The three of them muttered and plotted all evening.'

'How do you know they were plotting? Did you hear their discussion?'

'I caught snippets of it when I went to collect the empties. They were vexed, because some ruse to cheat the Lord Chancellor had gone wrong, although I cannot imagine why they imagined such an eminent personage would deal with the likes of them.'

So the scheme had involved four players, thought Chaloner: DuPont, Fatherton, Onions and someone who sounded like their leader. He recalled Onions' unease and his disinclination to return to Cheapside. Had he heard about Fatherton, and was afraid he would suffer a similar fate if he showed his face? So who was the leader? Baron? It would certainly explain why Onions was keen to keep a low profile.

'You say you did not see the third man's face, but did you notice anything else about him? His clothes? His size? Did he have an unusual gait?'

Hanson raised his hands helplessly. 'He kept himself wrapped in his coat all night. People do these days, as they hope it will protect them against the plague. Yet there was one thing . . .'

'Yes?' asked Chaloner, when the taverner trailed off.

'He hissed between his teeth once or twice. I think he was nervous. And who can blame him? I would not have been easy in company with such a pair either.'

'Hissed?' pressed Chaloner, recalling Landlord Grey's testimony: that DuPont's mysterious visitor had made a similar sound in Long Acre, shortly before the curber had made his final, fateful journey to Bearbinder Alley.

But Hanson could add no more, so Chaloner went to talk to Milbourn. The printer glanced up in alarm when the spy sat on the bench next to him.

'Your neighbours think you are dead,' said Chaloner, after he had assured the man that he meant him no harm. 'Incinerated in the fire that destroyed your workshop.'

'I wish I were,' said Milbourn miserably. 'It would be

333

better for everyone, including poor Hanson, who will never be paid for keeping me here. Randal promised to settle the bill, but he prefers to spend his money on himself.'

'Randal.' Chaloner pounced on the opening. 'I want a word with him.'

'You and a hundred others. Half to kill him, the rest to shake his hand. Which are you?'

Chaloner thought it best not to say until he knew the printer's views on the matter. 'Why did you agree to publish such a contentious work? Surely you could see it would bring you trouble?'

'Because Randal offered to eliminate half my debt to his father in return. But I should have refused, because how shall I pay the rest now that I have no printing presses? I cannot even sell the building, because it is a burned-out shell. I am ruined!'

'You cannot find work elsewhere?'

'Not as long as there are angry Roundheads itching to trounce me. I shall be trapped here for the rest of my life.'

Hanson would not be pleased to hear that, thought Chaloner. 'I understand that you printed advertisements for Baron instead of paying the Protection Tax. But he did not protect you, so he must be liable for the damage. Have you asked him about it?'

'Of course. Yet even though it was an obvious case of arson, he maintains that it was an Act of God, and he refuses to compensate me.'

'If I were you, I would leave London. Go to another city, take a new name and start afresh. Taylor probably charged you too much interest on your debt anyway, so it would serve him right to lose the rest.'

Milbourn gave a sickly grin. 'Perhaps I will. And

perhaps I will come back in a year with a scurrilous pamphlet about Randal. I *hate* him for destroying my life.'

'Do you know what possessed him to write such a poisonous tirade?'

'I do.' Milbourn's expression turned spiteful. 'He told me in confidence, but I do not see why I should keep his secrets now. His dearest ambition was to be a cook, much to the chagrin of his father, who thinks it a lowly profession compared to banking. It was Randal's proudest day when he was hired as a patissier in White Hall.'

'When was this?' But Chaloner already knew the answer. 'During the Commonwealth?'

Milbourn nodded. 'He served under Philip Starkey, but he had no talent, so Starkey refused to let him loose on the desserts. And Mrs Cromwell took one bite of a cake he had made, and decreed that he should never be allowed near an oven again. The pamphlet was Randal's revenge on them both.'

'Starkey did not tell me that Randal worked under him,' said Chaloner a little irritably.

'Randal enrolled under a false name – John Smith. He could not use Taylor, as they were a Royalist family, and his application would have been rejected.'

'So Starkey does not know that John Smith is really Randal Taylor?'

'Not a clue, although I am surprised he has not guessed. "John Smith" was livid when he was relegated to peeling vegetables, and made all manner of threats.'

'I really do need to talk to Randal,' said Chaloner. 'And while it will not help your troubles, I can promise to make our discussion very uncomfortable for him. It will be revenge of a sort.'

Milbourn brightened. 'Very well. But only if you break his legs.'

'Will you settle for me telling Spymaster Williamson where he is hiding instead?'

Milbourn considered, then nodded. 'Although you will have to swear to keep my name out of the matter – with Randal *and* Williamson.'

'You have my word.'

'He has a mistress who lodges on Bread Street. He is staying with her.'

'A mistress? He has only been married a few weeks.'

Milbourn smirked. 'Yes, and Joan will be outraged when she finds out. Perhaps you could mention his infidelity to her – you refused to break his legs, but she will not.'

Chaloner passed Oxley's house on his way to Bread Street, but the door and lower windows had been boarded up, and one of Williamson's watchers and two trainband men were stationed outside. An upper window was open, and a rope dangled out, ready to be tied to the next basket of food, but there was no sign of the occupants.

'All three have it now,' said the watcher when Chaloner asked for a report.

'Three?' asked Chaloner. 'There should be four.'

The watcher grimaced. 'The girl escaped, and I hope to God she is not carrying the disease or all our efforts will have been for nothing. Oxley tried to tell us that his wife was just sick from too much ale, but it was a lie. Misick saw buboes when he opened the door.'

The bell began to toll at that moment, and he and Chaloner automatically began to count, to learn whether the victim was man, woman or child, but the ringer was only announcing the start of the next Sunday service.

It told Chaloner that it was later than he thought, so he postponed his interview with Randal, and hurried to Fleet Street, where he found Swaddell waiting. The assassin was in his usual black, his pristine falling band so bright that it almost hurt the eyes. Chaloner pulled him away from the Rainbow quickly, lest any of the regulars should happen to notice who he was meeting. Luckily, Farr rarely cleaned his windows, so they were coated in a greasy brown sheen that made it all but impossible to see through them from the inside.

'I contacted some of my informants after we parted yesterday,' said Swaddell, then added glumly, 'But they told me nothing we do not know already.'

'Mine did,' said Chaloner, a little smugly. 'We are going to visit Nicholas Kelke, who is staying with his fiancée near the Bear Garden, across the river in Southwark.'

'Why?'

'He was one of Fatherton's tenants in Bearbinder Lane. Perhaps he will know who shot his landlord – and tried to have me incinerated. If he implicates Baron, Williamson may have enough evidence for an arrest.'

'The problem with Fatherton is that we do not have a body to prove our case – the fire burned so hot that it was never found. We would sooner charge Baron with *Wheler's* death.'

Chaloner was irked. 'Then what do you suggest we do?'

Swaddell pondered the question, gazing absently to where three of Williamson's men were struggling to light an enormous bonfire, but eventually he raised his hands in a shrug. 'You are right – Kelke is worth a try. How is your cold? You still sound hoarse.'

337

'It is all these damned conflagrations.' Chaloner coughed as a waft of smoke swirled around them. 'London's air has always been foul, but your plague measures have made it worse.'

'Not just ours. Many folk are starting to deploy their own, and some are positively toxic.'

He insisted on taking a hackney, because he did not want flying cinders to soil his clean falling band, and Chaloner agreed once he learned that Williamson would be footing the bill. While they clattered along, Swaddell talked amiably about his evening, which seemed to have revolved around sitting at home with his cat. It seemed altogether too innocent a pastime for an assassin, and Chaloner found himself wondering whether the animal had been encouraged to dispatch mice or birds for its owner's entertainment.

The driver took them along Thames Street, which was busy with the usual market carts; trading was technically forbidden on the Sabbath, but it was a rule that many ignored, especially those with perishable goods to sell. The road ran parallel to the river, and reeked of it, a pungent stench of seaweed, sewage and salty mud. Gulls circled overhead, their raucous cries inaudible over the rattle of so many wheels on cobbles. Then they were jolting down Fish Hill towards the Bridge itself. As always, traffic slowed to a standstill as it funnelled through the narrow gateway.

The tide was at full ebb, water roaring deafeningly through the great arches below, and Chaloner fancied he could feel the entire structure vibrating, although he knew that was unlikely from inside a coach. They crossed the open section known as The Square, the buildings of which had been destroyed by fire thirty years ago and

338

never replaced, then plunged into gloom when they reached the first of the houses and shops. These formed a thin tunnel, and towered overhead rather alarmingly, some to a height of five storeys. There was only just enough room for two vehicles to pass, and Chaloner winced when their driver edged left to avoid a wagon coming from the other direction, rasping his wheels along someone's window sill. He could see the residents sitting within, but scrapes were so commonplace that none of them looked up.

Then they jolted off the Bridge and turned right, moving slowly along Bankside. Southwark was very different from the city across the river, and was characterised by scruffy houses, rough taverns, seedy brothels and streets that never saw a brush or a bucket of water. Reeking pails of night soil were hurled from windows on a daily basis, and if the stinking mess was not washed away by the rain, it stayed until it rotted.

Shops and stalls were doing a roaring trade, but although the doors of St Mary Overie were open to entice parishioners inside, few bothered. No clerk was on duty to record names, and it occurred to Chaloner that he should take lodgings in Southwark if he did not want his own religious activities – or lack of them – monitored. Street performers were out in force: jugglers, singers, dancers and fortune-tellers, all desperate to earn enough for a meal or a bed for the night. Ragged children formed menacing packs, darting close to snatch at clothes and pockets, or to lob mud and manure if their victims attempted to fend them off.

Chaloner and Swaddell alighted at the Bear Garden. This was a place where tired and shabby bruins were tethered to stakes while dogs were sent to attack them.

Chaloner had approved of Cromwell's edict forbidding such hideous pursuits, but the ban had been lifted at the Restoration. He was glad to note that the posts were free of tortured animals that day, although patches of fresh blood on the ground told him that there had been plenty of 'sport' the previous night.

'Right,' said Swaddell, glancing around in distaste. 'Shall we start with that tavern over there? It looks like the kind of place that would appeal to the likes of Fatherton's lodgers.'

His insistence that people should answer questions on Spymaster Williamson's authority did not get them very far, so they were reduced to wrestling potential informants down alleys and putting knives to their throats. With Chaloner, the threat was hollow, as he rarely did more than prick, but Swaddell had to be restrained from doing serious harm. Chaloner hated working with such a violently unpredictable man, and it was a relief when they finally cornered someone who was able to tell them that Kelke's fiancée lived in a tumbledown cottage overlooking the river.

Swaddell hammered on the front door, while Chaloner went to the back, where he easily intercepted Kelke, whose response to the knock was to crawl out through a window. He bundled the pewterer back inside, and opened the door for Swaddell.

The house was tiny, with a single room on the ground floor that served as parlour, kitchen and bedroom for the elderly woman who dozed by the fire, presumably Kelke's future mother-in-law. The other residents slept in a loft reached by a ladder, although no one but Kelke was at home that day.

'We have questions,' said Swaddell in his silkiest voice, which made the pewterer – a puny, undersized man with bad teeth and two bandaged hands – quail in terror. 'Answer, and we shall all be happy. Refuse, and I will kill the crone.'

Chaloner was shocked, sure Swaddell meant it. So was Kelke, because he began speaking so quickly that his words tumbled over themselves in their haste to be out.

'Yes, I worked for Fatherton in Bearbinder Lane. I did curbing in my spare time, like all of us who roomed there. He told us where to go and when, but on orders from . . .'

'From Baron?' asked Swaddell, when he trailed off.

Kelke stared at him with frightened eyes. 'Christ help me! You will see me dead.'

'No one will know the information came from you,' promised Chaloner, although if Kelke believed it, he was a fool. He and Swaddell might keep the secret, but they had not been subtle in determining Kelke's hiding place, and word might well get back to the King of Cheapside.

'Yes,' whispered Kelke. Swaddell's eyes gleamed in triumph.

'What happened the day George Bridge died?' asked Chaloner. Kelke looked blank. 'Georges DuPont – George Bridge was his real name.'

'Was it? I am not surprised – his nose was too small for him to have been a real Frenchman. And when he was drunk, he sounded just like you and me.' He looked Chaloner and Swaddell up and down, then muttered, 'Well, like me.'

'So what happened that day?'

'He arrived at Bearbinder Lane sweating and groaning. Fatherton sent for Dr Coo, who said he had visited DuPont earlier that day and that he had plague. Well, none of us stayed long after we heard that verdict, I can tell you! I came straight here and—'

'Why did DuPont drag himself all the way from Long Acre?'

'For a free cure. Baron buys medicine for anyone took sick on Cheapside, and plague remedies are expensive.'

Chaloner was not sure he believed it, but for the first time he saw light at the end of the tunnel, and solutions began to come together in his mind. He just needed a few more details . . .

'Why did DuPont keep rooms in both places?' He recalled how Doe had taunted him for not knowing the answer, which had told him it was significant.

Kelke looked as though he would refuse to answer, but Swaddell smiled at him. Kelke blanched at its reptilian nature and began to babble again.

'Because he stole from over there, too. He had friends in St Giles, see, and they helped him. He was of the opinion that it is wise to have two separate bases of operation. I would do the same, but my pewtering keeps me busy during the day.'

Chaloner regarded him thoughtfully for a moment, then began the analysis that would tell him whether his tentative conclusions were right. 'It was you who set the fire in Bearbinder Lane. Your hands are bandaged, and I wager anything you like that they are burned.'

Kelke affected insouciance, although his eyes were uneasy. 'So what? There was no one in the building – except Fatherton, and he was already dead. Shot. I saw his body . . .'

'It was not empty,' said Chaloner softly. 'I was in it.'

Kelke gaped at him. 'You cannot have been! It was checked first, and we were told that no one was left inside except Fatherton, who was well past caring.'

'Told by whom?' asked Chaloner.

Kelke shrugged. 'The man in charge, but we all wore plague masks, so I never saw his face. And the masks muffled our speech, so I did not recognise his voice either, before you ask. We set our fires on each floor – I was in charge of the bottom one – and once they were going, we were ordered to make ourselves scarce. So we did.'

'You might have set the entire city alight,' said Swaddell accusingly.

'Never,' said Kelke with a flash of defiance. 'We were very careful, and the trainband were on hand to contain it with buckets of water and fire-hooks.'

'So who shot Fatherton?' asked Chaloner.

'Well, Baron, of course. Who else would leave a body in a house that was about to be burned down?'

'But *why* was the house burned down?' pressed Swaddell. 'It might have been old, but it was still bringing in rent. And do not say it was to get rid of a corpse, as I am sure Baron knows far less costly ways of disposing of those.'

'I think that was my fault,' said Chaloner. He shrugged at Swaddell's surprise. 'I asked whether the house was safe after DuPont had died in it, especially if the plague really is carried by invisible worms. Obviously, Baron took our conversation to heart and decided to eliminate a possible source of contagion.'

Swaddell turned back to Kelke. 'Who stabbed Wheler?'

'Joan, probably,' replied Kelke. 'Because she is part of the most powerful bank in London now that he is dead. She would not have dirtied her own hands but she knew plenty of killers through the trainband – killers who were once her husband's, but who are now Baron's.'

'But you do not know this for certain,' said Swaddell, disappointed. 'Then who killed Coo?'

'Baron, I suppose, in revenge for letting DuPont bring the plague to his domain. But if you go after him, you should be careful. He is a very dangerous man.'

'So am I,' said Swaddell softly. 'And Baron knows it. He will not harm us.'

Chaloner fully agreed with the first part, but was not at all sure about the last.

When they left Kelke, Swaddell wanted to go at once to report to Williamson, evidently of the opinion that they had just scored a major breakthrough. Chaloner did not think they had learned enough to warrant the journey, but accompanied the assassin anyway. Williamson was not at his Westminster lair on account of his cold, so they visited him at home. He lived in Hatton Garden, an exclusive area of handsome mansions that was removed from the stench and pollution of the city, yet still close enough to be convenient for business.

They were admitted by a servant, who led them to a sumptuously furnished bedchamber. The invalid lay in a vast four-poster bed wearing a frilled nightshirt and matching cap. He clutched a handkerchief to his nose, and the table next to him was full of patented medicines, all promising to relieve his symptoms. His wife, who had been reading aloud, seized the opportunity to slip away when they were ushered in, giving the impression that she was grateful to escape.

'You made me ill, Chaloner,' said the Spymaster accusingly, and sneezed.

'Not me,' replied Chaloner firmly. 'I was never obliged to take to my bed, so you must have someone else's sickness.'

It occurred to him that the Spymaster was simply less

hardy, or perhaps more inclined to cosset himself, but wisely did not say so.

'It is irresponsible,' Williamson went on sullenly. 'People with diseases should stay indoors, so they do not infect others. If I die from this, I shall haunt you.'

It was not an appealing prospect. 'Summon Wiseman,' suggested Chaloner, more from self-interest than compassion. 'He will sort you out.'

Williamson shot him an unpleasant look, but it slowly turned to pleasure as Swaddell began to summarise what they had learned in Southwark.

'Hah!' he exclaimed. 'We have Baron at last! Kelke will stand witness against him, and we shall be able to charge the King of Cheapside with murder and theft.'

'Kelke will disappear and you will never find him again,' predicted Chaloner. 'And even if you do, he did not actually *see* Baron kill Coo or Fatherton – he only assumed it. However, we might have solid evidence when I visit the Trulocke brothers tomorrow. I saw the gun that killed Coo, and Fatherton was shot by one with a similar bore – likely the same weapon. I hope the Trulockes will be able to identify its owner.'

'Why have you not mentioned this before?' demanded Swaddell accusingly. 'It is vital information. You should not have kept it to yourself.'

'I am telling you now,' said Chaloner coolly, suspecting that Swaddell and Williamson had a good deal that they were not sharing with him. 'And—'

'I will accompany you to St Martin's Lane,' said Swaddell, struggling to mask his irritation. He turned back to Williamson before Chaloner could object. 'We shall have Baron for arson, too, although he may have done us a favour by burning those particular houses.

345

Perhaps plague worms did lurk in them, but now they are purified.'

'It was reckless,' countered Williamson waspishly. He broke off for a bout of sneezing, and when he had finished, fixed Chaloner with reproachful and very watery eyes.

Swaddell had edged away from the bed to avoid being sprayed. 'If Kelke does vanish, we can use Baron's waning popularity to bring him down instead. People pay his Protection Tax to live in peace, but his domain seethes with unrest at the moment, particularly about the murder of Coo. If we put it about that Baron is the culprit . . .'

'People will refuse to pay him,' finished Williamson, nodding slowly. 'And without money he will be King of Cheapside no more. Yes! That might work.'

'We can use *The Court & Kitchin* as well,' Swaddell continued. 'Aggravate a few spats—'

'No!' hissed Williamson. 'Quarrels over Coo are one thing, but disputes between Royalists and Parliamentarians must be avoided at all costs. I do not have the troops to crush a rebellion, and we all know how fast the flames of revolt can spread once they are ignited.'

'Did you know that Randal has written a sequel?' asked Chaloner.

Williamson regarded him in horror. 'Christ God! You *must* stop him! So now you have three tasks, all urgent: stop Randal, depose Baron, and find out what is planned for Tuesday.'

These were tall orders, and Chaloner was not sure he and Swaddell could oblige. They took their leave, and he was relieved when Swaddell excused himself for a meeting with an informant, as it left him clear to pursue his own enquiries. However, it was difficult to buy information when he had no money, so he walked to Clarendon House to beg some from the Earl's accompter.

'Thank God you are here,' cried Kipps, seeing Chaloner enter the gate. The Seal Bearer's face was as white as snow. 'Someone has just murdered Neve.'

Chapter 12

There was pandemonium at Clarendon House. The servants were shocked and frightened, the Earl had locked himself in My Lord's Lobby, and there was an atmosphere of fear and uncertainty. The senior staff who should have taken control of the situation had retreated to the portico, where they formed a tight huddle. As he hurried past them to the hall, Chaloner wondered if they had chosen that spot so they could run to hide in the garden should more gunmen appear. Brodrick broke away from them to follow Kipps and Chaloner inside, where he immediately began to express his shocked indignation.

'I can scarce believe it! The villains just walked in and shot Neve at point-blank range. In broad daylight! Can you credit the audacity of it?'

'While he was hanging a Lely,' added Kipps in a hoarse whisper, as if this made the crime so much worse. He dabbed agitatedly at the spray of blood that covered the front of his otherwise immaculate uniform. 'I was there when it happened, Chaloner. Right next to him!'

'The rogues chose their time well – they struck when

the whole household was busy,' Brodrick went on. 'Otherwise they would have been challenged at the door.'

Chaloner frowned. 'What are you saying – that there were no guards on duty? The killers just walked straight in off the street? But why—'

'We were eating,' said Brodrick shortly, his aggrieved tone of voice indicating that the culprits had no right to strike at such an inconvenient time. 'The senior staff were dining at the back of the house, the Earl had a tray in My Lord's Lobby, and the servants were in the kitchen. The only ones not at table were Kipps and Neve, who were in the Great Parlour putting up the painting. Then a shot rang out . . .'

'There were two gunmen,' added Kipps. 'That I know for certain. But it all happened so damned fast! They shot Neve and were gone in a flash.'

Chaloner had seen no one running away when he had been walking along Piccadilly. There had been several coaches and pedestrians, but nothing out of the ordinary. He could only assume that the killers had fled west, towards Kensington.

'The Earl and Neve had quarrelled,' Kipps continued in an unsteady voice, 'because Neve wanted to resign. He was needed by his ailing mother in Devon, you see.'

'It was a lie,' spat Brodrick contemptuously. 'Even I could see that. The Earl was right – the real reason was that Neve had found himself a better paying post. My cousin had every right to be hurt and angry.'

'It was the Great Parlour curtains that started it,' said Kipps unhappily. 'The Earl ordered them taken down, which amazed us, as we all thought they were perfect. Neve offered to put them on the fire, but the Earl told him to leave them in the library instead.'

'Well, they did cost three thousand pounds,' sighed Brodrick. 'I would not have been happy destroying them either, and I do not blame him for wanting time to reflect.'

'Neve was vexed,' said Kipps. 'And sharp words were exchanged.'

Chaloner had no doubt that Neve had intended to take the drapery for himself, and cut his losses by selling it to someone else. Or perhaps by returning it to Baron. He could have retired on such a princely sum, so would naturally have been eager for the Earl to agree to their 'destruction'. Of course he had been irked when the Earl had demurred.

'It was then that Neve told the Earl he was going to leave,' said Brodrick. 'My cousin was piqued, and ordered him to stay.'

'His precise words were: if you abandon me, I will make sure that you never work for a wealthy household again,' elaborated Kipps. 'Afterwards, Neve told me that he was not sure what to do, but that he wanted to discuss the matter with you before making his final decision. God knows why – unless he wanted to see if you would be prepared to *forge* him a testimonial from Clarendon House.'

Chaloner winced. It had not occurred to him that the Earl would refuse to let Neve go.

'Then the Earl ordered Neve to hang his new Lely, and disappeared into My Lord's Lobby for something to eat,' continued Brodrick. 'The excitement over, the rest of us went to dine as well, but later than usual, which put us at the table the same time as the servants. As a consequence, certain duties appear to have been neglected . . .'

'Such as guarding the door.' Chaloner was disgusted. 'I cannot believe you were so remiss. You know the Earl

350

is unpopular, and there are many who itch to do him harm. What if it had been him who was shot?'

'We all thought Kipps was minding the entrance,' said Brodrick defensively. 'How were we to know that he actually went to the Great Parlour to gossip with Neve?'

'I assumed the servants would realise that the staff had been delayed by the quarrel, and would adjust their own mealtime accordingly,' snapped Kipps. 'And I did not go to *gossip* – I went to help with the picture. Neve was on a chair holding it, while I was telling him if it was straight. But suddenly, there was a tremendous crack, and his blood and brains spurted all over the Bishop of Winchester.'

Chaloner blinked. 'When did he arrive?'

'His portrait,' explained Kipps. 'I whipped around, and saw one man with a gun and another fellow behind him, so I dropped to the floor and covered my head with my hands. I heard their footsteps rattling away, but by the time I felt it was safe to look up, Neve was dead.'

'But you gave chase,' pressed Chaloner. 'If not to lay hold of them, then to memorise details that will allow us to track them down.'

Kipps regarded him coolly. 'I am a Seal Bearer, not a hunter of felons. Of course I did not hare about like some common ruffian! I had my dignity to consider. Besides, others had arrived by the time I had scrambled to my feet.'

'When we heard the bang, we had no idea it was gunfire,' added Brodrick. 'I thought it was the sound of the Lely being dropped, to be frank – Neve's revenge on the Earl for his harsh words. But then we arrived at the Great Parlour and saw him dead – and Kipps on the floor with his arms over his head.'

'I have sent for the palace guard,' said Kipps, while Chaloner reflected on the distances involved, and

351

concluded that the Seal Bearer must have spent a very long time cowering. 'They should be here soon, and then we shall all feel a lot safer.'

'But you must have seen *something* to identify the culprits,' said Chaloner, although not with much hope.

'Their hats shaded their faces and their clothes were dark,' said Kipps defensively. 'That is all I remember.'

'Did they speak at all – to you or each other?'

'One hissed something to his crony on the way out, but too low for me to catch his words.'

'Then can you describe the pistol?'

Kipps scowled. 'Yes! It had a nasty big muzzle and bullets came out of it.'

'Can you be more specific? This is important, Kipps. The Earl's enemies will make much of a murder committed in his home, and we need to find the culprit as soon as possible. You seem to be the only witness.'

Kipps stared at him. 'I suppose I am. I wonder if that is why . . .'

'Why what?'

Kipps swallowed hard. 'Why the gunman waved the dag under my nose as I lay on the floor, almost as if he *wanted* me to see it. I probably should have grabbed it, but . . .'

Chaloner refrained from remarking that he should, especially if it was spent and so posed no danger, but Kipps was clearly suffering pangs of conscience for his less than manly response and criticism would serve no useful purpose. However, Kipps had lied – the killers had not dashed in, shot Neve and raced off again, but had lingered long enough to make sure the sole witness to the crime had seen the weapon. Just as they had when Coo had been shot.

352

'So what did it look like?'

'It had an ivory butt and the barrel was etched.'

Chaloner's mind teemed with questions as he walked towards My Lord's Lobby. The most obvious suspect for the crime was Baron – Neve could not bleat the story of the stolen curtains in a court of law if he was dead. Yet Chaloner could not help feeling that Baron would have been more subtle, and it seemed uncharacteristically reckless to shoot the upholder in Clarendon House in broad daylight.

And what about the murder weapon, which the killers had taken time to brandish at the terrified Kipps? Chaloner had no doubt it was the same one that had dispatched Coo – and perhaps Fatherton, too. Had it just been an act of intimidation, a silent warning for the Seal Bearer to stay down until they had gone? Or had the intention been for him to see the pistol, and be able to describe it afterwards? In which case, its owner was unlikely to be the culprit, but someone who wanted him blamed.

Still mulling over the possibilities, Chaloner knocked on the Earl's door. He could hear his employer moving about within, but there was no invitation to enter, so he rapped again, harder.

'Go away,' came the Earl's trembling voice. 'Unless you are here to tell me that Neve's assailant has been caught, and is thus not in a position to shoot me.'

'It is Chaloner, sir. I have come to—'

He jumped when the door was whipped open. The Earl reached out, grabbed his arm and hauled him inside before slamming it closed behind them.

'Thank God!' he whispered, pale with fright. 'A man who will protect me! My other staff do not care – not one has come to ask after my well-being. Poor Neve! How long will it be before the culprits realise their mistake and come back to kill me – their *real* target?'

'You were not their intended victim, sir,' said Chaloner, thinking the staff might be more conscientious if the Earl did not treat them like dirt. 'First, I doubt any assassin would expect you to be hanging paintings, and second, you look nothing like Neve. He is slender, while you . . .'

The Earl regarded him frostily. 'I am what?'

'Usually wearing your robes of office,' finished Chaloner tactfully. He began to ask his questions before he could get himself into trouble. 'What did you see or hear?'

'I heard a crack, but I assumed something had fallen down. It did not occur to me that someone would be discharging firearms in my home. I hurried out, to see whether anything had been damaged, and saw . . .'

'Yes?' prompted Chaloner.

'Neve, lying dead on the floor,' finished the Earl in a whisper. 'And blood all over the Bishop of Winchester. It is a pity, as I had only just bought that painting. The Bishop sold it to repay some of his debts, and I had intended to give it back to him one day, as a gift.'

'You saw nothing of the killers?'

'They had gone by the time I arrived. What do you think happened? Could Neve have promised his services to someone else, who was then vexed when I refused to release him?'

'No, sir – Neve did not have time to tell anyone about your decision. After the argument, he went straight to hang your new Lely, and he was in company with Kipps until he was shot.'

'He had no business trying to end our contract,' said the Earl, shaking his head in bewilderment. 'He is the

354

finest upholder in the city, and Clarendon House deserves the best.'

'It was my fault, sir,' said Chaloner, supposing he could be open now that the truth could no longer hurt Neve. He outlined the dishonest arrangement the upholder had made with Baron, and the Earl listened in silence until he had finished.

'You should have told me,' he said accusingly. 'Then I would have dismissed him, and he would not now be dead. No wonder he was so good at securing bargain prices – he traded with thieves! And to add insult to injury, the rogue arranged for me to be palmed off with curtains that were stolen from a brothel! My enemies will crucify me!'

'They cannot, sir, not when they have been dealing with Baron themselves.'

'You managed to persuade them?' The Earl closed his eyes and breathed a heartfelt prayer of relief. 'So you think it was Baron who killed Neve?'

'It makes sense. Dead men cannot tell tales or stand witness in courts of law.'

'Yet you sound uncertain,' observed the Earl.

'I am. Baron is a ruthless and very successful criminal, and I strongly suspect that he *has* killed to further his ambitions. Yet I cannot shake the conviction that this is what we are meant to believe. I have no evidence to support my doubts, just a feeling . . .'

'Well, your feeling is wrong,' stated the Earl. 'It was me ending my association with him that sealed Neve's fate. I know about these professional felons. They grow nasty when crossed.'

'But Neve might have gone on to work for other wealthy households, whose masters are less scrupulous.

355

And why be so brazen about it, when Neve could have been dispatched quietly and his body buried with no one the wiser? His murder by Baron makes no sense.'

The Earl had no answer, so Chaloner took his leave and went to speak to the staff and servants, although it did not take him long to learn that no one had seen anything useful. Then he visited the Great Parlour, where the doors had been closed and a nervous guard stationed outside.

'I ordered it shut off,' said Brodrick, coming to talk to him again. 'I am not sure why, but it seemed the right thing to do. Neve is still inside, and nothing has been touched.'

Chaloner opened the door and went to examine the body. Neve lay where he had fallen, and the Bishop of Winchester would probably never be the same again. The wound in the upholder's skull was identical to the ones in Coo and Fatherton, and Chaloner regarded it thoughtfully. It was unusual for gunmen to opt for headshots – most chose the body, on the grounds that pistols were notoriously inaccurate, and torsos provided a larger target. Moreover, Neve had been standing on a chair, which would have made such a shot even more difficult to take. So what did that tell him about the gunman? That he was confident of his weapon? That he was an experienced marksman?

Brodrick had followed Chaloner inside and was standing by the window. The carpets were so thick that he had crossed the room without a sound, which told Chaloner how the killers had managed to come so close to their target without being detected – along with the fact that Kipps and Neve had been engrossed in a good gripe about their employer, and their voices had doubtless been loudly indignant.

'Will you arrange for Neve to be carried to the

Westminster Charnel House?' he asked. 'And see about hiring additional guards? I doubt the culprits will return, but we cannot be too careful.'

Restless and uncertain, Chaloner returned to Cheapside, where he hid opposite Baron's house, hoping to see some indication that the man had just ordered an audacious murder. He was not surprised when his vigil transpired to be fruitless. All he saw was the children bursting into tears when a horse similar to Caesar trotted past, and a vicious scowl from Baron that suggested Joan should probably watch herself.

He stared at the King of Cheapside, then started in surprise when Baron suddenly looked into the shadows, straight at him. He knew for a fact that he could not be seen, yet it was clear that the felon knew he was there. Disconcerted – especially as something similar had happened at Silas's soirée – he slipped away shortly afterwards, deciding to see what could be done about finding Randal instead.

Cheapside was more uneasy than ever, with angry voices discussing Coo's murder, the threatened invasion by the Dutch, the dishonesty of the bankers, and the rumour that old Parliamentarians were about to suffer heavier taxes. Backwell's handsome coach and four hurtled past, travelling quickly in an attempt to avoid some of the mud and stones that were lobbed at it. The financier's anxious face could be glimpsed within, and Chaloner thought him a fool for flaunting his wealth when it would have been safer to travel incognito in a hackney carriage.

'I hate that man,' Chaloner heard a grocer growl. 'He is a leech, bloating himself with riches on the backs of the poor. He should never have sold my debt to Taylor.'

357

'No,' agreed a crony. 'Last year, I deposited fifty guineas in his vault – it seemed safer than hiding them under my bed. Then I heard that all goldsmiths are thieves, so I went to get them back, but do you know what he told me? That I could not have them until next week at the earliest. He refused to give me *my* money!'

Further on, there were angry crowds outside Everard's home, which was being closed up with the plague. However, Chaloner saw a distinctive purple nose poking from under one hat, and watched the ex-banker slink away with a bundle tossed over one shoulder, doubtless aiming for the refuge offered by his mother in the country. An elderly couple leaned cheerfully out of an upstairs window, calling out that they were ready for the parish provisions now; Chaloner could only surmise that Everard had bribed the searcher to give a verdict of plague in order to secure faithful old retainers forty days of free food. A few doors down, the same thing was happening to Widow Porteous, but she was far from pleased.

'It is a sweating fever,' she howled. Perspiration shone on her face. '*Not* the pestilence.'

'You are being punished because of Wheler,' shouted Brewer Farrow, who always seemed to be to hand whenever there was trouble. 'Those greedy bankers think a debtor killed him, and this is their revenge. They aim to destroy us house by house.'

Chaloner continued to Bread Street, only to find it blocked by an enormous bonfire, which burned so wildly that the street had been closed in the interests of public safety. Reluctantly, he saw he would have to leave Randal until he could visit without fear of being incinerated.

The bell in St Mary le Bow began to toll as he returned to Cheapside, and a dreary procession made its way through the cemetery in the gathering gloom of dusk. The mourners wore scarves over their faces, and the coffin was interred with unseemly speed, the sexton shovelling soil into the hole long before the vicar had finished his prayers.

'That was Banker Vyner's gardener,' whispered a tallow-maker. 'But look at his house! Is he shut inside it, like the Oxleys? No! He is allowed a verdict of falling sickness, and goes about his business unfettered.'

Chaloner glanced across the road to the Oxley house, where the watcher was allowing Shaw to load food into a basket. No one was waiting at the window to haul it up though, and he wondered if everyone inside was already dead. Lettice was watching from the door of her shop.

'Oxley keeps asking for ale,' she remarked when Chaloner approached. 'No matter how much we supply, he still wants more. He will ruin us before the forty days are over.' She giggled, but it was a nervous sound, devoid of amusement.

'Perhaps fever gives him a thirst,' suggested Chaloner.

'Perhaps, but they are robust folk, and if any family can survive, it is them. We have sent up some of Dr Misick's Plague Elixir, which is excellent stuff and will soon put them right.'

Eventually, Chaloner turned for home. The last snippet of conversation he heard before he left Cheapside was between two beggars huddled in the porch of St Michael's Church.

'. . . will be settled on Tuesday,' one was saying with savage delight. 'Because blood will flow more thickly than in all the wars put together, and London will never be the same again.'

*

Chaloner arrived at Tothill Street to find his house completely empty, ready for the new tenants. Gram was in the kitchen, looking disconsolate, although he brightened when Chaloner walked in. They shared an apple and a salted herring, which was all that was left in the pantry.

'If you could learn who killed Wheler and Coo, Cheapside would be an easier place,' Gram declared, leaning back with a satisfied sigh, although Chaloner was still hungry. 'It is suspicion and rumour that are causing all the trouble. Have you tried asking Joan whether she stabbed her first husband? She is certainly a woman to kill, and Wheler was no great shakes as a lover.'

'How do you know?'

Gram made a dismissive sound. 'Everyone knows – it is common knowledge. Still, I am told she was fond of him, so perhaps you should leave her be.'

'What else have you been told?' Chaloner was desperate enough for answers that he was willing to listen to any old rubbish.

Gram shrugged. 'Nothing you will not have already heard – the bankers could be ousted from Goldsmiths' Row on Tuesday, because the poor do not like them. Which will please Baron, of course, as it will make him more powerful – word is that his authority is slipping, so he will want to regain it any way he can.'

'How will they be ousted?' pressed Chaloner. 'Exactly?'

'No one knows, but everyone is looking forward to it, so I imagine it will be spectacular. Of course, there are those who think it is *Baron* who will suffer on Tuesday, leaving the bankers stronger and richer. Or perhaps it has nothing to do with any of them, and we shall see King Jesus installed in White Hall instead. It is high time He came to finish what He started.'

Chaloner slept rolled in his coat that night, with a boot for a pillow, just as he had when he had been on campaign with the New Model Army. He dozed off immediately, and when he woke the following morning, he felt better rested and fitter than he had done in days. He was still hoarse, and there was the occasional cough and sneeze, but his head was clear and he could breathe. The cold was on its way out at last.

He had arranged to meet Swaddell at the Turk's Head Coffee House on Chancery Lane at eight o'clock, so he walked there briskly. The streets had been washed again, and smelled of damp earth and diluted manure, with the occasional sweeter waft of spring blossom from the open countryside to the west.

He reached the Turk's Head, paid for a brew with his last token, and sat alone at a table, earning disapproving glances from the other patrons who had hoped a stranger would provide them with new and interesting gossip. He ignored them, and studied his surroundings covertly, wondering what could be learned about Swaddell from the place, given that the assassin claimed it as his regular haunt.

It was much like any other such establishment – a single room with smoke-stained walls, seats polished from constant use, and an acrid fug. As it was near the hand-some mansions in Hatton Garden, it was full of people with loud views and good opinions of themselves. Will Chiffinch was there, relaxing after a heavy night of enter-tainment with His Majesty. In his self-important bray, he informed his fellow imbibers that all goldsmiths should be rounded up and thrown off London Bridge for the trouble they were causing at Court. The reason for his vitriol soon became apparent: Taylor had confiscated a fine brooch in lieu of payment on his debt.

361

'And he took my jewelled scent bottle on Friday,' he whined. 'I shall have nothing left if he persists. Damn him to hell!'

He was not the only one with complaints. Sir George Carteret was there, too, and related the tale of how he had been stripped of his buttons, valued at forty shillings each, in broad daylight on the Strand. The grumbles lasted until Chiffinch changed the subject to the plague, at which point there was a general consensus that the disease would never infect anyone of quality, but would confine itself to paupers.

It was unpleasant talk, and Chaloner flicked through *The Intelligencer*, hot off the presses that morning, so he would not have to listen to it. When he had finished and Swaddell had still not arrived, he borrowed pen and paper, and sketched all he could remember about the gun that had killed Coo.

'You are good at that,' remarked Swaddell, making him jump by speaking close behind him. The assassin had a very stealthy tread, because not many could sneak up behind Chaloner undetected, especially now his ears were functioning normally. 'It must be a useful talent. In counterfeiting, for example.'

'I would not know,' replied Chaloner, not about to admit to that sort of skill. 'However, if I lose my post with the Earl, I could always become an artist.'

It was meant as a joke, but Swaddell nodded earnestly, and Chaloner supposed he did not have a sense of humour. It was something to bear in mind, lest flip comments were reported as facts to the Spymaster.

'It is always good to have another career option,' the assassin said gravely. 'If ever I decide to abandon my own line of work, I shall become a perukier.'

Chaloner regarded him uncertainly. 'Really?'

362

'I have never made a wig, but how hard can it be? And everyone is wearing them these days, so it must be a very lucrative trade.' Swaddell nodded towards the drawing. 'Is this the weapon that killed Coo?'

'And Neve and Fatherton. Probably.'

'Then let us visit the gunsmiths and see if they know who owns it.'

It was a pretty morning, and Chaloner might have enjoyed the walk to St Martin's Lane had he not been in company with a dangerous assassin. The sun shone gently, birds sang and an early butterfly danced across the long, waving grass in Lincoln's Inn Fields. Then they reached Long Acre, which was being fumigated by two enormous bonfires that belched out choking white smoke, and all signs of spring were obliterated. With a pang, Chaloner noticed that two more houses had red crosses on their doors, including the one in which he had recently rented rooms. His heart went out to Landlord Lamb.

'It is not plague,' said an old woman, seeing him looking at it. 'It is dropsy. Unfortunately, Mr Lamb's lodgers left, which means he does not have enough money to bribe the searchers.'

'Oh,' said Chaloner guiltily.

'But perhaps he will be freed early,' she went on. 'Cheapside folk are talking about storming their shut-up houses and letting the inmates out. If it works, we might do the same here.'

'That would be reckless,' said Swaddell in alarm. 'The disease will spread for certain, and hundreds may die. Thousands, even.'

'Rubbish!' declared the woman. 'These measures are just an excuse for the government to stamp on the poor.

The idea probably came from the bankers, who resent us because we see them for what they are: greedy, unscrupulous scoundrels!'

Troubled, Chaloner and Swaddell walked to the end of Long Acre and turned down St Martin's Lane, where the premises of William, George and Edmund Trulocke, gunsmiths, was a seedy affair about halfway along. It was guarded by a fierce dog, which repelled all but the most determined patrons. But Chaloner had bribed it with bones in the past, and it remembered; it wagged its tail and licked his hand, allowing him and Swaddell to enter unmolested.

Inside, the shop smelled of hot metal and gunpowder, and displays of muskets and pistols adorned the walls, all secured with chains to prevent pilfering. It was full of shady customers, most of whom took care to keep their faces concealed, and who were almost certainly not the kind of people who should be in possession of firearms.

'Mr Swaddell,' said the largest of the Trulocke brothers. 'What can I do for you?'

Chaloner supposed he should not be surprised that the assassin was known to men who sold weapons. Swaddell was doubtless a regular and much-valued client.

'Tell me who owns this gun.' Swaddell handed him Chaloner's drawing.

'James Baron,' replied Trulocke promptly. 'We made him a pair of them about a year ago.'

'Well, that was easy,' said Chaloner, following Swaddell outside, and stunned by the speed with which they had gained their answer. He was used to prising information from the Trulockes piece by piece, using money or force. 'Can he be trusted?'

'Oh, yes,' said Swaddell. 'He knows the consequences

of lying to me, because he has done it before. His information will be accurate, you can be sure of that.' He shot Chaloner an admonishing glance. 'We should have followed this lead sooner – we could have had Baron in our cells days ago.'

Yet doubt niggled at the back of Chaloner's mind. 'I cannot escape the sense that someone is manipulating us, pushing us to draw these conclusions. Coo's killer waggled the gun at me, and Neve's killer did the same to Kipps, as if they *wanted* the weapon identified.'

'Well, I am happy with the solution, and Williamson will be, too. Once Baron is arrested and his operation crushed, you and I can concentrate on tomorrow's mischief.'

At that moment, a contingent of soldiers trotted past, wearing the distinctive buff jerkins and stripy sleeves of Williamson's troops. Their captain saw Swaddell and hurried over.

'We are summoned to King Street,' he panted. 'Randal Taylor made a speech to a lot of appreciative courtiers. Unfortunately, his words annoyed the local traders, who have Parliamentarian leanings, and the two sides are squaring up for a brawl. Williamson wants it stopped before the trouble spreads.'

'We had better come with you and arrest the villain,' said Swaddell. 'Damn him! Why choose now to make a nuisance of himself?'

'I doubt he will be there now,' predicted Chaloner. 'He is not the sort to linger when danger threatens. We should look for him in Bread Street, where he keeps his mistress.'

Swaddell glared at him, and the captain promptly slunk away to rejoin his unit, unwilling to remain while the assassin looked so deadly.

'And when were you going to share this information with me?' demanded Swaddell, acid in his voice. 'Christ God, Chaloner! We are supposed to be working together. How many more vital facts will you keep to yourself? Anyone would think you do not trust me.'

He turned away before Chaloner could respond and flagged down a hackney by leaping in front of it; Chaloner had no idea how the driver managed to miss him. Seething, Swaddell ripped open the door.

'Government business,' he hissed with such icy menace that the passenger within could not relinquish his ride fast enough.

He climbed in, gesturing for Chaloner to follow. The hackneyman sensed it would be wise to obey the order for speed, and set off at a tremendous pace, Chaloner clinging on grimly as he was flung from side to side. Swaddell scowled out of the window, and Chaloner, not sure how to make amends, did not try. They made the journey in a tense silence.

They alighted in Cheapside, and Chaloner was about to lead the way down Bread Street when he happened to glance towards the music shop. There was a red cross on its door and a watcher stationed outside.

All that remained of the great bonfire that had caused such concern the day before was a great pile of charred logs and a lot of ash; other than these, the road had returned to normal. While Swaddell began to question passers-by about Randal's lady, Chaloner went to the music shop. The watcher tensed and fingered his musket, so Chaloner raised his hands to show that he was not about to do anything rash.

'The wages of kindness,' the watcher whispered, patently

glad to talk to someone who had not come to rail at him. He nodded to the Oxley house next door. 'She went to tend the youngster in there, as his parents were dead and he was frightened. She nursed him through his last hours.'

'They have all gone, then?' asked Chaloner. 'Oxley, Emma and the boy?'

The man nodded. 'The girl, too. Me and the other watchers think she died of the sickness last night, and was buried secretly by family friends. And it really *was* the plague. No one can claim it was spotted fever, dropsy or drunkenness this time, as *they* do not carry off entire households in a day.'

Absently, Chaloner reached out to touch the cross on the Shaws' door. It was brighter than the others, perhaps because it was new. Or maybe it just seemed that way because the victims were people he knew. Then the window above it opened and Lettice leaned out. Shaw was behind her, his face even more gloomy than usual – and with good reason.

'Robin thinks me a fool,' she said with a hollow laugh. 'But the lad was afraid, and I could not leave him to die alone. It would not have been right.'

'I shall be on my way, then,' said the watcher, squinting up at them. 'My colleague down the road is having trouble and he needs help.'

He hurried away, leaving Chaloner staring after him in astonishment.

'We are responsible people,' explained Shaw bitterly. 'We can be trusted not to make a bid for escape, unlike the other folk who have been shut away.'

'Is there anything I can fetch you?' asked Chaloner. He would have to steal it if there were, as he had no money to make purchases.

'No,' replied Shaw, a little ungraciously. 'Misick has left us a flask of his Plague Elixir, which he says will keep us healthy.'

'He put extra alum in it,' added Lettice. 'I wonder if it came from your family's mines. I should like to think so, because it would be a good omen.'

'Those who owe us money will be pleased when they hear of our predicament,' said Shaw, while Chaloner decided to overlook Lettice's peculiar obsession with the mineral in the interests of compassion. 'They will not have to pay us if we die.'

On that note, he withdrew and Lettice followed. Chaloner hurried back to Bread Street, where Swaddell was having no luck locating Randal's woman. The assassin was angry, his restless black eyes burning with bad temper. As he was usually in icy control of his emotions, this was an unsettling development.

'What is wrong?' asked Chaloner warily, wondering if he was the sole cause of Swaddell's ire, or whether someone else had done something to annoy him.

Swaddell shot him a sour look and began to list his gripes on long, bony fingers. 'We are at war; the plague is spreading because people are too stupid to accept our measures; Baron's murder of Coo has outraged all Cheapside—'

'Baron's *possible* murder of Coo,' cautioned Chaloner. 'Yet I feel—'

'—the banks have generated so much ill feeling that they threaten the stability of the whole country; something terrible will happen tomorrow; Randal is stoking bad feeling between Royalists and Parliamentarians; and you withhold vital information. *That* is what is wrong.'

'It did not seem important to—' began Chaloner defensively.

'We took a vow,' hissed Swaddell, and something very nasty flared in his eyes. 'We are partners. We do not deceive each other.'

'I did not *deceive* you,' hedged Chaloner, hoping to heal the rift before Swaddell decided to renounce their pact. 'It was—'

'You take the east side of the road, and I will cover the west. Call me if you find her.'

Swaddell stalked away, colliding with a baker as he went, causing the man to scatter his wares all over the road. The man drew breath to remonstrate, but Swaddell whipped around with a glare of such malice that the words died in his throat. Swaddell strode on, and the baker quickly bent to gather up what he had dropped, evidently of the opinion that a little manure and ash never hurt anyone, before racing away as fast as his legs would carry him.

As knocking on doors and asking if Randal's mistress lived there seemed a poor strategy, Chaloner went to the lane that ran along the back of the road, and began to climb over garden walls, to see what could be learned from peering through windows.

Toys strewn around the first three suggested they belonged to families with children, and he doubted Randal's lady would have brats in tow, but the fourth was more promising. Discarded clothes lay on the floor, including petticoats and breeches. Had Randal received a passionate welcome after his rabble-rousing speech in King Street? Chaloner opened a window and climbed through: if Randal was within, he would fetch Swaddell and they would confront him together.

He found himself in a pantry that screamed of slovenly living. Vegetable parings sat in a festering pile on the table, and what was in the pot suspended over the ashes in the hearth did not look as though it had been very appetising before it had gone mouldy. The place reeked of decaying cheese, old fat and dirt. Then he heard voices.

They were coming from the floor above, so he aimed for the stairs, treading carefully so as not to make them creak. A shriek had him freezing in alarm, but it was followed by laughter, so he resumed his journey. He reached a bedroom, and peered around the door to see Randal and a woman lying in bed together.

The mistress could not have been more different from the wife – she was pretty, even slathered in cheap face-paints, and everything about her was sensual, brash and a little indecent.

Something pungent was burning in a brazier, so a smoky haze hung inside the room, accentuating its general air of seaminess. Unfortunately, the fumes irritated Chaloner's still-sensitive nose. He backed away, trying to stifle the irritating tickle, but it was no use. He sneezed.

The couple started in alarm, while he cursed under his breath. There was no time to fetch Swaddell now – he would have to tackle Randal alone. He flung open the door and strode in, sword in his hand. The woman screamed, hauling the bedclothes to her throat as if she imagined they might protect her. Randal dived for the gun that lay on the bedside table, but Chaloner reached it first. He grabbed it, then stared in shock. It had an ivory butt and an engraved barrel.

'Oh, it is you,' said Randal. He lay back and put his arms behind his head to show he was unconcerned. '*You* will not shoot me. Our mutual friend would not approve.'

'Temperance?' Chaloner sneezed again. 'She will never find out.'

370

'Oh, yes, she will,' countered Randal. 'And she will be livid. She likes me because I pay my bills on time, unlike most of her customers. Now go away. You do not frighten me.'

Chaloner supposed a sneezing invader was more ridiculous than intimidating. 'I will go as soon as you have answered some questions. Where is the second gun?'

'What second gun?' asked Randal warily.

Chaloner waved the weapon. 'This is one of a pair. Where is the other?'

'I have only ever had the one. It was a gift, but do not ask me who from, as I cannot recall.' Randal settled himself more comfortably. 'A great many people shower me with presents for writing *The Court & Kitchin*, and they tend to blend together in my mind.'

'Then do you remember *when* you were given it?'

Randal gazed at the ceiling as he pondered. Then he snapped his fingers. 'Last week! I went to a grand reception hosted by my brother Silas, and when I got home, that gun was one of several trinkets in my pockets. I imagine its giver made some pretty speech about what a fine token it is – they all do – but I was drunk and I cannot bring it to mind now.'

'When was this party exactly?' Chaloner sneezed a third time, wondering what foul concoction was being incinerated in the brazier.

'Sunday perhaps. Or Monday.'

'Dr Coo was murdered on Monday – with this gun or its partner. Am I to assume that you did it? And that you killed Neve in Clarendon House yesterday?'

Randal's eyebrows shot up. 'I have not killed anyone! Tell him, Polly.'

371

The woman nodded. 'He rarely leaves my side, and he was here all day yesterday.'

Chaloner looked at the weak-chinned, dissipated character in the dirty bed, and was inclined to suspect that Randal would be incapable of committing two bold murders in broad daylight.

'Was James Baron at this soirée?' he asked, struggling not to sneeze again.

Randal blinked. 'No, of course not! Silas's guests were merchants and courtiers. And bankers, of course. He knows lots of those, and they are always trying to curry favour with me in the hope that I will praise them to my father.'

Chaloner doubted Taylor would pay much attention to Randal's opinions. He shoved the gun in his pocket, sheathed his sword – he did not need either for Randal – and changed the subject, although he intended to return to the dag and its giver later.

'We did not finish the conversation we started in the brothel,' he began. 'You—'

'What brothel?' interrupted Polly angrily.

'It is not a brothel,' replied Randal irritably. 'It is a gentlemen's club – a respectable place, where men go to smoke and read newsbooks. Ignore him, Poll. He does not want me to publish my next book, and aims to stop me by causing trouble in my personal life.'

'I *will* stop you,' vowed Chaloner. 'For your own good as much as London's.'

'You mean for the good of the people I shall denounce,' jeered Randal. 'Well, they deserve it. I could have been master of my trade by now, but Starkey and Mrs Cromwell ruined me.'

Chaloner sneezed a fourth time. Exasperated, he

emptied a jug of water on to the brazier to put an end to its nasty reek. It hissed and sizzled, and Polly screeched her outrage.

'That is to prevent the plague! Do you *want* us to catch it?'

'He is a Parliamentarian so he probably does,' said Randal sulkily. 'Like all those who object to *The Court & Kitchin*, he considers himself Mrs Cromwell's champion.'

'Perhaps I do,' said Chaloner tartly. 'Because she is not corrupt or miserly, she never stole heirlooms from White Hall, and she certainly did not keep cows in St James's Park for making butter. Everything you wrote was a lie.'

'It serves her right,' said Randal, unrepentant. 'She and Starkey should not have told everyone that I cannot cook.'

'She left White Hall five years ago.' Chaloner went to open a window, because the stench from the wet brazier was worse than when it had been dry. 'Why wait until now to make a fuss?'

Randal shrugged. 'I needed to get my grievances into the open, to stop them gnawing away at me. It worked – I am much happier now.'

'You are,' agreed Polly. 'And best of all, neither Starkey nor Mrs Cromwell know why Randal Taylor should have taken against him. They still think you are John Smith.'

'Get dressed,' ordered Chaloner, thinking that Williamson could decide what was to be done with the petty Randal. He himself had more important matters to attend.

'No,' said Randal, folding his arms. 'You aim to take me to my wife and tell her about Poll. Well, I am not going and you cannot make me.'

Chaloner was sure he could.

'Your *what?*' demanded Polly.

'His wife,' supplied Chaloner, as Randal blanched at the inadvertent slip. 'Surely you knew? They were married a few weeks ago.'

Polly gaped at her lover. 'You bastard! You told me that once the sales of your book had made you rich, you would make *me* your lawful wedded spouse.'

Randal grabbed the hand that was flying forward to slap him. 'I will, Poll, I swear! I want *you*, not Joan. Just say the word, and we shall run away to Dorking together.'

'Dorking?' squeaked Polly, appalled. 'I do not want to go to Dorking! I want to stay here and be part of your family – to attend goldsmiths' feasts and be presented at Court masques. Like you promised.'

'You will,' Randal assured her. 'I will escape the contract, never fear.'

Chaloner drew breath to tell him again to dress, but the smoke was still irritating his nose, and he sneezed yet again. Unfortunately, it meant that he did not hear the person creeping up behind him, and by the time he did, it was too late. He whipped around to find himself facing a gun – the partner of the one that was in his pocket.

Chapter 13

Chaloner reacted instinctively when he saw the weapon. He lashed out with his fist, and although it did not connect, it was enough to spoil the gunman's aim. The dag went off with a crack that made his ears ring, but the bullet missed him. The attacker hissed his annoyance and Polly began to scream. A second assailant was on the heels of the first, pulling a knife from his belt. Both wore plague masks to conceal their faces.

The gunman hauled out a second pistol, older and less elegant than the first. Chaloner grabbed it and tried to wrest it away, but the accomplice began jabbing at him with the dagger. Using every ounce of his strength, Chaloner twisted the gunman around and used him as a shield. The gunman released a howl of pain as his friend's blade struck home, and the dag went off, showering all three with plaster from the ceiling.

Polly's screeches intensified, and there was a blur of movement as she hurtled forward to leap on to the gunman's back, where she battered his head with her fists. Leaving her to it, Chaloner whipped around to deal with the accomplice, only to find the fellow preparing to lob his dagger. At such close range, he could not miss, but a third shot rang out and he crumpled. Polly howled again as the gunman prised her off himself and flung her at Chaloner before racing away down the stairs. His hammering footsteps were punctuated by the bang of a fourth firearm discharging, followed by the sound of the front door being slammed shut.

By the time Chaloner had disentangled himself from Polly, the knifeman was dead, the gunman had escaped, and Swaddell was standing in the doorway holding two smoking pistols.

'I dislike firearms,' the assassin said, blowing on the weapons and stowing them in his belt. His sour mood had lifted, and Chaloner wondered if the act of killing had restored his equanimity. 'They make too much noise. However, they did alert me to the fact that you were in trouble, so I was able to speed to your rescue. Unfortunately, I arrived too late to help him.'

Chaloner glanced to where he pointed, and saw what had put Polly in such a frenzy. Randal lay on the bed amid a spreading stain of red; his eyes were open and already beginning to glaze. Chaloner sagged, thinking of all the information that had died with him.

But it was no time to assess what could have been done differently. He knelt by the knifeman and pulled off his mask. The face beneath was unfamiliar, and he knew he had never seen it before. He raised questioning eyes to Swaddell, who shook his head.

'I tried to lay hold of the gunman,' the assassin said, 'but the mask he wore . . . well, it unsettled me, to be frank. It spoiled my aim, and I failed to wing him as he fled past.'

'You only tried to wing him?' asked Chaloner, whose

experience with the assassin had taught him that Swaddell preferred such encounters to be fatal ones.

'He would have been no use to us dead.' Swaddell's expression hardened. 'However, none of this would have happened if you had waited for me, as we agreed.'

He had a point, and Chaloner acknowledged it with an apologetic nod. 'I am not sure if he and his friend came to protect or kill Randal. Regardless, the bullet intended for me hit him.'

'It did – so it is *your* fault he is dead,' snapped Polly. Her hair was in disarray, and angry tears had made a mess of her face-paints.

Chaloner ignored the accusation. 'Do you recognise him?' he asked her, beginning to search the knifeman's clothes for something that might reveal his identity.

'I have never seen him before in my life.' Polly glowered furiously. 'Now what will become of me? Randal was my future – I was going to be rich.'

'True love then, was it?' asked Swaddell acidly, then cocked his head at a rising clamour of voices in the street. 'We should go, Chaloner. People are coming to investigate, and we are too busy for lengthy explanations. Williamson will extricate us, but it will take time and we have more important matters to attend.'

'Williamson?' gulped Polly. 'The Spymaster? God help me! I shall never find a replacement for Randal if men think I entertain *his* creatures in my house! Get out before anyone sees—'

'Who gave Randal the gun?' Chaloner cut across her urgently.

Polly folded her arms defiantly. 'I will never help agents of Spymaster Williamson. It would be like colluding with Satan. Now leave.'

377

'Answer the question,' ordered Swaddell with icy menace. 'Or I shall tell everyone that you are one of his most valuable spies.'

Polly regarded him in dismay. 'But that would be a lie! And how would I make a living again afterwards? I should starve!'

'Then tell us what we want to know.' Swaddell moved towards the stairs and glanced down them. 'It would be inconvenient for us to be caught here, but that will be nothing compared to the trouble I shall cause you if you refuse to cooperate.'

'Randal was very drunk at Silas's party, and came home with no idea who gave him what.' Polly's voice was high with tension. 'He barely recalled being there, in fact. Now go.'

Chaloner pulled the weapon from his pocket, and a brief examination revealed that it was unloaded, so would have been scant use to Randal anyway.

'*That* gun?' blurted Swaddell. '*Randal* murdered Coo?'

He glared at Randal's body, and Chaloner was sure that had there been a spark of life in it, Swaddell would have stamped it out. Clearly, the assassin had been telling the truth when he had expressed a desire to see the saintly physician's killer caught.

'Coo?' gulped Polly, shocked. 'What black business is this?'

There was no time to explain, and the shouting in the street was growing louder. People would be in the house soon, clamouring to know what was happening.

'Where is Randal's next book?' demanded Chaloner.

Polly went to a drawer and pulled out a ream of paper. 'Another copy is already with a printer, although I do not know which one. However, I can tell you that the first editions will go on sale tomorrow. Now *please* leave before—'

'Tomorrow?' Chaloner glanced at Swaddell. 'That is Tuesday.'

Someone began to pound on the front door.

'Randal said it was timed to coincide with something important.' Polly spoke in a gabble as the hammering grew more insistent. 'But he did not know what. Now *go*, for God's sake!'

There was a crash from downstairs as the door was kicked open. Chaloner shoved Randal's book in his coat and hurried to the window, which overlooked a dismal yard. A quick glance revealed a series of conveniently placed sills – a burglar's dream – so he scrambled out and started to climb down them. Swaddell regarded him askance, unused to making undignified exits.

'Are you coming?' asked Chaloner.

Swaddell grimaced his distaste as he prepared to follow, then shot Polly a dangerous look when she tried to hurry him up by shoving at his back. She shrank away in alarm.

The ledges were slick with slime and the descent was not easy, although Chaloner swarmed down with an agility born of long experience. Swaddell climbed more cautiously, spider-like with his skittering movements and black-clad limbs. They reached the yard, opened the gate and made their way to the bustle of Cheapside, where they disappeared into the crowds.

The gunshots had done nothing to ease the tense atmosphere, and rumours were rife as to what had caused them – watchers shooting people escaping plague houses, a banker dispatching a hapless debtor, Coo's killer striking again.

'You should have waited for me before tackling Randal,' said Swaddell accusingly, giving vent to his annoyance once they were alone. 'You have made matters worse.'

Chaloner knew it and was sorry. 'You must have a list of city printers. Send soldiers to each one and seize Randal's book before it can be distributed.'

'And what if he has hired an underground press? Which is likely, because I cannot see a respectable one obliging him after what happened to Milbourn.'

'Then I imagine you have a list of those, too.' Chaloner thought, but did not say, that Thurloe certainly would have done.

Swaddell shot him a sour glance. 'We do not have the resources to track them all down at such short notice. However, if you had stuck to the plan we agreed, Randal would be alive to answer our questions.'

Chaloner started to explain what had happened, but it sounded lame to his own ears, so he did not insult Swaddell by finishing. The assassin stalked to a nearby coffee house, where he demanded pen and paper. The owner produced them with alacrity, unsettled by the malevolent glare. Chaloner leaned over Swaddell's shoulder, and watched him jot a short message in cipher.

'Is that to Williamson? What are you telling him?'

Swaddell made an irritable sound and switched to English, although he made no attempt to translate what had already been written. He scrawled a brief outline of their discoveries, then listed his conclusions, chief among which was that they now had enough evidence to arrest Baron.

'Trulocke's testimony proves that Baron owns the murder weapons,' he said when Chaloner started to argue. 'And yours proves that he used them to kill Coo, Neve, Randal and Fatherton.'

'It does not! Whoever shot Coo was smaller than Baron. So was the gunman in Randal's—'

'He sends minions to do his dirty work,' interrupted Swaddell irritably. 'Which is why we do not recognise the one I dispatched.'

'Then how did Randal come to have this dag? It makes no sense.'

'Of course it does. It was a gift from an "admirer" – Baron, who has encouraged Randal in his deluded scribbling for one purpose only: to foment unrest.'

'Why would Baron do that? He has nothing to gain from his domain exploding.'

'We shall ask him when he is in our cells. Hopefully, the situation here will ease once he is under lock and key. And arresting Coo's killer will certainly calm turbulent waters.'

'Or stir them up, if Baron transpires to be innocent.'

Swaddell made a dismissive gesture. 'He is not innocent and you know it. But his reign of terror is almost over, thank God.'

He took the gun and Randal's manuscript, wrapped them in a cloth, then went outside, where he snagged a passing soldier and ordered him to deliver them to the Spymaster with all possible haste. Then he leaned towards the man and whispered something Chaloner did not catch, accompanied by a clink as coins changed hands. The man grinned his delight and set off at a run.

'Now what?' asked Chaloner, wishing he was not saddled with such a moody and unpredictable partner.

'We wait for orders.' Swaddell favoured him with a wry glance. 'Preferably without doing anything else to aggravate the situation.'

'Very well,' said Chaloner stiffly, although he hated the notion of inactivity while the Spymaster decided what should be done.

'We shall continue to monitor the situation, of course – see what can be learned by watching and listening.'

Suspecting it would not take much for Swaddell's temper to erupt again, Chaloner maintained a wary silence as they walked along Cheapside, feeling the less said the better. Then the assassin nodded to where Taylor's coach was rattling past, although the banker was not in it.

'With luck, the Goldsmiths' Company will elect a new Master soon. Taylor is patently unsuited to the task – he refused to listen to government advice even when he was sane. Evan would be my choice of successor. He is much more malleable.'

'Evan could never manage such a post.' Chaloner was surprised that Swaddell should think he might. 'Backwell says London needs a strong Master at the moment and Evan is weak.'

'Silas, then,' shrugged Swaddell. 'He is energetic and decisive, and Taylor is a fool for favouring Evan over him. Still, Silas is one step closer to the family throne now that Randal is dead.'

Chaloner felt a cold tendril of unease course through his innards. Swaddell was right, of course, and Silas had always been ambitious – and bitter that he had been packed off to the wars while his older siblings had been allowed to stay safely at home. Was it possible that Silas had arranged for Randal to be visited by masked gunmen? He shook himself impatiently – Silas was no fratricide.

As they passed the White Goat Inn, a number of bankers emerged from a meeting – the Taylor coach was one of several that had come to transport them home. Liveried guards hurried forward to form a protective cordon around them, shielding them from the immediate hostile attentions of passers-by. The goldsmiths ignored the anger and resentment they attracted, and continued to chat.

'Fools,' muttered Swaddell. 'Flaunting themselves is asking for trouble.'

'It is Joan,' said Chaloner, glimpsing her mean little face in the financiers' midst. 'If she stopped talking, the rest would leave.'

'She must be very knowledgeable to keep them hanging on her every word,' remarked Swaddell. 'I am told that even Taylor regards her as a fiscal oracle.'

'Then he has missed out on her wisdom today, because he does not seem to be here.'

'By all accounts, he regrets his decision to wed her to Randal,' Swaddell went on, 'and wishes he had taken her for himself. Perhaps he decided to rectify the matter, and hired assassins to bring it about. Lord knows, he is mad enough to think he could get away with it.'

But Chaloner had already considered this possibility and discounted it. 'Even insane, I do not think he would harm his own son. Besides, he already has Joan at his side for financial consultations, which is all he really wants.'

Swaddell did not reply, and only watched the goldsmiths with silent disapproval.

At that moment, a groom appeared, holding the reins of Caesar. The horse stood docilely while they waited for Joan to finish pontificating, but suddenly its head went up, its ears pricked forward and it began to toss its head, so that the groom was hard-pressed to control it. The cause soon became clear: it had spotted Baron, who was walking along the other side of the road. It jerked forward in an effort to reach him, and Joan released a cry as she was knocked from her feet.

There was a brief kerfuffle, after which Caesar was whisked away and Joan was helped into her carriage by solicitous colleagues. Chaloner wondered how long the horse would survive the mishap, and Baron obviously did, too, as his face was a mask of open dismay.

Not long afterwards, Chaloner spotted Silas. His old friend was with Misick, and they had evidently indulged in a musical interlude, as both held flutes, although it did not seem that Silas had enjoyed the session, as his face was darker than Chaloner had ever seen it. Such an expression did not sit well on his usually jovial features, and made him look uncannily like his sire.

'I am no longer my father's son,' he said bitterly, when Chaloner went to ask what was the matter. 'He has disowned me.'

'He is not in his right mind,' said Chaloner soothingly. 'I doubt he meant it.'

'Oh, yes, he did,' countered Silas. 'And dear Evan was there to bear witness to the fact.'

'Randal is dead,' said Chaloner, hating to be the bearer of more bad news. 'I am sorry. He was shot during an altercation at his mistress's house.'

But Silas only shrugged, although Misick's jaw dropped in shock. 'He always did lead a chaotic life. Who did it? His latest whore? Or Joan, aiming to wed a better man?'

384

Chaloner had no answer. 'Before he died, he mentioned a soirée you held last week. One of your guests gave him a gun, which had been used to kill—'

'I know nothing about his antics with weapons,' interrupted Silas shortly. 'You will have to speak to his whores about them.'

'Then do you know who plans to publish his sequel tomorrow?' Chaloner grabbed Silas's arm when his friend started to stride away, tired of the discussion. 'It is important, Silas! He will have the city awash with blood, as it will provide the perfect excuse for a riot.'

Silas laughed harshly. 'They have plenty of excuses already, Tom. My brother's ravings will make no difference. Now, if you will excuse me, I need to speak to Backwell.'

He shouldered his way through a group of butchers' apprentices who happened to be in his way. Chaloner braced himself for trouble, but there was something in his savage mien that warned the lads against shoving him back. They scowled, but made no attempt to retaliate.

'Take no notice,' said Misick, clutching his wig when a passing urchin made a mischievous grab for it. 'He is upset over the spat with his father, but will soon return to his usual sunny self.'

'I hope so,' murmured Swaddell, 'because I do not like the sullen Silas at all.'

Neither did Chaloner, and Swaddell's earlier words kept coming back to him. With Randal dead, Silas *was* one step closer to the family throne.

'Have you heard about the Shaws?' Misick was asking. 'I told Lettice she should not have risked herself for the Oxley boy, but she would not listen. Now she has a fever.'

'Then give her more of your Plague Elixir,' said Chaloner. Unbidden, a memory of Aletta filled his mind, but he forced it down. He could not afford to be distracted when he had so much else to occupy his thoughts.

'She has had a hefty dose already,' said Misick. He looked sheepish. 'But it is not as effective as I had hoped, even with the extra alum. It did not save the Howard family either.'

Chaloner turned when someone tapped him on the shoulder. It was Backwell, who had Vyner, Glosson and several other financiers at his heels, although Silas had evidently decided against talking to the man, as he was not among the gathering. The bankers were attracting even more angry attention, and their guards were nervous. Several toted guns, and Chaloner hoped they would not be panicked into using one. Backwell was angry.

'You carry the government's authority,' he snapped, looking first at Chaloner and then at Swaddell. He held a coin, which he raised absently to his lips, like a talisman. 'So tell these folk to stop harassing us every time we step out of our houses. It is beginning to be irksome.'

'I am sure it is,' replied Swaddell, equally cool. 'But it is difficult to persuade them to respect Goldsmiths' Company members when you are ruled by a madman.'

'We are not,' retorted Backwell shortly. 'Not any more. It was decided that Taylor is no longer the man for the task, so an emergency election was called. Flatteringly, my colleagues voted me into office as Master.'

Chaloner frowned his surprise. 'You said you were too busy for such a role.'

'I am, but my fellow goldsmiths need me, so it is my duty to step into the breach.'

386

'Does Taylor know?' asked Swaddell.

'Joan will tell him when she gets home. But I am not the only one who needs to make sacrifices. You must emulate your bold uncle, Chaloner – *he* would not have stood by helplessly while the very foundations of his country crumbled. He would have acted.'

'And what would he have done?' Chaloner was willing to try anything to avert a crisis, although he doubted his reckless kinsman would have devised anything very sensible.

'Used his imagination,' replied Backwell unhelpfully. Then he glared, and Chaloner saw a darker, less pleasant side to the seemingly amiable financier. 'The King will not want a run on the banks, so think very carefully before denying our requests for help.'

'A run has already started,' said Glosson grimly. 'Someone began a rumour that I am on the brink of collapse, and my depositors are clamouring for their money back. The tale *was* untrue, but that might change if the tale persists.'

'And our failure means the fall of the government,' warned Backwell. 'So you two had better do something fast.'

'Go home,' ordered Chaloner, thinking the situation might ease if the goldsmiths did not parade their expensive clothes and armies of henchmen. 'It is—'

'Pah!' spat Backwell. 'You are no more worthy of your name than Evan is of his.'

'What is taking Williamson so long?' asked Chaloner agitatedly, as time ticked past and no word came from the Spymaster. 'You say arresting Coo's killer will calm Cheapside, but I am not sure that will be true for much longer – the situation will have moved past that point.'

'There is Baron,' said Swaddell, not answering. 'In the doorway of that tavern. Did you see his face when his horse bumped into Joan? She will order it destroyed and he knows it. Perhaps we should follow her, and catch him when he appears to blow *her* brains out.'

Baron was staring down Cheapside with an expression that was difficult to fathom. Then Doe and Poachin approached. Doe was limping and there was a bruise on his face, while Poachin's hair was less perfect than usual. Chaloner wondered whether their rivalry had spilled over into physical violence.

'He has seen us,' said Swaddell sharply, 'and is coming over. Not a word about the gun. He might run if he thinks we are on the verge of arresting him.'

Chaloner did not think so: Baron was not the sort of man to flee trouble, and besides, where would he go? Cheapside was his home, and he was far more likely to make a stand there. He watched the felon approach, Doe at his side, while Poachin lagged behind in a way that should have warned Baron that his partiality for the younger man had created a dangerous rift.

'I was sorry to hear about Oxley,' said Swaddell politely. 'I imagine you will miss him.'

Baron inclined his head. 'The plague is a terrible thing, and I pray to God that my own family will be spared.'

'Amen,' said Doe, although there was a smirk in his eyes.

'My trainband shut up three houses on Friday Street today,' Baron continued. 'All bankers. Williamson's searchers pretended it was something else, so we decided to act ourselves.' He patted Doe's shoulder. 'Look at my young friend's face – battered as he fought to seal these diseased merchants in their lairs.'

388

'But I won,' boasted Doe, puffing out his chest. 'They will not spread their filthy contagions among decent people again.'

'We do not want to die because the rich can buy favourable verdicts,' added Poachin. 'It would not be right.'

'Impoverished ancients will always be partial to bribes, I am afraid,' said Swaddell. 'Yet some are conscientious. They rooted out two cases on Cheapside this morning, which your own searchers seem to have missed, even though I am told they visited.'

'I shall look into the matter,' said Baron smoothly.

'Do,' said Swaddell. 'And remember that this is a deadly disease. We cannot afford to play games with it.'

'We shall do our bit,' replied Baron coldly. '*If* you ensure the rich do theirs.'

He gave a brief, rather challenging bow before sauntering away, his captains following. Chaloner stared after them. If Baron aimed to turn the situation into a war against the bankers, then perhaps he *had* murdered Coo – the saintly physician would certainly not have condoned locking healthy people away and letting infected ones go free on the basis of their finances.

'Perhaps I should go to Williamson,' said Swaddell, as more time passed and the mood along Cheapside grew increasingly tense. 'You are right – if we do not arrest Coo's killer soon, it will not matter, because there will be trouble here anyway.'

Chaloner agreed. 'I have never seen this road so crowded.'

'Nor have I, and one of the plague measures Williamson was ordered to implement is to prevent large gatherings

389

of people. You do not need me to tell you why: if one infected person moves among them . . .'

'Perhaps one already has,' said Chaloner soberly. 'If all these closed homes represent genuine cases of the pestilence – not other ailments, as most people believe – then it is spreading anyway. The measures are not working.'

'Perhaps not, but they are all we have. Or are you ready to give up and resign yourself to epidemics like the ones that ravaged Venice and Amsterdam?'

Chaloner did not know what to think, and looked at the nearest plague houses, which were Oxley's and the music shop. Some spectators were calling for the inmates to come to their windows, but none did.

'All dead,' shouted one crone. 'They were shut up and left to die.'

'Then you should be glad they perished inside, not out here among you,' called a nervous watcher, hoping to appeal to reason. 'We have no choice but to isolate suspected cases.'

He should have kept quiet, because his remark prompted an argument. It was confined to angry words, although there was some pushing and shoving at the back. Then Chaloner spotted a familiar figure.

'There is Taylor. What is he doing?'

The banker had snagged a passing mason, and was muttering in a way that had the fellow shying away in alarm. Taylor jabbed an irritable forefinger at what he wanted, and the mason handed over a sledgehammer, although with obvious reluctance. Taylor set his Plague Box carefully on the step of the Standard, picked up the sledgehammer, and dealt the door to the fountain an almighty blow. Nothing happened, so he did it again and there was a metallic screech as the lock disintegrated. He tossed the implement away, picked up his Plague Box and disappeared inside.

Intrigued by the unusual sight of a goldsmith laying siege to a public building, people began to gather around the Standard to see what would happen next.

'There is nothing inside except a cistern and a spiral staircase that emerges on the roof,' said Swaddell, puzzled. 'There is a rail at the top, but it has corroded from the foul air.'

'You mean Taylor might fall if he goes up there?'

'He might. And it is a long way down, so he will certainly die.'

'He must be having one of his turns. But here is Evan. He will coax his father away.'

Evan tried the door but it would not open, so he charged at it with his shoulder. He reeled away with a howl of pain when it held firm, and the onlookers laughed. Mortified, Evan snarled an order to his henchmen. One was Joliffe, who had the sense to use the sledgehammer. However, although the wood splintered, the door did not open, and it quickly became apparent that Taylor had blocked it from the other side. The crowd jeered mockingly when Joliffe's assault faltered.

Then Taylor appeared on the roof. He was an imposing figure, and eyed the people below with haughty disdain. Even from a distance, Chaloner sensed the power of the man, and the onlookers' merriment faded when his dark eyes swept across them. The banker nodded once, then removed a bottle from his pocket and treated himself to a sip.

'Is he drunk?' wondered Swaddell.

'Medicine,' muttered Chaloner, recognising the phial as one of Misick's. 'Let us hope it brings him to his senses before he does anything rash.'

'It will be too late – he is going to throw himself off! Lord! That will do nothing to raise confidence in the financial market!'

'No, it is worse!' breathed Chaloner. 'He is going to make a speech. We must stop him before he says or does something to cause a riot.'

'How?' asked Swaddell archly. 'If Evan's brawny followers cannot batter down the door, then we are unlikely to succeed. Or are you suggesting that I shoot him?'

'I cannot imagine that would help. Let us hope Evan is in time then.'

Taylor took another leisurely slurp from his flask, after which he tipped the remainder on to Joliffe's head. There was a roar of appreciative laughter from the onlookers, during which Taylor drew himself up to his full height. An expectant hush fell over those below.

'Debt is a terrible thing,' he boomed. 'And only fools allow themselves to be seduced into it. They should all be taken to Tyburn, and hanged by the neck until they are dead.'

'It is the bankers who should be hanged,' bellowed Brewer Farrow, his voice the loudest over the howls of indignation that greeted Taylor's remarks. 'They are the ones who lent the money in the first place, and who set crippling rates of interest. Wheler destroyed me before he was stabbed – and good riddance to him.'

There was a frenzy of cheers, although several financiers, safely behind a wall of henchmen, gave vent to yells of 'Shame!' Chaloner noticed that the crowd was growing larger by the minute, and its mood was ugly.

'Bankers are angels of God,' bawled Taylor, a claim that startled even his colleagues. 'I saw an omen – a three-headed serpent – and I know what the Lord wants me to do. I must save the world from debtors by unleashing the plague on them. I have it in here.'

He brandished the box and the crowd flinched backwards. Then he leaned against the rail, which flexed alarmingly.

'Plague worms and gold, gold and plague worms,' he chanted, shaking the box up and down so it rattled. 'The pestilence will cleanse the city of all vile vermin.'

'What vermin?' demanded Farrow. 'You had better not mean us.'

'Colburn,' hissed Taylor. He grabbed the rail with his free hand. It released a tortured shriek of protest, but miraculously did not tear from the wall. 'He started this evil, but I showed him. He is in his grave now, and the plague worms will eat him.'

'Lord! I hope he has not just confessed to killing Colburn,' muttered Swaddell. 'Williamson will not want me to assassinate the outgoing Master of the Goldsmiths' Company.'

'Misick's Plague Elixir,' yelled Taylor. 'I drink it every night. It will keep me clean, but the rest of you will perish in a stinking blackness of pestilence and—'

He stopped abruptly, because Joliffe had broken through the door and reached the roof.

There was a lot of jeering as Taylor was bundled un-ceremoniously out of the Standard and into a waiting coach. Chaloner glimpsed Misick's massive wig inside and medicines being proffered. Then the driver cracked his whip and the carriage rattled away. He supposed

Taylor would share the fate of his hapless colleague Johnson, and be packed off to Bedlam.

'Oh, God,' groaned Swaddell, as Evan took his father's place on the balcony. 'Now what?'

'Good people of London,' Evan began in a voice that was weak and high compared to his father's authoritative bass. 'You should not believe all you hear about—'

'You are a villain!' howled Farrow. 'Worse than a thief, because you are already rich, but you aim to make yourself wealthier on the backs of decent, hard-working folk. Shame on you!'

'Shut your mouth,' snarled Joliffe, striding towards him and shoving his face menacingly close. 'Or I will shut it for you.'

Unfortunately for him, far from being intimidated, Farrow took a swing at the tempting target. Joliffe reeled back with blood gushing from his nose, while the crowd roared its delight. Evan ducked back into the stairwell when a hail of stones flew towards him, wisely abandoning his efforts to make amends for his father's proclamations.

When some of the bankers' henchmen waded into the horde to extricate Joliffe, Chaloner braced himself for the start of a serious fracas, but Baron's trainband saved the day. They were polite but firm, and as neither guards nor onlookers were willing to fight the King of Cheapside, they began to disperse. Yet many did not go far: some congregated around the plague houses, muttering in low voices, while many formed sullen packs that lurked in alleys. Others walked with silent purpose down Friday and Bread Streets.

'Taylor's stupid opinions have provided the spark that folk have been waiting for,' said Swaddell in a low voice. 'I sense trouble looming.'

So did Chaloner. 'They are aiming for Goldsmiths' Row,' he said urgently. 'Come on!'

He and Swaddell hurried there, and arrived to find people clamouring at the doors of every financier for the funds they had deposited. The run had started.

'The banks are on the verge of collapse, and you will lose everything unless you take all your money out *now*.' It was Farrow again. 'Hurry! Reclaim—'

Swaddell grabbed his arm. 'Enough,' he said fiercely. 'You are not helping.'

'Not helping whom?' snarled Farrow. 'The goldsmiths? Who cares? They are maggots.'

'Very possibly,' said Swaddell. 'But if they fail, we will not be able to fight the Dutch.'

'Good! It was a stupid idea to go to war anyway.'

'Then think about the plague. The government will need to borrow from them to pay for watchers, bonfires—'

'If it comes, it will be *their* fault for not shutting themselves up when they were infected,' interrupted Farrow, stabbing an accusing finger towards the opulent houses. 'And the searchers' fault for claiming that everything is the plague unless someone bribes them to say otherwise. The whole city is corrupt, and we have had enough of it.'

Farrow's rant was drawing approving nods from onlookers, so Chaloner backed away, pulling Swaddell with him, as arguing was doing more harm than good. Then one of Williamson's officers arrived with a small unit of men and a brief, exasperated message saying there was a legal hiccup over the warrant – which had to be sound or the case against Baron would collapse before it had started. Swaddell and Chaloner were to keep the peace until the matter could be resolved.

'I expected more than this from cooperating with the Spymaster,' grumbled Chaloner, daunted by the scale of the task that confronted them. The mood of the multitude was growing more dangerous by the minute, and it was obvious that a serious riot was in the offing. For a start, many folk were wearing masks – ostensibly to protect themselves from the plague – which rendered them anonymous; it was common knowledge that those who believed themselves to be unrecognisable were more likely to misbehave.

Swaddell shot him a black look. 'He will be doing his best, but the wheels of justice do not always move swiftly.'

They did not seem to be moving at all as far as Chaloner was concerned, and there followed one of the longest and most trying days he could ever recall passing. Swaddell directed Williamson's soldiers in a complex game of cat and mouse with the ringleaders of the brewing unrest, while Chaloner spirited any number of troublemakers down dark alleys and advised them to desist. Between them, they managed an uneasy status quo through the afternoon and into the evening, but both knew that all bets would be off once darkness fell.

Shopkeepers thought so, too, and were closing their shutters. They were hampered by petty thieves, who worked in packs to dart in and steal. Baron's trainband was trying to stop them, but as soon as they had secured one business, another came under attack. The King of Cheapside was losing control. Was it because he was distracted by Caesar's probable fate? And why were more of Williamson's troops not on hand to help?

'Because we do not have enough men,' snapped Swaddell when Chaloner asked. 'We cannot keep the plague from spreading *and* quell unrest. It is not an army – just a few soldiers.'

Chaloner happened to be passing the Oxley house at dusk, and saw the plague cart arrive to collect the bodies. It was a grim vehicle, tall with high sides, operated by two men in masks and long cloaks. They had a brazier burning on the seat next to them, which released a noxious stench, and grey-white powder dropped from the back of the wagon each time it hit a rut in the road – the lime that was used as a disinfectant.

Shaw came to the window to watch, and a ragged cheer of encouragement went up from passers-by. He acknowledged it with a weary smile. He was wearing an old blue coat, which he hugged around himself as if he were cold.

'Lettice wrapped them as well as she could,' he called to the drivers. 'But she could not find enough big blankets, so please be careful. One is a child.'

There was no response from the men, who had doubtless seen other children that day. They adjusted their clothes, took deep breaths, and opened Oxley's door. Moments later, they emerged with a bundle. As they swung it into the waiting wagon, the blanket fell away. Chaloner braced himself for an ugly sight, but Emma looked strangely peaceful, her skin marble white. Oxley was next, followed by the boy.

'Do you have any dead?' asked one driver, glancing up at Shaw.

'Not yet,' came the whispered reply.

The wagon trundled away to its next port of call, while the crowd watched in silence.

*

397

Darkness fell, but still there was no word from Williamson, and householders and shopkeepers all along Cheapside lit pitch torches in the hope that the light would deter thieves. Throngs of men and women emerged from the alleys and adjoining streets to prowl, and although they pretended to be taking the air, Chaloner knew they were there to join the trouble when it came.

Then one of the Spymaster's captains arrived with four burly men in tow. They were not soldiers, but the louts Williamson engaged when he needed an intimidating presence, which meant they were neither loyal nor particularly trustworthy.

'Here is the warrant at last,' the captain said, handing a piece of paper to Swaddell. 'Mr Williamson wants it executed immediately, and he sent these fellows to help.'

'Baron has an entire trainband at his disposal,' remarked Chaloner, watching Swaddell scan the document quickly, then shove it in his pocket. 'I think we might need more than four hired hands to persuade him to leave his home and come with us.'

'Well you cannot have them,' retorted the captain. 'There is trouble in King Street, Drury Lane, London Wall, Fleet Street and Tower Hill. All London is in uproar tonight.'

'I thought it was just Cheapside,' said Swaddell.

'If only,' growled the captain.

'What about Randal's book?' asked Chaloner. 'Has Williamson found the publisher yet?'

'No, but he has risen from his sickbed to lead the search himself – he had no choice, given that he has no spare agents. He told me to hurry back and help him, so I had better oblige. Good luck.'

Chaloner thought they would need it. With the four

men lumbering behind, he and Swaddell ran to Baron's house, only to find it in darkness, its doors locked and windows shuttered. A passer-by explained why: Baron had decided that London was too dangerous for his wife and children, so he had sent them to the country.

'He is still here, though,' the man added. 'He would never abandon his kingdom. I saw him not long ago, heading for the Feathers.'

Unlike most taverns, which were enjoying a roaring trade from people keen to fuel their courage with ale, the Feathers was closed, and there was no sign of the doormen who were usually on hand to collect entry fees from guests. Chaloner and Swaddell crept to the back of the building, where light seeped dimly from under a single shutter. The rear door was locked but Chaloner had it open in a trice.

He indicated that the hirelings were to wait outside while he and Swaddell went to find out what was happening. The quartet nodded wordlessly, although they were patently uneasy, and he wondered how long their nerve would hold. Why had Williamson provided such paltry troops when he had claimed that quelling the trouble around Cheapside was important? But it was no time to ponder, because Swaddell was poking him in the back, prompting him to step inside.

The main part of the tavern was empty, but there were voices coming from the room that was lit. Chaloner padded towards it, Swaddell at his heels. The assassin had such a stealthy tread that Chaloner glanced around twice, just to make sure he was still there.

They reached the occupied room, a large chamber that was far more handsomely furnished than the rest of the inn. It was full of people, who sat around tables, all playing cards in an atmosphere of hushed concentration. They were drinking wine, not ale, and Chaloner understood why when he recognised the participants. Some, like Chiffinch, Bab May, Brodrick and Sir George Carteret, were courtiers; others included wealthy merchants, one or two clergymen and – somewhat unexpectedly – Misick. The game was primero, and the amount of money on the tables was more than Chaloner would earn in a decade.

'Such high stakes are illegal,' whispered Swaddell, as if he imagined Chaloner might not know. 'Although it is no shock to learn that Baron ignores the law.'

The felon himself was standing near the back of the room, watching the proceedings with a fatherly smile, although there was a glint of greed in his eyes. Doe was at his side, while Poachin prowled with a wine jug.

'No wonder these people are in debt,' murmured Chaloner. 'Doubtless, this is the kind of game that destroyed Colburn.'

Swaddell eased forward to get a better view but inadvertently knocked a tankard from a shelf. Chaloner watched in horror as it toppled and began to fall. Swaddell reacted with impressive speed, though. He twisted around and the vessel dropped neatly into his hands, so the clatter that would have betrayed them was no more than a click as the lid snapped shut. The games continued undisturbed, although Poachin excused himself to fetch more wine from the cellar.

'Good,' murmured Swaddell. 'Now there is only Baron, Doe and four of their trainband. We shall be evenly matched when I fetch our warriors.'

'You are not counting the gamblers,' whispered Chaloner.

'They will not fight for Baron – or against us.'

Chaloner regarded him askance. 'Of course they will! The alternative is being exposed for illegal gaming.'

'They would not dare. Besides, Misick is trained to heal wounds, not cause them, while Brodrick would never raise a hand against his cousin's man.'

'He might, if it means keeping the Earl in the dark about his antics. And Chiffinch and May would love an opportunity to kill me. We need to ask Williamson for more soldiers.'

'You heard: he does not have them to lend us. And this is perfect, Chaloner! Baron will never evade prison if we catch him in the act of presiding over illegal card games. Now fetch our troops while I keep an eye on him.'

Chaloner was deeply unhappy but began to creep back through the tavern. He was not at all surprised when he reached the street to discover that the hirelings had disappeared. Wearily, he started to return to Swaddell, but a creak made him whip around.

'Are you looking for me?'

It was Baron. Chaloner reached for his sword, but Baron had a gun and shook his head, tutting as he did so. Doe and Jacob were with him, the latter looking nothing like a footman with his unshaven face and rough clothes; Chaloner supposed he had reverted to the kind of person he had been before landing a cushy post in Tothill Street.

'It is all right, Baron,' said Swaddell, stepping out of the shadows. 'Chaloner knows nothing that can incriminate us. Shall we adjourn to your office to discuss the situation? I confess I am surprised to see you holding a meeting tonight. You did not tell me.'

'You will find a message waiting for you in Westminster, Mr Swaddell,' replied Baron, while Chaloner looked from one to the other in dismay. 'Do not worry. You will not lose out.'

Chaloner did not know whether he was angrier at himself for thinking that he and Swaddell might be on the same side, or with the assassin for being swayed by what were probably very large sums of money.

Chapter 14

Chaloner fought with all his might when Doe came to lay hold of him, ignoring Swaddell's pleas to surrender with good grace. Baron brandished his gun, but Chaloner ignored it, knowing the felon would not want to alarm his distinguished guests by blasting away with firearms. With a grimace, the King of Cheapside entered the affray with his fists, at which point Chaloner knew the battle was lost. He went down in a flurry of punches, but continued to struggle until a sack was pulled over his head and he was bound so tightly that he could not move.

There followed an uncomfortable journey tossed over someone's shoulder – he suspected Baron's, because he was toted as though he were made of feathers. He knew they were on Cheapside, as he could hear the bells of St Mary Woolchurch, while a choking stench from one of the plague bonfires permeated the sack, almost asphyxiating him.

Next there came the sound of doors being opened and relocked, and he was bumped roughly down some stairs. The temperature dropped, telling him that he was underground. His stomach turned to ice at the notion that he was being taken to a cell, and with Hannah living in White Hall and Thurloe away, no one would think to look for him for days, if not weeks. Panic made it more difficult to draw breath into his lungs, and he felt himself begin to black out.

The next thing he knew was that he was lying on a cold stone floor. The sack was off his head, and he was no longer tied up, although he had no recollection of being freed. He opened his eyes, and a quick check revealed what he had already suspected: that he had been stripped of all his weapons, probably by Swaddell, who would know where to look.

The faint smell of damp cloth told him that he was in the cellar below Baron's house, where the stolen drapery was stored. He sat up to see that one corner of the room had been converted into a little parlour, with an eclectic selection of fine furniture, including cushion-strewn benches and a table loaded with food and wine. Baron, Doe, Poachin and Swaddell were talking in low voices nearby, and when Swaddell saw that Chaloner was awake, he went to the table and poured a cup of wine. Chaloner did not take the proffered goblet.

'Now I know why you wrote part of your letter to Williamson in cipher,' he said coldly. 'It told him to ignore the following "plea" for help, which is why it took so long to arrive – and when it did, it comprised four hirelings who would disappear at the first sign of trouble. There was probably no warrant either. You are just another traitor, seduced by the scent of gold.'

Swaddell's restless eyes stopped roaming around the room and settled on him, which Chaloner found distinctly unnerving. They were cold and hard, like a shark's.

404

'An oath is an oath,' he said. 'My loyalties are—'

'Swaddell and I have an understanding,' said Baron, coming to join them and giving Chaloner one of his engaging grins. 'One that has been in force for some time.'

Chaloner recalled what the felon had said when he and Swaddell had visited the Feathers together – that he had made Swaddell the same offer that he had made Chaloner. Obviously, Swaddell had been less squeamish about accepting.

'Protection Tax,' explained Swaddell. 'Baron pays it as well as collects it.'

'Each month, Mr Swaddell here earns a nice little allowance in return for keeping the authorities from being too interested in what I do,' Baron went on smugly. 'All without the knowledge of Spymaster Williamson, of course.'

'Of course,' said Chaloner flatly. He was furious with himself for believing that Swaddell could be trusted. The man was an assassin, and such people were not noted for their sense of honour. Worse, Chaloner had even felt the stirrings of respect for him, and the sense that perhaps they might do some good together.

'You did well,' said Baron, turning to Poachin. 'I did not hear them prowling about.'

'It was the tankard falling off the shelf.' Poachin was obviously pleased by the praise. 'When it dropped, the lid snapped, so I went to investigate. I found four men outside, but sixpence saw them on their way.'

Doe was pouting jealously. There were more bruises on his face than there had been earlier, and Chaloner was glad that some of his punches had struck home.

'Poachin did *not* do well,' he snapped. 'He mishandled the situation badly. He allowed Chaloner to create a

405

rumpus that upset our visitors, and they called an early end to the games. It has lost us a lot of money.'

'It was you who caused the rumpus,' countered Poachin, nettled. 'I was about to slip up behind him and slit his throat, nice and quiet, but you started a brawl.'

'Doe was right to stop you,' said Baron sharply. 'Gashed necks are difficult to pass off as accidents, as I have told you before.'

'Was it card games run by you that ruined Colburn?' asked Chaloner, watching Poachin's face take on a murderous expression. It turned darker still when Doe smirked at him, and Chaloner wondered if he could use their enmity to his advantage.

Baron was nodding. 'I did suggest he rein back, but the urge had bitten him and he would not listen. We refused to let him play after he had lost all he owned, but he promptly went to the bankers for money.' He shrugged. 'Once he could pay his debts again, we let him return. It was not our fault that he ruined himself and others – it was his decision to keep gambling, and to lie to the goldsmiths about why he wanted loans.'

'We lost money in the end, too,' added Doe. He limped to the table, hand to his side, and poured himself some wine. 'He gave us a house to pay off one debt, but it was a place he had already sold to someone else. He cheated us.'

There was a rattle of footsteps on the stairs, and Jacob appeared. 'I saw all your guests safely away from Cheapside, like you ordered,' he reported. 'Except Misick, who wanted to stop at the music shop and leave more medicine for Lettice Shaw. But he was too late – she is dead.'

'And?' asked Baron, unmoved by the news, although Chaloner was sorry.

406

'Word is that the turmoil in the rest of the city has been quelled, but I suspect it is because all the troublemakers and malcontents have come here. They heard rumours that we are on the verge of a riot, see, and want to join in. I was told this by the several strangers who I stopped.'

'Who started these tales?' demanded Baron angrily.

'A man who kept his face hidden by a scarf,' replied Jacob wryly, 'which describes half the population of London at the moment. Regardless, his lying tongue has brought a lot of undesirables into our domain, and there are too many for the trainband to oust.'

Baron's expression was dark. 'What do they want? To loot our shops and businesses?'

'Some do. Others are here to support us in defying the government's unfair plague measures. But most came to protest against the bankers.'

'Taylor,' spat Baron. '*He* is the problem. People accused Wheler of being greedy, but he was a saint compared to Taylor. The other financiers profess to abhor his methods, but they will adopt them now they have seen how well they work, which will bring Cheapside even more bother.'

'There is bad feeling over *The Court & Kitchin* as well,' added Jacob, 'because of a rumour that its author has been murdered.'

'Then we had better go and sort it out,' said Baron tersely. 'With God and the trainband's help.'

'Shall we kill Chaloner before we start?' asked Doe, starting forward eagerly.

'No,' said Swaddell sharply. 'Unless you want the Lord Chancellor prying into our affairs.'

Doe backed off, although Chaloner doubted the Earl would give them much cause for concern. When he failed to report, his employer would simply assume he had either died of plague or had disappeared to avoid paying Hannah's debts.

'What shall we do with him then?' asked Baron, regarding Chaloner coolly. 'I do not want him working for me now.'

'Leave him to me,' said Swaddell, with a smile that made Chaloner's blood run cold. 'But first, we had better go outside to see what is happening for ourselves.'

The moment the door had closed behind his captors, Chaloner embarked on a frantic search of the cellar, but he discovered nothing he had not seen on his last visit. He was in an underground chamber with stone walls, no windows and a door that had been secured from the outside with a bar. He was trapped until Swaddell decided that it was time for him to die.

He was not hungry, but he ate some of Baron's victuals anyway, partly for something to do, but also because keeping up his strength seemed like a good idea. Perhaps he would overpower or outwit Swaddell. Unfortunately, he knew he was deluding himself: the assassin was no novice at sly murder, and Chaloner held no great hope of seeing another dawn. Indeed, perhaps *Swaddell* was the killer he had been hunting for the last week – after all, Wheler's death had allowed the assassin to make a profitable arrangement with Baron, while the other victims might have been sacrificed to ensure it could continue.

After he had eaten his fill, Chaloner sat on the bench, closed his eyes and cleared his mind of everything except his investigations. He started at the beginning, and reviewed all he had learned, painstakingly discarding hearsay and distilling fact from fiction. It was the first opportunity he had had for such an exercise, and gradually the glimmer of a solution began to appear.

Not long afterwards, there were footsteps and the door was unbarred. Baron strode in and went straight to the table for wine. Doe hobbled after him, although Poachin held back, and Chaloner sensed there had been a further falling out. Jacob was a silent presence at Doe's side, while Swaddell lurked behind them all, like a spider. For one crazed moment, Chaloner considered launching himself at the assassin. It would certainly mean his own death, but he was doomed anyway, and there was something very appealing about taking Swaddell with him to the grave.

Then he reconsidered. The sight of Swaddell had aroused in him a burning desire not to be the next victim. He wanted to survive, to thwart whatever was happening, so that Swaddell would not emerge victorious. But how? He glanced at Doe's battered face, then at Poachin. Again, he wondered how to aggravate the dissent between the two, and encourage one to his side.

'All is not well in your domain, Baron,' he said, beginning by testing the first conclusion he had drawn from his analysis. 'Someone has been betraying you.'

Baron's lack of surprise told him that this was not news. The felon said nothing, and poured himself another drink, which Chaloner took as permission to continue. Perhaps Baron wanted what he already knew to be repeated by an independent source. Chaloner did not look at the two captains, but was acutely aware that both were as taut as bowstrings.

'Oxley and his family did not die of the pestilence,' he went on. 'I saw Emma's body. It was white, and free from plague tokens. It means she was murdered and—'

'Nonsense,' interrupted Poachin impatiently. 'Not every victim of the disease is afflicted with buboes. Ask any *medicus*.'

'I shall,' said Baron, regarding him coolly.

'Perhaps *I* should look at the bodies,' said Doe. He had his hand to his side again, and was obviously in pain. 'I wonder what I would find.'

'Stay away from the plague pits, Doe,' said Poachin warningly. 'I do not care if you die, but I do not want you bringing the disease back to us.'

'Yet Chaloner poses an interesting question,' said Baron softly. 'Misick claims he saw buboes, but can he be trusted? He loves cards but has no money – he is so deeply in debt to Joan that he is obliged to jump every time she barks. So how could he afford to visit our tables tonight? Could it be that someone *bribed* him – a verdict of plague in exchange for a hand of primero?'

'Well, do not look at me,' said Poachin angrily. '*I* know nothing about it.' He stabbed an accusing finger at Chaloner. 'And do not listen to him either. He has a cunning tongue, and is trying to sow the seeds of suspicion, so we will turn against each other. Do not let him—'

'See how the rat scampers when it is trapped,' interrupted Doe, arms folded and a gloating expression on his face. He glanced at Baron. 'I told you he was betraying us.'

'It is you who is the traitor,' snarled Poachin, although there was unease in his eyes, and he edged towards the door. 'Do not listen to these lies, Baron. We have been friends for years, and you *know* I am loyal. We grew up together . . .'

'We did,' conceded Baron. 'But that was years ago. We are different people now.'

'*You* certainly are,' snarled Poachin, finally abandoning his attempts to convince. 'You have changed since Wheler died, and not for the better. Your wife thinks the same. She—'

With a roar of rage, Baron leapt at him, but Poachin had anticipated an attack and was ready. He raced for the door, slamming it so hard that the latch jammed. By the time Baron had wrenched it free, his captain was gone. Meanwhile, Chaloner had charged towards Jacob, aiming to have the cutlass, but the ex-footman darted behind a table, giving himself time to haul out the weapon. As Chaloner could not fight him empty-handed, he was forced to retreat.

'See?' Doe asked Baron, all smug satisfaction. 'I told you Poachin was no good.'

The felon glowered and the younger man had the sense to wipe the grin from his face. 'After him,' Baron ordered curtly. 'And bring him back. Alive. You go too, Jacob.'

'Do not worry about Chaloner,' said Swaddell, when Doe hesitated. He drew a pistol from his belt. 'He will not do anything reckless.'

There was silence in the cellar after Doe and Jacob had gone. Baron took a deep breath, and Chaloner wondered if he knew that Doe would ignore the last part of his order, and that Poachin would soon join the growing body count. He glanced at the door. Could he reach it before Swaddell shot him? A glance at the assassin's watchful eyes told him he could not. And even if the weapon flashed in the pan, Chaloner would have to pass Baron, and there were trainband men in the corridor outside. He would not escape by running.

411

Absently, he wondered what was happening on the street above. How many Londoners were doing battle over their grievances? And was Randal's deadly sequel even now being hawked around the local taverns and coffee houses? Although Chaloner doubted he could have done much to stop it, it was nevertheless frustrating to be locked up while the city turned on itself.

'Did you kill Wheler?' Chaloner did not know why he bothered to ask. Baron had not confessed when he had raised the matter before, so was unlikely to do it now.

But Baron surprised him. 'I did not,' he said firmly. 'I would have preferred him alive for a little longer. I never wanted to be King of Cheapside, and had made the decision to retire once he had died of lung-rot, leaving Poachin or Doe to succeed me.'

Chaloner regarded him sceptically. 'Then why did you move so fast to take control?'

'To protect what he and I had built – I did not want it to collapse just because Joan did not know what she was doing. When the current trouble is over, Doe can have my crown, because Poachin is right: I *have* changed since I took over, and Frances does *not* like what I have become. I have learned the hard way that power corrupts.'

There was something in the way he spoke that made Chaloner want to believe him. 'If you are innocent, then why have you made no effort to clear your name?'

'Why would I? My trainband is more likely to stay loyal if they think I am the sort of man who can eliminate wealthy bankers and leave no evidence. And Williamson cannot arrest me without proof – of which there is none, because I did not do it.'

'There is evidence for the murders of Coo, Neve and Randal, though,' Chaloner went on, wondering why

412

Swaddell made no effort to prevent him from interrogating his ally. 'They were killed with your guns, and that can certainly be proved.'

'The ones with the ivory butts?' Baron raised his hands in a shrug. 'Those were stolen.'

'How convenient,' said Chaloner heavily.

'They were a gift from Doe and I noticed they were missing a week ago. Few people have access to the private part of my house, where my family live. But my captains do. Poachin . . .'

'It is a blow when one cannot trust one's underlings,' said Swaddell consolingly. 'The soldiers I brought with me tonight were bought off with sixpence. Is that all I am worth?'

'And besides, I would never have killed Coo,' Baron went on. 'Not only because he physicked my trainband and my family, but because of Caesar . . .'

Chaloner frowned his puzzlement. 'The horse?'

Baron nodded. 'Coo was there when Wheler said I could have him. Joan honoured his wishes when Coo was alive – she did not want a saint to think badly of her – but the moment Coo died, she said there were no witnesses, and her lawyers took him back. So, you see, Coo's murder cost me more than you can possibly know.'

'I cannot imagine that old nag—' began Swaddell.

'You do not understand affection,' interrupted Baron harshly. 'Caesar is a member of the family, and therefore priceless.' He turned back to Chaloner. 'Poachin is unaware of what Wheler promised in front of Coo, because I never told him. Doe, on the other hand, is in my confidence. In other words, Doe knows that I would *never* have killed the physician; Poachin does not.'

'So Poachin stole the weapons from your private quarters with the express purpose of having you accused of murder,' surmised Swaddell.

Baron nodded. 'People loved Coo, and the rumour that I killed him has weakened my power. You may have noticed how my trainband struggles to keep order now.'

Chaloner saw a black, deadly anger in the assassin's eyes, suggesting he had been telling the truth about his liking for Coo, and really did want the physician's killer brought to justice.

'You sold Temperance seven pairs of curtains.' Chaloner lurched to another subject when Baron finished his wine and prepared to leave again. He wanted to keep him talking, suspecting he would not live long once the felon had gone. 'Then your curbers stole them back again, to peddle to my Earl.'

Baron's rakish grin reappeared. 'She did not like them much anyway, but he thought they were glorious. Where lay the harm? Neve was a rogue, though. He told Clarendon they cost three thousand pounds—'

'Whereas you charged him twenty-nine hundred. Yes, I know. However, he *did* buy nine pairs, no matter what your ledger was altered to say.'

Baron raised his hands in a shrug. 'It was worth a try. Unfortunately, Doe made rather a mess of tampering with the books – Howard the milliner was far better at it. But your Earl will have his drapery. I was not lying when I said my brother-in-law was making more.'

'So you killed Neve,' stated Chaloner. 'For taking a commission without your consent.'

Baron laughed. 'I might have been vexed if he had taken his commission out of *my* money, but he took his Earl's, and that is none of my business. If you want his

414

killer, look to Poachin. And before you ask, I did not dispatch Fatherton, Milbourn or Randal either.'

Chaloner knew Baron had not killed Milbourn, because the printer was still alive, but he was not sure what to think about the others. He said nothing, and Baron continued.

'However, I admit to burning down the houses on Bearbinder Lane. I decided you might be right about the plague worms, especially after the Howard family perished. You may not think much of me, but I look after my own, and those buildings posed a risk to my people.'

'Did you know I was in it at the time?'

Baron's surprise seemed genuine. 'Really? Why, when you said it was full of the plague?'

'Howard,' said Chaloner, declining to answer when he saw a way to strike at Swaddell instead. 'Did you know that he was spying on you for Williamson?'

'He would not have dared,' declared Baron, and Chaloner saw the gleam of relief in the assassin's eyes. 'I am sorry you rejected my offer of employment, Chaloner. We could have worked well together. Come with me, Swaddell. I want a private word.'

With growing despair, Chaloner heard the bar fall into place on the other side of the door a second time, and Baron's voice receded along the corridor. However, only seconds passed before it was removed again, and the door swung open. It was Swaddell.

415

Chapter 15

Chaloner said nothing as Swaddell entered the cellar, unwilling to give the assassin the satisfaction of knowing that he was talking to delay the inevitable. Then he saw that although Swaddell had two pistols in his belt and a sword at his side, none were in his hands. Hope surged through Chaloner. He could win a fist fight.

'Come on, quickly,' whispered Swaddell urgently. 'I expected our four hirelings to warn Williamson of what is afoot, but the cowards appear to have let Poachin intimidate them into disappearing. Damn them for their cowardice!'

'What trick now, Swaddell?' asked Chaloner, making no move to do as he was told.

'Trick?' Swaddell regarded him in confusion, then his jaw dropped. 'Surely you do not imagine I am really on Baron's side?'

'He certainly seems to think so.'

Swaddell continued to gape. 'But you and I exchanged blood and promises!'

'You probably exchanged them with Baron, too.'

The colour drained from Swaddell's face and when

he spoke it was in a tight whisper that shook. 'I should kill you for that insult! I take vows seriously and I thought you did, too. Yet even so, I thought you might be uneasy, so I virtually *told* you to trust me.'

'You did?'

'I said "an oath is an oath" to remind you of our pact, and to assure you that I had the matter in hand. You played your part splendidly, convincing everyone that I had betrayed you. Now I know why: you believed it!'

'Why should I not?' Chaloner flashed back. 'You took bribes from Baron to look the other way while crimes are committed.'

'Of course I did! It is called "going undercover". Surely you are aware of the practice?' Swaddell was working himself into a frenzy. 'However, every penny Baron gave me is recorded in a ledger, and the money has been ploughed back into the intelligence services.'

'So I could go to Westminster and inspect these records?' asked Chaloner sceptically.

Swaddell bristled. 'This very minute if you like, although I think we both have more important matters to attend.'

With utter amazement, Chaloner realised that the absurd ritual they had played out in Maidenhead Alley had actually meant something to Swaddell. As Chaloner himself had lived a good part of his adolescence and all his adult life in situations where betrayal was the norm, it came as a shock to learn that there were people who honoured such promises. Swaddell's principles made him feel old, jaded and rather grubby.

'You and I are blood brothers,' the assassin went on. 'I would never betray you. God's teeth, Chaloner! I expected more of you. Williamson told me you were a man of integrity.'

417

'Did he?' Chaloner found that hard to believe. However, this was a discussion that should be held when they were not in the cellar of a vicious criminal who would kill them if he knew what was happening. He indicated with a gesture that it was time to leave.

'It is always the same,' Swaddell went on bitterly, ignoring him. 'Just because I occasionally eliminate certain undesirables, people think I am immoral. Well, I will have you know that I am an extremely ethical man, and I live by values that are far higher than most.'

'Oh,' said Chaloner, wishing he would lower his voice. 'Well—'

'I cannot begin to express the depth of my disappointment in you. And you had better thank God that our vow means I will not harm you, because at the moment I am sorely tempted to stick a knife in your gizzard.'

He scowled with a malignancy that was unnerving, and Chaloner saw he was going to have to say something conciliatory or Swaddell might inveigh at him until Baron reappeared, in which case they would both die.

'I am sorry,' he said, trying to sound sincere. 'I judged you by the standards I expect from others. It will not happen again.'

'It had better not. Now follow me. We have wasted too much time already, and tomorrow is Tuesday. We shall discuss your deplorable behaviour later – *if* we are both still alive.'

He tugged the door open, then recoiled in shock: Baron was standing on the other side, and the black expression on the felon's face told them that he had heard every word. Chaloner cursed himself for starting the discussion in the first place. Why could he not just have gone with Swaddell and confronted him once they were

418

outside? Now, even if he survived Baron's wrath, Swaddell would not.

'I thought as much,' said Baron, eyeing the assassin icily. 'You refused to take an oath of allegiance to me on the grounds of your faith, and being a religious man myself, I respected your wishes. But I should have known that you were not devout.'

'In my line of work,' said Swaddell with admirable cool, 'one cannot afford to be. I would spend all my time worrying about hell and eternal damnation.'

Baron whipped out a cutlass, but Swaddell jerked back, so the felon's first swipe went wide. The assassin drew his rapier, but its slender blade was no match for the thick implement in Baron's brawny paws, and it snapped in the first parry. He yanked out his pistols, and hurled them at Baron when impotent clicks reminded him that he had neglected to load them. Chaloner grabbed a lamp and flung it hard, but Baron batted it away impatiently, and his glittering attention did not shift from Swaddell for an instant. In desperation, Chaloner took a leaf from Polly's book, and leapt on to the felon's back, trying to batter him senseless with his fists.

Unfortunately, Baron was as strong as an ox, and while Chaloner was no weakling, he still found himself plucked off and hurled against the wall as though he were no more substantial than straw. The room swam before his eyes, and when his wits had stopped spinning he heard a gurgle. Baron had grabbed Swaddell, and his massive hands were around the assassin's throat.

Chaloner staggered to his feet and raced forward, butting Baron powerfully enough to make him loosen his hold for the moment that Swaddell needed to wriggle free. They exchanged a glance of understanding, then attacked together, but Baron was impervious to their thumps, punches and kicks. The ones he gave back, however, were debilitating, and Chaloner knew that unless they did something fast, they were going to be pummelled into oblivion.

He glanced around wildly and his eye fell on Swaddell's pistols. He snatched one up, and managed to dart in and deliver a sharp blow to the side of the felon's head. Baron collapsed to his knees, reeled for a moment, then crashed to the floor.

'Good,' muttered Swaddell, retrieving both guns and indicating that Chaloner should take the cutlass. 'Now follow me.'

They did not get far. When they reached the top of the stairs, they saw Doe at the end of the hall with Jacob and several other members of the trainband. Chaloner and Swaddell could not pass them, so they ducked into a conveniently located coal cupboard. They would have to wait until the coast was clear. Then Baron staggered up the stairs.

'Swaddell has betrayed us,' he said in a low voice that nevertheless held considerable rage. 'Find him. He will not be far.'

'Later,' said Doe, pulling a gun from his belt and pointing it at Baron. 'I have dealt with Poachin. Now it is your turn.'

Baron gaped at Doe. So did Swaddell, although Chaloner had guessed the identity of the traitor during the discussion about Caesar. Baron had made an erroneous assumption: that Doe would not have killed the witness who heard Wheler bequeath him the horse. He had overestimated his protégé's affection for him, and the truth was that Doe did not care that Coo's murder had lost Baron an animal for which he had formed a very deep attachment.

'You have killed Poachin?' asked Baron hoarsely. 'I told you to bring him back alive.'

Doe limped down the passageway. 'He will die tonight and so will you. You are too old for this business, and the time has come to yield to a younger man.'

Before Baron could respond, Doe lurched forward and dealt him a blow with the pommel of his dagger. It would not have landed had Baron been himself, but he was still dazed and went down hard. Scenting victory, Doe was on him like a wild animal, kicking and punching.

'The trainband will never follow a weasel like Doe,' hissed Swaddell to Chaloner in the darkness of their cupboard. 'His coup will be a disaster. Baron is the lesser of two evils – we shall have to save him.'

'For what?' Chaloner whispered back. 'Williamson to hang?'

Swaddell grimaced. 'You kept saying that someone *wanted* us to think Baron guilty of murder. Well, it seems you were right.'

Chaloner knew it. 'Doe is the killer. He shot Coo to turn people against Baron, which means he probably also killed Randal, Neve and Fatherton.'

'Well, he will not get away with it. Now *think*!'

Chaloner assessed the situation. Doe had five armed men; he and Swaddell had a cutlass, two unloaded guns and the element of surprise. The odds were not good.

Meanwhile, Baron had mustered enough strength to push Doe away and take refuge behind a chest. Doe stood with one hand to his side – the assault had hurt him as much as his victim.

'I should have known.' Baron's eyes glittered with rage. 'All those sly words about Poachin . . . but it was you who plotted against me.'

'For my rightful inheritance,' stated Doe. 'I stabbed Wheler so that *I* could take over, but you seized control before I could act.'

'You shot Coo,' said Baron, his voice thick with disgust. 'A good man. God help you!'

Doe shrugged. 'I used your gun and waved it all along Cheapside, to make sure people saw. Then I gave it to Randal, saying it was from you, in the expectation that Williamson would see it when he visited him to discuss *The Court & Kitchin*. But stupid Williamson never did find Randal, which meant I had to get the weapon back . . .'

He rubbed his side again, and then Chaloner understood exactly how he had been hurt – at Polly's house, when he had been used as a shield against his knife-wielding crony. It was how his face had been bruised, too – not from locking plague-ridden bankers in their houses as he had claimed.

'How could you have used a sot like Randal to further your plans?' sneered Baron. 'Fool!'

'It was a mistake,' acknowledged Doe. 'However, there were no misjudgements with Neve. I killed him with your other gun, and soon everyone will believe that you are the culprit.'

'I suppose you burned Milbourn's workshop as well. That was stupid – tame printers are useful.'

Doe shrugged. 'I told him not to publish Randal's book, as I could see it would cause trouble, but he ignored me. I shall tell everyone that you did it – and that you killed Fatherton before incinerating his corpse in Bearbinder Alley.'

So Noll had run to Doe when he had been told to fetch the constable, thought Chaloner. But there was no time to ponder the lad's betrayal, because Baron was speaking again.

'No one will believe you. I have no reason to want Fatherton dead.'

'I shot him in the head, which is how you killed Parliamentarians during the wars. It is more difficult than aiming for the body, and you always did love to show off your skill as a marksman. Unfortunately, no one has made the connection yet, but I will make it known when I am King of Cheapside.' He hissed between his teeth as he took a cudgel from Jacob. 'It is a pity you will not be alive to see how well my clever plot will work.'

Swaddell glanced at Chaloner. 'It has to be now. Ready?'

Chapter 16

Swaddell exploded from their hiding place, and his flailing pistols knocked one man insensible and caused two more to stagger back in alarm, while Chaloner slammed into Doe so hard that the cudgel cartwheeled from his hand. It was caught by Baron, who raised it above his head with a roar of triumph. Chaloner whipped around to deal with Jacob, dealing the ex-footman a kick that sent him sprawling.

Swaddell fell to a savage punch, so Chaloner stood over him, fending off attack after attack, while the assassin blinked frantically to clear his vision. Baron laid about him like a madman, and Jacob was struck stone dead as he tried to struggle to his feet. Doe glanced at him, which was his undoing – he did not see the knife in Baron's other hand. He shrieked in pain and fury as it entered his innards, and once he was down, the fight went out of his surviving men. They backed away, then fled. Baron was after them with a vengeful howl.

'Baron is doomed,' whispered Doe, as Chaloner crouched next to him. 'The murders of Wheler, Coo, Fatherton, Neve, Randal, the chaos here on Cheapside – all will be blamed on him.'

'You should not have killed Coo,' said Swaddell coldly. 'He was a good man.'

Doe squinted up at him. 'This is your fault – if you had been halfway efficient, you would have arrested Baron . . . But Taylor will put everything right, and Cheapside will be . . .'

'Will be what?' demanded Swaddell.

Doe coughed weakly. 'I am not sure, but it will happen today. I met him not half an hour ago and he told me. He wore his hooded cloak and spoke with the voice of doom. He told me that he manages everything with a song. For vengeance.'

'He is rambling,' said Swaddell in disgust. 'Leave him. There are more urgent matters—'

'*Now* I know why DuPont went from Long Acre to Bearbinder Lane,' said Chaloner, recalling how Doe had gloated over him for his ignorance. 'It was not for free medicine, but because Doe paid him to go. Doe *wanted* the plague brought to Cheapside.'

'No, I wanted it brought to *Baron*,' corrected Doe softly.

'Landlord Grey told me that DuPont had a visitor who wore a plague-mask,' Chaloner went on. 'Doe has one – he donned it to shoot Randal. Grey also said the visitor's clothes were respectable without being showy, which describes those of a felon who makes a decent living. He wore the mask when he ordered Kelke and his cronies to incinerate Bearbinder Lane as well.'

Doe grimaced. 'You should have died when I locked you in DuPont's room. I cannot imagine how you contrived to escape.'

'And then there was the hissing,' Chaloner went on, ignoring him.

425

'Hissing?' queried Swaddell.

'DuPont's visitor hissed, which Grey thought was a sign of unease; Coo's killer hissed when he saw me; Neve's killer hissed in Clarendon House; Randal's killer hissed when he met trouble; and Doe hissed when he was about to bludgeon Baron. A hissing man also met Fatherton and Onions in the Green Dragon to discuss stealing documents from Dutchmen.'

Doe scowled. 'That was an ingenious plan. It should have worked.'

'It was a ridiculous notion,' countered Swaddell harshly. 'Not *one* of your overly elaborate schemes stood a chance of succeeding, and you have done untold damage in the process. I suppose the deaths of the Oxley and Howard families were part of this stupid intrigue, too.'

'No – they died of the plague.' Spite flashed in Doe's eyes. 'And so will you. Taylor has the disease in his box. He told me so, and he will release it today . . .'

Baron returned and Chaloner tensed, not sure the felon would be in the mood to appreciate who had rescued him.

'There is trouble afoot,' Baron said tersely. 'My train-band cannot stop it and neither can Williamson's forces. Tear up the warrant for my arrest, and let us work together to save our city.'

Swaddell hesitated, but then pulled the piece of paper from his pocket. Baron snatched it and ripped it into shreds.

'Shake hands,' he instructed, 'as a mark of our alliance. Just until this crisis is over, of course. After that, all bets are off.'

Chaloner's hand was grasped first by Baron's meaty

426

paw, and then by Swaddell's limp, damp one. So could they be trusted? He supposed he would find out.

Chaloner was assailed with a sense of the surreal as he padded along the dark streets with Swaddell on one side and Baron on the other, the trainband streaming at their heels, and he wondered at the quirks of fate that had led him to join forces with a criminal and an assassin.

It was the deepest part of the night, perhaps one or two o'clock, and Cheapside was eerie, because it was full of people at a time when it was normally quiet. It was brightly lit in parts, where the wealthier houses and shops were illuminated with pitch torches; the watchers had done the same with the plague houses, to deter anyone from attempting to storm them. In other areas, the darkness was absolute, especially in the alleys.

Everywhere was the sense that something was about to happen. Many folk strutted along armed to the teeth, their faces taut with anticipation; others skulked in the shadows. Another crowd had gathered around the Standard, where several people had followed Taylor's example, and were making speeches. Their competing voices meant that none could be heard very well, which was fortunate, as not one was saying anything sensible.

Chaloner glanced at the music shop as he passed, and saw that the plague cart had stopped outside it. The door was open, and he skidded to a halt to watch two men emerge with a body wrapped in a sheet. They failed to swing it high enough to lodge on the corpses already there, and it slithered off again, landing on the ground with a thump.

'Get back!' barked one, when Shaw started forward

with a cry of dismay. 'You are law-bound to stay within your own four walls.'

'Please!' Shaw whispered hoarsely. 'That is my wife. My Lettice . . .'

The men threw the body upwards again, and this time it stayed. A dead, white hand slipped out, and Shaw closed his eyes tightly.

'There,' said one of the men gruffly. 'It is done. Now go back in.'

'I hate this city,' said Shaw in a low voice. 'How could this have happened? It is a cruel place, and nothing is fair.'

He trudged inside and shut the door. Then Swaddell gave an angry shout, calling Chaloner on to Goldsmiths' Row, where the bankers' henchmen were struggling to keep an enormous crowd away from their employers' properties. Several scuffles had broken out, and Chaloner was alarmed to note that the arrival of Baron and his trainband had done more to exacerbate the situation than calm it. Baron knew it, and thrust through his people to stand at the front of the screaming protesters, armed with nothing but the force of his personality.

'Go home,' be bellowed, and the sheer volume of his voice quelled much of the bickering. 'There will be no trouble tonight.'

'We are not going anywhere,' yelled a man who wore a scarf over his face, although he was still recognisable as Brewer Farrow. He was surrounded by cronies who were similarly disguised.

'The bankers have bled us dry,' added a cooper, identifiable by the tools in his belt. It was evident from the restless way he fingered them that he did not have barrelmaking in mind that night. 'I cannot make a profit from my business, because they take it all.'

428

'And now they refuse to return what we deposited with them,' called a clerk. 'They plan to keep *my* money for themselves. And to top it all, Taylor says he will give us the plague.'

The resulting roar of outrage was so loud that Chaloner fancied it rattled the nearby windows. The bankers' guards drew weapons, and Chaloner recalled what Silas had told him – that they were well paid for their loyalty. He hoped his friend was right, because if not, there would be nothing between the mob and the riches within. Swaddell darted forward and grabbed Baron's arm.

'The whole country will be plunged into chaos if the goldsmiths are ruined by looters. We need economic stability, or we might as well surrender to the Dutch right now. *Do* something!'

Baron tried again. 'Disperse, or as God is my witness, I will—'

'We are not paying your Protection Tax any more either,' hollered Farrow. 'We want Doe instead – he has offered to halve it.'

Cheers vied with the trainband's howls of indignation, and whatever else Baron bawled was lost in the racket. Someone lobbed a stone, and although it did him no harm, his followers reacted with fury. They shoved forward, trapping the crowd between their weapons and those of the bankers' sentries. No blows were struck, but it was clear that a fight would not be long in coming.

Chaloner watched Baron struggle to regain control. Then he spotted two familiar figures 'hiding' at the entrance to White Goat Wynd: Wiseman and Misick.

429

'Taylor has lost his reason,' said Misick worriedly. He had tied his wig under his chin to prevent it from being snatched off, and the effect was bizarre. 'Evan insisted on summoning help, so Joan told me to fetch Wiseman, but we cannot reach the house – we keep being pushed back.'

'Why me?' grumbled Wiseman. 'I am a surgeon, not a mad-doctor. Unless she wants his head amputated.'

Given the embarrassment caused by Taylor's unpredictable behaviour, Chaloner suspected the family might be by no means averse to such a solution.

'I hope there is someone inside who can stop him from coming out and making another reckless speech,' Swaddell said anxiously.

'Yes – Evan,' replied Misick.

Wiseman snorted his disbelief. 'You think *he* can control Taylor? You should have sent a servant to fetch me and stayed by your patient's side.'

'I have only been gone for a few minutes,' objected Misick. 'And—'

'I imagine it takes longer than that to play primero in the Feathers,' interrupted Chaloner, unwilling to stand by while the physician told brazen lies.

'The Feathers?' echoed Wiseman, regarding the physician accusingly. ''But you said the other day that you would never set foot in such a place.'

Misick grew angry. 'First, I did not leave Taylor's side until he was asleep – it is hardly my fault the noise of this rabble woke him. And second, what I do in my spare time is none of your business. It is not illegal to gamble.'

'It is when the stakes are so high,' countered Swaddell.

'The government has no business dictating how I spend my own money,' snapped Misick. 'I would not have to

430

visit such places at all if it fostered a more enlightened attitude.'

'It is right to impose such laws,' said Wiseman, and nodded to the seething crowd. 'It was reckless games of chance that ruined Colburn and precipitated this nonsense.'

'No! Taylor precipitated "this nonsense" by offering to give everyone the plague,' argued Misick.

'By threatening to release plague worms,' scoffed Wiseman. 'But everyone knows they cannot be gathered up like caterpillars, so no one believed him.'

'Oh, yes, they did,' countered Misick. 'And he *does* have some worms, anyway – he collected items of clothing from plague victims, ones that teem with the things.'

Chaloner looked at Wiseman. 'Would that let him spread the disease?'

Wiseman was suddenly pale. 'Taylor would never—'

'There he is!' breathed Swaddell in alarm. 'His family have let him escape, and he has a pair of guns! Christ God! If he fires one, we shall have a riot for certain. Misick, go and give him some of your calming medicine. Quickly!'

'Me?' squeaked Misick. 'How am I supposed to tackle an armed man? I am a physician, not a warrior.'

Taylor stood alone, looking around with detached interest. He wore an odd combination of nightclothes and riding boots, while the top of his box poked from the bag he carried over his shoulder. Then Evan and Joan appeared. Evan tried to take his father's arm, but Taylor roared in fury and pointed a gun at him. Evan cowered away, so Taylor lowered the weapon and went back to surveying the crowd, allowing Evan and Joan to

431

scramble to safety. Chaloner started towards him, but the gun came up a second time, forcing him to retreat. Tensely, he assessed the distance between them. Could he cover it and disarm the banker without triggers being pulled in the process?

'I told you that particular sleeping draught would not be very effective,' snapped Evan at Misick. 'Especially after doses of your Elixir, Venice Treacle, Goddard's Drops, Mithridatum, Turpentine Pills and tobacco.'

'Taylor has swallowed all that?' cried Wiseman, shocked. 'Then no wonder he is raving! These quack potions are dangerous on their own, but when mixed . . . What were you thinking, Misick? It is *you* who has driven him out of his wits – with a cocktail of poisonous ingredients!'

'Oh, come,' interrupted Joan dismissively. 'Medicines cannot harm anyone. They are—'

Evan cut across her. 'Father was perfectly rational before Misick came along. He would never have bought the other bankers' bad debts if he had been sane. Nor would he have ordered such extreme measures to collect on them.'

'Oh, I see,' said Misick wearily. 'You were happy to implement his decisions when people were too cowed to object, but now they are in revolt, you aim to shift the blame to me. You—'

He stopped abruptly as Taylor approached. Chaloner eased a knife from Wiseman's belt. Could he disable Taylor without the guns going off? He tensed, ready to lob it, but the banker read his intention and aimed a dag at Swaddell.

'Money,' he announced. 'Give me some or I shall blow his brains out.'

'Come inside,' coaxed Misick, although from behind Wiseman. 'I will make you a—'

'Give me money *now*,' hissed Taylor. 'Or Williamson's creature dies.'

Chaloner could see he was in earnest, so he pulled out Maude's cabochon, hoping she would forgive him. 'I have no money, but will this suffice?'

'Oh, yes.' Taylor fixed it with manic eyes. 'Almandine garnets prevent the plague.'

He reached for it with one hand and struck Chaloner under the nose with the other, an unexpected and sly move that caught the spy by surprise. His eyes watered furiously, and by the time he had blinked them clear, the cabochon had been wrenched from his fingers and Taylor had disappeared down White Goat Wynd. Swaddell and Misick had tried to stop him, but had tripped over each other in the process.

Chaloner hurried after the banker, Swaddell at his heels. They emerged on Cheapside, bright and thronged with people, but Taylor was nowhere to be seen.

'Now what?' muttered Chaloner. 'He will cause a riot for certain if he wanders about robbing people at gunpoint.'

'I think we will have one anyway,' said Swaddell, looking wildly this way and that. 'Especially if Randal's sequel makes an appearance.'

Back on Goldsmiths' Row, the mood of the mob was growing uglier, although the guards continued to stand their ground. Baron was doing his best to disperse the protesters, but he and his trainband were too few to make much of an impact. Swaddell stalked towards the doorway where Evan, Joan, Misick and Wiseman had taken cover.

'Evan, find your father,' he ordered. He turned to Joan and Misick. 'You two stay here, lest he tries to go home. He *must* be apprehended.'

'What am I supposed to do against a lunatic armed with pistols?' demanded Evan.

'And I must protect my bank,' added Joan.

'*Whose* bank?' demanded Evan sharply.

Joan regarded him with dislike. 'Mine – the one made powerful with *my* inheritance and *my* ideas. Do not argue, Evan. You know I have been running it while your sire has turned mad.'

'Discuss it later,' barked Swaddell. 'Now do as I say – all of you!'

Evan and Joan looked as though they would argue, but a glance at the assassin's face warned them that this would be ill-advised. Scowling, they and Misick slouched away. Swaddell started to give orders to Wiseman, too, but Chaloner interrupted urgently.

'Doe misled us. He claimed he met Taylor not long ago, wearing a hooded cloak, but Taylor is not sane enough to disguise himself. Moreover, Doe said that Taylor was managing everything "for vengeance". But—'

'Later!' snapped Swaddell. 'This is not important now.'

'Yes, it is, because all this mischief is being deliberately orchestrated by someone – each sly rumour is specifically designed to enrage. And Doe actually met the culprit – a person purporting to be Taylor, although Doe was too dim-witted to question the claim.'

Swaddell stared at him. 'You are right,' he breathed. 'Someone *has* been sowing the seeds of dissension. And I know who: Silas, the strongest and cleverest of Taylor's sons.'

Chaloner wanted to disagree, but was painfully aware

434

that Silas had lied about his association with Backwell and had declined to answer reasonable questions. He also had good reason to want vengeance, given the shabby treatment he had received at the hands of his family. But—

'Advance!' howled Farrow. 'Take what is yours. Then we shall free the folk shut up in their houses because the bankers left them no money to bribe the searchers.'

The multitude bayed its delight and pressed forward. The cordon of guards buckled but held.

Swaddell's voice was urgent. 'I will go to Cheapside and try to keep the plague houses shut. You must find Silas and stop him causing more mischief. Can you tackle him alone?'

'Chaloner will not be alone,' said Wiseman grandly. 'He has me.'

'Wait!' shouted Chaloner, as Swaddell raced away, but there was too much noise, and the assassin did not hear. He tried to follow, but another surge towards the shops blocked his way.

'Where will Silas be?' asked Wiseman. 'His home? A tavern?'

'Silas is not the culprit,' snapped Chaloner, taut with agitation. 'Misick is.'

Wiseman gaped at him. 'No! He is neither cunning nor audacious enough to have devised such a plan. I have known him for years.'

'He *deliberately* fed Taylor potions to make him insane – even I know that mixing different remedies is dangerous, so a physician certainly will. Moreover, you are a surgeon, who knows nothing of diseases of the mind, so why summon you, when he could have called someone better qualified? Because he did not want a *medicus* who would see what was really happening!'

'I did, though,' said Wiseman smugly. 'But it was not his idea to fetch me – it was Joan's.'

'Joan!' exclaimed Chaloner, as all became clear at last. 'Of course! She is cunning and audacious, and she was the one who hired Misick in the first place. He owed her money, and she offered to cancel the debt in exchange for his services.'

'I heard her giving him orders – brusquely. I wondered at the time why he put up with it.'

'His lack of funds leaves him no choice, and his situation is unlikely to improve if he continues to gamble in the Feathers. Then there is her husband Randal – I cannot imagine it is coincidence that his sequel is due to be released today.'

'But these reckless antics threaten the safety of her bank. Why would she—'

'You heard her answer that yourself – with Taylor ill and Evan minding him, who has been running the business? She has! And she has a plan for it, although I have no idea what it might be.'

It was not easy for Chaloner and Wiseman to fight their way through the mob to where Joan and Misick were supposed to be on the lookout for Taylor. They arrived to find no sign of either. Then Chaloner glimpsed movement in White Goat Wynd – the pair were turning down the tiny alley that provided the residents of Goldsmiths' Row with rear access to their properties.

'You grab her, while I tackle Misick,' growled Wiseman. 'And if he is punched for trying to use me to further his nefarious plans, then that is too bad.'

But Joan and Misick had too great a start, and had disappeared through a door long before Chaloner and

436

Wiseman could reach them – a door that was now locked and barred from within.

'Taylor's house,' remarked Wiseman. 'Can you break in?'

Chaloner tried, but it was a bank – specifically designed to thwart invaders. He turned his attention to an adjacent window instead, although it took his expertise and Wiseman's strength before they were able to prise it open. He climbed through it quickly, then turned to the surgeon.

'Find Swaddell. Tell him what we have reasoned and ask him to send help.'

Inside, the ancient stone walls muted the racket from the street at the front, rendering the building eerily silent. He lit a lamp and began to explore.

The kitchen was enormous, and had several pantries leading off it. Two were locked, suggesting that there was something inside worth seeing. He picked the mechanism on the first to discover a great stack of pamphlets entitled *More Tayles from the Court & Kitchin*. At least they had not been distributed yet, he thought.

He relocked it, then moved to the other, which was empty except for a pallet bed, where the body of a maid lay. He edged closer, then jumped at Wiseman's voice close behind him.

'Plague,' the surgeon said, using a poker to examine it. 'With running buboes and filthy dressings that will certainly give the disease to anyone rash enough to touch them.'

Chaloner jerked away in alarm. 'Did you deliver my message to Swaddell?'

'Cheapside is so crowded that finding anyone would be impossible, so I decided to help you instead.' Wiseman gestured to the corpse. 'There has been no report of plague here, which means her sickness has been concealed

437

from the searchers. Or the searchers have been bribed to look the other way.'

'The house appears to be deserted, which means her fellows have fled – perhaps taking the disease with them.'

'Then God help us all,' breathed Wiseman.

Chaloner pushed him out and refastened the door. 'Now we must find Joan and Misick.'

Moving stealthily, Chaloner and Wiseman searched the ground floor, but their caution was unnecessary: there was no one to stop them. The jewellery displays had been dismantled and the door to the vault was ajar: a glance showed it was empty. Had Taylor's people stolen everything before they had fled? Then there was an angry roar from outside, audible even through the thick walls. How long would it be before the horde forced its way past the guards? Chaloner only hoped that he and Wiseman would not be in inside when it did.

The first floor was also full of the signs of hasty abandonment – inkwells on their sides, ledgers and papers scattered across floors, and a half-eaten pie on a table. Then Chaloner heard voices coming from Taylor's office. He crept towards it, indicating with a wave of his hand that the surgeon should stay back.

The door was open, so he peered around it. Inside were Joan and Misick. The physician's wig was dishevelled, presumably from its passage through a hostile crowd. Joan's ferrety face was malevolent in the flickering lamplight, and her eyes flashed with anger.

'You should have stopped him,' she was snarling. 'You know what is in his Plague Box. How could you let him wander off with it?'

'I thought you *wanted* him loose in the city with the

thing under his arm,' Misick snapped. 'He will be torn to pieces when he is recognised.'

'His jewels are in it. I wanted to take them out first.'

The crack of a stone hurled at a window warned Chaloner that it was no time to eavesdrop. He surveyed the room quickly, and saw that while there was a handgun within grabbing distance of Joan, Misick was unarmed. He flung open the door and dashed in.

Joan moved fast, yet Chaloner would still have reached the pistol first if Misick had not reacted with impressive speed. The physician hurled himself forward, knocking into Chaloner and unbalancing him just long enough to allow Joan to seize the weapon. Hope of rescue evaporated when Chaloner saw that Wiseman had not stayed put as ordered, but had followed him.

'There is no time for this,' he said, when a second pebble hit the glass. 'Those people will storm this building soon, and anyone they find inside will be—'

'They will not touch me,' declared Joan. 'I am not responsible for Taylor's excesses.'

'I doubt they will see it that way.' Chaloner wondered if she had been at Misick's medicines herself, for it was a naive remark. 'Now put down the weapon, and come—'

'Tie them up, Misick,' Joan ordered. 'We do not want them getting in our way.'

Misick stepped forward with cords from the curtains. Chaloner started to back away, but Joan pointed her gun at Wiseman's head. Would she shoot, knowing that the sound might precipitate an attack by the rabble outside? He looked at her ruthlessly determined face and suspected she would. Thus there was nothing he could do as Misick secured his hands behind his back. He clenched his fists, though, aiming to prevent the cords from being pulled

439

too tight, but Misick guessed what he was doing and compensated by making a slip knot and hauling on it as hard as he could. Then he did the same to Wiseman. As an additional precaution, both prisoners were then roped to Taylor's desk to prevent any sudden lunges.

Wiseman regarded Misick in distaste. 'What led you to take such a dark path? Dosing patients with dangerous concoctions, throwing in your lot with those who mean London harm . . .'

Misick shrugged. 'I have an expensive lifestyle and medicine does not support it.'

Chaloner twisted his hands frantically behind his back, but Misick had done his work well: his knots were rock-hard and the cord so taut that there was no give in it whatsoever. Then a third stone hit the window, and this time the glass shattered. When both Misick and Joan swung towards the sound, Chaloner used the opportunity to lean towards a pot of writing implements on the desk.

As his hands were behind him, he could not see what he was doing, although he managed to snag something before Joan and Misick turned back again. Unfortunately, it was not the quill-sharpening blade he had been aiming for, but a 'fountain' pen – a new-fangled invention with its own supply of ink. The upside was that its nib was metal and fairly sharp; the downside was that it was not very big. He began to saw at the cord anyway, praying that it would be equal to the task.

'Misick's motives are greed and self-interest, but what about yours?' asked Wiseman, treating the physician to another contemptuous glance before addressing Joan. 'The same?'

'She objected to being fobbed off with Randal,' supplied Chaloner. He spoke calmly, but behind his back he was frantically scraping the makeshift blade against his bonds. 'She thought she deserved better.'

'*Taylor* should have married me,' declared Joan. 'Then we could have ruled my first husband's empire together. But he gave me his least appealing son, then refused to take back what Baron had stolen from me. He and Evan will not survive today.'

Outside, Farrow was yelling, and although Chaloner could not make out the words, he could tell the mob was loving them. Through the broken pane, pitch torches illuminated upturned faces – at least two hundred, probably more. He sawed harder, trying not to wince when the pen slipped and cut his hand. There was a wet cascade over his fingers as the ink drained out of the reservoir.

'Enough,' he said urgently. 'Or do you want to die? Cut us loose and—'

'It is you who will die,' snapped Joan. 'You are Swaddell's creature, whereas I am just a helpless woman. Who do you think the mob will kill?'

'All of us,' said Chaloner desperately. The pen was slippery now, and difficult to manipulate. 'And even if by some miracle you do survive, you will have nothing left – this building will be razed to the ground, and every coin and scrap of gold will be gone.'

'Yes, this house will burn, but we will sue the city for a new one. And looters will not find a penny – I emptied the vault and hid the treasure days ago. But they will find something else.'

'Pamphlets to cause a rumpus, and the plague,' put in Misick with a chilling smile.

'You *want* people to die of the disease?' asked Wiseman, shocked. 'But you are a *medicus*!'

441

'Nothing will happen to those who stay outside,' said Joan icily. 'But those who break in to loot will suffer a fate that serves them right.'

'And what happens when these "robbers" return to their wives and children?' asked Wiseman. 'Are innocent babes to be punished with death as well?' He pressed on before they could reply. 'But I doubt all this is your idea. You have not had time, what with managing the bank, gambling at the Feathers and poisoning Taylor.'

They declined to answer, but he was right, of course. Chaloner knew he should concentrate on escaping, but he could not leave the question alone. So who *was* directing their actions? Was Silas at the heart of the mischief after all? Or Backwell?

Out in the street, Farrow was still yelling, and Chaloner saw Joan smirk her satisfaction.

'He is in your pay,' he said in understanding. 'Your personal rabble-rouser.'

'He is so desperate to avenge himself on the trade that ruined him that I did not even have to give him any money,' she gloated. 'Just whisper in his ear and point him in the right direction.'

'But it was your first husband who destroyed him. Why would he listen to you?'

'I do not treat with such people myself,' she said disdainfully. 'I delegate to minions.'

'Minions like your husband, I suppose,' said Wiseman in distaste. 'A weak man, who obligingly wrote inflammatory tracts.'

Chaloner recalled Randal's claim. 'It was Joan who told him that he would feel better once his grievances were out in the open.'

'He did feel better,' smirked Joan. 'He has thoroughly

442

enjoyed the stir his stupid pamphlet has caused.' She jumped at a sudden clatter of stones on the windows.

'We should ready ourselves,' said Misick uneasily. 'I am not sure the guards can hold them back much longer.'

'Staying here flies in the face of all reason,' said Chaloner, desperately looking from one to the other. 'Which means you are under orders from someone else – someone who does not care about your safety. You are being used, as you have used others! How can you not see it?'

'Shut up!' shouted Joan, although uncertainty flared in her eyes. 'Of course we shall survive. I am needed to lead London's *only* bank.'

At that moment, there was a cheer from outside: the guards' line was disintegrating. Scenting victory, the mob surged forwards.

'There are more people here than I expected,' gulped Misick. 'Are you sure we have to—'

'Yes!' hissed Joan urgently. 'Or all our work will have been for nothing. Now hurry!'

Chapter 17

Chaloner's pen was so slick with sweat, blood and ink that he was afraid of dropping it. It meant he was forced to rub slowly and patiently at the cords that bound him, which was difficult when every instinct screamed at him to hack as hard as he could. Joan and Misick were mad, he thought, to think they would be spared when the horde reached the office.

He tried to think rationally, to guess what they planned to do, but it was hopeless, so he concentrated on moving his makeshift blade instead. Were his efforts paying off or was he wasting his time? He could not tell, but it was the only chance he had, so he persisted. Meanwhile, Misick busied himself at the table. Chaloner could not see what the physician was doing, although it was something that involved foul smells.

Joan grabbed a coat from a bench and began to tug it on. It was an ancient thing, which covered her finery and would render her indistinguishable from the invaders. It was also flecked with silvery grey hairs.

'Slasher!' exclaimed Chaloner, recalling the dog's unusual pelt. 'That is Oxley's coat. You say you never dealt with Farrow yourself, so someone did it for you – Oxley, a lout who would do anything for money. I saw him here when Taylor hurt his toe. Now I know why: to receive orders from you.'

Joan did not affirm or deny the charge, but the knowledge allowed the last piece of the puzzle to fall into place, leaving Chaloner so stunned that, for vital seconds, he neglected to saw at the cord.

'But Oxley is dead,' Wiseman pointed out. '*He* has not been prompting Farrow today.'

'He and his family were murdered.' Chaloner started working on the rope again when the protesters began to pound on the door; it was sturdy, but it would not withstand such an onslaught for long. 'Which means that Lettice could not have nursed the boy in his final illness. Shaw was lying – and *there* is the real mastermind behind the madness! Not Taylor, but someone pretending to be him, and who told the gullible Doe that he "manages everything with a song". Shaw! A talented singer.'

'Shaw?' asked Wiseman doubtfully. 'Really?'

Chaloner recalled the paint on the music shop door, different to that on the other houses. And why? Because Shaw had put it there himself! Then he had persuaded the watcher that he and Lettice were responsible folk who would not leave their house. But Shaw *had* left it, of course. For a start, he had been wearing a coat when he had been called to his window, and who wore coats indoors?

'He killed two birds with one stone,' he said, answers coming thick and fast. 'First, he silenced a family who knew the truth about him. There were no buboes on Emma—'

Misick turned to smirk at him. 'But everyone believed me when I said there were.'

445

'And second, if everyone thinks that Shaw is locked up with the plague, then he is free to wander about as he pleases, to stir up trouble among people with grievances.'

Chaloner tried a second time to see what Misick was doing, but the movement caused the pen to skid out of his fingers and drop to the floor. Joan looked sharply at him, so he began talking to distract her while he frantically twisted his hands this way and that in the hope that he had sliced through enough of the cord to allow him to snap it.

'Shaw speculated in tulips—'

'He did,' said Misick, turning to nod. 'And lost everything, poor soul.'

'Which he would not have done had his fellow bankers stood by him. He claims to be happy selling music, but how can it be true when he and Lettice have to endure the condescending patronage of men like Backwell?'

'Backwell means well,' said Joan. 'But he is insensitive.'

There was a loud crash, followed by a triumphant cheer. The door had fallen in.

'They lost a child.' Chaloner looked at Misick. 'Because they could not pay for a physician.'

'I would not have charged them.' Misick held up a glass flask and inspected its contents. 'But they did not know me then. Now Lettice has suffered a similar fate.'

Downstairs, the looters' excited cries turned to disappointment when they discovered the shop devoid of riches. How long would it be before they broke into the locked pantries?

'Misick!' barked Joan, her voice cracking with tension. 'Hurry!'

446

'I am going as fast as I can,' the physician snapped back.

'You will be too late,' warned Chaloner. 'The rioters will be here at any moment, and you will be torn to pieces.'

'They do sound angry,' said Misick nervously. 'Shaw cannot expect us to die on his account, so perhaps we should leave while we can.'

Chaloner was too fraught to be satisfied by the confirmation of his suspicions. He could hear footsteps on the stairs, along with an increasing cacophony of frustrated yells, and his wrists burned from his frenzied struggles to free them.

'All will be for naught if we do not carry out his commands,' snapped Joan. 'You heard him: we follow his orders to the letter or not at all.'

'He is tying up loose ends – he wants you dead so that you cannot betray him.' Desperately, Chaloner turned to Misick, hoping to appeal to the weaker of the two. 'Whatever you are doing will not work, so stop before—'

'Yes, it will,' interrupted the physician. 'My Plague Elixir explodes when mixed with spirit of turpentine, so all I have to do is insert fuses of cloth, which can be set alight . . .'

'And then what?' demanded Chaloner, when hammering footsteps indicated that the invaders were scattering through the offices. 'Throw them at people while they just stand there? You must see this is madness!'

'Farrow will lead the looters in here, but he has outlived his usefulness, so the first bottle will be for him,' replied the physician. His voice was unsteady and he scowled at Chaloner. 'The second will be for you. The fight will go out of the rest once they see you burn, and we shall

447

escape down the back stairs during the ensuing confusion.'

'What happened to turn you so bitter?' asked Wiseman pityingly, while Chaloner was so stunned by the ludicrous nature of the plan that he was momentarily lost for words. 'Joan?'

'I have more talent than all the other bankers put together,' she snarled. 'But will I ever be Master of the Goldsmiths' Company? No. However, things will be different tomorrow. Shaw has a powerful sponsor who will reward me for all I have done these last few weeks.'

'There is no powerful sponsor!' cried Chaloner, astonished that she should believe such a wild claim. 'If there were, Shaw would not be selling music from a shop that reeks of sewage.'

Joan addressed Misick urgently as the rioters entered the room next door. 'Is that the last one?'

Misick nodded, but at that moment a stone flew through the window and sheer chance saw it knock the flask from his hand. It fell to the floor, where it smashed. He dabbed at the droplets on his wig and reached for another, but anxiety made him careless and he inadvertently bumped against the lamp. His hair ignited with a dull whump.

He issued a horrified shriek and tried to pull it off, but it was fastened too securely. Then the flames caught his coat and within seconds he was a human torch. He howled in pain and terror, while Joan surged forward in an effort to rescue the remaining flasks.

Panic gave Chaloner strength, and he twisted his hands with all his might. Suddenly he was free. He grabbed the quill sharpener from the desk and slashed through the cord that held Wiseman. Rage blazed in Joan's eyes as she prepared to lob the missiles she had grabbed, but Misick knocked into her. Plague Elixir and turpentine slopped out, and the inferno that was Misick did the rest. There was another dull whump, and then there were two burning people in the room. Chaloner started towards them, appalled.

'No – it is too late,' shouted Wiseman.

At that moment the door flung open to reveal Farrow, whose savagely vengeful expression suggested he was not about to listen to reason. Chaloner put his head down and charged, sending the brewer sprawling back into his cronies. Yelling for Wiseman to follow, Chaloner clambered over the chaos of arms and legs, and turned left, hoping the back stairs were where he expected them to be, or he and Wiseman were doomed. They were, and he took them three at a time, Wiseman lumbering at his heels.

The stairs led to the kitchen, where a dozen men were laying siege to the locked pantries, clearly in the belief that gold was stockpiled within.

'We must stop them,' breathed Wiseman, aghast. 'But how?'

Chaloner put a hand to his head, which ached with tension, and saw that his fingers were a mess of blood and ink. It gave him an idea. He smeared it on his neck, hoping the light would be too dim to expose the ruse. Wiseman grasped the plan immediately, and flung himself into action.

'Plague!' he bellowed, while Chaloner reeled into the kitchen. 'He has the plague!'

There was a concerted dash for the back door, but other would-be looters had just succeeded in battering it down. There was a collision, followed by a frenzied skirmish as each group tried to force its way past the other. Smoke billowed into the kitchen, while the crackle of approaching flames and the screams of those trapped on the upper floors did nothing to calm the situation.

Then there was a booming yell, and every head swivelled towards it. There was silence, then suddenly everyone was running in the same direction. Baron and his trainband had arrived.

'Need help, Chaloner?' asked the King of Cheapside mildly.

The blaze in Taylor's shop spread to the adjoining buildings with horrifying speed, and the beautiful façade that had inspired poets was quickly lost behind a wall of flames and smoke.

'At least Randal's book will be destroyed,' wheezed Wiseman, his eyes streaming. 'Along with that plague-dead maid.'

A figure approached, his hair a soggy mess that straggled down his back. It was Poachin. Baron clapped a comradely hand on his shoulder, so Chaloner supposed the rift precipitated by Doe had been mended.

'The worst troublemakers are not Cheapside folk,' Poachin reported. 'They hail from the Fleet and St Giles rookeries, enticed here by the promise of loot by a man in a blue coat. He kept his face hidden, but Gabb and Knowles say it was Shaw. Yet I cannot believe . . .'

Wiseman gave a terse account of what had happened, while Chaloner struggled to think. Where was Shaw now? Among the masked rioters, watching the mischief he had caused?

'I always thought his music shop was an odd concern,' said Baron. 'His customers were courtiers who seldom

450

pay their bills, and I never did understand how he made enough to survive.'

'He brought Colburn to the Feathers, even when the man bleated that he had no more money,' added Poachin, while Chaloner thought about Hannah's flageolet. Perhaps he should have been suspicious sooner of a creditor who let forty pounds remain outstanding for so long. 'He kept promising that his luck would change with the next hand. It never did, of course, and when Colburn was finally ruined, I had the sense that he was pleased.'

'And now we know why,' said Wiseman. 'So his debts would destroy the bankers.'

'Plague,' said Baron tersely. '*That* is the terrible thing Shaw has planned for today – his ultimate revenge on the whole city.'

'And he might do it,' said Wiseman, 'if Taylor's box really does contain infected cloth.'

'Get this fire under control,' Baron ordered Poachin. 'I will look for Taylor.'

'Go to the Standard,' suggested Poachin. 'He was there not long ago.'

Baron began to run, moving with surprising speed for a man his size, Chaloner trotting next to him and Wiseman ploughing along behind.

They reached Cheapside to find it full of howling rioters. Some were attacking the wealthier mansions, while others clustered around the plague houses, and there was a great cheer when a man arrived with a bucket of whitewash and painted over the red cross on Widow Porteous's door. When it was done, he marched on to the next one.

'Where are the watchers?' cried Wiseman, horrified.

451

'Fled for their lives,' replied Baron. 'Although the plague is not in most of the houses the authorities have shut up, so there is no real danger—'

'There *is* danger!' yelled Wiseman. He jabbed a finger at Widow Porteous, who was at her window calling down to the crowd. 'Look at her! You can see she has a fever from here.'

'There are fevers other than plague—'

'Would you let her touch Frances or your children?' demanded Wiseman. 'No? Then I suggest you keep her in her house, where she belongs.'

They stood face to glowering face, and for a moment Chaloner thought Baron would refuse. Then the felon nodded assent, and turned to Chaloner.

'Find Shaw before he causes any more mischief.' He whipped around to Wiseman. 'And you must stop Taylor. I will try to contain matters here.'

Chaloner reached the music shop to find that the cross had been daubed out, but the windows and door were still nailed shut. He hurried to the back, and was not surprised to find the rear gate unlocked. Damp footprints on the step indicated that it had been used recently.

He entered with every nerve in his body taut with tension. The shop was deserted, but then he heard someone talking in the cellar. He aimed for the stairs. There was a light at the bottom, but it was feeble, and the glow it cast did not allow him to see much. However, it did show that work had continued apace since he had last been there. The cellar floor had been raised by another ten feet, and comprised an evil, reeking soup of molten mud. It almost reached the scaffolding, which

452

now formed a narrow walkway running around all four sides of the room. Above it all hung the massive leather bucket, mostly full and almost ready to be poured.

Taylor was squatting near the base of the steps. His nightgown was filthy, and there was blood on his sleeves. His handsome face was flushed and his eyes were too bright, while his hair was a wild mat that stood up in all directions. He was muttering to his box in an unsettled, agitated way, fiddling with the hinge. Chaloner swallowed hard. Had he already opened the thing, and touched its filthy contents? Was that why he was feverish?

'You should not be here.' Chaloner whipped around to see Lettice on the stairs above him. She held a gun. 'There is plague in this poor, benighted house.'

Chaloner gaped at her. 'I saw your body tossed on the cart . . .' But all he had seen was a corpse wrapped in a blanket and a cold white hand. Understanding dawned. 'It was Oxley's daughter. She was supposed to have run away . . .'

Lettice giggled. 'She served a higher purpose.'

'So you killed the whole family, then told Misick to say there were buboes on Emma so the house could be shut up.' Chaloner looked for Shaw. It was too dark to see, but he could sense the man's presence. 'Oxley never demanded lots of ale, and nor did you send it to him – he was dead the whole time. And he was telling the truth when he claimed that Emma was suffering from the after-effects of too much ale—'

'If they had been better neighbours, we might have let them live. Stand still, Mr Chaloner. I *will* shoot you if you move.'

Chaloner had stepped towards Taylor. 'I need to take his box away. You must know what the plague—'

'I do – better than most,' interrupted Lettice bitterly. 'My daughter died of it, if you recall.'

'Then you will not want it inflicted on anyone else.'

'Oh, but I do!' Her voice was hard, and the hand holding the gun was rock steady. 'Our fellow goldsmiths could have saved us from the Tulip Bubble, but they did nothing. Well, now *they* will know what it is like to lose everything. And *their* children will die of that vile disease.'

'But so will others who are not bankers—'

'I do not care! Let the plague take this whole, filthy city.'

Chaloner scanned the darkness desperately. Where was Shaw? Did he have a gun, too? And how good a shot was Lettice? Would she hit him if he made a dive for Taylor's box?

'You have been clever,' he said, wondering if he could distract her with words. 'You have created unease and ill-feeling with rumours—'

'We *created* nothing. We merely exacerbated what was already there. People were angry with the bankers and the plague measures anyway.'

'And you used Joan. Through her, you controlled Misick, Oxley, Farrow and Doe.'

'Not Mr Doe. He acted for his own interests, although we might have given him the occasional prod. Robin appeared to him tonight, for example, in a hooded cloak.'

'But there is no powerful sponsor. That was a lie, to convince Joan to do your bidding. Who did you claim? A member of the Privy Council? Another banker?'

Lettice giggled. 'Spymaster Williamson, who is the kind of fellow to initiate clandestine plots. Robin told her that he would ensure she had everything she had ever wanted if she followed our instructions. She is a

454

clever lady, but too greedy, twisted and ambitious to be wise. As if Williamson would work through the likes of us!'

Chaloner listed all they had done. 'You fomented trouble over *The Court & Kitchin* and organised a sequel; encouraged your "good friend" Colburn to run up huge debts; started rumours about the integrity of the bankers that made depositors demand their money back—'

'All so easy.' Lettice adjusted her hat, the one with the feathers that the Court milliner had made, and something else snapped clear in Chaloner's mind.

'The tale that something would happen on Tuesday came from Howard,' he said. 'And who was his last customer? You!'

'I might have let something slip when he handed me his final creation. It has served to heighten tension, and these things are often self-fulfilling.'

Chaloner started to edge towards Taylor again, but stopped when someone materialised at Lettice's side. It was Shaw, holding a pitchfork with wickedly sharp tines. The couple exchanged a glance, and Chaloner sensed their excitement as the plot marched towards its climax.

'It is time for Mr Taylor to walk along Cheapside again,' said Lettice. 'He will open his box to—'

'No!' begged Chaloner. 'You cannot—'

'And when the bankers are dead or ruined, we shall rise from the ashes,' finished Shaw. 'We shall begin to reclaim our fortune with the Chaloner alum mines.'

'*Our* alum mines now,' corrected Lettice, smiling triumphantly at the spy. 'Mr Howard forged a will in your name before the plague took him, one that leaves your interest in them to us, in lieu of Hannah's debt.'

455

'Then you will remain destitute,' warned Chaloner, 'because I do not—'

'Do not lie,' said Shaw coldly. 'We had the truth from Hannah and your uncle, and we believe them over you.'

'The soul of London!' sang Taylor suddenly, lurching to his feet. 'Pretty, bright things.'

'Open the box!' called Lettice, her voice full of malice. 'Bring out your worms, and give some to Mr Chaloner. Do you remember him? His wife owes you a fortune, but he aims to cheat you of it.'

Taylor walked towards Chaloner, who tried to back away, but Lettice made a sharp sound with her tongue, warning him to stay put. The mad banker came closer, and Chaloner watched in horror as he began to lift the lid. He flinched as the goldsmith held it out for him to see.

'Pretty, bright things,' Taylor chanted again. 'The soul of London.'

The box contained nothing but treasure.

Chaloner stared into Taylor's box, while Lettice's mocking laughter echoed around him. There was Bab May's hatpin, Brodrick's watch, Chiffinch's scent bottle, Carteret's buttons and Hannah's pearls. He rubbed his head tiredly. Of course it contained jewels – Joan had been angry with Misick for letting Taylor wander off before she had had the chance to raid it. He tore his eyes away from the gaudy glitter and glanced upwards.

'There is no plague in it,' said Shaw scornfully. 'How could there be? The theory about worms is a nonsense – it is carried in a miasma. But Taylor *will* take the disease into the city today – on his person.'

'But he may not have it. You should know – it was you

456

who encouraged Misick to dose him with a deadly mixture of medicines. That is what ails him, not the pestilence.'

'Nonsense,' said Lettice. 'But you are beginning to annoy me. It is time to end this pointless chatter and be about our real business.'

She took aim and fired, but the gun flashed in the pan, causing her to jerk back with a squeak of surprise. Chaloner lunged at Shaw, aiming to grab the pitchfork, but Shaw stabbed so hard that the spy almost toppled backwards into the pit. Chaloner thought fast. Hoping Lettice did not have a second dag, he wrenched the box from Taylor's hands, opened it up and seized a handful of buttons.

He lobbed them into the mud. They lay on the surface for a moment, then sank. Taylor gave a wail of distress. The Genovese watch went next.

'What are you doing?' cried Lettice in horror. 'Stop!'

'Then come and get them,' taunted Chaloner, holding Bab May's hatpin aloft so that they all could see it, then letting it drop. He dipped into the chest again and pulled out a crystal salt cellar. Was it the one Starkey had left as a pledge? Regardless, into the muck it went.

Taylor released a great bellow of dismay and leapt into the pit after it, sending up a fountain of thick brown sludge. He vanished beneath the surface and did not reappear. Chaloner gaped in disbelief, imagining the terrified struggle that would be taking place beneath. He had not intended that to happen!

'Enough!' roared Shaw, running down the steps and raising the pitchfork threateningly. 'I will kill you if you do it again.'

Defiantly, Chaloner tossed a cameo of Good Queen Bess over his shoulder, although he could not bring himself to do the same with Hannah's pearls – those went in his pocket. Shaw howled his anger, and aimed a wild jab that came nowhere near its intended target, while Lettice hurried down the steps after her husband and knelt on the walkway. The salt cellar lay tantalisingly close, and stretching out, the tips of her fingers could just brush it.

But it was a fraction too far. She lost her balance and toppled in. The mortar was thicker around the edges than the middle, so she sank more slowly than Taylor had done.

With a howl of rage, Shaw raced towards Chaloner, jabbing furiously with the tines. Chaloner backed around the scaffolding and in desperation tossed the box and all its remaining jewels into the pit, hoping Shaw would abandon him in the hope of salvaging something. But Shaw came at him again and again, driving him back, step by step.

'Stop!' Chaloner shouted. 'Save Lettice!'

His foot slipped on mud that had slopped up when Taylor had jumped, and he only just avoided the savage lunge aimed at his chest. He scrambled upright, then struggled to retreat fast enough as Shaw surged after him again.

'Lettice is drowning,' he yelled. 'She will . . .'

He faltered when he realised that Shaw had been driving him on for a reason – to reach the lever that would release the next batch of mortar. He made a spectacular leap that saw him just clear when it gushed out, narrowly avoiding being washed off the walkway and driven to the bottom of the pit.

Furious that his plan had failed, Shaw resumed his advance. Chaloner turned to run – they had travelled three sides of the cellar and one more would see him at the stairs again. He reached the steps but had no more than set his foot on the first when a hand fastened around his ankle. It was Lettice, using him to pull herself upwards. Shaw jabbed with the pitchfork at the same time, and Chaloner fell.

Seeing his quarry trapped, Shaw lifted the deadly tines. Chaloner twisted away, and the pitchfork bit into the wood so deeply that Shaw could not tug it free. Cursing vilely, he heaved with all his might. As it came loose, Chaloner punched his knee.

Shaw toppled into the sludge. He tried to spread his weight, but he had landed badly – his legs were already caught and he began to sink fast. He clawed frantically, but to no avail.

Chaloner had problems of his own. No matter how hard he fought, Lettice would not let go of his foot. He glanced behind him but could see nothing of her except an arm. Was he going to be towed to the bottom by a corpse? He flailed wildly for a handhold but his hands were foul with mud and he could not gain purchase.

'You will die with us,' came a weak voice.

Chaloner twisted around to see mud ooze up Shaw's neck, then reach his mouth and nose, until only the top of his head remained. He recoiled at the hatred in the music-seller's eyes before they finally slid from view.

He returned to his own plight. Was Lettice still gripping his leg? He could not tell, but it did not matter because he was going down regardless. Then he felt powerful hands fasten around his shoulders, and he began to rise. It was Wiseman, bellowing with the effort of pulling him free.

'How did you . . .' Chaloner could manage no more, and lay gasping on the walkway.

'Baron sent me to tell you that we were too late,' whispered the surgeon hoarsely, and Chaloner saw his face was deathly white. 'The fools freed Widow Porteous, who staggered out shaking hands and breathing into faces. Then she fell down in a faint, and was discovered to be filthy with plague tokens.'

Chaloner glanced at the pit. The surface was ruffled, but gravity was already working, and he imagined it would soon be perfectly smooth, with no evidence of the terrible fate that had befallen three misguided people and jewels belonging to half of London. Then what might have been a hand broke it, and twitched slightly before slipping out of sight.

'Who was that?' asked Wiseman hoarsely. 'Which of them?'

'I do not know,' said Chaloner with a shudder. 'And nor do I want to.'

Epilogue

Three days later, Cheapside

Chaloner stood with Wiseman on the steps to the music shop's cellar, watching Yaile smooth the surface with a long-handled tool. The builder was still angry that a mischievous rioter had released the lever on his leather bucket, because the resulting finish on the new floor was inferior, but it would be impossible to dig out so many tons of material, so it had to stay as it was.

'Mind your clothes,' he instructed. 'Your wives and sweethearts will not be pleased if you go home covered in muck.'

'I imagine Hannah will have other things on her mind,' muttered Wiseman to Chaloner. 'Such as how to pay her debts.'

Chaloner smiled, the first time he had done so since the terrible events on Tuesday morning. 'That particular problem is resolved. I do not know if Williamson kept his word or the record of her loan was lost in the fire. Regardless, our slate is clear.'

'The other bankers profess themselves to be appalled

by what happened – not just Joan's selfish ambitions and the bitter revenge wreaked by Shaw and Lettice, but the craven greed of Taylor himself. They have established rules regarding interest rates, and honourable men now regulate them. Trouble like this will never happen again.'

'Their good intentions will erode over time,' predicted Chaloner. 'Others will see there is money to be made from borrowing and lending at high rates, and the whole cycle will start all over again.'

'Yes, but not in our lifetimes,' said Wiseman comfortably.

'Are you sure about Taylor, Lettice and Shaw?' asked Chaloner, glancing uneasily into the pit. 'That their bodies will dissolve?'

Wiseman nodded. 'Quite sure. There is quicklime in Yaile's mixture. Of course, it will take time. If someone comes with a spade in the next year or so, there will be questions to answer.'

'Taylor did not deserve to die so horribly.' Chaloner was still appalled by what had happened, and the fate of all three haunted his dreams. 'It was hardly his fault that Misick poisoned him.'

'He had been gouging his customers for weeks before Misick came along, taking over where Wheler left off. He was not a good man, Chaloner, and I doubt there are many who will miss him.'

'Not miss in the sense that they want him back, but they are certainly interested in his whereabouts. Silas and Backwell have both paid for searches to be made.'

Wiseman smiled. 'Williamson has started a rumour that he fled to France, so that should satisfy them for a while. They will give up when they find no clues at the ports.'

Chaloner stared into the pit. 'And what about the plague?'

'There were seventeen new cases along Cheapside this morning, with twenty more in St Giles and in the Fleet rookery. The worms are out of the bag, and they will not be easily encouraged back in again.'

Both fell silent when the bell of St Mary le Bow announced the death of another parishioner. The number of chimes indicated a dead woman, and it was followed by two children. In the distance, there were more.

'There was a fortune in Taylor's box,' said Chaloner, turning his attention back to the cellar. 'There are many who would dig up this pit with their fingernails to lay hold of it.'

'True,' acknowledged Wiseman. 'But we are the only ones who know it is down there, and I will not be telling anyone. However, the situation must be galling for you.'

'Must it?'

'A donation from Taylor's Plague Box would have soothed the Earl's ire with you for not preventing a run on the banks and an outbreak of plague – and for proving Baron innocent of Wheler's murder, which means the Earl himself is still vulnerable to a scandal involving stolen curtains.'

'He will just have to trust Temperance to keep that tale to herself. She promised she would.'

'He is fortunate she is your friend,' said Wiseman. 'But regardless, you must resist the temptation to come here one night with a spade.'

'You need not worry about that,' said Chaloner fervently. 'And if the hoard ever does come to light . . . well, its discoverers will just have to wonder how it came to be here.'

463

Wiseman smirked. 'No one will ever guess the truth!' Then the grin faded. 'But it was a nasty affair and I feel soiled by it. Doe was the worst – he killed Wheler so he could be King of Cheapside; he shot Coo, Fatherton and Neve to turn people against Baron—'

'In revenge for Baron seizing control of Cheapside before he could grab it himself,' put in Chaloner. 'Although he need not have bothered: Baron had planned to retire when Wheler died of lung-rot, and the chances were that he would have named Doe as his successor anyway.'

'He killed Randal with a stray ball during the struggle in Friday Street,' Wiseman went on, 'and he planned to murder Baron and Poachin during the riots. Perhaps we should have let him. They are not men we want in our fair city.'

'I like Baron,' said Chaloner. 'He is a thief, a liar and a bullying extortionist, but there is a certain charm about him. And he did risk his life to save London.'

'True. Will Williamson arrest him? I am told there were more stolen goods in his cellar than there are curtains in the whole of White Hall.'

'Who knows what Williamson will do?' Chaloner had had scant contact with the Spymaster since he and Swaddell had made their report three days ago. He supposed the truce was over, and they could return to their usual state of mutual antipathy.

'Well, Baron is certainly happy for now,' said Wiseman. 'Silas gave him his horse back.'

Chaloner was glad. 'I thought Silas – and Backwell – were the villains at one point, but they met only to discuss the looming crisis and devise ways to handle it. Silas will make an excellent head of the family bank. Better than Taylor, Joan or Evan.'

'Evan! Silas certainly avenged himself on *him* for that dead-end post in Harwich – he is sailing to New York as we speak, fearful that he will be blamed for the disaster surrounding his father. But Silas deserves his triumph. It was due to him that the city escaped financial ruin – there *was* a run on the banks, but he managed to stall it. So the King will have his war money, and there will be funds to fight the plague – as far as we can.'

'I still cannot believe the lengths to which Shaw's hatred drove him,' said Chaloner. 'He used any opportunity that arose to spread fear and unrest – Doe's murderous spree, the bankers' greed, the unpopular plague measures, Randal's book. He was like a leech, latching on to anything and everything, and turning it to his own ends. And he used Joan, Misick, Oxley, Farrow . . .'

'They did not have to do what he suggested – it was their own decision to follow dark paths. And Misick, for one, should have resisted. He was a *medicus*, for God's sake – a higher being than other mere mortals.'

'Maude is not very pleased that I gave away the cabochon she lent me,' said Chaloner gloomily, segueing to another subject. 'I have no idea how to replace it.'

Wiseman waved an airy hand. 'Oh, do not worry about that. I told her that those particular gems are attractive to plague worms, so she is grateful to you for ridding her of it. In fact, she is so glad that she has arranged for you to receive a certain gift.'

'Christ!' muttered Chaloner. 'When the truth comes out—'

'What truth? Can you prove that my considered medical opinion is wrong? No? Then keep your amateur opinions to yourself. Besides, it is high time that Maude

465

and Temperance put their money towards something more worthwhile than fripperies like curtains.'

'Curtains,' said Chaloner disgustedly. 'The Earl has forgotten that his upholder cheated him, and blames me for the fact that Neve's replacement is not as talented. My next assignment is with the fleet that is about to fight the Dutch – a case of missing funds from the navy coffers. I am sure he wants me drowned or blown up.'

'We need every penny we can muster if we are to defeat the enemy,' said Wiseman sternly, 'so he is right to send his best man to root out the thieves. But you will like Maude's gift, I promise. It involves the redemption of certain items from a shop on Foster Lane . . .'

'My viols?' asked Chaloner, his heart quickening.

'They are waiting at the club. Shall we go there now?'

It was a pretty day when Williamson and Baron met in the Smithfield Meat Market. Both had promised to go alone, but each knew the other had henchmen in the vicinity. Baron attended the meeting openly, but the Spymaster wore a disguise. It was not a very good one, and Baron smothered a grin.

'To business,' said Williamson briskly, not bothering with pleasantries. 'I am a busy man, and cannot afford to squander time.'

'No,' agreed Baron mildly. 'Although you could do worse than delegate to your henchmen. Swaddell and Chaloner are able men.'

'Chaloner is not my henchman. He has a fine array of talents, but he is too honest for my line of work. It is an annoying trait, especially as it seems to have rubbed off on Swaddell.'

'Swaddell is honest?' asked Baron doubtfully.

466

Williamson grimaced. 'He recorded every one of the bribes you paid him, and has used them to buy information for the Dutch war. It is good of him, but it makes me very uneasy.'

Baron nodded understanding. 'A minion's integrity can be a nuisance if it makes one's own conscience prick. But you did not come here to discuss the ethics of our chosen trades. How may I be of assistance? Do you have a house that requires some drapery, perhaps?'

'No,' said Williamson irritably. 'I came to discuss your operation along Cheapside. It is illegal to demand a Protection Tax from residents and shopkeepers. It is also illegal to operate gambling dens that play for such high stakes – high enough to ruin Colburn and half the Court.'

'The laws that restrict what a man may bet are foolish,' declared Baron, a little dangerously. 'We are all adults, and should be allowed to decide for ourselves how we spend our money. It is none of the government's affair.'

'It is when it bankrupts a goodly number of its ministers,' Williamson shot back.

'Would twenty per cent of my takings change your mind?'

'No, it would not,' declared Williamson indignantly.

'Thirty per cent?'

'Done.'

Historical Note

On 18 June 1912, workmen made one of the most remarkable discoveries in the history of London archaeology: a mass of jewellery and other precious objects, which had lain undisturbed beneath 30–32 Cheapside for at least two hundred and fifty years. No one knows who put it there or why, but it is one of the best collections of Elizabethan and Jacobean treasure ever found – a fabulous jumble of necklaces, cameos, jewels, rings, cabochons, scent bottles, salt cellars and brooches. There were also twenty-four diamond and ruby buttons, a hatpin in the shape of a ship, pearls and a Genovese watch. Known as the Cheapside Hoard, they are held in the London Museum.

A number of theories have been proposed for why someone should have hidden such wealth and neglected to recover it – plague, the Great Fire, the civil wars, or even a burglar, executed before he could tell anyone what he had done – but until more evidence comes to light, all must remain speculation.

The house may have been owned by one Richard Taylor, who was accused of producing 'fowle and course' wares in 1606, and faced dismissal from the Goldsmiths' Company. He suffered a spell in prison, but returned to his work and took a lease on a shop in Cheapside, where he stayed until the 1650s. His partner was Richard Wheler, whose widow Joan is recorded as renting a similar property two doors down. It was somewhere between these two premises that the hoard was discovered, although there is no evidence to say that it belonged to any of the three.

Captain Silas Taylor (no relation) was a Parliamentarian soldier who was Storekeeper of the Harwich Shipyard, as well as an amateur composer and a personal friend of the musician Matthew Locke. He was known to Samuel Pepys, and often appears in the Diary. Evan Taylor (or Tyler) was a printer who worked in the Cheapside area in the mid 1660s.

Another Taylor, also unrelated, was Randal, who wrote *The Court & Kitchin of Elizabeth, Commonly called Joan Cromwel, The Wife of the late Usurper, Truly Described and Represented, And now made Publick for General Satisfaction*. It was printed by Thomas Milbourn on St Martin le Grand in 1664, and republished in 1983 as *Mrs Cromwell's Cookery Book*. It is a peculiar pamphlet, presumably intended to prove the author's Royalist convictions by mocking the dead Cromwell's wife.

There is a theory that Randal had worked in the White Hall kitchens during the Protectorate, and was dismissed ignominiously, but this has never been conclusively proven. Philip Starkey was one of Cromwell's master-cooks, paid twenty pounds for each ambassadorial function. Mrs Cromwell died a few months after the book was published, at the home of her daughter and son-in-law in Northamptonshire. There is no evidence that she ever saw Randal's scribblings.

As there were no banks as such in the 1660s, goldsmiths took it upon themselves to store and lend money, keeping it in their vaults, and loaning it to other customers at rates of between six and ten per cent. Some of their stockpile went towards paying for the war that had been officially declared on the Dutch on 22 February 1665 – a month later than portrayed in this novel.

Edward Backwell was one such goldsmith, a founder of our modern-day banking system. He was the government's chief financial advisor during the Commonwealth, a role he continued after the Restoration. He arranged the money side of the sale of Dunkirk (an unpopular transaction that turned many people against the Earl of Clarendon), managed the payment of war subsidies, and lent the government money to pay the Tangier garrison. His 'bank' suffered a near-collapse in 1665, when he was out of the country on government business and the clerk he had left in charge (Robin Shaw) died of plague. He was finally ruined in 1672, when the King put a Stop on the Exchequer – *de facto* admission that the government was bankrupt. Shaw was probably in Spymaster Williamson's pay. Other great goldsmith–banking dynasties of the 1660s include such names as Vyner, Angier, Hinton, Glosson, Johnson and Meynell.

James Baron was a linen-draper who married Frances Bott in 1650 and died in 1667. Francis Poachin was landlord of the Mitre on Cheapside in 1667, and lived on Cornhill; he suffered catastrophic losses to his business in the 1680s. Charles Doe lived on Cheapside between 1641 and 1671; his business failed shortly after the Great Fire. Nicholas Kelke was a pewterer who married a Southwark lass, while Mr Yaile paid twenty pounds' rent for his house on Cheapside in 1638.

470

The Earl of Clarendon did build himself a princely home in Piccadilly, sneeringly called Dunkirk House. And the vintner Nicholas Colburn bought a country estate in Essex, where he was living in February 1665. Thomas Chaloner, father of the regicide, did discover alum on his estates at Guisborough in Yorkshire; they subsequently passed to the Crown, and an unfair takeover has been suggested as one reason why his heirs might have sided with Parliament.

The Intelligencer for 24 April 1665 records the unfortunate lot of Dr Misick, who was severely burned while reaching for a glass of spirit and turpentine. His maid suffered the same fate trying to save him, and it was feared that both would die. Francis Neve was an upholder active in the Cornhill–Threadneedle Street area in the 1660s. Famous courtiers include Bab May, Will Chiffinch, Winifred Wells, Lady Carnegie (rumoured to have given the Duke of York a 'shameful pox') and the Duke of Buckingham, while Sir George Carteret was Treasurer to the Navy.

As in most conflicts, the propaganda machines were busy during the Second Anglo-Dutch War. The rumour about the fifteen hundred drowned Britons was hawked around the city until it was discovered to be a lie and its originator punished. Similar rumours were propagated in Holland at the same time. Omens and portents were rife, and included comets, coffin-shaped clouds and other celestial phenomena, all reported with grave precision in the newsbooks. Pepys records being told about a sea-battle heard on 14 April, during which Captain Teddeman had his legs blown off, but there was no truth in it.

The parish registers of St Mary le Bow record several burials in the spring of 1665. They include Robert and

Sarah Howard, George Bridges and Abner Coo, physician. Another early victim was Margaret Porteous, buried on 12 April 1665. Daniel Defoe's *A Journal of the Plague Year* contains a tale of a Frenchman who caught the plague at his lodgings in Long Acre, and who then went to Bearbinder Lane off Cheapside, thus transporting the disease from one parish to another. However, Defoe was still a child when the Great Plague of London raged, and his account was written almost sixty years later, intended as fiction.

There was a riot in London over the double standards imposed by the authorities during the plague, although it happened in the area surrounding St Giles-in-the-Fields, not on Cheapside. It stemmed from the fact that the searchers could be bribed to record a death as something other than the pestilence, which would release the house from the forty-day quarantine.

Regardless of their efforts, London was essentially powerless to combat the disease, mostly because contemporary medics did not understand how it was transmitted or how to treat it. Various theories were put forward, including one that said it was caused by a deadly miasma, and another that blamed tiny worms invisible to the naked eye. Cures and preventatives were myriad, and many were advertised with great confidence in the newsbooks, although it was to no avail. The disease advanced relentlessly as the weather grew warmer, leaving thousands dead in its wake.